Also by Andrea Lee

Lost Hearts in Italy: A Novel
Interesting Women: Stories
Sarah Phillips: A Novel
Russian Journal

RED ISLAND HOUSE

A Novel

Andrea Lee

SCRIBNER
New York   London   Toronto   Sydney   New Delhi

Permissions

Naivo, "Beyond the Rice Fields," translated by Allison M. Charette, Restless Books, 2017.

Lee Harding, *How to Read a Folktale: The Ibonia Epic from Madagascar*, Cambridge, UK: Open Book Publishers, 2013.

"Old Merina Theme," by Flavien Ranaivo, and "Lovely Woman," by Esther Nirina, translated by Marjolijn de Jager, from *Voices from Madagascar: An Anthology of Francophone Literature*, edited by Jacques Bourgeacq and Liliane Ramarosoa. Copyright Ohio University Press © 2003 This material is used by permission of Ohio University Press, www.ohioswallow.com.

To Alexandra, Charles, Harry, and Marie

This island of Madagascar affords all the necessaries of life . . . The seas around it are well stor'd with fish, the woods with fowl, and the intrails of the earth are enriched with mines of excellent iron . . . and doubtless there are both gold and silver mines in the mountains . . . The soil will produce sugar, cotton, indigo and other growths of our American Colonies, at a far inferior Expence . . . Negro slaves in Barbados are 30, 40, 50 (English) pounds per head, and I dare answer that 10 shillings in European Goods will purchase a Negro slave at Madagascar . . . The natives are, or seem to be, very Human.

—Captain Charles Johnson (probably Daniel Defoe),
A General History of the Pyrates, vol. 2

This is a sacred country, but it is adrift, at the mercy of outside interests

—Naivoharisoa Patrick Ramamonjisoa (Naivo),
"Beyond the Rice Fields," translated by Marjolijn de Jager

Contents

The Packet War

I am a big house seen from afar
Not even a whole crowd can take it apart
but if they do, it takes revenge.
And when those from across the sea catch sight of me
I add them to my servants.

—"Ibonia," traditional epic of Madagascar,
translated by Lee Haring

There are houses you don't want, that, nevertheless, enter your life and bring with them other lives, whole other worlds. There are countries you visit that lay hold of you and don't let go, even if you diligently attempt to remain a tourist. These thoughts have been incubating in the mind of Shay Senna ever since she—a Black American woman with scant interest in the continent of Africa except as a near-mythical motherland—unexpectedly and unwillingly became mistress of the Red House, a sprawling household in northwestern Madagascar.

It is because of the big house and its bad fortune that she is at present in a dreamlike situation, hurrying under the calescent subequatorial sun through the back lanes of a fishermen's shantytown on the island of Naratrany, in pursuit of a tiny Sakalava girl in a white satin gown.

In the light-soaked stillness of the hottest noontime hour, when mongrel dogs lie flat as puddles in patches of shade, the barefoot child, who looks like an eerie carnival figure in that glaring dress with its flounces and ribbons, skips in and out of sight through a maze of tottering bamboo huts. Occasionally she turns her little braided head and makes a cheeky, beckoning motion with a spindly brown arm as she guides Shay and Shay's head housekeeper, Bertine la Grande, to the home of the man referred to, usually in whispers, as the Neighbor.

The tall, stately Bertine, also barefoot, also Sakalava, leads the way. Dressed in a sweeping print *lamba*, her geometrically knotted hair hidden by a big, sun-faded newsboy hat that gives her a curiously regal air, she chuckles softly each time the small white apparition flashes into sight, then treads on casually as if engaged in an everyday errand.

Shay stumbles along in her wake, hampered by the long skirt she was told to wear, and hobbled as well by her American common sense, which is struggling with the awareness that she has crossed a threshold into the deep unknown. Her woven shoulder bag, concealing a wad of *ariary* bills and the small gift Bertine suggested, bangs against her side, as she tries not to think of the fact that she is seeking out the Neighbor, a notorious conjurer, in hopes that he can lift the spell on her house.

2.

How has this peculiar quest come about? You could say it is because of something else that hasn't come about: the housewarming ceremony that Shay's husband, Senna, a rich but stingy Italian businessman, neglects to hold when he finishes building his fantasy vacation residence on Naratrany. So tightfisted is Senna that not even one zebu bull is slaughtered for the local villagers, not one festive step danced, not one glass of rum poured on the ground for thirsty ancestors, when the last thatch has been laid on the big villa he constructed on what was formerly Colonel Andrianasolo's lot on Finoana Beach.

Naratrany, a very minor part of Madagascar, is a small lush island with a central crater that gives it from afar the look of a squashed green fedora. Framed by coral reefs, it is one of a chain of ancient fumaroles that in the Tertiary period arose to become satellites to the huge main island. Though defined by cartographers as part of Africa, Madagascar really belongs only to itself, having developed its independent character over the millions of years since the primeval continent of Gondwana broke apart and abandoned the shield-shaped landmass in the sea between Mozambique and India. The topography of the country ranges from deserts of lunar desolation to swathes of emerald rice fields; from allées of baobabs to impenetrable forested uplands; but its coastal fringe of palmy islets is perhaps loveliest of all. In a letter from the early 1900s, a French priest (and amateur poet) stationed on Naratrany describes it as *"un petit morceau du paradis, tombé des cieux."* He notes as well that the name Naratrany seems to mean "broken" or "wounded," though it is unclear whether this refers to a forgotten battle or the island's craterous shape.

Located on an ancient Indian Ocean trade route, the tiny dot of land has for centuries been a magnet for explorers, missionaries, pirates, and plunderers of all descriptions. It is the territory of the Sakalava, one of Madagascar's nineteen peoples, a linchpin in that martial tribe's vast kingdom, which once covered all western Madagascar. Sakalava lived on Naratrany before the earliest Indian merchants arrived; were present with their zebu cattle when the pirates Tew and Avery sailed through; were there when their powerful rivals the Merina, aided by British guns, swept down from the highlands to conquer the coast; were in residence when France annexed all Madagascar as a colony, and still there in 1960 when the colony won independence.

This history connects to the story of the Red House, since the swathe of beachfront that Colonel Andrianasolo sells to Senna belonged, a century earlier, to a Malagasy nobleman, a cousin of the Sakalava queen. A now-forgotten quarrel cut short the life of this gentleman and one of his retainers, and their remains still rest discreetly in a far corner of the property, concealed by the roots of a huge kapok tree.

Colonel Andrianasolo, a Merina whose father snapped up the property just after independence, knows all about the hidden graves when, after intense bargaining with the wily Italian, he signs the *certificat d'achat*. But the colonel prudently keeps silent about the unusual feature of the terrain. He only expresses a neighborly hope—Andrianasolo vacations on the next beach over, in a properly exorcized 1970s bungalow—that Senna's future housewarming celebration will include the proper formalities, and the sacrifice of two zebus.

But, like many self-made men, Senna is willful in strange ways. Much of his youth was spent helping his family hustle their way out of postwar poverty in the malarial rice fields of Vercelli, and, now in middle age, he is contentedly ensconced as ruler of his own profitable company that brokers repair services for agricultural machines all over Europe. A wiry Lombard with a brawler's crooked nose, he has a steel-trap mind and shrewd green eyes able to ferret out the scurviest tactics of his competitors. But unlike most Italians of his hardscrabble generation, he has an early life that includes an odd chapter: as a teenager, he spent a year in Rome in the dolce vita era, working for a cousin who was a cameraman at Cinecittà. The immersion in the magical atmosphere of golden age Italian cinema, the sight of film stars walking the earth amid the rubble of a world war and the ruins of imperial Rome, awakened a dreaming side in young Senna. But when his father suddenly died and he had to return to the rice lands, he put this part of his nature under wraps. There it remains for decades, until he has divorced his first wife, and his savings are snug in discreet refuges around the world.

Then, in his forties and free at last to indulge in midlife folly, he sets off on a six-month fishing trip around the Indian Ocean with a buddy from his military service year, a weathered sea dog of a Calabrian baron, born in Italian Somaliland. Crossing the Mozambique Channel, en route from the Comoros islands, their sloop draws up upon the eastern coast of Naratrany, and at first sight of the island, Senna is struck with a raw mixture of feelings: a roundhouse punch of mingled amazement, ambition, lust: what he imagines the early explorers felt, staring dumbfounded from their caravels.

Motionless at the rail, he gazes over Finoana Bay to a low-rising land formation that is dazzlingly, virginally green, as if it is the first time that color has been used on earth. Its undulating slopes are stacked with shadowed rain forest and the kinetic lighter hues of sugarcane; the shoreline is hemmed with a string of palm and casuarina and a long curve of empty coral beach, white and perfect as a fresh slice of apple. Senna isn't religious, but the arc of beach recalls to him the pale folded hands of the Baroque statue of the Holy Mother that was the sole treasure of his childhood parish church. And he, the astute business-man who knows the value of instinct, then and there determines to buy that beach and build a house. Decides this with the violent sense of yielding that an aging man feels when he plunges into an infatuation with a young girl.

"Be careful," warns his Calabrian friend, an old Africa hand. "Places like this aren't ever as simple as they look! Especially here. These people are part Bantu and part Indonesian, and part something else that is just pure strangeness. You can never tell where you are with them."

Of course, Senna knows nothing about Madagascar, not one thing about the country's epic geological past, nothing about the quirky evolutionary journey of its fabled wildlife, or the nineteen tribes and their language with its recondite Swahili-Polynesian roots. Like many Italians, he adores the tropics, and over years of growing prosperity has vacationed with his family and friends in the Bahamas, Thailand, Bali, and Tahiti.

He sees these places of coralline seas as a single landscape, flat as a Rousseau painting. A backdrop against which to bring to life his youthful adventure fantasies, rooted in his love for the pulp novels of Emilio Salgari, the best-selling nineteenth-century bard of the exotic. Salgari never actu-ally traveled out of provincial Italy, but his fevered descriptions of Asian, African, and South American jungles and lagoons are as detailed as ency-clopedias can make them. The author's swashbuckling heroes, who battle headhunters in ancient temples, commandeer Moghul treasure ships, and rescue swooning heroines from seraglios, fired the imaginations of genera-tions of boys in Latin countries—boys including Gabriel García Márquez, and Che Guevara. And Senna.

Added to these fantasies are yarns he has heard of Libertalia, a seventeenth-century colony said to have been founded in Madagascar by an idealistic crew of European pirates. Legend describes Libertalia as a raffish utopian settlement, in which all property was shared and all license allowed. What with dusky concubines, commodious bamboo residential huts, communal chests of gold, freed African slaves, and high-minded gentlemen buccaneers who frequently discoursed on the rights of man, Libertalia seems to have offered everything. But did it ever really exist? Senna likes to think it did.

"Think what you want," says the Calabrian. "But true or false, the old story ends badly. The local Malagasy tribesmen get sick of the settlers and wipe out the colony in one night. Not a stick or a bone left. Happens over and over again in places like this."

But Senna ignores this implied warning. The Calabrian, he reflects, hasn't even had the brains to hang on to one cent of his family's prewar coffee fortune.

Senna himself is a man who gets things done fast. He's quite used to skipping cultural niceties and clinching overnight business deals with foreigners—often Chinese or Russian—using the internationally respected language of brutal haggling. Thus, he gains the startled admiration of Colonel Andrianasolo, and in record time has in hand an exquisitely hand-copied French-Malagasy deed of purchase for a swathe of beachfront with rice paddies and cane fields behind it.

Finoana Beach is not, as he first thought, empty. Behind the palms are two villages, Finoana and Renirano, full of fishermen and cane workers, and a whole network of life, complete with markets, a tiny mosque, a Catholic church, and a ramshackle French-built elementary school. To Senna, this means only that he'll have more men for construction, at weekly wages that would barely pay for coffee for workmen back in Italy.

So the house goes up with almost magical swiftness. The terrain has not been built on before, but has been extensively planted: coconut, mango, jackfruit, tamarind, banana, as well as flowers: jasmine, frangipani, hibiscus, ylang-ylang. The pleasure Senna derives from this profusion of color and fragrances leads him to christen the place Villa Gioia. Though he knows it's a commonplace name, better suited to a second-rate pensione in Rimini, he reckons it will be the only one on this island.

He alone designs the house, though he works out a deal with a local construction kingpin, a Karan Indian from Diego Suarez, whose fleet of *boutres*, fat wooden schooners, swing into the bay to deliver concrete as well as timber from Madagascar's shrinking forests. Senna is dizzied by the infinite possibilities offered by using First World money in a Third World country, one of the poorest on earth. Like a djinn out of the *Arabian Nights*, he summons up a structure of fanciful grandiosity, a pastiche of tropical styles from around the world. There is a soaring peaked roof suggesting a palm-thatched circus tent, inspired by the dramatic huts of Sumba, Indonesia; an interior with one end dominated by a grandly swung double staircase, like that in an Antiguan plantation house, rising to a mezzanine with a curving lineup of bedrooms; a sweep of open-plan ground floor separated from a wide veranda only by tall jalousies, like a certain inn in Trincomalee. At the garden entrance stand tree-trunk pillars carved with leering primitive faces—copied, Senna cheerfully admits, from a ride at Florida's Disney World.

Like most big tropical residences, the place is a compound: breezeways lead to a separate kitchen and other outbuildings, including a bungalow for the house manager. But most striking is the expanse of floor that a visitor faces when entering. This floor is concrete: sanded, stained with many coats of iron-oxide paint, which, waxed and polished, acquires a warm maroon hue that glows in the shade of the cavernous roof almost like something alive. Because of it, nearby villagers immediately begin to call Villa Gioia *ny trano mena*—the Red House. La Maison Rouge. In any language, the appellation is such a natural fit that nobody, not even Senna, ever uses anything else, or after a short while even recalls that there was an earlier name.

Of course Senna's acts of architectural hubris are minuscule in comparison to those of pharaohs, sultans, and Aztec kings. He brings his vision to life with the glee of an eighteenth-century English lord adding follies to his ancestral acres, or an American robber baron transplanting parts of dismembered chateaux to Newport. And in the end, mysteriously, it all works.

Though it could have looked cartoonish, the big roof rises with undeniable majesty above the feathery line of palms between the cane fields and the beach. Unlike anything built by the Sakalava, the Indian merchants, or the colonial French, it nevertheless appears plausible in that landscape, and Senna is delighted to see his creation up there against the sky. He isn't a bad man; but after long years spent peddling irrigation valves, his soul is thrown off-balance by the possibilities of a country where he is not just a successful businessman, but a nabob.

So in a fit of arrogance he declares that he, Senna, won't be guided by the broad hints of Colonel Andrianasolo and the local village headmen; will not inaugurate the new house with the customary feast for the construction workers, neighbors, and friends. Not until such time as he feels like it. Maybe never. And he will certainly never go to the trouble and expense of butchering a pair of black and white zebu bulls just to honor a lot of superstitious claptrap.

And so the islanders—the fishermen, charcoal burners, cane workers, hotel maids, gardeners, mechanics, market vendors, prostitutes, woodcarvers, middle-class shopkeepers, and professionals—observe this neglect of the proprieties without rancor, but with a sense of inevitable consequences. Particularly the Sakalava feel this way. They are the abiding ones, the *teratany*, residents essential to the place as volcanic bedrock, for generations washed over by the caprice and varied abuses of the *vazaha*, as they call the foreigners who come and go on the land. These locals know all about the disrespected dead, and they watch, unsurprised, as the Red House begins, even before it is furnished, to accumulate an evil atmosphere. It happens bit by bit, just as dust and litter build up in the corners of an unswept room.

And finally, as is so often the case, it becomes a woman's job to clean things up.

3.

Shay Gilliam, Senna's second wife, doesn't imagine when she first sees the Red House that because of it she'll soon be engaged in a life-and-death struggle, swept up in an occult battle that devolves on mastery, on many kinds of possession.

What are mastery and possession after all, but advanced forms of desire? And Shay, a university instructor raised with staunch East Bay political correctness amid the progressive Black middle class of Oakland, California, has, emphatically, never desired a tropical manse like a jumped-up plantation fantasy. Throughout a bookish childhood and beyond, Shay, always known as the flighty one in her family, has cherished many peculiar wishes (an ability to walk through walls is just one), but not once has she pictured herself as the chatelaine of a neocolonial pleasure palace, conjured up on African soil.

But the Red House has been in her husband's life longer than she has. During their first meeting, at a wedding in Como, Senna boasts of his Madagascar project to Shay, as she flirts with him from under the brim of an extravagant couture straw hat, and their unlikely romance begins. Unlikely because the tall, mischievously smiling Fulbright scholar with her Ivy League degrees seems to have nothing in common with the short, pushy Lombard businessman whose sole diploma is a high school *ragioneria* certificate. Yet this odd couple surprise themselves, and those who know them, by promptly falling in love, with an intensity that precludes anything but joining their lives together.

Shay is bowled over by a man so different from the cerebral American and European lovers she's had since she left her first brief marriage to her college boyfriend, a Jamaican medical student whose evangelical views on wifely submission emerged once vows were spoken. Senna is like no one she has known before: a man her father, a professor at Mills, disapproves of not because Senna is white and foreign—the family tree with its high-yellow Virginia roots includes many a Caucasian ancestor and their Oakland neighborhood is peppered with international marriages—but because he didn't go to college. To Shay, fresh out of graduate school, Senna is a new experience: this cheeky, charismatic Italian a decade and a half older than she is, a businessman with an unfaltering grip on the concrete facts of life; a man who deals (in some mysterious commercial way) with agricultural machines; who buys land—has bought part of an actual island. A man who hustled his way out of poverty, the way so many Black Americans have had to do. A man, she early discovers, who conceals behind his pragmatic exterior a vein of wayward fantasy that matches her own.

Senna, a sensualist by nature, at first pursues Shay for her physical beauty—the length of her, her body with its gleam of terra-cotta, her shallow-set eyes that render her face both stern and childlike—beauty that could belong to many hot terrestrial places where different races intermingle in seaports. Moreover, she is American, like the film actresses he worshipped as a kid at Cinecittà. He is impressed by her fancy education, her fluent Italian and French, her schoolmarmish air of familiarity with all corners of the far-flung landscape of literature. But mostly he is drawn to an unknown quantity, a recklessness he finds deep in her gaze.

The construction of the Red House runs parallel to their courtship, something that by unspoken agreement remains behind the scenes, almost like an erotic secret. Shay visits Naratrany on their first trip together, passing through from Cape Town to Mauritius; she sees a concrete foundation and a beautiful blank beach and hardly thinks of it again.

But Senna, privately, remains obsessed. He feels, somehow, that the house is a task he has to complete before he can properly embark on this second marriage. He travels back and forth from Italy to Madagascar and, on a business trip to Hong Kong, fills a container with old Macau furniture and has it shipped to the island. He hires an unemployed Greek hotel manager named Kristos to act as foreman for the construction and, later, to run the place. In the back of his mind, he holds an evolving image of his creation: the lofty framework of the roof rising bare as a giant hoopskirt between the hills and the ocean. Lilliputian figures of palm thatchers clamber nimbly over the wooden ribs, filling in the spaces.

For her part, Shay is distracted by love, by marriage, by remapping career plans. Her thoughts are overwhelmed by the whole new direction of her future—a circumstance she is aware that she courted years earlier, when she began to focus her studies on Black expatriate writers like William Demby, and came to Rome for dissertation research. Now she, too, has chosen the expatriate path, and in this whirlwind of change the idea of a connection to a construction site far away near the Tropic of Capricorn is too much to contemplate. Italy is enough of a challenge, with its labyrinthine family dynamics, its sunlit surfaces concealing shadowy Catholic taboos. She assumes that her relation to Madagascar will simply be an extension of the European culture she is learning to negotiate; part of the custom—slightly shocking to industrious Americans—of long vacations, the idle existence of the watering place, the *villeggiatura*. In her early view of this new life, Naratrany features simply as a decorative detail: a wallpaper print, like an exotic toile de Jouy.

Only Senna's mother, a sturdy, good-humored widow, reveling in prosperity after a youth spent stitching rice sacks, sees the connection between the amiable, brown-skinned American *professoressa* her son has presented her as a second daughter-in-law and the property he has acquired in hot, brown, and heathen Africa. Like many Italians, she has few qualms about race and quickly grows fond of Shay, who impresses her as ladylike, if a bit high-strung; but, knowing her boy, she predicts that things will not go easily for his new wife—as things will not go smoothly with that wasteful and unnecessary vacation villa he has built in the jungle at the dangerous ends of the earth. It's the fault of those Salgari books, she thinks, and she's right. But she keeps her mouth shut.

4.

"Look what a palace I built for you!" boasts Senna, when Shay first sets eyes on the Red House.

It is July in the late nineties, before there are direct charter flights from Italy to Naratrany. Husband and wife, married six months, have made the overnight haul from Milan to Paris, then Paris to Antananarivo, the capital in the rugged interior of Madagascar. Awaiting their connecting flight to the coast, they spend a day and a night in an old French colonial hotel, their moods cast down by the cold up-country climate. The air is full of history and ghosts there in the City of the Thousand, sacred highland seat of the Merina kings and queens, ancient scene of sanguinary clashes with religious heretics and intrusive Europeans. Though the streets pullulate with crowds and decrepit vehicles, there is an otherworldliness to the place, with its stark azure skies, the stone arches of its ruined palace, its brick houses stacked along the hillsides like toy blocks, its beggar children gazing through blowing dust with the shining eyes of angels. Shay studies the faces around her, with their mixture of Asian and African traits, and feels that she is somewhere unlike any other place on earth: a city aloof, melancholy, and—despite its decay and festering poverty—emanating a strange, secret purity.

At dawn they fly to the coastal islands. In dazzling sunlight, the Indian Ocean reveals from above its deep patterns of blue buried in blue and Naratrany draws closer, rolling with green pelt of cane and forest, coral beaches blazing like sudden smiles, mangrove swamps bleeding mud into the sea. Then the descent from the small plane onto the macadam airstrip and the first caress of tropical air like an infant's hand on the face.

On her first brief stopover, Shay found Naratrany a place of standard postcard beauty. But today in the coastal heat, she finds the same powerful atmosphere of secrecy and innocence as in the cold highlands. The morning air has an almost supernatural clarity as she and Senna head out of the tiny airport in a dusty Toyota pickup and jounce along a once-paved road through a landscape out of the morning of time. Falling away from each side of a high ridge are green declivities that cup dense groves, crowned with flambeaux of red blossom and hung with giant lianas bearing seedpods the length of a man's arm. She can imagine the rare animals hidden deep in the leaves, their jeweled eyes veiled against the sunlight: lemurs, aye-ayes, dwarf chameleons, flying foxes—arcane species alive nowhere else on earth.

Shay, typically, has consulted no guidebooks, but instead skimmed a motley assortment of writing on Madagascar: annals of early Chinese and

Persian explorers; records of Dutch slavers; convoluted accounts of Merina and Sakalava alliances with England and France; yellowed treatises by amateur naturalists and missionaries like the redoubtable James Sibree; histories of adventurers like the shipwrecked seaman Robert Drury, or Jean Laborde, the French industrial wizard and lover of the Merina queen. From this patchy research has come one clear idea: outsiders always want something from Madagascar. The emotion is always the same, whatever the thing desired: whether it is to establish the country as a locus for fabulous legends of gigantic birds and man-eating trees; or as a source for gemstones, rare butterflies, rosewood, spices, slaves; or as fertile ground to produce sugar, vanilla, raffia, cocoa; as a foothold for ascendancy in the Indian Ocean; or even—as Hitler once planned—as a convenient penal colony for the exiled Jews of Europe.

These thoughts are in her mind as they pass Saint Grimaud, the harbor town. Once a French administrative center, it is now a crumbling backwater where zebu graze in the weedy promenade, and washing is spread to dry on the battered cannons above the port. Near the central market, vendors and customers in bright *lambas* stream by bearing baskets of vegetables and sacks of rice on their heads, pushing past schoolchildren in tattered smocks, bush taxis crammed with passengers, mud-caked tractors transporting field hands. A turn at a crossroads lined with food stalls leads past an overgrown European cemetery, then across a river where half-clothed women pound washing against stones. And soon the dusty brick-colored road bursts into open country, carrying them through a roiling sea of sugarcane, dotted with abandoned hulks of dead machinery.

"A few more years and this cane will all be gone," remarks Senna. For this arrival, he has already assumed his vacation persona: hair in a military crop, camouflage vest, and a pair of mirrored sunglasses that suggest that to complete the look he should have an AK-47 slung across his back. "Since independence, the sugar bosses have been getting by with the old French machines. Even when the Marxists were in power back in the seventies, they didn't turn their noses up at colonial leftovers! But it's been too long— the soil is worn out, and the gear is falling apart."

"Can't your company help?" asks Shay, thinking of the clanking combine harvesters somehow connected to Senna's work. She sees sugarcane as an emblem of historical evil, but she is sure that the abrupt death of an industry will create extreme misery.

Senna laughs and pats her knee. He has no sentimentality when it comes to business. And he loves to explain things to his overeducated wife, robust truths about the way the world functions outside of books. "We charge actual money, which nobody has here," he says. "No, it's going to happen: the cane will die, this land will go up for grabs, and tourism will close the gap. Golf courses, big hotels, like on Zanzibar and Mauritius. That's the future for places like this. But *tesoro*, you know we're not here for work. Did I tell you the story of Libertalia?"

"Libertalia is a myth," says Shay mildly, for the umpteenth time, as she settles her sunglasses and tightens her scarf to protect her short hair from the blowing dust. She doesn't go into the literary genealogy she found when she sourced the legend: how it appears in just one book, *A History of the Pyrates*, posited to be the pseudonymous work of Daniel Defoe; how the tale fits into the utopian travelogue tradition that runs back beyond Thomas More, to Plato and Eusebius. And how she was surprised to discover that, in modern times, William Burroughs chose Libertalia as the setting for his apocalyptic novella *Ghost of Chance*. But Shay has no inclination to lecture her husband about literature. He wouldn't listen anyway, and, strangely enough, this is one of the things she admires about him.

Senna has gotten increasingly worked up as they approach the Red House and his big reveal; he schusses the truck around the pits and gullies of the broken road like a kid on a dirt bike. They pass a congeries of discolored cement huts built for fieldworkers, where ducks and chickens wander, women pounding rice in tall wooden mortars look up curiously, and small ragged children run out waving. "*Salut, vazaha!*" they holler.

Dust billows as Senna jolts to a stop beside a half-buried railroad trestle road once used to transport cane. At the crossing is a corroded warning sign still displaying the faint image of a small locomotive, like a nursery school drawing. There the land rolls downhill and offers the first view of the roof of the Red House rising above treetops against the impossible blue glare of the sea beyond.

"Look what a palace I built you!" Senna makes his proclamation now, throwing his hands open wide in an impresario's grand gesture.

And Shay is surprised to feel her breath catch in her throat. Conflicting emotions seize her: a flare of feminine pride that Senna should have tried so hard to impress her, but also alarm. She realizes that she's been hoping the house wouldn't be beautiful—has vaguely felt that it would be easier to accept if it were tasteless: overblown, like a reception hall at a tacky beach resort, or cramped, like a badly proportioned summer cottage—the kind of place you end up loving like an annoying relative.

Instead she sees a lofty thatched roof peak, with something impressive about its isolation and its size, taller than the tallest palms that fringe the long bay. Shay recognizes the harmony of the proportions, and in the same moment feels that something about the place is all wrong. Not its architecture, but its mere existence is an error in a way she can't yet define, but which goes far beyond being an emblem of wealth in a land of poverty. What she does know, immediately, is that—of course—it was never built for her. The reality is that here, in this remote corner of the world, her new husband has raised a monument to an unseemly private fantasy. And now that she has seen it, she somehow shares the blame.

Into her mind comes the opening line of *Out of Africa*, a book that she has both loved for Blixen's lapidary prose style and deplored for the grandiose paternalism that shapes the author's vision. "I had a farm in Africa . . ." As a college freshman, eager to establish herself as a cultural warrior, she once wrote a passionate essay describing those few words as the rallying cry of imperialist oppression. For what does *had* mean, eighteen-year-old Shay typed furiously, but the act of rape?

Now these thoughts dissolve as Senna leans over the gearshift and hugs her uncomfortably against the pockets of his camouflage vest. "Well, what do you think?" he demands.

"*È bellissima,*" Shay tells him. Because that is the truth, and for now other truths are unsayable.

5.

B ut it does happen that when she first steps onto the veranda of the Red House she feels a chill. Just a feather of cold air that brushes her skin. Uncanny, there and gone. For an instant it dizzies her, nearly makes her stumble. Probably a touch of heat exhaustion or migraine after the endless trip, instantly forgotten as she rights herself, lets go of Senna's hand, and steps under the roof. Ever afterward, coming in from the blazing sub-equatorial sun to the deep shade of that house, Shay has the same sensation, which she'll come to recognize as the signature of the place. With time she'll welcome the feeling, think of it as marking a change in dimensions, an entry into penumbral solemnity, like entering an old Italian church.

Now her dazzled eyes adjust to take in the dim sweep of space, the double staircase up to the encircling gallery, the soaring ceiling of rafters and braided thatch. With its ground floor framed in open shutters, the place seems like a way station between indoors and out, walled with the mingled greens of tropical foliage, with a northern view over rice paddies and cane fields and a southern view down a palm-shaded walk to the sea. She stands in the center, staring around her, silenced by the realization of what Senna has achieved here. The spaciousness and air of comfort, the islands of gleaming colonial furniture, the richly colored kilims, the occasional statue: it is all just right, so much so that the usual wifely tasks of decoration have been abrogated. Except: "Why are the floors red?" she blurts out.

Senna, who's been watching his wife's reaction with childish eagerness, looks pained. He goes into a long, testy explanation of how this crimson painted finish is traditional around the Indian Ocean, and how much trouble it took to achieve it. And Shay dispels his annoyance by grabbing and kissing him while pouring out praise. Above all concealing her first unnerving impression: that the ground is covered with blood.

A flicker of movement reveals that the two of them are not alone—as no one ever is in that house. From behind the left staircase emerges a small group of Malagasy people, moving toward them a bit hesitantly: three men dressed in T-shirts and shorts and six women in blouses and floral *lambas*, their hair braided or knotted in twists. They are the domestic staff of the Red House, and they are all looking with intense curiosity at Shay.

What do they see? A tall, almond-skinned young woman dressed in crumpled Italian linen, her short kinky hair held back with a wide striped band like that of a sixties film actress. A pretty woman whose mixed-race looks could place her origin as Réunion Island or Mauritius, except for something American in her loose-jointed stance, her eager, unshielded gaze.

They themselves, this cluster of men and women, have skin tones that run the Indian Ocean gamut from sulfur yellow to Black-brown, and later, as she gets to know them, she will be able to trace in their lineaments the various tribes of Madagascar. But for now, she sees them as people who in some way look like her. People of color, similar to those who, passing her on streets in Italy and elsewhere around the world, exchange with her the swift, coded nod of diasporic cofraternity. Men and women who would not be out of place in a gathering of her relatives in Oakland or Washington, DC.

The difference from Black Americans being, she thinks—as she has on her trips to Ghana and Senegal—that the eyes of these residents hold a deep stillness, that they move through the world with the impeccable poise of people who live where their ancestors did, who have never been stolen or scattered.

"Ah, voici l'équipe! Bonjour, bonjour!" calls out Senna in a loud, joking tone, which is evidently the established way he relates to them. On her first trips abroad with Senna, Shay was at first mortified by the clowning persona he often adopted but has found to her surprise that his buffoonery works surprisingly well in countries where, in any case, Europeans are considered barbarians. The typical reaction is that Senna is at first tolerated with the indulgence reserved for children or lunatics, and then, slowly, an unexpected intimacy is born. Shay sees immediately from the expressions of the Red House staff that her husband is well liked, if not quite respected.

When, with the air of a ringmaster announcing a trapeze artist, he introduces her—"*Et finalement—la plus belle fleur de l'Amérique: ma femme, Madame Shay!*"—they address her in a sonorous chorus that sounds rehearsed: "*Bonjour, Madame!*"

But when she in turn greets them in painstakingly rehearsed Malagasy—"*Mula tsara!*"—they all burst out laughing.

It's a pure expression of appreciation, and she and Senna find themselves giggling too. To Shay this spontaneous peal of laughter is an unlooked-for gift that offers a shining glimpse of connection, of possibility. Perhaps indeed things will work out here.

But just then the dark faces close up like shutters, as a fat white man with a walking stick stumps onto the veranda. A loud European voice barks: "*Qu'est-ce que vous en faites là, à rire comme des couillons?* What are you all doing standing there laughing like fools? Where are the drinks for Madame and Monsieur?"

This is how Kristos, Senna's right-hand man in Madagascar, first appears before Shay, at the entrance to the house that will become their secret battlefield. Kristos the Greek, the house manager. Majordomo. *Governante*. From the start, her enemy.

He is Shay's first live example of the kind of pan-European rogue who turns up in African backwaters and in every derelict former outpost of empire. Claims to be a Greek from Thessaloniki, speaks Italian with a Pugliese accent, French with a Marseille slur, and a disconcerting amount of English with an Australian twang. Officious, devious, an expert snitch and bully, he embodies the first mate of every pirate ship in B movie history. Shorter than Senna—who is not tall—he has a grand vizier's belly that strains the waistband of his khaki shorts, a limp from some nameless catastrophe, a bulldog face purpled with rum, a bristle of stained mustache, and wispy, colorless hair bound back with a shoelace. And, like any stock character, he has props: a walking stick crudely carved with a coiling serpent; a neck chain displaying a coin he claims is a Roman aureus. When in the sun, he wears a sinister pink Panama hat.

Presented to the wife of his boss, he kisses the air over her hand as

Europeans of social pretensions do. Behind his greeting there is a stony challenge that she'll recall in future days, when she has begun to dread him. Why does he hate her so promptly? The answer is obvious: because her skin is as dark as that of the people he lords it over.

A thin smile crosses his lips as one of the younger housemaids hurries up to Shay and Senna with a tray bearing a pair of neon-colored drinks: canned pineapple juice tinged with grenadine syrup, served in tall glasses topped off with bougainvillea blossoms and plastic straws. This, he announces, is his own idea: to celebrate arrivals with a welcoming cocktail, as they do at swanky hotels in the Caribbean.

Shay and Senna exchange amused glances at this vulgarity. But Senna only says that they've thought from the start that it would be a fine thing to make use of the Red House, in the off-season, as a bed-and-breakfast, a *chambre d'hôtes*. That is their future plan. He adds that, now that Shay has arrived, the place will finally have the benefit of a woman's taste. Shay is surprised by the mild tone which her husband—usually brusque with Italian employees—adopts with his manager.

"Ah, but Signora Shay must be completely on holiday when she is here," counters Kristos smoothly. He spreads his ropy arms to indicate the staff who have scattered about their various duties. Around the edges of his squat, khaki-clad figure, Shay can glimpse the garden, a *hortus conclusus* dense with leaf and blossom. "The Signora won't have to lift a finger," adds the Greek.

6.

That night, when the watchmen have closed and locked the downstairs shutters, Senna undresses Shay ceremoniously by a flickering hurricane light in the master bedroom. Not exactly undresses, because she's wrapped her naked self up in the embroidered bedcover so that he can un-wind her, as Caesar is said to have freed Cleopatra from the fabled carpet. Senna has a hibiscus flower stuck behind one ear. It's perhaps the best time they will ever have in the Red House. They're drunk on Three Horses beer and vanilla rum; they're stuffed from feasting on coconut rice and oysters chipped from rocks at the far end of the beach. They're sunburnt from snor-keling. They're worn out from looking over the house and playfully arguing about rooms for the children they haven't yet had; from weaving plans for their friends who will arrive later in the summer, from discussing fishing trips, and overland treks, and motorcycle excursions into the backcountry.

When Shay stands stripped and giggling in front of him, Senna looks her over with an intent air of discovery.

"Well, *monsieur le patron?* Do I suit?" she demands. "I know you think I'm the last piece of furniture!"

"*No, no—tu sei la madonnina*. You're one of those holy statues—you know, a Madonna, a saint—like the country people used to build into their farmhouse walls back in Vercelli."

"A Black Madonna?"

"A *professoressa* like you doesn't know about the wonder-working Black Madonna? She has shrines all over Italy!"

"Let's forget about Italy," says Shay, yanking the flower out of his hair.

Tired as they both are, they charge into each other like teenagers that night, with uncontrollable laughter and a transcendent feeling of arrival.

But deep in the night, Shay, a seasoned traveler who usually sleeps well even in bare-bones hostels, wakes up to the crash of the tide beyond the garden wall. Over the nocturnal chorus of frogs, it sounds annunciatory, as if a single solemn phrase were being repeated over and over again. She frees herself gently from Senna's embrace and lies staring into darkness through the mosquito net of the huge four-poster bed. The disquiet she felt on the hillside this afternoon returns and becomes a wanderer's desolation at waking in a strange place. The strangest of places, this Madagascar—whose very name, like Timbuktu or Samarkand, is used by Americans as shorthand for the very farthest away one can be. And suddenly Shay is homesick, but for where? For the shingled house in the Oakland Hills where she spent her happy childhood? For the assortment of East Coast student digs she occupied after that? For the Milan apartment where she has chosen to start a new life?

Certainly, this big barracks of a villa on the shore of the Indian Ocean could never offer such comfort. She pictures how the crested roof must look silhouetted against the night sky inscribed with Southern constellations. And then she imagines the dark island: cane fields whispering in the breeze, the forest alive with the glittering wakeful eyes of the small beasts; the villages sheltering the sleep of men and women like those she met today, all in mute dreaming conversation with ancestors. In those huts no one has to wonder where home is. From the ground under their dwellings their history rises and cradles them.

Lying there in the darkness beside her, Senna himself seems an unknown country. What does he feel about this house besides satisfied vanity? What does he find in this distant land, and in these people—and what of value is he bringing here?

And for herself she wonders: How the hell did I end up in this place? And: What do I owe? For something is owed, she feels certain.

For a long time she lies awake, listening to the waves and nervously twisting a lock of her short hair, until dawn comes with the clamor of cockcrow, a brief dogfight, and the call of a distant muezzin. All the time, she has been thinking. Thinking: *I have a house in Africa . . .*

7.

So Shay steps reluctantly into her role as the foreign mistress of the Red House. Guiltily she admits to herself that, with regard to Naratrany, she'd prefer to be a tourist—that word that, once upon a time in student days, she used as a gibe. But now, being a respectful tourist seems like a decent alternative to delving into the soul of a place where she senses she may be far out of her depth. Her unacknowledged desire is to skim over the surface of life in this new country, as she does when she swims over a reef: breathing outside air, observing through a mask.

She and Senna quickly make the Red House the center of their vacation months, a setting for the ritual leisure of the holidays, when Italians flock out of the cities to Riccione or the Red Sea resorts, or the mountain valleys of Aosta. Friends and relatives make the long trip to stay with them, passing July and August weeks filled with diving, fishing, sailing to the Radames archipelago, stalking lemurs with cameras, traveling to the big island to explore the *tsingy* of the Ankarana or paddle pirogues down the Sambirano River. The guests always have a great time. At the house, they roast themselves into a sunburnt stupor on lounge chairs facing Finoana Bay, sit lazy hours around the long dining table on the veranda, smoking, drinking beer and wine, chattering in French and Italian and English throughout Pantagruelian creole-style meals of pasta, smoked white tuna, *romaẓava, poulet à la vanille.*

These vacations are part of the new life Shay assumes with what her mother insists on calling her "conversion to Italy." The larger picture includes negotiating the provincial Vercellese culture of her in-laws; refurbishing the rambling apartment she and Senna have bought near Corso Magenta; putting on hold her plans to turn her dissertation into a book, as, in the drafty halls of the Università Cattolica, she finds herself suddenly teaching a wildly popular introductory course on Black American literature.

In the midst of all this, there is no way to define what Madagascar means to her. Certainly, she can't place it under the heading she knows well from her upbringing: the conventional African-American reverence for a romanticized and undifferentiated ancestral continent. She has tried, and failed, to connect this newly introduced East African country to her emotions about the regions of West Africa that she believes were home to her own ancestors—to link it to the anguished spirits she clearly sensed while visiting the slave palaces of Gorée. But Madagascar is itself, with its own bloodstained warp and weft of tribal and slaving heritage; not to be defined by foreign myths—whether the myth of Libertalia or that of a uniform African experience.

Still, the Red House refuses to be ignored. It intrudes into her dreams as she lies in bed on foggy nights in Milan, and pops into her head as she coaxes her students through *Cane* and *Native Son,* or sits eating osso buco with Senna's family on rainy Sundays. She envisions Naratrany island not as it appears in the balmy dry season of June to November, but in the February monsoon period. The time when the house is shuttered, tended by a skeleton crew of caretakers coughing with the maladies that run through the villages. Cyclone season, when tempests march up from Australia, inflicting floods and starvation. There in Europe, she pictures the Red House at its worst: swarming with winged termites, its furniture cloaked in sailcloth, roof thatch stripped off in stray gales. The waves on the beach frothing yellow, laden with debris, and the roads transformed to arteries of mud. It is then that, from thousands of miles away, the house calls out to her like a feverish child in the night.

Oddly enough, Senna, creator and official master of the place, seems to feel nothing of the sort. The minute it is built and furnished, it loses its urgent central role in his imagination. It becomes just a vacation retreat, as richer Italians possess in far more fashionable foreign resorts, an exotic status symbol to boast about at parties. Of course, he considers it a responsibility and an expense—though not much of the latter, given the minuscule cost of living in Madagascar, where a good yearly salary would cover the price of a pair of trousers in Milan. And there is not much responsibility, either, since, to keep things in trim, they luckily have Kristos, that great guy. *Quel bravo ragazzo.* That is how Senna has taken to describing the house manager.

Senna says it's Shay's fault that she doesn't get along with the Greek. Part of the eternal wifely inability to tolerate *gli amici del bar*: male buddies, the great guys of the world. He himself, from the start, finds in Kristos a boon companion. Together, they embark on fishing expeditions in the murky shark-infested waters off Analalava. Kristos has convinced Senna to invest in a second truck, a massive Defender pickup with a rhino bar, and in this ostentatious vehicle they make backcountry excursions on Naratrany to seek out village woodcarvers who can add to the decorations of the house. Along with Aakash, a young Karan Indian who owns the garage in nearby Renirano village, they begin a fascinating hobby of salvaging and rebuilding vintage French motorbikes. These pastimes take Senna away from Shay, but a man's vacation is his own, right? Shay has plenty of company, with all the friends they invite from Italy and the States. Not only that, adds Senna, but she is mistress of a magnificent villa where her word is law.

But the fact is that after two years of holidays, Shay finds that not only is she far from understanding what being mistress of the Red House entails, but also her rapport with Senna—that ineffable bond between a husband and wife, nourished on a mysterious balance of affinities—disintegrates when she is there. A few days after arriving on Naratrany, Senna becomes unrecognizable: cold, critical, subject to ferocious explosions of temper. Shay is at first incredulous, then furious. After that, as is her way, she takes it inside of herself. She avoids Senna. She sleeps badly beside him, the mere sound of his breath pitching her into agitation. Underlying everything is her peculiar inability to find a role of authority at the Red House; and at the center of it all, like a prehistoric stone under the altar at a shrine, is the house manager.

Kristos is never overtly rude, yet in her bones she knows that he hates and undermines her. With a flash of his wolfish pale eyes, he smoothly accedes to whatever request she makes, and then ignores it. Whatever questions she asks, he finds a way of not answering.

And there are many questions. From childhood on, Shay has absorbed a fascination with old-fashioned housekeeping from her dauntingly practical mother, a county administrator for a network of public libraries, who collects volumes of Victorian household lore, which she melds with domestic wisdom passed down from her own Black southern grandmothers. Shay has found the tradition of efficient house management alive and well both in Italy and in other big households in Madagascar.

But in the Red House, things stumble along. Why, for example, in a place with guests coming and going, with eight bedrooms, and countless outbuildings, is there no dedicated laundry room? What happened to the washing machine ordered from Mauritius? Why are the maids obliged to scrub clothes and household linens in plastic basins in a back courtyard, and to iron while squatting on the storeroom floor? Why is the concrete of the outdoor steps already crumbling? Why is the generator so poorly wired that the overhead fans, refrigerator, and freezer shudder to a halt three or four times a day? Why are the trucks, motorcycles, and motor launch always out of gas? Why are they endlessly buying food and supplies?

Back in Milan, Shay would have put a quick stop to this mismanagement, but here she finds it curiously difficult to get a grip on the situation. When she brings up any of these concerns to Senna—the kinds of things they work out easily at home—he flies into such a rage that she begins to wonder about his sanity. And anything she attempts on her own is met with an odd ineffectiveness, as if she is trying to grasp smoke. And with smirking resistance from Kristos.

She knows of course what the house manager's role is in her plantation fantasy: he is the overseer, the noxious intermediary between the gilded bubble of the gentry and the sweat and blood of the slaves. She sees this clearly as she watches him strut through house and garden with his bloated belly swelling his fussily ironed shirts and khaki shorts. Or sees him tearing around in the Defender, wearing that revolting pink hat. Or catches him hollering at the staff (out of earshot of Senna) as he brandishes his serpent-carved walking stick.

Somehow, the Greek has created an occult reign of terror among the soft-spoken employees of the Red House. He barks orders at them all day long in French and Malagasy, swears at them with obscene inventiveness, calls them savages, keeps them well beyond working hours set by government law, and constantly exacts fines from their salaries for an array of petty damages and presumed crimes of which he alone knows the details. Between Shay and Senna, only Shay seems to see all this.

In Italy she has come to terms with the culture of domestic help: the rigorously unionized maids and housekeepers, who, along with intrusive in-laws, are an accepted part of Italian middle-class life. But here in Madagascar, where the houses of the prosperous tend to sprawl, to attract entire families of workers, and where the atmosphere of colonial France still hangs heavy in the air, she feels as if she is witnessing a shadow play of the experiences of her own enslaved ancestors. And so the injustice under her roof gives her a double sense of shame.

Anjatoky. Celestine. Lova. Cyprien. Bakoly. Landry. Kiady. Camille. Zalifa. Benjamin . . . Shay by now knows their names, the people whose workdays are spent on the Sennas' holiday comfort, whose joint efforts keep the Red House sailing along like a galleon headed for an unknown shore. The people who are unfailingly benign and courteous to her, but who seem to be asking her a silent question: Why is she allowing things to proceed like this? They, and she, know that there are other large households in Madagascar run in dignified ways, by mistresses both brown and white.

Once or twice one of the youngest housemaids comes weeping to Shay in private over some accusation—say, of pilfering rice or laundry soap— and begs her to intercede with Kristos. But when Shay attempts to resolve the matter, she once again faces the mocking resistance of the Greek and the incomprehensible rage of Senna—who accuses his wife of bending to the crocodile tears of the servants, and interfering with the manager's authority.

So Shay's initial wish for superficiality has been granted: she is a guest in her own house. She feels it in the mornings as she drinks her coffee at the head of the table covered with serving dishes swathed in gauzy fly covers. In the afternoons and evenings, when she hangs out reading and chatting on the beach with her own guests, or kicks around a soccer ball with the Finoana village kids, or comes back salt-soaked from diving in the outer islands, or sits long over dinner on the veranda, as citronella candles flicker in glass shades. At all times, she sees the people who work for her looking at her over a barrier. A barrier of her own impotence and two white men.

How has this come about? How has Shay—known since childhood

for being irrepressible and irreverent inside and outside the classroom—turned into this easily silenced person in Madagascar?

Yet all returns to normal when she leaves for Italy. The intense anger and frustration, hardly remembered, evaporates so quickly, unremarked by Senna—who returns to being the man she loves—that it seems like a dream. It is all so vague that she has been unable to discuss it even with her mother and sister.

She has spoken of it only with a Malagasy friend, Angélique, an elegant, vivacious Betsileo woman, who is the pharmacist in Saint Grimaud. Angélique knows all the island gossip and has dire things to report about Kristos. For one thing, no one believes he is really Greek. The story is that he is a small-time Calabrian thug who got in trouble with some Albanians, and fled first to Saloniki, then to Johannesburg, and finally to Madagascar, where he knocked around Toamasina and Saint Marie, fleecing tourists, before washing up on Naratrany.

"Your husband was most unwise to hire that crook!" exclaims Angélique, in one of these conversations, adjusting her stylishly eccentric French glasses. Educated in Grenoble, she is tall and thin and has glowing high-country skin and chic, chemically lightened hair. She is divorced and runs her pharmacy and her own large family with impeccable control.

She describes Kristos as the worst kind of racist, one who hates *"les nègres"* more than the most retrograde Frenchman on the island. He has been overheard at the Fleur des Îles café describing Madagascar as a filthy sewer; particularly he inveighs against the poor prostitutes who, as in every seaport in the world, struggle to make their meager living—calls them insects, filth. But at the same time his appetite for those despised girls is boundless; he is always hustling them out onto the dark beach behind the Finoana billiard hall. Old Madame Revelle's housekeeper reports that he goes to bed with the old lady on Sunday afternoons, then cheats her out of big sums of money at cards. It's common gossip as well that during the construction of the Red House, Kristos was selling off sacks of concrete, cinder blocks, copper pipes, lumber, and even household appliances. His companions in thieving are a pair of Comorean sisters from Anjouan, owners of a string of dry goods stores around northern Madagascar: dangerous women, rumored to have connections to drug syndicates in Mahajanga and, still worse, to practice powerful Black magic.

And the airs Kristos gives himself when the Sennas are back in Italy! Angélique casts her large eyes dramatically toward the ceiling. "He swans around in that big flashy truck of yours, telling everyone that the Red House is his. You *have* to do something!"

Shay, who during this diatribe has been standing with her elbow on the pharmacy counter, looks down past the overpriced French sun creams to her sandaled feet on the gleaming tile floor. The place looks like any drugstore in Europe except that in the corner dozes a white cat with its eyes stitched shut with blindness and, outside in the dusty street, women pass by bearing bright-colored plastic buckets on their heads. "I can't," she whispers.

"*Tu ne peux pas?* But why?"

"I don't know. I just can't do anything."

"What about Senna?"

"It's like he's hypnotized," Shay confesses. "He believes everything Kristos tells him. He says Kristos is a great guy. And—well, he seems to hate me. I can hardly say a word to him."

"And back home in Italy?"

"Then he's a different person."

"Aaah," exclaims Angélique on a peculiar rising and falling note. "And if I may say, you seem worn out and your looks are suffering. (I never did like those twists you do with your hair, but *ça c'est la mode Américaine.*) This is very bad, *ma chère. Ça devient dangereux.* Why didn't I think of it? I should have seen it from the first. You absolutely have to—"

Just at that moment, a noisy group of South Africans from a cruise ship pours into the pharmacy, and Shay never learns what that urgent advice is.

Certainly there's a sense that things are fast slipping out of control. Every morning when she wakes in the Red House, she seems to have proceeded further into a skewed dimension.

For one thing there are the plants and the statues.

When Senna and Shay arrive in July of their second year, they find that Kristos has replaced a third of the garden with a planting of cacti—prickly pear, agave, and other thorny succulents—set into an expanse of pulverized black volcanic rock from the quarries up the coast so that the place under the midday sun is a miniature desert. "Let the fellow do what he wants—he knows what's best for the house!" roars Senna, when Shay objects.

And week by week over that summer, Kristos encourages Senna's newfound passion for wooden sculptures, urging him to commission dozens from backcountry artisans. These works share a family resemblance: nearly life-size and not particularly well crafted, created in a faux-primitive style that Kristos seems to favor, like cheap figurines at souvenir stands all over Africa. The statues are set up along the garden paths and inside the house. Teak women with big breasts and protuberant behinds, bearing platters and bowls. Naked men with half-erect penises and slouched hats. Some have serpents coiling around their bodies, like the snake that decorates Kristos's walking stick; and indeed, a rosewood beam adorned with a large, undulating python soon replaces the original lintel over the house entrance.

The growing number of statues gives the house a crowded, public feeling, like a train station, and sometimes at dusk, as guests gather on the veranda, and the maids move around lighting mosquito coils and preparing the dinner table, Shay has trouble distinguishing the real people from the wooden. She has an unpleasant recurring dream, in which she is lost in a dim multitude buzzing with rumors over a guilty secret of hers. In the daytime, a lowering cloud seems to hang in the atmosphere. But though the Sennas have friends and relatives staying with them, no one else seems to notice.

Shay's lethargy increases. A mist seems to lie between her and the rest of the world. She feels dragged *à rebours,* against the grain, as if her cells have been pulled out of alignment. She wonders if she has malaria or dengue fever. But this is a familiar feeling, one she knows will lift when she returns to Milan. She'll hardly remember it, just as the peculiar rift between her and Senna will almost instantaneously heal and be forgotten, leaving them as content with each other as any couple married just two years. But here and now, Senna's attitude toward her is one of cold disfavor radiating from the farthest corner of the big bed, where he sleeps withdrawn from her as if by religious conviction.

8.

One July afternoon when Senna is off fishing, it all comes to a head. Shay has just stepped out of the shower when she hears a commotion coming from the beach. She pulls a sundress over her bare body and hurries to see what is going on. On the sand just below the stone garden wall she finds two of the maids and the two gardeners bending over a moaning, thrashing figure she thinks at first is a sick animal. But it turns out to be a girl who seems to be having a seizure.

She is one of the beautiful young Sakalava women who are as thick on the island as butterflies around a buddleia plant. But now her deep brown face is overlaid with a ghastly pallor and her braids are matted in sand where in her paroxysm she has ground her head into the beach. And a large dark stain is spreading at the crotch of her flimsy Chinese-made jeans.

"*Ventre! Ventre!*" exclaims Landry, the younger of the two gardeners over his shoulder as Shay dashes up. Stomach? thinks Shay. The girl seems to be hemorrhaging. A miscarriage?

They are trying to move the girl onto a straw mat spread on the sand. Shay, ablaze with the energy of crisis, shouts at them to wait, that they have to get her to the clinic run by Dominican nuns on the port road. Both of the house trucks are in use, so she grabs Landry by the arm and dashes with him a hundred yards down the beach to the Gargotte P'tit Coin, a combination café and food stall where there are always a few bush taxis. With shouts they wake up the dozing driver of the least decrepit vehicle, and, after Landry translates Shay's directions, the battered Renault 4 trundles down a rocky incline to the edge of the beach by the Red House, followed by a slowly growing swarm of curious onlookers—villagers, staff from the house and from the café.

Somehow they lift the groaning, writhing girl into the cramped backseat, a towel under her backside and the two Red House maids crowding in to support her. And Shay, who has sent for her handbag, has opened the front door to climb inside when a shout stops her.

It is Kristos, returned from town, who seems to have popped up from the sand like a malevolent genie.

"*Non, Non,*" he shouts. "*Non! Madame ne va pas! Pas avec la salope, la— Allez! Allez!*"

His face is purple with fury, and he actually strikes the hood of the taxi a loud wallop with his walking stick. The little knot of onlookers stands frozen. At his sudden appearance, Shay, to her lasting shame, jumps away from the car and stands before him like a child caught in a misdeed by a parent.

"We have to get this girl to the Dominicans! She may be dying!" she cries in Italian, straight into his face.

To this, the Greek replies with a broad, bitter smile that shows his discolored teeth. "She'll live, she'll live—you've seen to that," he says softly.

"Let's take her in the truck—it'll be faster!" urges Shay, but the odd smile never leaves Kristos's face.

"No," he says, as if he has every right to say it. "And you won't go either."

He turns quickly, bangs shut the door of the taxi with his stick, and barks out a peremptory order. As the driver immediately starts to back up, Shay reaches suddenly into her bag and before Kristos can stop her, tosses a wad of *ariary* notes in through the Renault window. "*Pour le docteur!*" she cries as the taxi jounces away.

Kristos is shaking his head in a chiding way that increases her rage. The little crowd of onlookers has melted away and the two of them are left facing each other on the beach, in the blinding sun and the deep afternoon hush of low tide.

"You encourage things you don't understand," he says to her in Italian, still in that infuriating soft voice. "Now every little whore on the island will show up on our doorstep asking for money to go to the clinic. Let them go back to their villages—the old women know what to do."

"Sei senza cuore," whispers Shay. "You are heartless."

"And you understand nothing," he says, and this time the contempt he feels is undisguised.

"Get out of my sight!" Shay suddenly shrieks, not caring who overhears.

But the Greek looks completely unperturbed. He gives a mocking bow and turns away with the words "As the Signora prefers."

And a half hour later, anyone in the Red House can hear Senna berating his wife at the top of his lungs. Fortunately, they are in a hiatus between guests, but there are still plenty of staff to eavesdrop near the closed doors of their bedroom as the Milanese hollers mad, disjointed accusations, completely comprehensible in any tongue. Senna, raging, shouts that Shay has been unforgivably rude, given offense to the good man who is their only hope in this benighted country; that she is maliciously trying to bring the whole house down around their ears because of her American presumptuousness, and he, Senna, is disgusted by such behavior.

"We need Kristos!" bellows Senna at the end of his tirade. "Do you know how hard it is to find a white man to run things in Africa?"

Then the bedroom door crashes open, slams shut, and he storms out to the parking space where the Greek stands calmly beside the Defender, leaning on his stick, and smoking.

"Get in," the cook, who understands Italian, plainly hears Kristos say in a commanding tone to his employer. "And drive me to town. I need cigarettes."

Shay doesn't hear this, but she is already in shock. No one has ever spoken to her as Senna has just done. She prides herself on being a staunch fighter, and has engaged in plenty of stormy scenes with men throughout her life. But this one—where she has found herself mute while enduring a rant that sweeps far past offensiveness; words that have broken through into a mad new world—has severed the last link allowing her to believe in any manageable reality.

She sits on the edge of the bed, tears of rage and desperation running in sheets down her cheeks, and stares blankly at her phone. Outside the windows, the quick darkness of the tropics has descended and she can hear the crash of the rising tide and clattering of palm fronds as the offshore wind strengthens. It sounds like a tempest, but she knows that if she steps outside she will find above the furiously buffeted trees a star-studded sky of uncanny serenity.

She needs to act, to call someone, but who? Cell phones barely work here. Her mother in Oakland and her sister in Ann Arbor will be lost in their time zones, two small scratchy voices fading in and out at the other end of the line. Neither of them has yet visited Madagascar; her marriage and passage into Italian life has already widened the distance between them, and this further dimension of new experience is something impossible to explain. What is she supposed to shout over the patchy satellite connection: that she thinks—no, is almost certain—that her husband is possessed?

She could pack a bag and go, but where? The next flight off the island is five days away. She could take the truck and go stay in town with Angélique, who would indeed understand, but she imagines the lecture she'd receive, the gossip spreading exponentially.

She is still sitting there in the darkened room, staring blankly at the phone as if she expects an oracular message to appear, when there is a tap at the door and a soft voice asking in Malagasy for permission to enter. *"Hodi."*

Shay remembers that it is time for the maids to turn down the beds and light mosquito coils for the night. She composes herself so as to have a shred of dignity, and calls out the polite response: *"Karibu."*

9.

The door opens. But instead of one of the young chambermaids she expects, there enters an older woman, one who usually does not do such tasks.

This woman's name is Bertine, and she is in charge of the household laundry and storerooms: directing the washing, ironing, keeping of the linens, and organizing general supplies. She holds an undefined position of authority among the rest of the staff, somehow even respected by Kristos, who never raises his voice to her. Shay has always found her slightly intimidating—watchful, silent, omnipresent, like a shadow.

One of Kristos's odious observations that Shay has overheard is that, on an island of beauties, he has never seen a homelier woman than Bertine. But Bertine is not at all ugly; rather, she is imposing. She is pure Sakalava, born in the north of Naratrany, the thickly forested hill territory that the locals refer to as *la montagne*: a region where there are no roads, and lemurs still abound. At nearly six feet tall, she has broad shoulders; slim, sinewy hips; and large, emphatic breasts—hence her nickname: Bertine la Grande. Her dark skin has a bloom on it like that of a ripe plum, and she has a round face with a tiny, upturned Sakalava nose, a mouthful of strong teeth yellowed from smoking, and small ears that stick out like jug handles.

She could be any age from thirty to fifty, but she dresses like an older woman—never in the flimsy polyester minidresses and tight Chinese-made jeans the younger maids wear when off duty, but always a long skirt, or a print *lamba* with a starched blouse on top. Her hair is never straightened in European fashion or sewn onto long extensions, a style just becoming fashionable on the island, but severely divided into six neat knots.

En route to work, to keep her hairdo free from blowing sand and dust, Bertine wears a puffy, oversize man's visored cap, the shape of a pimp's hat in a seventies blaxploitation movie. But hers is weathered to an indeterminate organic color. This colossal piece of headgear rests above her protuberant ears in a way that could be comical, but instead gives her a peculiar majesty, her tall silhouette instantly identifiable as she strides up and down the beach from her home in Renirano village.

Hatless now, she comes into the bedroom carrying a saucer holding a lit mosquito coil that trails bluish smoke. With a quiet *"Bonsoir,"* she puts it down on a small table, turns on a lamp, and sets about closing the window shutters. Meanwhile Shay sits as if transfixed on the bed, clutching her phone, and keeping her spine straight, as if these two things might give her strength. She cannot not pretend that the whole household has not overheard everything.

"Madame," she hears Bertine address her in a soft voice. *"Madame. Ça va pas bien.* Things are not going well, Madame. In this house."

The silence, the pretense at normality, has been broken. Shay's eyes once again overflow with sheets of tears, and, abandoning any attempt at composure, she bows her head and manages to choke out the word "No."

Her shoulders shake with sobs. In America or in Italy, anyone seeing this might pat her head with a maternal gesture, murmur some word of comfort, even offer her a hug. But Bertine la Grande stands quietly in front of her and simply waits until she is calmer. Standing there barefoot in all of her height, looking gravely down at Shay on the bed, she seems not a housekeeper but a dignitary about to make a pronouncement.

"It's that bastard Kristos," whispers Shay.

"Not just that man," says Bertine, regarding her intensely with her large dark eyes set in slightly bluish whites. From the start, Bertine rarely refers to the Greek by name, preferring to call him "that man," or "that one." "That one has called in others. And they have opened the gate."

"What?" says Shay, feeling she has descended one more step into madness.

"Don't worry—*ne t'inquiètes pas.* It is not for you to understand. Not yet."

It will take several conversations before Shay notices what sophisticated French the woman speaks, in comparison to the other Malagasy people working in the house. Right now, she just sits and absorbs what she is hearing in the lamplit room.

"It is very bad for you," repeats Bertine. Like everyone on the island, she always uses the informal *"tu,"* but here it sounds deliberately intimate.

"And for my husband?"

An almost mocking smile flickers on the other woman's face. "No," she says, carelessly. "Senna"—she tosses off her employer's name as if speaking of a child—"is not important here. That man is using him, nothing more. But the real danger is for you. Look at you, Madame—you're thin, getting sick."

A chill runs through Shay, because she knows it is true. "Why is he doing this?" she asks. "Kristos. What does he want?"

Bertine shrugs. "He wants everything. He wants the house, the land. That is how he is."

"But that's not possible! It's against the law!"

"Anything is possible here. The law doesn't always work, not even for white men. Things like this have happened before, many times."

Shay feels a surge of anger. "I want to get out of this place," she says between her teeth. "Never come back! Leave Senna, too."

Bertine looks very grave. "No, you must not do that. We want you here in Madagascar. We like you. We think that you should be a real mistress to this house."

"We?" Shay looks at her uncertainly.

"All of us in the Red House. We who work here and earn a good living. We who live on the island. We *teratany*. We think you should stay with your husband. Come back and forth for nice holidays as you do now. A few months a year—that's the right amount of time for *vazaha* to be in Madagascar—otherwise the sun makes your brains go wrong. You will have children, and become really the queen of this house, as it should be."

"But how?"

"That man must go. The house will be cleaned, and will be yours. Your husband will come back to you."

"How?" repeats Shay.

"I will help you. I'll speak to some others. We will help you. It will be . . ." Bertine pauses and gives Shay a significant look, as if she is reminding her of something forgotten. "It will be work we women do. Just between women."

In a quick, low voice, she gives Shay a few instructions, to which Shay listens obediently, and then Bertine turns to go. But Shay detains her. "Why are you helping me?" she asks.

Once again Bertine faces her. "Because we are women and we all have the same problems. And, Madame, you helped me."

"How?"

"*La fille à la plage*. The girl on the beach."

In her disarray, Shay has almost forgotten the girl of that afternoon. "The one I sent to the clinic?" Once again she pictures the blind look of pain in the girl's eyes, her agonized, thrashing body. "Is she all right?"

"She is my sister's daughter, and she will be well now."

"Was it a . . ." Shay doesn't know the French word for miscarriage.

"She was bleeding because she was losing a child."

"An accident?" asks Shay awkwardly.

Bertine la Grande raises her chin slowly, her eyes fixed on Shay's. A gecko croaks somewhere high in the rafters, and the lamplight gleams along the curve of her cheek. "A child who could not be born," she says obliquely.

"And the father?" asks Shay in a faint voice.

Bertine holds her gaze. *"À qui penses-tu?"*

The rest of that evening and the next two days are surprisingly tranquil in the Red House. Shay regains her composure after her conversation with Bertine, of which everyone working in the house somehow seems aware, though no one else alludes to anything by even so much as a meaningful glance. The older woman has instructed her to be calm and dignified and act as if nothing at all has happened; to be distant, but pleasant, with Kristos, and act charitably toward Senna, whom it is best to think of as a small boy with some undisclosed ailment. This is all easy for Shay because Senna, under the thumb of the Greek, seems truly not to recall their dispute. And Kristos, puffed up with triumph, is fawningly courteous to her as if he feels he can now afford to be generous.

Bertine's further instructions are both specific and cryptic. Shay is simply to wait for the right day, sometime soon, when a woman from Bertine's village will come by with a basket of fruit or vegetables, and will invite Shay for a walk. "When this happens, you must put on a dress with long sleeves, and a hat, and go with her. Don't tell anyone. Just be ready."

10.

At midmorning of the second day after the household drama, the wind picks up. It begins as a normal tidal breeze but doesn't subside after a few minutes—instead, grows stronger, as if it is February and a cyclone is charging in from Indonesia. But the sky holds nothing but blue. Palms clatter and bend, women's *lambas* flap like flags, and out past the reef, small fishing pirogues, square sails bellying, rocket along toward safer harbors beyond the headlands.

As the sun sinks lower, a violent gust races through the garden and rips off a big branch from the kapok tree at the left side of the house. It crashes down on the stone walk to the beach, just missing the edge of the roof. Another hurricane gust sweeps through the house, knocking over lamps, rattling pictures, and sending a fossilized Aepyornis maximus egg, set decoratively on a table, flying off its wooden pedestal to roll across the floor like a stone football. The two kitchen cats go shooting up and down the staircases, with eyes ablaze and fur on end. The air crackles with electricity, and the fallen branch fills the garden with a powerful smell of fresh sap.

"Maybe," remarks a luncheon guest, a Frenchman who runs a restaurant in town with his male Malagasy lover, "Maybe it is time to call in the medicine man!" He says this in the manner of someone making a joke to express a truth he expects no one will discern.

The next day, as the gardeners are chopping up the fallen branch and dragging off the chunks of bright yellow wood, one of the housemaids brings Shay the message that a village woman called Fayeda is asking for her down on the beach. This is the signal Shay has been waiting for. Quickly, she changes into an outfit prepared two days earlier: a long blue and white striped peasant dress that she usually wears open over a bikini. Now, severely buttoned, and worn with hat and sandals, it seems like garb she'd wear back in Oakland to go with her grandmother to Shiloh A.M.E. Church. (Shay's parents are easygoing California agnostics, but as a child Shay loved being in a Sunday morning forest of old people at Nana Gilliam's side.) She picks up the woven shoulder bag that holds a small amount of money and the modest present that Bertine has indicated she should bring along: a pair of silver earrings.

It is just after lunch and the Red House seems as empty as it will ever be. Kristos and Senna have left for a day of fishing north of Nosy Mamoko. It is Bertine's day off. Except for the gardeners, absorbed in dismembering the fallen branch, the household staff are squatted peacefully under the mango tree behind the kitchen, chatting over their midday rice. Shay feels invisible as she whisks through the crowd of wooden statues and across Kristos's cactus garden, and steps onto the sand. Waiting here beside a market basket of papayas is Fayeda, a gaunt Sakalava woman with a *lamba* hooded above her face, which is thickly smeared with reddish clay against the sun. They exchange Malagasy greetings, and Fayeda, who clearly speaks no French, simply says "Bertine," then in a single practiced movement sets the huge basket on her head and sets off down the beach with Shay.

Shay has often seen and photographed these market women who pass by every morning: living caryatids who balance their piled wares effortlessly on their superb straight necks and backs. But walking beside a bearer of one of those big straw hemispheres is something else, like being part of a grand procession. Yet there is hardly anyone to see in this burning noon hour, as she and Fayeda trudge silently across the sand toward the creek that runs through mangrove flats into the sea. Only a few children in tattered school pinafores greet them shyly, and stare at Shay. It is the lowest of low tides, what the islanders call *la grande basse,* and far out beyond the naked shell-strewn expanse, the Mozambique Channel lies in perfect repose, and farther still, below a bank of cumulus clouds, stretches the undulating violet silhouette of the Grande Île. All is hushed and distances seem close.

When they turn inland on the path along the estuary, Shay sees Bertine in the distance, unmistakable in her oversize hat. Bertine is festively dressed in a two-piece yellow skirt and *lamba* suitable for a Sunday, and she stands smoking a cigarette beside a battered taxi, a Renault sunken so low to the ground that it seems to have no wheels at all. Bertine waves, and then, to Shay's surprise, Fayeda, with astonishing swiftness, turns off on a narrow side path leading in back of a small hotel. In a few seconds, she and her huge basket have vanished among the mangroves.

"Seulement nous deux," says Bertine, tossing away her cigarette butt, as Shay reaches her. With an ease that would be unthinkable in the Red House, she greets Shay in the Malagasy way, with two kisses on the left cheek and one on the right. And Shay, for the first time, breathes in the scent she will afterward always think of as the soul of Bertine: cigarettes—the harsh brand popular on Naratrany, called Good Look—and laundry soap.

"Where are we going?" asks Shay, as they pry open the tinny doors and cram themselves into the stifling backseat.

Bertine arranges her yellow skirts and settles her puffy hat formally on her knees the way a woman in a limousine might set down her evening purse. She gives a few instructions to the taxi driver, a long-faced man with an elaborately sculpted beard, then turns to Shay: *"Allons chez le Voisin,"* she says. "We are going to see the Neighbor."

Among all the events of that extraordinary day—a day that, it would not be too much to say, forever changes Shay's view of life—she hardly remembers the strangeness of that ride, when, in the suffocating heat of the tiny backseat, squeezed up against the body of another woman who until recently has been a distant acquaintance, she recognizes that a mysterious thread of attachment has spun itself between the two of them. More than that, there has been a power shift. Bertine is clearly in control of the situation, now more mistress than servant as she sits composedly there in her holiday attire, her work-twisted dark hands like roots clutching her cap. She sits there, knowing. Knowing, as Shay does not, where they are headed and what they will find.

The shockless Renault trundles along the old broken colonial road in the direction of Siramatany, the sugar mill town, where there are no tourist hotels, just an expanse of millworkers' and fishermen's huts. Bertine is chatting with the driver, apparently having informed him that she is taking the foreign lady to bargain for embroidered curtains made by the fishermen's wives. She points out a tiny roadside Catholic church as the place where she was confirmed, and Shay thinks of how little she knows of Bertine's life. Whereas the other woman, in the manner of domestic workers, knows intimate things about Shay. Is Bertine married? Does she have children? What does she see when she gets home each night?

The taxi makes its way into the ugly dilapidated town, past the half-derelict sugar mill, past tangles of rusted machinery, past godowns and garages and a sun-flayed marketplace, where in the noonday heat vendors doze in the shade of stalls hung with fly-encrusted strips of meat. Bertine and Shay pay the driver and get out near the elementary school, a once-plastered colonial building now scaled and flaking with a hundred shades of rot. Here, in the humming stillness, Bertine settles her cap on her head and leads Shay between the shanties.

As they advance into the labyrinth of bamboo huts patched haphazardly with bits of wood and metal, the path changes from trodden earth to sand; Shay can hear the sound of waves on an invisible shore nearby. She recalls that the beach here is notorious among foreigners because the townspeople, in the old island manner, still use it as a toilet. The sun beats down savagely on the shanties, for there are no trees, just occasional thornbushes stuck with trash. And not a soul is visible except for sleeping dogs and a few lean, wandering chickens. But suddenly up ahead comes a flare of moving light, and as Bertine laughs softly in recognition, a vision flashes into sight: the little girl in the white dress.

After a minute, Shay sees that the dress is one of the cheap sateen gowns sold in the Chinese dry goods stores for first communions, but so startling is the appearance of a child thus attired, in the sunlit lanes of poverty, that she seems like an emissary from another world. Later Shay will liken the sight to unexpected apparitions of children in art—the little girl in the darkness of Rembrandt's *Night Watch,* the tiny red dress flickering through the black and white Holocaust in *Schindler's List.* But now, swimming deep in oneiric single-mindedness, she simply follows Bertine, who in turn follows their small guide.

After many twists and turns, Bertine pauses and gives Shay a big smile that shows her cigarette-stained teeth. *"Nous sommes arrivées,"* she says. "But first let's buy some Coca-Cola and some candy for the children, at the store."

Store? Shay's puzzled gaze falls on a small wooden flap unlatched on the side of one of the huts, to form a rudimentary counter with a tiny window behind it. Laid out on the counter are a cake of brown soap, the inevitable pack of Good Look cigarettes, and a big old-fashioned screw-top jar full of hard candies. Inside, she can just see the outline of a face and she realizes that her progress through the village has been marked by a series of just such hidden gazes out of the shadows. She produces a bit of change, and buys a big glass bottle of Coke, then fills her skirt pocket with miniature hard candies, whose wrappers, she is amused to see, have an American flag design.

The little girl has vanished, but immediately another odd figure appears in the distance. A small, skinny Sakalava man, wearing a ragged polo shirt and tattered red shorts, his head topped with what looks like the ruin of a trucker's cap, comes jogging toward them with a peculiar bouncy gait, a clownish, crazy prance that sometimes turns into a spin—not as if he is drunk, but as if he's enacting a playful pattern choreographed in his mind. Again, Bertine seems unsurprised and greets him softly. The man's bearded face is impassive, but he salutes them with a gesture that is careless, even flippant, then suddenly vanishes behind a hut somewhat bigger than most, with a cinder-block foundation and a roof of corrugated aluminum.

"*Ici,*" says Bertine, leading Shay around a corner to a doorway in the same hut. Here, after Shay leaves her sandals beside a blue plastic washtub, they mount a rickety step and, when Bertine has asked permission, push aside a doorway curtain of coarse white cotton cut out and embroidered in the island version of Richelieu style.

Inside, Shay's dazzled eyes encounter a crowded dimness. Five or six people kneel on straw mats or sit with their backs propped against the side of a double bed of carved reddish wood, the kind that Indian merchants sell along the port road. She sees a middle-aged woman with a round face and plaits coiled over her ears, a teenage girl with slanted antelope's eyes, a thin old woman with gray braids brushing her shoulders, and two little girls. One of the girls is the child who led the way earlier, her white dress gleaming like a ghostly flower.

And cross-legged in the center of the half circle is a man—a fat, solid bare-chested man with a beard and a close-shorn graying head—who is busy knotting a *lamba* around his bulging paunch. He has the same impassive Sakalava face as the skinny dancing eccentric who greeted them outside, but of whom there is no trace, though Shay can see the tattered trucker's hat hanging on one of the bedposts. Yes, though the cheeks are full and the slightly slanting eyes are set deep in fat, the features are identical. Can it be the same man? How can a man one minute be skinny and dancing manically along like a live scarecrow, and then be as plump and solidly planted as an overfed house cat?

"Welcome to the Neighbor's house," says Bertine. "This," she says, indicating the man, "is Abu Nasdeen. Did you ever see such a big belly?"

The Neighbor nods regally, pronouncing a word of welcome, and the members of his family offer smiles displaying flashing white teeth; the two small girls rise shyly and bob respectful little curtsies. No one speaks more than a few words of French. Shay and Bertine crowd in to kneel on the mat, and as Bertine makes polite conversation, Shay senses the attention of the company netting her in intense curiosity. She particularly feels the watchful eyes of the little girl in the satin dress, whose gaze seems unchildishly deep and solemn; and those of the old woman, who carries her head and bony shoulders with a curious airy grace, like a young dancer. Shay, accustomed to being the object of scrutiny in Madagascar, busies herself absorbing the small details of the single room. Tacked on the bamboo walls are magazine pictures of Bollywood stars and Will Smith; suspended at the head of the bed is a machine-made tapestry depicting a stag in a Nordic forest; on a bench flickers a silent color television showing, at intervals, a grainy drama of Indonesian actors sporting rococo nineteen-eighties hairdos.

A big pot of *romazava* appears. Shay, crushed warmly between Bertine and the teenage girl, finds herself awkwardly scooping up the soupy rice and bitter greens in her fingers, to the politely contained amusement of her hosts. The Coke is poured out into two glasses, which they pass around and share. Somehow time has begun slowing down, and she has no idea whether this meal lasts for hours or just a few minutes.

When the pot is empty, at a nudge from Bertine, she hands out the American flag candies to the delighted little girls, then presents her gift of silver earrings to Abu Nasdeen. The Neighbor studies the small hoops with grave approval, then to Shay's surprise, turns to the old woman beside him, and begins to insert them in her ears. Silently the woman pushes back her thin gray braids from her strangely youthful jaw and shoulder as Abu Nasdeen pushes each hoop through an earlobe. And suddenly Shay realizes, with a chill, that this is a painful process: whatever pierced holes the old woman once had have grown closed and are being forced open by the wires of the earrings. Still, her face is expressionless. Once the hoops hang from her ears, she inclines her head formally to Shay, while a single tear escapes to run down her gaunt brown cheek.

The Neighbor also inclines his head to Shay. "Now," he says, as Bertine translates. "Now you have eaten rice with Abu Nasdeen."

As if the proprieties have been observed, he rises and beckons to the two guests, and Shay obediently follows him and Bertine out of the hut. They descend the rickety steps and file into an outbuilding, a small hut behind the larger, thatched the traditional way and not raised off the ground. Except for a small vent, the place is windowless, empty and severe. A working space. Light filters in through the cracks between the sticks of the walls and the sole decoration is a broken plastic wall clock, arrived from its original Chinese manufacturers by who knows what strange roads, its battered face printed with a faded black and white yin/yang design.

The three of them kneel on a worn mat stretched over bare earth, and Bertine launches into a very specific sounding conversation with the Neighbor, as if she is in a doctor's office. In the quick flow of Malagasy, Shay hears her own name and that of Kristos, and once, Senna.

But here time slips completely away from Shay. As the voices drone in the shadows, she is caught up in a ripple of existence, an unstoppable process that could be playing out equally over long seconds or brief hours. An ineffable element of communication, like electricity, flows among the three of them. She is afterward unable to recall anything more than glimpses of Bertine talking quietly and earnestly to the Neighbor, the other woman's worn dark hands gesturing as the man with his close-shorn graying hair and magisterial belly listens closely. Actions are performed: a coin placed, a few tattered playing cards positioned, a book opened, dried leaves crumpled and burnt, dust sprinkled, something written carefully on paper, a word or two set adrift on the air.

Then another lapsus, and Shay, with no recollection of having left the hut, or of saying goodbye to the Neighbor, finds herself walking beside Bertine in one of the sandy lanes through the shantytown. She is surprised to discover that night has fallen. There is the sound of high tide pounding the invisible beach, and the previously deserted lanes are full of women squatted cooking over braziers emitting choking charcoal smoke, of children playing, of khat-chewing men lounging off to the lamplit market stalls. Passersby call cheery greetings to Bertine, but look through Shay as if she were invisible.

Confused Shay may be, but she knows that deep in her shoulder bag she holds something powerful: a tiny packet barely bigger than a Chiclet, folded out of coarse, lined school-notebook paper, with a short length of crimson thread wrapped tightly around it. This is the result of the day's excursion, and Bertine has already given detailed instructions as to how to use it. Tomorrow morning before sunrise, Shay is to go out to the front gate of the Red House, dig a deep hole in the earth to the left side of the threshold, and bury the packet. "Then," says Bertine, "we will see what *that man* has to say."

11.

A nd so in the dark of the next morning the scene unfolds. The crowing roosters, the muezzin calling from the village, a single church bell, the chorus of frogs from the rice paddies, the hush of low tide. The way the scene seems to freeze around her as, with no thought of waking Senna or being observed by the night watchmen, Shay leaves the bedroom, pads barefoot down the stairs and across the cool floor, careless of centipedes and spiders and undisturbed by the wooden statues, who at this moment seem as benign as a grove of trees. She steps over the threshold, descends the shallow steps, and then squats down and plunges her fingers into the loose sandy soil in the posture of her mother thinning perennials back in California. And then the small hole is dug deep, and the tiny packet, planted like a seed, has become part of the landscape.

She pats the earth back in place, sprinkles a few pebbles, then stands to look up at the portentous architecture of the sky, where time is measured in light. She believes fully in the importance of what she has just done—that is the great change that came over her sometime yesterday in the shantytown. In her bones she knows that this problem of Kristos and the house is part of a greater problem, a very real matter of propitiation, of settling otherworldly accounts. It is a comfort, now, to have taken the first step. So, she calmly brushes the dirt off her hands and returns to bed, settling back beside the warmth of Senna's indifferent body and fading into sleep just before the daytime staff arrive.

Morning is a quiet space. Senna's nieces from Bergamo have arrived for a three weeks' holiday, and Shay spends her time after breakfast on the beach with the two sweet provincial teenagers, one giddy and rambunctious, and the other tattooed and morose. At lunchtime, the family has gathered on the veranda to sit down at the table, when all at once Kristos can be overheard in his bungalow shouting into his cell phone.

In the next moment, he hustles out of his door, with his pink hat on his head and a small traveling bag in his hand. And then—amazingly—he departs. Just leaves. Not in one of the trucks, but in a bush taxi that has pulled up in that moment. The explanation he gives to the dumbstruck Senna is that an emergency has arisen on a property he owns near Diego Suarez, and that he must at all costs catch the ferry to the Grande Île.

Then he is gone, and a shocked peace descends on the household. That day, Senna complains for the first time about how disrespectful and high-handed the Greek is. Meanwhile, Shay struggles to keep a straight face. She is amazed and jubilant over what seems to be a new dispensation of power. She has followed magical directions, and, as if a button has been pushed, her enemy has been ejected.

"You mustn't get a swelled head over this," Bertine tells her, when they meet for a moment among the sun-heated sheets hanging in the drying yard. "This is just the beginning. *That man* was surprised by the first touch of what we did, but he'll be back soon, and he will fight. There's a long way to go. But don't worry. The Neighbor does good work."

Three days of tranquillity go by—the windy August days of the Feast of the Assumption—and then, without warning, Kristos returns. As Bertine has predicted, he returns as if he'd never left, with his usual bluster amped up. He returns with a new wooden statue—a life-size figure of a man playing an accordion—and two dozen mildewed brocade curtains that he claims were once in the Portuguese embassy, and that he wants Senna to purchase at an exorbitant price. He returns with a preposterous business plan to turn the Red House into a luxury spa.

Strangest of all, he comes bearing a present for Shay: a lovely white silk dressing gown made up by a Malagasy seamstress, with a palm tree and the name Villa Gioia embroidered on the left breast. A prototype he says, of the robes they can provide for their future spa clientele. He speaks of how well made the garment is, and the reasonable cost and good quality of the imported silk. Smiling, he urges Shay—whom he has greeted as if they are great friends—to try it on.

The Sennas and their guests are scattered across the veranda, drinking and chatting before dinner. In the background, near the breezeway that leads to the kitchen, Shay can see Bertine standing, vigilant. Catching Shay's eye, the Sakalava woman gives a shake of her head. Laughing, Shay declines to put on the robe, saying that the person who should really model it for them is Senna's pretty niece, Lucia. Lucia, always a show-off, giggles, thrusts her arms into the sleeves, drapes the silk over her scanty shorts and tank top, and skips around the gleaming red floor, striking poses. The others laugh and whistle, except for the Greek, who looks glum. Fingering his grizzled ponytail, he insists in a soft voice that he brought the robe for Shay.

"I'll try it later!" she says, thanking him with a saucy bow, as if thoughtful presents are a usual thing between the two of them; however, she lets the robe lie on the couch where Lucia leaves it.

Bertine later tells her to keep it for a few days, but never to put it on. "Then we can cut it up and throw it in the sea."

"It's pretty, though," says Shay. "What's wrong with it?"

"Something strong, maybe in the sewing," replies Bertine.

"Another little packet?" asks Shay.

Something in her tone—something flippant, born of her growing confidence—causes Bertine to look at her reprovingly. *"C'est pas une blague, tu sais,"* she says. "It's not a joke. These are dangerous matters."

The next day, Senna is furious over the fact that seventeen-year-old Lucia, who, to be sure, has always been a precocious little tease, is flirting outrageously with Kristos. She tags along with him into town, and demands he buy her cocktails at the Fleur des Îles café; and back at the house, attired in a minuscule bikini, she trails around puppyishly after the Greek. Senna has to exert his severest avuncular authority to keep her from pursuing the house manager to the billiard hall, that den of iniquity. Kristos, to his credit, simply looks embarrassed by the girl's attentions.

Shay, no longer surprised by anything, lets her mind drift through myths and legends where enchanted garments play a role, clothing that can bestow invisibility or even death. What might Kristos have desired to achieve through his robe? Certainly not seduction. No, he wants to stop her resistance.

On Sunday, Senna sets off with friends on motorcycles for a day of exploring the bush up north beyond the airport. This is the first time he hasn't included Kristos, toward whom his friendly feelings seem perceptibly cooler. Apparently unperturbed, the Greek makes the surprising announcement at breakfast that he'd like to take Shay and her two nieces out to lunch at Chez Odile, a little restaurant at the other end of the beach.

This is the first time he has ever invited Shay anywhere, and with her newfound sense of confidence, she sees no harm in accepting. She wonders what his next move will be. Trying to spike her food or drink? She has heard that magical potions are common on the island, but surely such an attempt would be easier at home? As the four of them stroll down the beach and then settle around a table on the shady, crowded restaurant porch with its weather-beaten blue paint, she realizes that the Greek has no attack in mind. He just wants to observe her outside the house and know what he is dealing with.

Throughout their delicious meal of zebu fillet with green peppercorns, as giddy Lucia rattles on and her moody sister, Gemma, stares out to sea, Kristos keeps his gaze fixed on Shay. His pale eyes set so deep in his jowly purple face—a face that until recently she has loathed and feared—have lost their wolfish intensity, and now hold a look of wondering confusion, increasingly mingled with an expression of almost doglike entreaty.

Shay sits savoring her meal, elated by this turn of events. The little restaurant is packed with a Sunday crowd of French, Italians, Malagasy, South Africans, many of whom wave to her, and call out greetings; she feels surrounded by island friends and neighbors, uplifted. Odile, the Mauritian proprietress—so renowned for her big breasts and backside that she's had a cartoon of herself painted on the sign outside—bustles up and gives Shay a hug.

Meanwhile, Kristos downs beer after beer, forks up his food with the finicking delicacy that has so often unnerved Shay at the Red House table, and sets out to thrill the two teenage girls with lurid Madagascar adventure tales: rapine and murder in the western sapphire mines; bone-moving ceremonies among the Hova in the highlands; bandits and zebu rustlers in the southern wastes; pirate ghosts in the cemeteries of Île Sainte-Marie.

He is quite a raconteur. Did they know, he asks, that, in the center of this very island, there is a sacred lake that no outsider is allowed to see? Near the lake is the tomb of a Sakalava queen, protected by a village of sorcerers. The whole interior of Naratrany is said to be full of witches, he says, his gaze fixed on Shay.

Shay smiles blandly back at him. She smiles because all the while quite another conversation—one without words—is going on between the two of them, as the Greek silently demands to know what she is doing to him, then starts to ask—then implore—her mercy. Although Shay is not sure where her new power is coming from, it buoys her up to see this gross bully visibly deflating.

She straightens her spine and cuts into her exquisitely tender fillet, contemplating her enemy at bay. Whenever she is tempted to feel even a tinge of pity—he really is such a toad in his craven bewilderment—she recalls the Sakalava girl writhing on the beach. The shift in strength is palpable. Even young Lucia senses it, and abruptly stops her flirting.

The very next morning, Senna—sunburnt, sore, and irascible from his daylong motorcycle jaunt—suddenly stalks into the little household office adjoining Kristos's bungalow and demands to go over all the Red House accounts. A furious argument ensues, and soon the staff is agog, as the garden resounds with the unfamiliar music of the boss thundering out questions counterpointed by a placating rumble from the Greek.

Shay feels triumphant, but when she meets Bertine in the usual corner of the drying yard, the other woman shakes her head and says that it is still not over.

"What more is there?"

"You'll know," says Bertine. "And remember what I said. *C'est pas une blague.*"

That night, Shay wakes up into thick darkness. She can feel that she is in her big bed in the Red House, but there is none of the usual dim light from the mosquito coils, and she cannot feel Senna beside her, or hear the whir of the ceiling fan. Instead she senses the darkness itself, like some heavy element weighing upon her skin. There is a small clicking sound, and then a spark of light appears and grows into a dull glow on the left side of the room, where there is a window that every night is closed and shuttered from the inside. But Shay sees that this left-side window is now unshuttered and wide open. And through the window something is coming into the room: a huge black serpent, thick as a man's thigh, is pouring its great length over the windowsill with a silent, riverine motion like pouring tar.

Dread freezes Shay's body. But then, unaccountably, she is able to move. She reaches to her right side, and there in the place of her husband lies a big knife, a machete—what the Malagasy call a *coupe-coupe*—with a worn wooden handle that feels familiar, even pleasant, to her touch. She rolls out of bed, grabs the *coupe-coupe* in both hands, and not swiftly, but deliberately—no longer fearful but full of uncanny strength—in a single stroke hacks off the head of the serpent. The severed head looses a single piercing shriek and spins away like a soccer ball into the darkness. Then sleep falls on Shay like a curtain of lead.

When she wakes in the early morning, she finds Senna beside her looking at her with an air of dazed recognition as if he has just rediscovered her existence. Numbly they contemplate each other for an instant while Shay grows aware that there is more light than usual in the bedroom. At that moment Senna complains that the left-side shutter is open, not just the shutter but the window too. "If that," he fusses, "is the way the maids close up at night, it won't be long before every local thief is shinning up the wall!"

Banging slightly in the freshening breeze, the loose shutter lets a long slice of sunlight into the room. And for an instant, Shay feels her hair actually stand on end.

After that, nothing can surprise her. At breakfast, Kristos announces that he is quitting. Effective immediately, for he plans to take up the offer of a far more prestigious job as director of a luxury hotel in Tulear. He cannot stay, he declares dramatically, in a place where he is not trusted, where the heart and soul he has invested in his work is disrespected. Before lunch he rolls off grandly in a gleaming Range Rover driven by one of the two Comorean sisters said to be his lovers and magical accomplices; the woman's beautiful flat brown face is masklike below her head wrap as she maneuvers out of the Red House gateway. The household staff watch silently as Kristos departs.

"What will happen to him?" Shay asks Bertine.

"Oh, he'll wander around the Grande Île, working, leaving. Always trying to take what isn't his. Men like that will never have anything for long. He is empty, like an old calabash. He may even come back to Naratrany, but he won't set foot in this house. He opened the gate once, but never again."

"I can hardly believe he's gone," whispers Shay. The two women are silent for a moment, then she stumblingly adds: "Bertine, I have to repay you for this. What can I give you?"

The other woman gives a quick glance over her shoulder at a maid polishing the dining table with a coconut-fiber brush. *"Ca, c'est facile,"* she says, without even a hint of demurring. "I would like something for *my* house. A new roof, to keep out the rain during the cyclones. An aluminum one, like the Neighbor has, the kind the Indian sells at ten euros a sheet."

"Of course," says Shay, a little nonplussed at this brisk specificity. Involuntarily she glances up at her own huge roof, and feels ashamed that she has hardly ever thought of where Bertine lives.

"You'll see my house one day," says Bertine, as if she has read her mind.

12.

The Greek leaves behind him a mountain of bills, mainly for things the Sennas thought were already paid for. He leaves his pink hat and, surprisingly, his serpent walking stick, which Landry the gardener saws into pieces that are unobtrusively flung onto the bonfire a week later, at the Red House housewarming.

For they finally host the big fête that should have been given two years before. A few minutes after noon on the day of the August full moon, headmen from the two villages stand with Senna on the beach in front of the Red House and slaughter two thrashing, bellowing black zebu bulls with white chests. As the blood of the poor beasts cascades to the sand, Shay, faint with revulsion, shudders and squeezes her eyes shut; but her French, Italian, and Malagasy friends—including the pharmacist Angélique, in her chicest sundress—and the household workers, who have pushed her to the front of the crowd—cheer and clap and burst into song.

That night the Sennas, their staff, and friends sit crammed together at a long makeshift table set up on the beach. As the moon rises and the towering bonfire blazes, they feast on zebu *brochettes* washed down with rivers of beer and powerful *toaka gasy* rum shipped in from Amoron'i Mania. The sugarcane has been harvested and the stubble burnt off, and islanders stream in over the ash-strewn paths, as the crowd dances far into the night to the live music of a popular *salegy* trio. At one point, Shay and Senna find themselves performing a clumsy solo jitterbug in the middle of a screeching, clapping circle of onlookers.

"It's good for the house for the husband and wife to be dancing," Bertine tells her approvingly, when Shay, sweaty and disheveled, encounters her finishing a cigarette in a deserted corner of the garden that smells strongly of urine. Like Shay, Bertine is half-drunk on the strong tamarind rum, and totters a bit, but her six Sakalava hair knots are gleaming and impeccable. Shay grins and starts to move back to the party, but the other woman catches her by the arm. "There is one more thing you have to do," she says.

She pulls Shay deeper into the shadows and presses a familiar-feeling small packet into her hand. "Inside is a powder. Put it in a cup of water and pour it over your body. Then you should make love with your husband. Tonight."

"What if he's not interested?" Shay thinks of the peculiar limbo in which she and Senna have lived together since the departure of Kristos, a kind of benign fog of distance through which neither of them finds any inclination to navigate. "More important, Bertine, what if *I'm* not interested?"

Bertine chuckles. "He'll be interested. And as for you—well, Senna is a decent man, and that is all that matters. We women are the ones who choose to love or not. We are the ones who count."

Shay for the first time feels annoyed by Bertine's oracular tone. "You always say that," she protests. "But the Neighbor is a man!"

Bertine, who really has had a lot to drink, gives a scornful whoop of laughter. "You think that?" she says. "The Neighbor could never be a man!"

Shay stares at her through the darkness. "But Abu Nasdeen—"

"*Il fait le travail*. He does the work. He is a kind of—"

"Servant?" whispers Shay. "But then who—"

"You ate rice with her."

Shay recalls the female figures clustered around the pot inside the shanty—the little girl with the white dress and the grown-up eyes; the old woman with her young girl's neck and shoulders—and her head seems to spin. Which one was she?

Bertine touches her arm. "Don't ask any more about these things," she says. "A *vazaha* can't understand. Just remember to do what I said."

And lighting another Good Look, she heads back onto the beach, her tall dark figure soon lost in the crowd of silhouettes dancing in the firelight. Shay carries Bertine's gift to her room, noticing as she does that the musicians are taking a break, and that someone has turned on the sound system, which is blasting, not *salegy* or *tsapika*, but what sounds like old-school American hip-hop: A Tribe Called Quest, if she is not mistaken. This is also a happenstance that is almost unbelievable, but Shay is too tired to go and find out how music from her country has traveled over land and sea to wash up, this particular evening, on the shores of this tiny island. She is already terminally amazed. I'm drunk and mystery lives under this moon, she thinks: that is all. And she tucks the tiny packet away in her beauty case.

13.

During the last week of August, before the Sennas depart for Italy, statues flow out of the Red House. Given away or sold, they are lugged off through the main entrance or across the garden, where Landry and the other gardeners are replacing cacti with banana plants and bougainvillea. Shay discovers a new passion for haggling when she sells six of the largest sculptures to a Belgian developer for a new beach resort at Bevalava. Senna pitches in to off-load the pieces he helped collect, grumbling that he doesn't know what that son of a bitch Kristos thought he was doing, wasting money on this cheap tourist crap. Colonel Andrianasolo buys a musician holding a bamboo zither, and the South African owner of the Rêve Bleu dive center acquires the big serpent carving, saying that it will keep prowlers from breaking in, since Naratrany islanders have a horror of snakes.

Shay and Senna have fallen into a curious equilibrium, a kind of casual tolerance usually shared by couples who have been happy for decades; at night, though, they find themselves fucking with the unhinged intensity of strangers overcome by lust in, say, an airplane toilet. They hardly remember this in the mornings, but it is not at all a bad thing.

And the atmosphere in the Red House feels lighter as the house begins to breathe, inhaling and exhaling with the tides.

"So it's done," Shay remarks jauntily to Bertine on the Sennas' last morning. The suitcases are packed and loaded into the back of the pickup, salaries paid, and the usual gifts distributed among the staff. Senna is off talking to the new managers Shay found with the help of Angélique—a Malagasy husband and a French wife who will begin renting rooms to travelers in a *chambre d'hôtes* system, and will keep the house in repair through cyclone season.

Shay, hair dried out and skin darkened by two months in the tropics, has a strong autumnal urge to travel north. To return to life in a big city; to wake to the rattle of streetcars on mornings when fog presses in on the nineteenth-century windows of the apartment so full of familiar comforts. To return to work, riding her bicycle through Milan traffic to the university, where she will take up once more the hopeless but gratifying task of imparting to her eager Italian students a minimal sense of the legacy of outrage that informs Black American literature—her own literature, her own people's pain. To be back in the part of the world where reality has fixed parameters and, foreigner though she may be, she knows the rules.

Impatience hangs over her as, dressed for travel, she stands facing Bertine in the bedroom where so much took place. Already, the events of the summer seem far away, like happenings in a folktale. Bertine herself, for weeks the most vivid presence in Shay's life, with her big body, her draped *lamba*, her knotted hairstyle, this morning appears somehow faded, like an illustration in an old geography book.

And now Shay longs to feel satisfied. Haven't battles been won and debts paid? She has given Bertine enough money for three new roofs. And just now she has given her a pair of Italian gold ear hoops, big enough to make the rest of the staff jealous. To the Neighbor—whoever she may be—Shay has sent more money, concealed within a pink plastic doll from the Saint Grimaud market. In a very American fashion, Shay wants to be quits; and surely being generous with gifts is the best way to accomplish that. Although, for some reason she can't explain to herself, those gifts feel just slightly like bribes.

"No," says Bertine, looking at her steadily. For the first time, Shay notices that each of the other woman's eyes has a ruddy spark deep in its darkness, like a campfire seen from far away. "It's not done."

"But he—Kristos—is gone. The house is quiet. I feel it." Shay says this with a sharp intonation that she instantly senses is presumptuous, as Bertine continues to regard her with those deep-lit eyes, her bare feet—strong, with each toe clearly defined—set firmly on the red floor.

"No," says Bertine. "It wasn't for *that man* to decide whether a house is quiet or not quiet. He opened the gate, that's all. He wanted something that wasn't his. And so he—and those Comorean women he went to—tried to make a way. Ha! He soon learned."

"You keep talking about the gate, but I don't understand what you mean," says Shay.

"You can't understand. All I can tell you is that it has to do with things you see, and things you can't see. The more time you spend here, the more you'll know. You are in a good position now—we've made sure of that. Still, you'll have to work with us to keep it."

"Work with you? What do you mean? It's our house—our property!" breaks in Shay impetuously. She suddenly feels impatient at the fact that this simple, practically illiterate woman should be lecturing her.

Bertine la Grande doesn't look away or change her expression but seems to grow taller, and solider in her stance. And suddenly Shay feels intimidated—a very different emotion from the schoolgirl terror she felt toward Kristos.

"It's the house you *vazaha* built, on the land you bought," Bertine says, very quietly. "But that doesn't count for everything. You are young and rich," she continues, without bitterness.

"And fortunate, and you'll have children who will be fortunate. We've made you queen of the house, in our way. But this land—*eh bien*. Let us say . . . let's say that it is yours, for now."

Just then comes the sound of the truck horn, signaling that it is time to leave for the airport. Shay throws her arms around Bertine, kisses her three times in the Malagasy style, breathes in the older woman's powerful scent of laundry soap and tobacco, and, driven by some impulse she hardly understands, whispers: *"Merci, ma soeur!"*

Bertine presses her close for a bare instant. "Don't worry," she says, withdrawing. "I'm here, and so is our Neighbor." Quickly she reaches for Shay's shoulder bag and drops something small into it: a final packet. "Don't open it. Just put it away, and keep it where you live—*là-bas en Italie.*"

The staff of the Red House call goodbye and wave, as Senna and Shay jounce slowly out of the courtyard in the truck, with Landry the gardener dreamily chewing khat as he balances atop the luggage in the back. At the head of the driveway, Senna, whose phone is already buzzing with messages from his office, brakes as he always does, and gazes down over the treetops at the house. "Well, it's goodbye to this old place until Christmas," he says, in the elegiac tones of any husband leaving a fishing lodge anywhere. "It was a great summer in the end—right, darling? True, we had a bit of a problem with that asshole Greek, but things like that happen in these primitive countries."

Shay hardly hears him. There will be time enough back in Milan to decipher what kind of respect she will preserve for Senna. But now she is looking down at the roof of the Red House and what flashes through her mind is Libertalia. The Arcadian fantasy of perfect freedom, which in one meretricious form or another has washed up on so many shores over the centuries, opening the way for hordes of thugs far worse than Kristos. Libertalia, a tale of rapine disguised by lofty dreams; a theme not unique to Madagascar but also buried in the history of her own family, her America.

She thinks of the people at work under that big thatched roof: the true landowners, who know the secret contours of the terrain. The Malagasy, garbed as servants, who hold together the newcomers' aspirations like dark stitches closing a wound; who have set her up as mistress—within their private limits and definitions. Then she thinks of Bertine, whom she has just called "sister." And again and again during the drive through the burnt cane fields, Shay wonders what the other woman thought of her words. *Was she offended? Pleased? Did she think it was funny? Did she hear me? Did she?*

The Children

If ye touch at the islands, Mr. Flask, beware of fornication.

—Herman Melville, *Moby Dick*

The adventure of the lost heirs begins when Shay and her friend Giustinia run into Harena at the Fleur des Îles café. This encounter happens one summer day in the early aughts, a time when the Sennas have settled with relative serenity into the ritual of vacations at the Red House, which by now is almost four years old. In the same period, Naratrany is experiencing a bizarre crime wave: a maniac at large on the island is cutting off people's heads. The mysterious beheadings are not connected to the events recounted here, except to establish the lawlessness always present behind the dazzling Naratrany panorama of sugar-white beaches and cobalt sea. The crimes begin to surface on a hot January morning, as a French hotel manager is taking his predawn constitutional along Finoana Bay and spies through a mist of sand flies something just above the tide line that looks like an unhusked coconut. It turns out to be a human head, one that was last seen on the shoulders of a part-time sweeper at the Frenchman's hotel. In the next months, four more severed heads are discovered, hideously marooned near grounded pirogues, on paths through the sugarcane, and even on the rocks that are used by villagers as public toilets. The victims are all men from various Malagasy tribes: Antandroy, Tsimihety, Sakalava—night watchmen and grounds-keepers of so low a status that no one bribes the island gendarmerie into investigating their deaths.

This is the state of affairs when Giustinia arrives from Florence to spend two weeks with Shay on Naratrany before embarking on a trek through northern Madagascar. It is the middle of June, and the two of them have the Red House to themselves: most of the staff is on leave, planting rice or visiting relations on the Grande Île, and the place is empty both of paying guests and of the swarm of family that will come from Milan in August; Senna will arrive later in the month. Giustinia is a poet and a critic, an elegant woman who became friends with Shay when Shay translated some of her essays for an American magazine, and they discovered that they shared a passion for Victor Segalen's eccentric, early-twentieth-century monograph on exoticism. But while Shay, prompted by her own life path from America to Europe to Africa, finds her interest drawn to restless ex-patriate artists of color, Giustinia, whose noble family has ancient roots in Tuscany, most often writes about the inescapable pull of a place to which you belong entirely. Her regal air is quite unconscious, based mainly on the authority with which she can speak about famous authors she knows. In spite of her worldly connections, she has the unexpected ingenuousness of those rare aristocrats who are still safely contained within their insular history. Shay, whose tolerance for the violent mysteries of life has grown exponentially since she first set foot in Madagascar, intends to shield her guest from the news that there is a serial killer at large.

A week into Giustinia's visit, the two friends go food shopping in Saint Grimaud and, after the heat and the stench of the outdoor market, stop for a cold drink at the Fleur des Îles. Harena is just leaving the café as they pull up in the truck. When she sees Shay, she calls out a greeting in her childish voice, raises one slim brown hand, and flashes her incandescent smile. Then she floats past the one-legged beggar perched on the Fleur des Îles steps and climbs into an odd-looking customized dune buggy, where a bald middle-aged Frenchman sits beeping the horn impatiently.

"What a stunning girl," Giustinia remarks, as she and Shay chase flies from a sticky table on the veranda and settle themselves where they can keep an eye on the baskets of vegetables and bread in the back of the pickup.

"Yes," Shay says. "She's half Italian." And, acting in her role as exasperated hostess—for, during the week with Giustinia, there has been no rococo tropical sunset, no rare lemur or chameleon, no gaudy market stall, no fluorescent coral or blinding expanse of beach that has dispelled her guest's queenly, slightly bored air of expecting something more—Shay sketches out the story of Harena, which is a sort of legend on Naratrany.

The girl is presently about seventeen years old. Her father, Leandro, is a heroin addict from a noble Roman family, a family that shipped him off to Madagascar as a remittance man when he was in his early twenties. For a few years, he lived on rum and drugs out in the bush at the north of the island with Heloise, a Sakalava seamstress, and during this time Harena was born. When Harena was three or four years old, Leandro's father died, and Leandro returned to Italy, where he'd inherited an estate in what Melville once called the "accursed Campagna" of Rome.

He soon cut off contact and stopped sending money, and when Heloise, who had taken up with a French merchant from Saint Grimaud, perished suddenly after a miscarriage, the girl was left at the mercy of her grandmother, who wasted no time in settling her gray-eyed, barely pubescent granddaughter with Hans, an affable middle-aged German, who sold construction materials. Shay first saw Harena with him one Saturday night, when the girl must have been about fifteen, standing forlornly on the crowded concrete dance floor of Tonga Soa, clutching a large vinyl handbag, while Hans cavorted in a karaoke show onstage. Harena, even then, was extraordinarily pretty, with fawn-colored hair and skin, long spindly legs, acerbic breasts, and a beauty mark beside an arched nose that looked as if it belonged on an ancient marble statue in a museum thousands of miles away.

Shay is warming to the subject when Giustinia suddenly interrupts. "Wait!" she exclaims, and then, incredibly, adds, "I know this story. I didn't remember that it happened here. I know him—Leandro. The father."

It is almost noon, and the Fleur des Îles is filling up with rich Malagasy and Indian kids from Notre Dame lycée, devouring *pains au chocolat* and monopolizing the three back-room computers. Outside in the glaring dusty street, ragged boys hawk trays of samosas and Comoran women with laden baskets on their heads file down to the port.

Shay watches them as Giustinia tells her that, in the tight circles of old Italian nobility—which are as closed as kinship groups can be on Naratrany—she's met Leandro a few times, at weddings. Moreover, one of his sisters is married to a cousin of Giustinia's husband. Leandro is a sort of Italian Sebastian Flyte: extravagantly good-looking, a hopeless addict, and now a doomed recluse. What made him notorious was that eighteenth-century-style exile, imposed by his family, to an island that no one had ever heard of, in the north of Madagascar.

"I'd like," Giustinia says, gazing into the dregs of her glass of papaya juice, "to meet this Harena."

Later, Shay wonders why she saw no harm in this. It has to do, she thinks, with the general trifling nature of her behavior in Madagascar, where her brown skin and her American expansiveness lend her a false sense of familiarity with the people of color around her: people of the island, whose language she doesn't speak, and whose values and motives she will never fully understand.

Shay mentions to Romolo, the Italian proprietor of the Fleur des Îles, that she wants to talk to Harena, and, sure enough, early the next afternoon she catches sight of the girl making her way down the beach toward the Red House, in the indolent manner of a cat that has just decided to roam in that direction. She is dressed in white jeans and a tight sleeveless top that drapes from a metal ring around her neck, and her pale, kinky hair, free of extensions for once, is caught up at the crown of her head in a pouf that is very becoming.

When Harena, Giustinia, and Shay sit down on the veranda, Shay can see that her friend is, for once, at a loss. It is one thing to take an impulsive interest in someone whose life seems like a fairy tale, and it is quite another thing to have that beautiful young person sitting in front of you with shining, expectant eyes and a valiant, determined poise. Giustinia, who this afternoon has been writing an essay on Octavio Paz, is a handsome brunette in her late thirties, presently barefoot in a bathing suit, with a pair of tortoiseshell glasses perched on her freckled nose. She looms over Harena like a dowager empress over a royal pretender.

After ascertaining that Harena understands Italian, she tells her that she is acquainted with Harena's father, and that Harena much resembles him.

The effect on the girl is electric: she begins to tremble. And Shay thinks that this is exactly the wrong way to go about it: making such a statement is like promising a shower of gold. For years, Harena has nourished herself on the myth of her Italian father, and now it is impossible to keep the subject within the bounds of simple conversation.

Then Harena begins to tell the two women something that Shay has never heard before. That when she was sixteen, her first lover, Hans—who always treated her with great respect, she says, as he would have treated a white girl—gave in to her pleas and took her to Italy. And there she actually made it to the gate of the country villa near Nemi from which her father, years before, had sent her a single letter. The gatekeeper, a peasant who spoke mainly dialect, told her that the house was closed and the family abroad. Through the gate, she could see up a long road, bordered with umbrella pines, to what looked like the gleam of parked cars. She told the gatekeeper that she was Leandro's daughter, and he told her to go away. She left a letter stuck in the gate, and afterward wrote from Naratrany, but there was never a reply.

Soon after recounting this tragic story, Harena finishes her Coke and departs, but not before giving Shay and Giustinia three kisses each, Malagasy style, with fervent emphasis, as if her fate were now in their hands. She leaves the Red House through the back entrance, which leads to the road through the rice field, where Shay can hear the tootling horn of the Frenchman's dune buggy.

Speechless, Giustinia and Shay stroll down to the edge of the sea. It is close to sunset, and low tide, and they stand in the warm water and watch a little band of village children drag-fishing in the shallows with a length of tattered cloth.

"She does look like Leandro," Giustinia remarks, after a pause.

"What are you going to do?"

"I suppose I should contact the family. His sister . . ."

But she sounds vague. Shay also has conflicted feelings. She knows that Harena is who she says she is, yet it is difficult to believe the tale of that trip to Italy. First, it is too hard to imagine that Hans, the eminently practical German, would go through the byzantine process of getting a tourist visa for a Malagasy girlfriend he didn't intend to marry. Second, Harena told the story in the same histrionic tone that Shay has heard her use, at several parties, in tipsy rants about the wealth and power of her Italian father.

"You've opened Pandora's box!" Shay's next-door neighbor, Madame Rose Rakotomalala, exclaims when Shay and Giustinia go over for tea the next day. Madame Rose is a wealthy Merina from the capital and has scant esteem for the Sakalava and other coastal peoples. "She is not at all a nice young woman! She takes after the mother, who was no seamstress but a bar girl, plain and simple, and she drinks and smokes *rongony* all day long. Harena acts innocent, but she starts fights, even with bottles, right in the road. Now that Hans has disappeared, she goes from one white man to another, except when she is working changing money for those Comoran hoodlums. We've all seen her in the café, counting out stacks of cash."

Here Madame Rose gets up from the table and leans her slim waist over the railing to harangue two of her maids, who are hanging out clothes beside the generator. She resumes, "If you start trying to help that girl, it will be one thing after the other, and none of it good. Besides, if you go tracking down all the white men who leave children behind, that, too, will never end."

Giustinia, more spurred on by Madame Rose's ominous warning than anything else, stubbornly emails her husband's cousin with the news of her discovery of Harena. But she seems relieved, as is Shay, when the days pass with no reply, and her departure from the island grows nearer.

Still, a curious social electricity now seems to surround Giustinia and Shay. Harena comes by twice, breezing into the garden with casual assurance, making no requests but simply regarding them with that same ecstatic, expectant gaze. Meanwhile, Shay begins to notice Malagasy people she has never seen before standing on the beach and staring at the Red House. And, whenever she and Giustinia pass through Finoana village in the pickup, they cause a palpable ripple of interest. A Sakalava woman who runs a used-clothing stall tells Shay that word has spread that Giustinia is really Harena's Italian grandmother, a rich and titled matriarch, who plans to take the girl back to her father's country or, failing that, to shower her with enough wealth to build a big house for herself, her uncles, and the rest of her family in Madagascar. (Though youthful Giustinia would be insulted at the supposition, the islanders afford enormous prestige to grandmothers.) Feeling the gathering energy, Shay wishes intensely that she could consult her imperturbable friend and confidante, Bertine la Grande, head of the Red House staff. But in this season, Bertine is deep in her private life, far away with relatives in Djangoa, harvesting rice. And so Shay, as is just, must make her way through this unsettled atmosphere by her own wits.

Naturally, she says nothing to Giustinia about all this, and the rest of her friend's visit passes quickly—without, to Shay's intense relief, another attack by the headhunter. Shay introduces Giustinia to Père Jobeny, a priest from Diego Suarez, who is the author of a lengthy treatise on Jean-Joseph Rabearivelo, Dox, and other early Malagasy poets, and the three spend a delightful evening discussing the Négritude movement, Machado de Assis, and James Baldwin. On the morning of her departure, Giustinia has still heard nothing from Leandro's sister, but she promises to make a round of telephone calls when she gets back to Italy. "I feel strangely under obligation," she confides to Shay.

"You're trying—what more can you do?" Shay replies, also feeling weighed down by a peculiar burden of duty. One thing she has learned in her few years of sojourning in Madagascar, with its convoluted history and its pulse of dark magic concealed just under the skin of events, is that, in this country, whatever happens close to you—under your roof, say—becomes part of you, though you may not realize it at the time.

Giustinia departs, with kisses and effusions, leaving behind an envelope containing the generous sum of thirty euros for Harena, as well as an almost new beach dress.

The next day, Shay doesn't receive a visit from the girl, as she half expects to, but while she sits reading after lunch she hears a subdued hubbub from the far end of the garden, near the gate to the beach. Soon, Tumbu, the old man who fills in as factotum when there are few guests in the Red House, calls out to her that there is someone down by the water who wants to speak to Madame Shay. When Shay asks who, he mumbles confusedly that it is someone from the Grande Île.

Squinting against the high-tide wind that rattles the palms, Shay follows Tumbu's grizzled head and bare, wiry back down to the seawall at the end of the garden. There she finds waiting a tall, unbelievably handsome teenage boy whom she has never seen before but recognizes immediately, for he is almost a twin of Harena. He has the same fawn coloring and sculptural nose, but his eyes are the clouded turquoise of certain Alpine lakes, which gives him an oddly blind look in the blazing subequatorial sun. He is barefoot, dressed in long shorts and a tattered Italian football jersey, and his sandy hair is clipped close to his skull. Shay greets him in French, asking him his name, and invites him into the garden, but he stands staring at her with those eerie eyes and replies in a Malagasy dialect that Shay doesn't understand.

"He doesn't speak much French," Tumbu explains, rather condescendingly. "His name is Didier, and he is from Morondava, far south of here, and he wants to see the mother of his father, who is the Italian Leandro."

Didier will come only a single step inside the Red House gate, so Shay stands with him near the threshold and, as Tumbu interprets, learns that the boy is sixteen and was born, on Naratrany, to a young woman of the southern Sakalava tribe, named Adi, who worked as a hotel maid. Leandro never lived with Adi, but "he loved her" and, after the boy was born, paid for her to return to her family on the big island, promising to join her there. Of course, he never appeared or contacted her, and eventually, leaving her son with her people near Morondava, she found work at a shrimp fishery in Mahajamba Bay and soon afterward died there of malaria, as so many do in that harsh line of work.

A week ago, word somehow reached Didier's grandmother that Leandro's mother, and possibly Leandro himself, had arrived at the Red House on Finoana Beach, on Naratrany, and that finally the Italian father wanted to lay eyes on his children. So Didier left Morondava and traveled north, for four days and nights, by foot, bush taxi, and ferry. Once on Naratrany, he walked the six kilometers from the port to Finoana Beach.

As Shay listens, she becomes more and more furious. With herself, with Giustinia, and with a tall Italian phantom who seems to have been summoned up from the ground beside her. Now that she has seen two of Leandro's children, she can imagine exactly what he, the absent father, is like: his aristocratic height; his useless blond beauty; his addict's vacant face; his idle concupiscence; his suzerain's habit, bred in the bone, of taking whatever he wants; his ruthless indifference to everything that isn't the chemical in his veins.

And now, she wonders, what to do with this magnificent son out of the famine-ridden south, who has traveled across land and sea, chasing a rumor? A rumor that she, Shay, helped start?

"Does he know Harena? His sister?" Shay demands of Tumbu.

"He knows who she is."

As the boy continues to stare at Shay with those mineral-colored eyes, panic seizes her. "Tell him," she says to the old man, "that his father and grandmother are not here. That the woman who was here is not Leandro's mother, and she is gone now, anyway. That woman is only a friend who knows the Italian family of his father. She is a friend who promises to look . . . who will help find . . . No, tell him that I myself will help . . ."

Shay stammers in confusion, suddenly gripped by a cinematic vision of snatching this beautiful youth out of his present life, as if she were conducting a helicopter rescue at sea. In an instant, she pictures schools, clothes, university, some grand career, where that flawless face would gleam in the high marble halls of European tradition. Later, she will tell herself that this is a maternal impulse, but it is as selfish and intoxicating as sex.

That Didier shows no surprise or disappointment increases Shay's confusion. "Ask him what he needs," Shay tells Tumbu. "Money, food, a place to stay?"

Soon, the old gardener, with a hint of a dry smile, informs her, "He needs nothing, Madame. He has a job as an apprentice mechanic, and in two or three months he will go to Mahajanga to work on trucks."

"Will he stay now with his sister—with Harena?"

"No. He'll go back home immediately. You can"—the old man pauses, and then announces in a formal tone, as if affording Shay a rare privilege—"you can pay the price of his journey."

Shay doubles the sum, but even so it is a laughably small amount. When she gives the notes to the boy, she notices that his hands, too, are beautiful: long and slender, though already rough from labor, and scarred with what appear to be burns. As she comes close to him, he suddenly looks her straight in the eye, with an intensity that feels like a blow, and says something in a low, forceful voice.

"He wants to know," Tumbu says, impassively, "why it is that his father has not once come to look for him."

Shay stammers that Didier's father has been sick for many years in Italy.

And, before her shame at this transparent falsehood has evaporated, the boy coolly bids her farewell and turns away. Shay watches his tall, sculptural figure and cropped head departing down the three kilometers of beach, skirting the incoming tide. He walks like a king in exile, seeming to cast a sort of furious solitude around himself. And, as he grows small and disappears in a distant crowd of fishermen, she thinks of how much the life of an island is about watching for those who arrive and dreaming of those who depart. About waiting, sometimes forever.

Madame Rose Rakotomalala and Shay's other friends on the island are of the opinion that Leandro has fathered no more children in Madagascar. But in the following days, and even after Senna arrives, Shay gets jumpy whenever she hears visitors arriving at the Red House; she has visions of an army of gorgeous bastards pouring into her garden. She tries to avoid places where she might run into Harena, whose face grows more and more piteously crestfallen as the weeks pass with no word from Giustinia. One morning in September, just before the Sennas leave for Italy, Shay sees the girl at the Fleur des Îles, heavily made up and dressed in a theatrical Comoran *lamba* and headdress, deep in conversation with a quartet of South African tourists. Clearly she has thrown herself wholeheartedly into her money-changing, and she nods to Shay with haughty indifference.

Back home in Milan, Shay at last sees Giustinia. And, after some excited talk about a poetry festival in Johannesburg, she informs Shay, "I finally got in touch with Leandro's sister, and the news is bad. Leandro is dead— has been dead for a year, though this is the first I've heard of it. Overdose or AIDS—though they're very vague about it. There must have been a funeral, but when a family like that wants to keep things quiet . . . It's as if he died ten years ago."

"Did you tell his sister about Harena and the boy?"

"When I told her, she just laughed. She reminded me that, before they shipped him off to Madagascar, Leandro spent a year in the Caribbean, skippering in the Islas los Roques. She said that, over the past few years, the family has had letters from a pair of Venezuelans claiming to be his children—"

Shay breaks in. "But there is no doubt that these two kids are his!"

"Yes, but what exactly does one do? Arm them with lawyers and fly them to Rome for DNA tests that they can use to lay siege to relatives who will never accept them? And for what? Between you and me, that family hasn't got anything left. Just land that is all tied up with taxes and entailments, and some sculptures of popes that no one wants, and acres of architecture that costs too much to restore. Oh, and titles. They have titles to spare."

Shay envisions a Princess Harena changing money at the Fleur des Îles, and a Prince Didier, with his aristocrat's hands, dismembering truck engines in Mahajanga. Madagascar has its own kings and noblemen, whose polysyllabic names lie deeply rooted in the historical conquests and ancient migrations of each tribe, but none of those revered Indian Ocean pedigrees belongs by birthright to either of the half-Italian children. And, on the tourist island of Naratrany, what, without money to back it up, would a hereditary Roman certificate of rank be but a meaningless piece of rubbish, another plastic bag blowing down the beach?

"They could send something—pay for education!" Shay persists.

"Believe me. They will do nothing."

Giustinia and Shay look fiercely at each other, aware that they are so indignant over the neglect of Leandro's progeny because they feel guilty about their own role in stirring up false hope: in bringing that tremulous, starry look to Harena's eyes, and spurring Didier to travel for days over land and sea for nothing.

They sketch a plan to raise the situation with the Italian and Malagasy consuls, and they both send letters to which no answers come. And so, bureaucracy performs its traditional task of transmogrifying action into inaction, and the two women lose themselves in their own busy lives.

At Christmas, when Shay and Senna travel to Madagascar, Shay is pregnant with their first child. This makes her the center of attention, but she still keeps up with the gossip, and the first thing she hears is that Harena has married a half-Chinese musician, who has taken her to Mauritius, where his band plays in the smaller clubs and hotels. It is a love match, and Harena is said to be always dressed up and much admired, but drinking more than ever and doing hard drugs. Shay is told that, when some visiting Italian finally gave Harena the news of her father's death, she flung bottles, clawed her own face, and screamed that it wasn't true; that even now she talks about Leandro as if he were coming to fetch her. Her husband is patient with—maybe even proud of—what he calls her European behavior, but people on Naratrany say that she is possessed. Nothing good, they say, will come of her.

As for Harena's half brother, Didier, the phone number he gave Shay is out of service, and no one can discover his whereabouts in Mahajanga or Morondava, though there can't be many mechanics like him. So, the lost heirs who came into Shay's life are just as suddenly gone.

Around the same time that Harena got married, the murderer who had been cutting off heads was caught hiding out in the cane. He was a lunatic from Toamasina, a Betsimisaraka dockworker of fearful strength, whose whole family perished in the catastrophic floods of a few years back. He was, they say, obsessed with the idea of chasing *vazaha* out of Madagascar, of eliminating the rich Europeans and Indians who were offending the spirits of the ancestors and who for so long had plundered the wealth of the country. His twisted methodology was to kill Malagasy men who worked for the foreigners. But he had no chance to expound on this in a trial, or even to languish for more than a day in the medieval hell of Naratrany's prison, because on his way to the courthouse he was seized by a mob of islanders and promptly lynched, torn to pieces, burnt, and cast into the sea.

Bertine, Tumbu, and the rest of the staff at the Red House all have a gentle air of pitying the murderer as a man cursed by madness, and placidly seem to accept the idea that justice has been served. With no newspapers to pick up the story and with both criminal and victim at the bottom of the social scale, talk of the drama soon fades away.

Shay herself cannot help associating the unspeakable murders with the plight of Harena and Didier. But is it a plight? Wrong was certainly done. By miserable Leandro, and by his stony-hearted family. But also by Giustinia and Shay, with their frivolous intervention—they were like magpies who settle on cattle and peck open wounds.

———————

During the next years, as more hotels are built and charter flights arrive from Rome and from Paris, prosperity steals over the island like a gilded mist, and pale half-European babies become a more common sight in the villages and on the beaches. Some of them are loved, legitimized, and even taken away to live comfortable lives in France and Italy; others grow up amid conflict and squalor. The situation of Harena and Didier, no longer unusual, fades into the constantly rewoven fabric of gossip and fantasies that makes up island history.

By this time, Shay and Senna have a small son and daughter of their own, who, being half Italian and half African-American, are often, during their holidays on the island, mistaken for mixed-race Malagasy children. With the births of Roby and Augustina, Shay suddenly knows the crushing force of that incomparable love that, when the parents are from different worlds, brings with it all the shadows of historical conflict, in custom and color and speech.

Darlings of fortune, adored by their Italian and their American grand-parents, Shay's children grow up fluent in two languages. They are at home in Milan and in her native city of Oakland, and also in Madagascar, where they pick up rudimentary French and Sakalava dialect as they splash in the warm Naratrany waters. From the kids they play with on Finoana Beach, they grow used to hearing lurid stories of sorcerers and ghosts—even the horrific tale of the headhunter—and, because the disgraceful mis-adventures of foreigners are the villagers' entertainment, they absorb the details of intricate scandals as well.

Buried somewhere amid all the other unsuitable anecdotes that her son and daughter bring home, Shay suspects, is a distorted account of the Leandro story, but she is certainly not going to bring it to light.

Sometimes she sits at her little writing table at the end of the garden and from the deep tamarind shade watches Roby and Augustina at play on the dazzling sand with a horde of village and tourist children, the hollering crowd expanding and contracting with algorithmic logic, like a flock of starlings, as they splash in the waves, play *raboka*, race hermit crabs, or draw mysterious labyrinths in the sand for the island version of hopscotch.

Her son and daughter are always the focus of her vigilance, with their wild sunbleached hair, their faces bearing the stamp of distant continents; children healthy and loved, who play in front of the house of wealth that they will inherit; who, in short, have everything. And from time to time, as Shay watches them, she'll unavoidably envision a boy and a girl who are their shadow twins: Didier and Harena, the beautiful children who have almost nothing. And then she holds a guilty circular conversation with herself, a kind of call-and-response.

"What more could we do?"

"We did what we could."

"What did they need?"

"They needed to be found. Of course."

"Was that our job?"

"Who knows if it was?"

"We could have tried harder."

"We did what we could."

Like a lullaby or a nursery rhyme, the sequence of excuses blends into the voices of the kids on the beach. But this is one song Shay doesn't sing aloud. She is well aware that, on the journey toward separation that is life with even the best-loved children, it is all too easy to lose their respect.

Blondes

She is the daughter of the king of the Palace of Crystal, who lives on yonder island. Every morning, at the break of day, she combs her golden hair; its brightness is reflected on the sea, and up among the clouds.

—From the Slavonic fairy tale, "Golden Hair,"
translated by John Naaké

S hay is sitting with her feet soaking in the plastic pedicure bucket when Caroline la Blonde shows up at La Joconde to have her weave resewn. There are constant arrivals at La Joconde, the most expensive beauty parlor on Naratrany: a white-tiled cubicle with a single sink, a rickety hood dryer, and a doorway that opens directly onto the dust and noise of the taxi rank at the crossroads of the Finoana market. Flies come and go from the zebu meat hanging like red rags at the nearby butchers' stalls, wandering dogs push through the long strips of plastic shielding the threshold, ragged child vendors arrive with trays of fritters and samosas to tempt the two Malagasy beauticians: plump, solemn Thérèse, and her thin, vivacious sister, Gisèle.

Customers at La Joconde are a varied lot, many of them women of the island gentry—Malagasy, French, Italian, South African, Indian, Mauritian—who pull up in Land Rovers and gleaming SUVs with blacked-out windows. The salon is popular with anyone who can pay the price—exorbitant for Madagascar, but in euros, remarkably low—for the benefit of the sisters' skilled hands, trained in Rome and Toulouse; for their beauty products imported from Nigeria and France. Women on vacation, desperate for a blow-dry or a retouch of nail polish, are initially terrified by the rudimentary look of the place, but soon find themselves reassured by the strict cleanliness and the intense, near-religious attention to details, which is the same in serious beauty salons everywhere. The aesthetic creed of Thérèse and her sister is summed up by the emblem on the plastic sign that swings amid the market dust and blazing sunlight outside the door: printed in crude two-tone brown and blue is the image of Leonardo's *Mona Lisa,* from which La Joconde proudly takes its name.

"Salut mes poupées!" calls Caroline as she swans in. She is the most gorgeous of the bar girls on the island this year. Small-boned and slender like most Malagasy women, but unusually tall, with that seductive Saka-lava bubble-butt in tight white French jeans, a tiny nose, heart-shaped lips, commanding eyes, skin with the healthy gleam of dark syrup, and in contrast to it all, the source of her nickname: that dramatic fall of yellow hair to her waist. Hundreds of euros' worth of natural blond tresses shorn from some distant Eastern European head, hair that cloaks Caroline in glory, all the more powerful because it is so clearly hers not by nature but by choice: a pirate's swag of plundered gold arrived by who knows what channels from the far north. Outrageous, improbable hair out of a Grimms' tale, which strangely suits her midnight beauty.

Rapunzel, Sleeping Beauty, thinks Shay. During this vacation stay, she has seen that head of hair many times around the island, gleaming like a banner through the kinetic shadows of dance clubs like Chanson de la Mer, and flashing by in the big Cayenne belonging to her latest lover. Caroline la Blonde is strictly deluxe. One never sees her on foot in the market buying a basket of manioc greens, or haggling at a used clothing stall. And she is serious-minded: said already to have used her considerable earnings from infatuated foreign men to build her family a sizable house in their village on the Grande Île near Port-Bergé.

Shay greets Caroline, and Caroline, seating herself gracefully in a wobbly salon chair, replies *"Bonjour!"* with the peculiar mixture of pride, deference, curiosity, and barely hidden resentment with which island women like Caroline address Shay, and other wealthy women of color. On Naratrany, Shay occupies a high-ranking position as the foreign mistress of a luxurious house, yet to Caroline she looks much like any mixed-race hussy who takes the boat in from Diego Suarez during the tourist season, to steal business from locals.

Normally the conversation would end here, but Shay, mesmerized by those rippling golden waves, which Gisèle is now deftly brushing out and clipping up to show the intricate pattern of extensions sewn onto braids against the scalp, exclaims: *"Ils sont vraiment jolies, tes cheveux!"*

And Caroline gives a little start of surprise at the compliment, and looks directly at Shay in the wavery mirror. *"Merci!"* she replies. Adding, with a mock-regretful sigh: *"Malheureusement, pas les miens.* Unfortunately, not mine."

As if, thinks Shay, anyone were under any illusion that it was really your hair! But as Gisèle begins snipping the old stitching, and pulling out the tracks of extensions that will be resewn, Caroline catches Shay's eye in the mirror and winks.

The squatting manicurist, a very young Sakalava girl who seems to be a relative of the two beauticians, is using a pumice stone to scrub Shay's heels with agonizing slowness; manicures and pedicures take hours at La Joconde. To lessen the suffocating midday heat, the overhead bulb in the tiny salon has been turned off, and in the half-light from the doorway and the somber glow of the mirror frame, the arrangement of the five women in the small space seems deliberate, as if they are enacting a mysterious rite, or are part of an old allegorical painting.

They are all absorbed in what they are doing: the young girl with her knobs of neatly parted hair bent over Shay's feet; beautiful Caroline, straight-backed, chattering noisily away in Malagasy, as, with a keen eye toward the mirror, she watches the weave swiftly stripped away, and her dark, sculptural close-braided head emerge; Gisèle, skinny in a floral sundress, her own hair straightened in a pert sixties bob, hands flashing in a graceful repetitive movement as if she is harvesting a crop, as she removes the lengths of golden waves, gives them a quick practiced shake, and drapes them over a hairpin stand; plump, ponytailed Thérèse, in green leggings and a ruffled top, deftly seizing each track of hair, swiftly shampooing it in the small rickety sink, then pinning it up on a rack that seems to be exclusively for weaves; Shay, the American spy, wearing batik trousers from Bali, her own hair a mass of natural kinky curls that her husband loves, but that she herself sometimes refers to as "the jungle."

The long mirror seems to double the number of figures in the dim little salon and the crowded effect is increased by the models in the posters for foreign hair products pinned up on the walls: Nigerian women, Indian women, French women, all eerily submerged in their own perfection. But the hypnotic focal point of the scene is that disembodied blond hair, now being held aloft and painstakingly blown dry by both sisters in a way that suggests that they are handling a holy relic—Saint Veronica's kerchief, thinks Shay frivolously, or the Turin Shroud.

She notices that Caroline ignores the extensions once they are off her head, and sits contemplating her flawless face and natural hair with the same complacent satisfaction she had when wearing the weave.

Shay pulls her other foot out of the bucket, and, as her endless pedicure proceeds amid the monotonous rise and fall of women's voices and the tinny *salegy* music on Radio Fanambarana, she closes her eyes and falls into a reverie about blondes.

Like many women of color, Shay has been bothered by blond hair all her life. Since the time she noticed that her favorite fairy tales were filled not just with golden treasure but with golden tresses adorning the heads of imperiled princesses. Since elementary school days back in Oakland, when all the fourth-grade boys at Bentley had their foolish hearts tied up in the long yellow plaits of the Kosslowski twins. Since the afternoon when, shopping with her mother, Shay asks for a T-shirt in blue, her favorite color, and her normally considerate mother informs her that blue is for little blond girls.

A free-floating resentment of blondes is of course just part of the endless Black American discourse on hair: a wilderness of mingled opinion and tradition whose borders touch politics, aesthetics, folklore, shame, sex, and love. Shay has been immersed in it her entire life, especially when, at an early age, she begins experimenting with what grows on her own head. Braiding it, straightening it, encouraging its natural texture, growing it waist-length, or cropping it to her skull, dyeing it pink in high school, adding clattery beads—even trying out blond highlights herself, in the period when Black female hip-hop stars are going through a Marilyn moment.

But now at La Joconde, she is pondering what yellow hair signifies in Madagascar. Blondes, she muses, have always been fetishized in art and literature encompassing colonial themes, as emblems of sacred white womanhood—the apex of European civilization, shining in contrast to a tenebrous background of savagery as Fay Wray did in the grasp of King Kong. Even little Naratrany has had its legendary blondes. French residents of the island still talk of the daughter of the French sugar mill owner who in colonial days used to gallop her horse up and down Finoana Beach, pale tresses streaming in the wind. In an early guide to the Mozambique Channel, a Belgian marine biologist unprofessionally included a color print of his wife afloat in a transparent Naratrany lagoon, bright hair haloing her head like a *Cyanea capillata*.

And there is the one renowned Madagascar blonde whom Shay knows quite well: Helle, who has been visiting the Red House since the Senna children were toddling bare-bottomed on the beach. The arrival of Helle is heralded by the sputter of an ancient Land Rover at the gate, and the subsequent groans and quick disappearance of Senna and any other Italian man. "*Cazzo*, no, she'll talk us to death! You deal with her, Shay!"

Then there will come a shrill warbling "Yoo hoo!" as over the threshold sweeps a tall, corpulent woman in her seventies, bundled into a safari vest, golf trousers, hiking sandals, a frilly blouse, and an old-fashioned graduated string of pearls. Her short, poodle-curled mass of whitening fair hair crowns an eager, sun-creased, unmistakably German face, which in its time must have been of show-stopping beauty. Born in Essen at the apex of the Third Reich, she was, at her postwar peak, a belated blossom of the Aryan ideal.

"Shay, my angel, it's me, Helle! Just stopped in for a swim! You know, my beach over there at Havoana is terrible, just terrible. The villagers are still sneaking out to do shit on the rocks, you can't imagine how un-hygienic, the wretches!"

Helle chatters in English with only a slight accent, or in fluent French, since her long-dead husband, a shipping magnate who once owned much of northeastern Madagascar, was originally from Briançon. In her wake, bearing a basket full of beach towels and presents for the Senna children, trots a diminutive, round-faced Betsimisaraka chauffeur who looks about sixteen, and whom she refers to as *"mon petit"*—with such frequency that everyone calls him Mompty.

Helle, who passed much of her life out in the bush on the Grande Île, believes in good old colonial-style visits, the Kiplingesque kind where settlers are described as riding hundreds of miles across the wilderness to "see a white face." She'll breeze into the Red House of a morning, take an early swim and then lie soaking up sun on Finoana Beach, her huge breasts solidly propped in an old-fashioned balconette one-piece, her tow-colored ringlets spilling out from a kerchief tied peasant-style. She stays for a long, gossipy lunch, stretches out in a bedroom for siesta, takes tea with the Sennas' neighbour Floristella—once, long ago, a lover of hers—and then, in high spirits, sits down to dinner with the Sennas.

She acts grandmotherly to the Senna children, bantering and flirtatious toward Senna, and effusively maternal toward Shay, who takes her with more than a grain of salt, convinced that only an accident of historical timing kept the older woman from being an ardent *Grossdeutsch* patriot. Undeterred, Helle—who adores visiting the Red House—heaps Shay with compliments, and offers her a constant stream of antediluvian advice on housekeeping in the tropics: how a proper memsahib does things.

"You have to be on guard every moment!" she tells Shay, sitting on the edge of a beach chair, and vigorously rubbing her huge, maculate knees with a towel, her breasts and curls bouncing, as Shay tries not to stare at so much exuberant Teutonic flesh discolored by so many years of sub-equatorial sun. "Your servants are children, and you have to take charge: not just to keep them at work, and to prevent them from stealing—they all steal—but to make sure they eat properly, and go to church. (The Muslims are observant, it's the Catholics you have to push.) And you have to keep an eye on who they sleep with—you can't have them making babies all over your compound—and guide them when it's time for them to marry. I chose a wife for Mompty and he is very happy!"

Shay's chest contracts with outrage as she listens to the recitation of these plantation homilies, but at the same time she finds it perversely fascinating to hear a voice straight out of another epoch—like watching a live tyrannosaurus lumber across the landscape. Helle herself is blithely unaware of saying anything untoward.

In the 1950s, her husband, Fabrice Gagne—a gnomelike, immensely rich trader who made his wily way unscathed from enjoying close wartime ties to the short-lived Madagascar Vichy government to enjoying close postwar ties to the fledgling Malagasy Republic—set up his ravishing young German wife in a palatial compound surrounded by coffee and clove plantations in the Atsinanana uplands near Toamasina. Lonely European men stationed in remote outposts traveled for days just to gaze at Helle at dinner in a low-cut evening dress. Her renown extended outside Africa, to some very high places. She tells Shay: "Once, in Venice, when I was at a concert in Piazza San Marco, the king—Vittorio—leaned back and told me a naughty joke right there in public. I had to smack him!"

And Shay knows the story to be true—that even kings became smutty little boys to punish, when Helle was at the height of her golden power. As Toamasina with its bustling port became Gagne's fiefdom, his wife ruled the upper strata of European-Malagasy society from Antananarivo to Fort Dauphin. But as the twentieth century wore on, the nationalist revolution and old Gagne's series of strokes arrived at the same time. After the government seized his plantations and freighters, Gagne ended his life half-blind and babbling on his veranda, overlooking a sea of dying coffee trees on land swiftly being reclaimed by starving villagers eager to plant manioc.

In his last years, he found comfort in the arms of Malagasy concubines, whom Helle had sometimes literally to chase out of her house. She talks scoffingly of this to Shay, advising Shay to ignore any little tropical amours into which Senna may stray. She titters: "You know what they are like, these Malagasy hussies! They're simply a housekeeping problem—like bedbugs."

Shay looks incredulously at her when she says these things, wondering if Helle has actually forgotten that she is talking to a Black woman. But it has long been apparent that Helle's obsessive monologues are not really addressed to her, Shay, but directed toward a crepuscular lost dimension of history.

Nowadays, after years of widowhood, her beauty demolished by time and overindulgence in Three Horses lager, Helle comes and goes between Toamasina and the healthier climate of Naratrany. On the small island she owns a beach bungalow and, like all the other old-time Europeans, occupies her days with property speculation and complicated lawsuits against her neighbors. Everyone, villagers and foreigners, knows her, and she is greeted with a kind of amused homage along the dirt roads as she hollers greetings from the Land Rover, yellow curls still valiantly bobbing in the wind. Shay has always found it mystifying that Helle, living relic of colonialism, is so well liked among the Malagasy of all classes. Both the opinionated Madame Rose and the fastidious Bertine la Grande show her warm approbation, while burdened Mompty serves her as if she were an elderly relation. Perhaps this arises, Shay thinks, from the respect that islanders seem to have for people who are unabashedly true to themselves—those who follow a strict code, though that code may be a hateful one and belong to a world that no longer exists.

One night Helle turns up for dinner at the Red House with an unexpected companion: another woman, much younger and thinner, with straight dull yellow hair cut off sharply at her shoulders, dressed in an odd overlapping array of voluminous clothes. The Sennas and their friends are stunned to learn that this is Helle and Gagne's daughter, Erika, who has always lived in France. Who even knew they had a child?

"*Poverina*, they kept her a secret," says Senna, sotto voce, to Shay. "You can see why."

Though Helle offers no explanation, it is immediately apparent that her daughter suffers from a grave systemic disorder: below her flaxen fringe, blue eyes stare out from growths like reddish coral that encrust her face, and the same growths gnarl her hands and what can be seen of her arms. Proteus syndrome, Shay hears later: a lifelong affliction.

It is an uncomfortable evening, as the Sennas' guests cannot bring themselves to engage in the usual lively gossip with Helle, as if her daughter's disfigurement somehow extends to her. And although Erika, in the few remarks she exchanges with the women of the party, shows herself to be a charming and highly cultured person, still it takes resolution to look at her. Mother and daughter leave early, as Erika, who cannot stay long in tropical temperatures, must fly out in the morning. Shay walks them to the entryway, thinking how like specters the two pale-headed women look, as, lit by Mompty's flashlight, they vanish inside the car.

All this has flashed through Shay's memory by the time she drowsily stretches out her newly polished nails to dry, and watches the hairdresser's scissors trimming the ends of Caroline la Blonde's waist-length weave. Only tiny amounts are snipped away, little tips of gold littering the floor, because the weave represents millions of *ariary*, more than an average year's salary in Madagascar. It is a literal fortune, this top-quality hair that has been bargained for and sold by the gram, like drugs. Hair that was harvested, probably, in a village of Moldavia or the Ukraine: a place just as poor as a village in Madagascar, the kind of place from which girls with similar corn-colored tresses are trafficked to become prostitutes in Western Europe and the Middle East.

Track after track of rippling gold, newly washed and dried, is swiftly stitched with cotton thread onto Caroline's natural strong, blue-Black Sakalava hair, which has been braided into spiraling cornrows as Malagasy women do before ancestral ceremonies. Just a narrow frame of her original hair, bleached to the shade of the extensions, is left free around the edges and the parting. After these edges have been flat-ironed, pomaded, and blended to disguise the stitching, the two sisters, working together, run a curling iron through the long tresses. And finally Caroline stands up in all her Goldilocks glory, dark face glowing with satisfaction, loose flaxen ringlets cascading to her slim hips.

And then the two hairdressers, their little assistant, and Shay exclaim, *"A-ʒa-la!"*—that inimitable Malagasy ejaculation of admiration and wonder. And Caroline rocks back and forth on her platform sandals, swinging her shining cloak of hair and laughing her little girl's laugh. She is, after all, very young—maybe nineteen at most.

Just then, a tall shadow fills the doorway, and a man pushes through the plastic strips. He is Caroline's boyfriend, a Frenchman in his fifties, whom Shay knows as the owner of the Chambord, one of the few elegant hotels on Naratrany. He is a handsome sun-bronzed man with a forthright face and an air of wealth and authority, but as he enters his shoulders slump and his eyes immediately fasten on Caroline with an imploring look, like a dog begging mutely for a treat.

Shay greets him, but he ignores her and every other woman in the room but Caroline, whom he approaches with unnatural slowness and heaviness, as if some invisible current is dragging him to her side.

"Ah, c'est toi," says Caroline, in a bored tone, still swinging her weave and not bothering to look at him. She indicates Thérèse with a curt nod and commands the man: "Pay!"

The sleepy atmosphere in La Joconde suddenly crackles with strange energy as the sleekly barbered Frenchman, dressed in a fashion that suggests golf or sailing at some expensive European resort, fumblingly opens his wallet, yanks out a mass of *ariary* bills, and, eyes lowered, hands it to the hairdresser.

"Bien," says Caroline la Blonde, with queenly indifference. "Now—go and wait."

Shay stares, and all the Malagasy women burst into giggles, as the man obediently turns and exits the shop.

Outside in the market square is the big gleaming Cayenne, and Caroline, after adjusting her lipstick, exchanging a bit more banter with the hairdressers, and offering a friendly goodbye to Shay, takes her leave. Through the fly strips, Shay watches her saunter outside and issue a careless command to the Frenchman standing like a footman beside the car: "Well, what are you waiting for? Open!"

Shay catches sight of her own reflection in the dim wavery mirror and finds she has lifted her freshly polished fingernails up to touch her unruly curls, which for an instant seem coarse and dull, after the extravagant false locks she has been admiring. She is reflecting on a number of things—on beauty, subjugation, and the perverse and fascinating mystery of how and where they intersect—but what also comes to mind is an image of Helle. Helle, who has toppled from her pedestal and outlived the epoch of her own gilded dominion, riding along beside her tragic daughter, their hair blowing like dry-season pasturage as the battered Land Rover passes along the roads of dark people, who wave to them with unreadable smiles. Has Caroline, with the aid of her chimeric tresses, snatched back even more of the power, avenging the Black and brown women Helle has despised?

The market is closed for the afternoon, vendors curled up asleep in the shade of their stalls. As Shay slips her sandals on her freshly pedicured feet and opens her bag to pay her own bill, the sudden breeze of high tide sweeps in from the bay, rattling the La Joconde sign with its faded image eternally smiling out at the dusty thoroughfare.

"Ah, Caroline! Comme elle est belle!" murmurs Gisèle dreamily, as she takes Shay's money. And the little manicure girl, with her thick hair twisted into careful knots all over her head, squats and sweeps up the centimeters of trimmed golden weave, collecting them into a small basket as if they will not be thrown out but weighed up, then locked away, like bankable treasure.

Sirens

Here she stands
her eyes reflecting crystals of sleep
her eyelids heavy with timeless dreams
her feet are rooted in the ocean
and when she lifts her dripping hands
they hold corals and shimmering salt.

—Jean-Joseph Rabearivelo, "Here She Stands,"
translated by Miriam Koshland

There are two women on the island that Shay thinks of in the same beat, unfailingly, as one thinks of twins or certain married couples. These two aren't related, except by an ever-evolving hatred. Still, Shay feels they are the same kind, the same peculiar species, and their fates are intertwined. She first sees this on the day she drives Blue home.

One morning Shay comes out of the water from her early swim and finds the boy Blue sitting up in the tamarind tree. He knows the tree because he has played there often, aloft in its branches with her children, Roby and Augustina; there is even a rough plank platform that they nailed up between two of the thick boughs. From there, accompanied by a scrambling host of Malagasy children from up and down Finoana Beach, they holler shrill piratical challenges and military directives, while raising and lowering bananas and bottles of lime and honey water on a rope. But at the moment the Senna kids are thousands of miles away, spending a summer month with their grandparents in California, and there is no sense of play in the way Blue crouches aloft like a mournful young lemur, peering down at Shay through the dense, feathery leaves.

"Ciao!" he calls out in Italian, in his high-pitched voice. "I'm kind of hungry! Do you have any of those fried potatoes?"

It is barely seven in the morning, the sea is a flat azure tray, and land shadows still stretch long fingers of coolness over the beach. It is her favorite time of day, when Senna and their guests are just getting up, the fishermen and the dive boats already departed, the sand deserted except for market women passing with baskets on their heads, and hotel gardeners quietly raking the tide line. Shay with mask and flippers has swum the length of Finoana Bay just inside the reef, the water smooth as cream, the surface already sun-warmed, a sting of nighttime chill lingering in the depths.

"Ciao, Blue!" she says, trying to keep alarm out of her voice. His hair is a burnt rusty gold, thick as a chow dog's. His lips are full as a girl's, and, in the greenish shade, the enormous sky-colored eyes that give him his nickname resemble those of a child saint from an old painting. "How'd you get here?"

Blue lives with his mother, Giusy, who runs a notorious beach bar on the next bay over.

"Oh, I got a ride up to the crossroads on one of the Siramamy trucks," he says, meaning the big tractors that carry the workers back and forth to the sugar works. He brightens visibly at the memory. "They all know me."

Everyone on the island knows him, in fact, every cane worker and fisherman and hotelkeeper and petty port official and backcountry peasant, as do the prostitutes, who for his whole life have dandled him on their knees in his mother's bar.

"Oh. And so what time this morning did you leave home?" Shay asks carefully.

"Well, it was last night," he admits, clambering nimbly down the tree trunk and presenting himself for Shay to kiss on each cheek with a confident, ceremonious air, as if he's a prize she has just won. He is sturdy, healthy-looking, deeply tanned, wearing a normal outfit of surfer shorts and a Billabong T-shirt; dirty, but no dirtier than any other ten-year-old boy.

Shay wraps a towel around herself and takes him into the Red House. There she gets him a glass of honey water, and has Gaethon, the cook, who has just arrived, fry him up a plate of potatoes. She is tamping down any rage she feels toward Blue's mother. Shay doesn't have Giusy's phone number, and in any case, she won't be awake yet. Shay adds toast and two scrambled eggs to his plate, which the boy cheerfully pushes aside. He chatters to her in Italian with a rather posh accent, and in French and Malagasy with Gaethon.

Then Shay puts him in her pickup truck and drives him home, up the hill past the charcoal makers' settlement, through Finoana village, past the Muslim cemetery and the hippie hotel Chez Bebèle, to the beginning of Sokatra Beach, where, between the village road and the sand, stands a thatched concrete building with a wide entryway closed off with a steel grille that makes it look prison-like in the daylight. On the damp-stained plastered wall facing the road, an island artist has painted, in slapdash style, a ten-foot-long reclining mermaid with explosive green hair, brown skin, muscular arms crossed firmly over invisible breasts, and a jaunty, twice-curled, forked tail like a cross between that of a sea serpent and that of a barracuda. She is of no identifiable race or age, and, almost eyeless, she squints into the distance with her huge crimson mouth opened in a smile of rapacious glee. Running along the upper curves of her figure, neon letters—a rarity on Naratrany—spell out the name of the bar: Chanson de la Mer.

In the daytime this all looks tawdry and grotesque, like a weather-beaten circus poster. But at night, when the pink neon glows, and *salegy* music blares out over the scraggly palms, and the kerosene lamps of vendors selling *brochettes* and samosas glow in the dark crossroads, and the young people who are too poor to afford an entrance fee dance in a throng in the road outside the forbidden doorway, every fiber of their bodies pulsing with the beat—well, then the painted mermaid takes on glamorous substance and the appearance of life: a resplendent, if scaly, mistress of the revels.

Chanson de la Mer is Blue's home, the only one he has known since he first arrived in Madagascar, a baby with a flamboyant Italian mother, but no identifiable father. Here he has grown older, and can be found any night the club is open, sitting at the bar at one, two, even three in the morning, sipping a Coke, watching the scrum of old white tourists and young Black prostitutes on the dance floor, falling asleep with his head on his folded arms. People of all colors and social classes on Naratrany deplore how Blue lives, but there is really nothing anyone can do. He seems healthy and literate, goes with fair regularity to the École Notre Dame, and his mother, Giusy, is quick to tell any critics to fuck off.

"Little Boy Blue, come blow your horn . . ." The nursery rhyme pops into Shay's head whenever she encounters the boy, though no Malagasy or Italian knows it, and it seems of an otherworldly innocence compared to his circumstances.

As Shay pulls up to the club and Blue hops out of the Mitsubishi, the warped wooden side door leading to Giusy's private living quarters bursts open, and Giusy—who is usually never seen before late afternoon—darts out and grabs her son with a movement suggesting a moray eel shooting out of a rocky underwater den. She is a small, freakishly skinny woman with a mane of multicolored dreadlocks, and although she is not much taller than her son, she manages to envelop him in a total embrace, as if she wants to yank him back into her body. At the same time—Shay watches this multitasking with a kind of maternal awe—Giusy administers two tight slaps, which she somehow incorporates into an avalanche of kisses on the boy's scarlet, dodging cheek, accompanying all this with a tearful litany of curses and endearments.

"Piccolo stronzo . . . amore mio . . ." You little asshole, my treasure, where have you been? Saida woke me up, and told me you didn't sleep here. I have been dying, dying of worry, do you understand? I called everybody, I sent Umar and the boys out looking for you!"

Blue starts bawling, too, loudly, like a calf calling its mother, and blubbers out an explanation: he went chasing crabs out on the beach after midnight with the two Belgian boys from the hippie hotel, who have a new, powerful flashlight, and when the boys went to bed, he wasn't sleepy so he hiked down to Renirano to watch the fishermen set up their pirogues for the predawn excursion, and then, followed by a friendly pack of stray dogs, he strolled through the little shuttered village toward the Saint Grimaud road, where he was uproariously greeted by the cane workers on the tractor as the sun rose, and thought it might be fun to take a ride to visit the tree house he'd built with Roby and Augustina.

Shay is sitting in the driver's seat of the truck with the door open and her legs hanging down the side, broiling in the nine o'clock sun. Village women are walking by with *sobiky* baskets and plastic washbasins on their heads, and the bush taxi drivers always parked near the club are lounging up against their battered Renault 5s. Everybody is observing the scene with enjoyment: Giusy—with her bird's nest of purple and green dreadlocks, her spidery sunburnt limbs covered with sleeves and leggings of dense tattoos that somehow give her, for all of her coarse deportment, the delicate beauty of an otherworldly captive, a real mermaid, perhaps—berating her errant son.

Shay experiences a surge of something like relief at the thought of her own faraway kids, whose only danger this summer is of being spoiled by adoring grandparents as they test the tame limits of computer camps and adventure playgrounds out there in the straw-colored Oakland Hills. She finds peculiarly disturbing the sight of this entwined mother and son, in which there seems to be something ominous, vaguely reminiscent of Laocoön and his doomed offspring. Her uneasiness increases as Blue breaks away and scuttles into his door, and Giusy throws her overwrought effusions of gratitude in Shay's direction.

"*Tesoro, grazie, grazie!*" she sobs into Shay's neck, having drawn her out of the truck and into a clinging embrace. "You're a marvelous woman, such an angel, always looking out for my sweet boy!"

Through Giusy's skimpy halter and shorts, Shay can feel her bony body, which, despite the morning heat, is strangely clammy. Giusy smells of cigarettes, some unsuitably girlish floral cologne, coffee, and a tinge of Dzama rum. Shay knows that Giusy comes from a rich manufacturing family somewhere in the Marche region, and is a former addict. Despite her present histrionics, there is a hard practicality in this woman, a quality that has been invaluable in running the biggest dance club on the island; nowadays her pleasures come not from drugs but from the thrill of wielding power in her own domain, from drawing in and manipulating men through a sea of gorgeous Black hookers years younger than she is.

Giusy is pressing Shay to accept a cappuccino, some papaya juice, or a beer, when a jeep pulls up, blocking the road in front of the club. It is a peculiarly customized jeep, with fat tires and beachy wooden panels cut low and open on the sides, and a bright green chameleon painted across the hood.

The driver is Marisa, the other woman in this story. She is instantly recognizable by her thick black Dutch-girl chop of hair, and her habit of dressing in layers of starched white linen, as if she is living out some Happy Valley colonial fantasy. A thin, dour Sakalava woman in a print head wrap, her housekeeper, sits bolt upright beside her. The vintage memsahib image is perfect, at least until Marisa opens her mouth, which is pure back-street Neapolitan.

"Ciao, Shay!" she hollers. *"Che ci fai qui con sta sgualdrina?* What are you doing here with this slut? I hear her kid was roaming around the island all night. Well, well, what do you expect with a mother like that?"

"Fuck off, you lurid bitch!" shrieks Giusy, and flings herself toward the jeep, but Marisa just smirks, takes a newly lit cigarette out of her mouth and flips it deftly onto the dirt road in front of the other woman, then roars off, scattering a crowd of marketgoers. The taxi drivers crack up laughing, and one of them strolls up and retrieves the cigarette. In a couple of hours, news of this encounter will be all over the island, though it is not anything that hasn't been seen before.

Giusy and Marisa rule an appreciable part of the nightlife of Naratrany. They don't really compete for clientele, yet for years a bitter enmity has simmered between them. Marisa owns a popular restaurant, Le Caméléon, built on bad land just a short walk down the beach from the Red House. The land is bad because it was originally not even solid earth but a tidal stream that flowed in and out of the backcountry, complete with mangroves, mud, crabs, and shrimp larvae. An Italian developer, whom everyone calls just "the Abruzzese," years ago filled in the channel and did a perfunctory drainage of the surrounding wetland; then Marisa, newly arrived from Naples, bought the terrain and built her small thatched establishment. It has a lot of quaint island charm: waxed plank floors, lightbulbs caged in baskets, tables and chairs knocked together in a primitive, appealing way, furnishings fit for an arty beach bar on Mykonos or Formentera. *Caméléon* of course means chameleon, and a wooden carving of the creature, painted bright green and magnified to the size of a crocodile, hangs over the entry-way. Chameleons are everywhere on the island, often stopping traffic as they cross the road with their halting mechanical gait, but they are *fady*—taboo—among the Sakalava and other tribes, considered harbingers of misfortune. The neighboring villagers, whose stream has now become a stagnant marsh, speak darkly of Le Caméléon.

But things have gone well for Marisa. Italian and French locals flock with the eagerness of the desperately bored to fill her ten tables or crowd around the tiny counter, to devour her excellent Neapolitan and creole dishes: *pappa al pomodoro* with a touch of piri-piri, calamari pizza—somehow she has set up a wood-burning oven that achieves the proper intensity—dark chocolate mousse with lychees.

It is rumored that Marisa is a criminal and can't go back to Naples, or anywhere in Italy. Undeniably there is something dangerous about her, but she also has a powerful charm, though at forty-something she is angular and weathered, a wicked little *Arlecchina* with pointed nose and sharp grifter's eyes under her dyed black fringe, and an antic flow of Neapolitan blarney. Like Giusy, she has that seductive ability to alternate raucous good humor with stony impassivity: a talent typical of barmaids and other women who spend their lives in crowds of drunken men. And, like Giusy, she has a young, vulnerable creature unhealthily attached to her.

Not a child, though. Marisa's dependent is a Swiss girl named Hélène, in her twenties and already a hopeless alcoholic; fair-haired, weak, rich, and rumored to be Marisa's lover, though Marisa is ostentatiously heterosexual. But how else to explain the older woman's demonic hold over this creature with her refined manners, who hums Mozart and efficiently superintends the dessert making in the restaurant kitchen, before indulging in wild drunken scenes, and collapsing sodden on the beach? Pretty Hélène, with her tubercular pallor and wistful smile, the girl whose money paid for Le Caméléon, and who continues to invest in Marisa's dodgy projects: a sapphire mine near the Baie des Russes, a burger franchise in Mahajanga.

The day Shay sees Marisa and Giusy skirmish with each other in the road, it occurs to her that the patterns of their lives are similar, that they are the same kind. In Shay's hyperactive and playful imagination, they become not just two louche women, but relics of a mythical race: bleak-hearted enchantresses, with magnetic powers over ordinary humans.

So why do they hate each other? Part of it is fighting over lovers. There is the Belgian dive instructor; the handsome Merina director of the agricultural school; an array of good-looking young fishermen, musicians, Peace Corps workers, boat hands. All captured and retaken like pawns in an unending game of chess. Recently, it is said, they've been battling for possession of a *moraingy* boxing champion, a Bara who is said to be the handsomest man in Madagascar.

"A pair of ball-breakers, those two gals," says Shay's husband, Senna, in his usual blunt way. "They're territorial, like monk seals. There's only room for one of them on the island."

The Sennas are relishing these weeks without the kids, a holiday meant to reestablish harmony after a year in which Senna's business trips to China and South America—and, Shay suspects, his casual affairs—have been too frequent. Here in the incomparable beauty of Naratrany, diving, poking around the trackless backcountry as they both love to do, they've started to enjoy each other again. Things are good, in spite of the onerous presence of guests from Milan, of whom the women spend fretful hours smoking on sun loungers and in world-weary tones reiterating the eternal Italian litany: that marriage is a vale of tears and neglectful husbands part of the natural order.

In contrast to these martyred wives, Shay finds Giusy and Marisa suit her mood. In some ways, she can't stand them—she's heard from friends that Giusy refers to her behind her back as *Our Holy Virgin of America*, and Marisa is just as catty. Yet at the same time she is fascinated by the unshakable autonomy of the two women, their dance of shifting domination and their deepening feud.

It's the week of the yearly music festival, when stars from all over the Indian Ocean crowd Naratrany, and, day and night, mobs of ecstatic dancers sweat up the brickcolored dust in the barren terrain near the Saint Grimaud port that serves as football pitch and fairgrounds, crazy with *salegy, twarab*, and wild hip-hop fusion from Mauritius, Comoros, Rodrigues, and all regions of Madagascar.

There are six of them, the Sennas and their friends, crowded around a table in Le Caméléon, as the cold June tidal breeze rattles the basket lampshades, and a local trio that Marisa hired in honor of the festival plays unendingly on a bamboo tube zither, a four-string guitar, and a frenetic accordion in a corner of the room. The place is packed with diners planning to go on later to hear some serious music at Chanson de la Mer or get down and dirty with the three-day-old crowd at the fairgrounds, though Marisa, darting between tables, black bangs bobbing, acts as if her restaurant is the destination of the century.

Hélène has squeezed in next to Shay, who breathes in the castile soap fragrance of the girl's feathery hair as she leans on Shay's shoulder and chatters—in English with a posh L'Aiglon accent—about the recipe of the vanilla tart they are gobbling down. Hélène is always drunk but never smells like it, and Shay wonders if this is connected to her age. How old must she be? Twenty-three or twenty-four, practically a child in this middle-aged European crowd. How did this little debutante end up marooned on a remote beach, a willing victim of Marisa?

Just then, a young man with headphones around his neck, carrying a pair of speakers, steps off the dark beach onto the restaurant veranda, and conversation dies down. He is Malagasy, with a high-angled face that looks not Sakalava or Antandroy, but some other tribe bred to the point of divine symmetry of feature; hair in short vertical twists; skin the color of polished iron; a heroic body of chiseled muscle and sinew. He is a living statue, and either completely unaware of the effect he creates or showing off, since he's shirtless on that windy night. "Oh Lord, look at *that!*" blurts out Shay, who has had a drink or two herself.

A few people laugh at this rambunctious remark, including Hélène, who murmurs into her ear, "It's Tomy."

But Marisa, standing at the table next to Shay's, gives her a hard glance with her *Arlecchina* eyes and says in a knife-sharp tone: "Do you mean my husband, Shay?"

This, then, must be the boxer she has been contesting with Giusy. Everyone bursts out laughing, and Shay pretends she knew all along, and greets the sculptural Tomy, who replies with grave formality. Senna turns the whole thing into a joke, in a way that makes Shay's gaffe seem witty. Hélène lolls on her shoulder, giggling and explaining in a loud whisper that of course the two are not really married, but Tomy is now Marisa's property. And everybody knows how jealous Marisa is.

Later on, the Sennas and their guests head over to Chanson de la Mer. The place is in an uproar, infected by the mad carnival spirit. Three bands are playing off against each other, and the dance floor has been enlarged—a simple matter of expanding the picket walls beyond the roofline so that you can dance not just on the concrete inside floor but on trampled dirt under the riot of stars.

Everybody is in a fever, agog over rumors of the imminent arrival of Raydar, a huge hip-hop star and Naratrany homeboy, who always makes the rounds of his old clubs. Gate-crashers mill on the outer edges, shoving against the village thugs that Giusy employs as bouncers, and girls in hot pants and skintight jeans are up on tables dancing with full beer bottles on their heads, or on the ground in the position of prayer, asses raised and fluttering in unbelievable *maputo* moves. Fights break out, mainly staged between prostitutes trying to impress tourists, but one girl actually takes off her high heel and slashes another on the shoulder.

The Sennas make it through to the bar, where the island toffs have gathered: Shay sees Paranaky, the Merina senator, his shaved head glazed with sweat, talking with Georges, who owns the Chambord hotel, and Janine, who runs the malaria foundation. At the heart of the tumult is Giusy, calmly slinging drinks along with her motley trio of bartenders, a Malagasy, a Mauritian, and a New Zealander who somehow washed up on Naratrany. Giusy is wearing one of her Greek-looking dresses, her tattooed shoulders poking through cutouts, her multicolored dreadlocks pulled up in a spiral tower. She looks slit-eyed like a cat with enigmatic contentment, and occasionally leans over to murmur something to her latest boyfriend, a handsome Sicilian she is said to have pinched from Marisa.

And of course there is young Blue, seated on his usual high stool, but this time, because of the chaos, behind the bar. He is sipping a Coke and, completely absorbed as if he were alone, playing on a Game Boy. Seated beside him is a handsome white-haired man Shay has never seen before, wearing a crisply ironed striped dress shirt. He is ignoring the music and the wild scene, and talking to Blue, who barely acknowledges him.

"Who's that?" Shay asks Angélique the pharmacist, who is decked out in a jumpsuit and peacock feather earrings.

"That's Giusy's father. He's here from Ancona, and everybody is talking about how he wants to take his grandson back to live in Italy. Giusy won't have it, though it would be a good thing for *ce pauvre* Blue."

Shay studies Giusy, her father, and her son through the cigarette smoke and tumult. She can sense the Olympian respectability of the old man, the hesitant attraction of Blue to the privileged life his grandfather offers, the furious resentment of Giusy, the former addict, toward her father, and her passionate maternal clutching at her son. It's a mess of a situation, a tragedy in the making. But at the same time Giusy has never looked more triumphantly at her ease than she does right now surrounded by music and chaos and men.

A few days later, Shay steps out of the shade of the Red House garden into the buzzing reverberation of noon, feeling herself a small figure against the hard blue sky; the shrunken shadows; the bay, flat as a prairie at low tide.

In the shallows, a pair of catamarans and a fat-bellied *boutre* sit still as monuments. She needs to get away from the annoying chatter of her guests, who are roasting themselves alongside the pool. Heat leaking through her sandals, her head spinning from the dazzle of the sand, she sets out down Finoana Beach toward the black-lava headland visible two miles away. A few squatting village children and snoozing souvenir vendors cluster in the scant shade of the palms and sea pines, but otherwise she has the beach to herself.

Passing in front of Le Caméléon, Shay looks across the little terrace, and sees, at one of the tables inside, a sight that startles her. The profile of Giusy's father, unmistakable with that precise white haircut, seated at a table with Marisa, Giusy's archnemesis. With them sits Hélène, her hair pulled up in a tiny bun, smoking in her *jeune fille rangée* fashion, and sipping a beer. And in the mangrove-lined hollow abutting the restaurant Shay can see Tomy, a Riace bronze figure come to life, changing a tire on Marisa's jeep.

Shay pauses, amazed by Giusy's father's presence in the camp, so to speak, of his daughter's enemy. And then Marisa spots Shay, and summons her with a wave that like all of her movements has a commedia dell'arte dash to it. Shay knows that getting involved in this situation is unwise, but still she trudges up to the restaurant through the blistering sand.

Introduced, Shay sees that Giusy's father embodies the man of virtue, as Lorenzetti's frescoes illustrate *il Buon Governo*. He owns a shoe factory near Ancona and has a businessman's pragmatism that Shay recognizes from her own husband. Blond eyelashes gone white with seventy-five years or so, a face expensively weathered in sailboats, mouth corners downturned with the tortured angle that parents of addicts develop, and the same sky-colored eyes as his grandson, Blue. He has a big gold chronometer on his sun-spotted wrist, and sits in front of his beer without touching it.

"Signora Shay just loves your grandson!" Marisa tells the old gentleman vivaciously, crinkling her brilliant dark eyes. Today she is wearing a crisp white linen sundress, and resembles—if you don't know her—a warmhearted hostess. "Adores him! Blue is a close friend of her children. That is Shay's big villa down the beach, and the dear boy considers it a home away from home. He showed up there once in the morning, didn't he, Shay? After running away from Chanson de la Mer and wandering the island all night, poor darling. So dangerous, in this wild place. His mother didn't even know he was out."

Shay reluctantly admits this is so.

The angle of Giusy's father's jaw grows sharper. *"Non è possibile!"* he mutters.

"But the boy does love his mamma," ventures Hélène, and then stops suddenly like a guilty child, as Marisa gives her a stinging glance.

"We gave up on our daughter years ago," the old gentleman says abruptly. It is clear that he is normally a reserved person, at the moment cast into one of those confessional moods that tropical climates inspire in some visitors. "But our grandson, our only grandson, *perbacco, no!"*

"Ce pauvre petit," he adds—suddenly switching from Italian to orotund French as if he were presenting a case at the Cour d'Appel—"that poor child will no longer live in these depraved circumstances. There will be legal measures, I assure you!"

Marisa nods with feigned sympathy, and Shay feels the afternoon wind pick up, rattling the straw shades of the veranda as if a current of the element of pure life—the crazy element that creates unstable situations, makes things, even terrible things, happen—had suddenly raced through the little restaurant. Shay finishes her cup of bitter Neapolitan coffee, excuses herself, and goes on with her walk. When she passes by some time later, Giusy's father is gone.

Soon afterward the Sennas leave Naratrany for Italy, and, as always, it is as if a door shuts on a different dimension. In August they rent out the Red House, and head to California to take the kids camping across the national parks. Once back in Milan, Shay, immersed in her usual round of teaching, translation work, shepherding Roby and Augustina between school and sports, has no time to think of Madagascar. Odd scraps of gossip reach her like messages in bottles. One of these is that Blue is now back in Italy, living with his grandparents.

Briefly Shay wonders how this has happened, reasoning that Giusy probably saw the light, and agreed to let the boy spend the school year in Ancona. She doesn't find out until she returns to Naratrany at Christmastime that, following her father's visit, Giusy lost custody of her son. International lawyers were involved, and the Italian consul.

Blue is no longer on the island, and the Senna children soon stop asking about him. The official story is the tame one that Shay first imagined: that Giusy and her family decided it was best for him to prepare for his middle school exams in Italy. But her island informants, chiefly Angélique and the all-knowing Bertine la Grande, soon enlighten her as to how bribes were offered, gendarmes called in from Diego Suarez, scandalous information dug up about drugs and underage prostitution at Chanson de la Mer. They tell of ugly threats; an attempted escape of Giusy and Blue to Mauritius blocked at the airport; scenes of screaming and yelling, and officers tearing away a boy too big to be clinging to his mother.

People are appalled, but, as usual, Naratrany life goes on. Over the Christmas holidays, when the island is full of Europeans and South Africans, Giusy is there behind the bar every night, as if nothing has happened: she appears a bit scragglier, but unbowed, with a new tattoo—the name Blue—covering the left side of her neck. As always, she is immersed in men. Heartbreak or not, she continues to expand her business, bringing in music talent from all over the Indian Ocean; the hip-hop star Raydar even records a hit track about Giusy and Chanson de la Mer.

Meanwhile, at Le Caméléon, Marisa is also doing good business, looking trendy with a new hairdo—shaved on one side—her eyes sparking with schemes, bouncing about like the little circus performer she resembles. She seems more than usually pleased with herself; it's common gossip that she is the person who actively encouraged Giusy's father to snatch his grandson away from Chanson de la Mer.

That year, rains come a month early, in late December, and the displaced tidal stream beside the restaurant swells to a powerful muddy torrent, sometimes thigh-high, that you have to cross on the beach to get there, but people flock to the place anyway, laughing and splashing like adventurers. Marisa has enlarged the veranda onto the beach so that it sometimes seems as if you are eating afloat in the high tide. Hélène has gotten an ice cream machine, and has the cook making passion fruit and lychee sorbets. Somebody writes up the place in an important travel guide, and backpackers take detours to eat there.

Hélène has also had her hair cut, in a schoolgirl bob, and she is drinking more than ever. Staggers all over the place in the evenings, sometimes flinging herself onto the laps of customers. Marisa, as always, treats her with offhand affection, as one would an impossible little sister, deploying the cook and waiter to cart her off and lock her in her bedroom when she gets too raucous.

All at once, though, there is an unpleasant rumor in circulation, one that Shay expected to hear much earlier: that Marisa's handsome boyfriend Tomy is having an affair with Hélène. Word has gotten around that the amorous couple have been seen at night in a truck parked up beyond the airport, near the collapsed archway that leads to an abandoned ylang-ylang plantation. And that, back at the restaurant, when Marisa is away, they shut themselves up in the kitchen toilet.

On Naratrany, nasty gossip like this circulates about everyone, including Shay herself, so Shay discounts it. She doesn't think that Hélène would be so stupid as to put herself in an inflammatory situation with a woman so clearly dangerous as Marisa. Yet it is true that, when she has a few drinks, Hélène loses track of things. The rumors just hang in the air of those unusually hot and wet early January days, and then the Senna family heads back to Milan.

One night in early spring, Senna comes home from work with staggering news: Hélène is dead. Senna has learned this in a phone call from his friend Raza, a Réunionnaise auto dealer and aspiring triathlete who roams Naratrany on a flashy trail bike. It seems that the day before, at dawn, that peculiarly eventful moment on tropical beaches, Raza came upon Hélène's body in front of Le Caméléon, her head in the torrent that runs past the restaurant, where the land water meets the incoming tide. She'd been dead for hours, soaking wet, her long dress pulled up half over her face so—Raza added this salacious detail—the whole world could see she was wearing no undergarments.

The commissioner who acts in forensic matters (at least for white people and rich Malagasy—the poor are left to their own devices) on Naratrany determines that she drowned while intoxicated, which anyone who knew her can understand. Hélène greeted more than one sunrise while passed out on the beach. It is impossible to interview Marisa, who at the time of the death was off in the capital buying supplies; she is said to be devastated, and in seclusion. Tomy, that week, was competing in a *moraingy* boxing match in Diego Suarez.

Shay was never a close friend of Hélène's, but tears fill her eyes when she hears this news. Imagining the poor girl sprawled in the wet sand like a piece of trash, like one of the tattered strips of *lamba* cloth you sometimes find washed up at the Finoana tide line, of no use even to the poorest of the poor. Later Shay hears that Hélène's family in Zurich won't even pay to ship her back from Madagascar. The Swiss consulate has to get involved, and for days the body lies disgracefully marooned on ice in the primitive morgue of Naratrany, where other friendless foreigners have lain.

Just weeks after Hélène's death, Marisa abandons Naratrany, moving to the Grande Île, somewhere far down on the coast near Tulear. It seems that Tomy has family there, and the pair has invested in a terrain planted with oil palm. With what money no one knows, just as no one ever learns what happened to Hélène's savings, and her pearls, and her gold signet ring.

The owner of the hippie hotel Chez Bebèle buys Le Caméléon's quirky furniture and the kitchen equipment, and the restaurant sits boarded up on the beach. It falls apart quickly, a template of abandoned structures in the tropics, having fulfilled all the villagers' predictions about the bad luck of the name. Occasionally a little Sakalava girl is seen dreamily sweeping the veranda, but weed piles up on the sand in front, and the watercourse clogs with debris. The painted wooden chameleon, displayed so boldly across the entrance, changes color through the cyclone season, as if it were slowly going through all the gradations of the real animal, fading from bright green to a yellowish pallor, to gray.

Later, a canny developer from Johannesburg buys up the property, knocks down the building, has the terrain properly drained, and builds a trio of luxury condominiums, which he has no trouble marketing as peaceful havens to European tourists scared by terrorism at Red Sea resorts.

Of course, the chattering classes of Naratrany, whose epicenter is the Fleur des Îles café, are convinced that it is Marisa who—driven by her notorious jealousy, and employing some dark agency of Neapolitan vengeance—murdered her protégée. But there is, of course, no proof. In the swirl of conjecture, one person Shay never hears mentioned is Marisa's sworn enemy, Giusy. Is Shay the only one who suspects that it was Giusy who started that ugly rumor of Hélène's affair with Tomy?

When Shay sees her in summer and winter vacations afterward, Giusy always looks well: hair more serpentine than ever, drawing in a tide of lovers and customers of all colors and nationalities. With her usual acuity, she takes advantage of the restaurant gap left by the departure of her rival, by hiring the former Caméléon cook and opening a brasserie.

Some years pass, and when Blue is eighteen, he comes running back to Madagascar, to the louche life from which he was torn. Giusy, ecstatic, throws a huge party and free concert that overflows her club and floods out onto the crossroads and down to the beach. But in the end Blue proves a torment to his mother. No longer a child content with sitting at the bar, he picks fights with his mother's boyfriends, disrupts her carefully nurtured rapport with musicians, brings in serious drugs, and gets in big trouble with Comorean gangsters. He is one of a crew of rich island kids who race Jet Skis off Sokatra Point, and one day he has a bad crash that fractures his jaw and right leg so that he has to be helicoptered out to Réunion for surgery. He returns with a frozen face, a limp, and a pill habit that his mother despairingly feeds as he lumbers around Chanson de la Mer, pudgy and bloated, his big, fringed eyes blank.

Giusy seems to absorb the shock of her son's injury into herself, and begins to deteriorate. She keeps her odd beauty but becomes skeletal, her tattoos mingling with the veins wrapped around her bones, her hair still bravely polychrome, but the whites of her eyes taking on a bronze tinge. It's said that she is using again; it is said that she has lung cancer, cirrhosis of the liver; but no one knows for sure because she shuts herself up at home. She hires a German as manager, and without her charismatic presence, Chanson de la Mer loses business.

One morning, Giusy and Blue get on a plane to Cape Town, a common destination for moneyed islanders with medical problems. They are never seen again, and news spreads that she has sold the club to the German. Nobody learns what fate the mother and son meet in South Africa because, although everyone on Naratrany knows Giusy, she only had lovers and customers, never any friends.

The new owner makes no success out of Chanson de la Mer. He tries to charge a percentage from the bar girls, and to take over the night market where the village kids dance for free; but people simply move to other clubs. Finally, he renames the place Le Vieux Phàre and whitewashes over the old sign. In daylight, though, passersby can see through the paint the barely visible outline of the figure with the swirling tresses and barracuda tail.

It seems there will be no more news of Marisa and Giusy, but one July afternoon after Giusy has left the island, Shay is reading in a hammock near the seawall of the Red House when a woman comes up out of the dazzle on the sand, and calls her name. She is Italian, and has very long, straggly hair, badly dyed a coal black that has turned rusty in the tropical sun, held back by a wide headband; she is barefoot and wears white Indian trousers and a T-shirt. Her gaunt face is pitted with scars from sand fly bites, and were it not for the sly tilt of her black eyes and the jaunty set of her shoulders, Shay wouldn't recognize her.

"Marisa!" Shay exclaims.

"So you didn't know me?"

Shay lies and says she knew her immediately, invites her in, offers her something to drink, but Marisa can't stay. She's restless, amped on khat or something stronger, bouncing around on the balls of her feet, her eyes roving up into the tamarind tree as if she is looking for a trapeze to catch hold of.

She replies evasively to Shay's questions about how she is, what she has done over the past years, and Shay quickly stops asking. Marisa doesn't want to talk to her anyway: she came by to look for Senna. "Shay, it's a business deal, something really big, that maybe he might . . . Not the oil palms, nothing to do with sapphire mines, no, this is something new."

Shay tells her Senna is still in Italy and won't arrive for another week, and Marisa, rude as always, immediately turns to leave. But Shay keeps her talking, asking whether she has seen the new condos on the site of Le Caméléon. At this, Marisa gives a harsh laugh, and mutters something in dialect, something like *"Quello ho vinto io"*—"I won that one . . ."

Someone calls Shay from inside the Red House, and Shay excuses herself, telling Marisa to wait, but when Shay returns, the other woman has disappeared. Shay squints into the sunlight down the beach, and makes out a small figure walking toward the Finoana headland, loose trousers and hair fluttering in the breeze. Then, just around the level of the former Caméléon, Marisa makes a quick turn to the side, an eerie flicker of a movement, and disappears into the palms.

Shay asks around, and it turns out that she is the only person who saw Marisa. No one else even believes she was on the island, and Shay begins to think that the whole encounter was a dream she conjured up in the hammock, while dozing and jotting down teaching notes on *Beloved*. Except that it's exactly the kind of thing Marisa would do: drop by to hustle money.

A few months later, Shay hears through her usual channels that Marisa is dead—of cerebral malaria picked up down there in the wilds of Tulear; the Italian consul can't even track down her body. The enigmatic Tomy, however, is said to be alive and well.

Shay doesn't want to calculate exactly when Marisa was supposed to have died, because it rattles her to think that, on the beach, in broad daylight, she might have been visited by a phantom. And anyway, why should she be the one to encounter that particular ghost? She determines to forget the whole thing, but what sticks with her is the uncanny swiftness with which Marisa, at that last sighting, flickered and vanished, like a fish into a crevice in a reef. It is very like a move Shay saw Giusy make one night on the crowded dance floor, slipping off with a man she'd just met. A sidelong glance, a slight shimmer as of hidden scales, a flourish of snaky locks, and the lady of Chanson de la Mer, along with her hapless conquest, is suddenly not there.

On Naratrany memories are short, and the islanders have long stopped discussing Giusy and Marisa, as gossip turns to fresher topics: election riots in the capital; a scourge of *muti* killings spreading from Mozambique; rosewood smuggling and vanilla wars.

But Shay, both at the Red House and back in Italy, finds the two women fixed in her mind. It's an odd thing, because she didn't like either of them. But in spite of this, what she has seen of their lives and their strange feud exerts over her the fascination of things only partially visible, like the spires of a submerged city. Shay has never lost her childhood passion for myths, and the impression lingers with her that she's been privy, not just to the vendetta of a pair of amoral women, but to the duel of two other-worldly beings, with their own cold-blooded female motives and alien code of conduct. For some reason she has been able to discern their curious life cycle: deadly conflict, chance victims, flaunted triumph, swift dissolution.

Of course this is purest fantasy, and as Shay pictures the face of Blue staring at her through the tamarind leaves, and the body of Hélène sprawled on the sand, she also sees the pointless destruction the two women managed to spread around them. And this in turn begs the question: What, in the end, was gained by anybody involved? But here, Shay, whether on or off the island, finds herself at a full stop. Neither her compassion, her febrile imagination, nor her skill at translation is of any use in deciphering what is either grotesquely tangled human history or the annals of mermaids— which are written in seawater if they are written at all.

Voice

To speak a strange tongue is a blessing or a curse. Shay comes across this cryptic adage in an old collection of Malagasy proverbs, translated and privately printed by a long-dead Lutheran missionary. Books of this sort—the work of nineteenth-century French and English clergymen once deployed in remote corners of Madagascar: foxed and musty-smelling volumes of notes on folklore and ethnology, whose amplitude suggests scholarly devotion and appalling loneliness—are full of the famous *ohabolany* proverbs, which once formed an underpinning of practical tradition in village life. But this particular statement (who knows how badly translated?) intrigues Shay because she feels it suggests another aspect of Madagascar that she has noticed upon becoming a frequent visitor: how everything there—earth, air, water, and sentient life—seems to flow with intermingling communication. And how, in this permeable atmosphere, the Malagasy—like the Inuit and countless other peoples of shamanic and animistic faith—are well accustomed to receive greetings, counsel, even scoldings from other worlds, often through a human medium.

Shay has seen something of this. On several occasions she has been privileged to visit the hidden Sakalava village of diviners and sorcerers that lies at the very heart of Naratrany island, where whitewashed royal tombs are guarded by a circle of teetering huts, some with jars of crocodile fat set out on their thresholds. Here during long ceremonies she has witnessed men and women wreathed in cigarette smoke, entranced by hours of invocatory clapping and singing to the tunes of reedy accordions and sacred drums, bamboo zithers and wooden rattles, suddenly possessed by the great *tromba* spirits, so that they become other than themselves. She has seen how, using oracular tones and gestures that come from beyond the wall of time, they pour forth, in whispers and murmurs and laughter and shouts, the pronouncements of long-dead queens and kings.

But although Shay's hair has been plaited against her scalp in the proper design and her body modestly draped in a cotton *lambahoany*, and though she joins her hosts in their drinking and songs, she naturally feels herself at all times an outsider: the foreign guest, honored, but unable to appreciate sensations beyond the suffocating heat, the tedium, the creeping skepticism interspersed with lightning flashes of amazed conviction, all of which keep her at an observer's distance.

But there have been a few times in Madagascar when a voice out of an unknown region has spoken directly to her.

One time is when she is driving around the wild northern coast of Naratrany with her friend Felice. Felice is Malagasy, some years younger than Shay, and from a high-ranking Merina family of Antananarivo. Her father is a diplomat, and she spent her multilingual childhood in Washington, DC, and Paris, and graduated from Georgetown. Now she works for an international health organization and has come to Naratrany shepherding a pair of French optometrists who run free weeklong clinics every year all over Madagascar. All three are now staying as guests of Shay and her husband, Senna, at the Red House on Finoana Beach. Shay and Felice have just dropped off the female doctors at the small whitewashed annex loaned by the Notre Dame lycée near the port, and have been impressed by the long, quiet line of villagers from all over the island who have been waiting since daybreak for their eye examinations and free glasses.

"It's unfortunately just a fashion," says Felice, as they jounce out of the dusty school compound and Shay turns the Mitsubishi toward the Naratrany airport and the unpaved roads beyond. "Offer anything free to a Sakalava or an Antandroy, even treatment they don't need, and they come running."

"I'm sure it helps some!" protests Shay, amused by how snobbishly her friend talks about Malagasy peoples other than her own.

"I'm saying this privately to you, because these initiatives are my job of course—but I tell you, this is one of the more pointless ones. The serious cases—trachoma, river blindness—rarely show up at these clinics. They go first to the *moasy*, the village herbalists, then to the spirit healers, and only then to clinicians, and so it's usually too late—maybe they go blind. At this clinic here, people get diagnosed for myopia or astigmatism that has never, ever bothered them before—and they get free glasses and swagger around for a few days. Until they get tired of the weight on their faces, and then they lend them to their brothers and sisters and cousins, and then the glasses are worn as a decoration until they break, and of course there is no one to fix them, and so it goes—more trash. Until next year's clinic. There's pleasure in it for both sides. The villagers get status and the doctors get a tropical vacation."

"So young and so cynical!" says Shay, remembering, however, how the entire staff of the Red House strutted around proudly in new glasses for a week before discarding them.

"I can talk this way because it's my country. Just like you can say 'nigga.'"

Shay gives a hoot of laughter. Felice, small, round, and pretty with a coppery Indonesian-looking face, straight hair cut in a stylish bob, and a tiny, impudent, turned-up Merina nose, has a steely intelligence and a wicked sense of humor. She is engaged to a preposterously tall Swedish bacteriologist she met in Nairobi, and she is one of the few friends Shay has who can understand her own restless leapfrogging between languages and cultures.

"Felice, you know as well as I do that it is a matter of credibility. You can say 'nigga' just as I can. You are from an African nation. You grew up in the States, right there on the fringes of our diaspora. A generation earlier in DC, you would have endured segregation. And in college you pledged Alpha, for heaven's sake!"

"Yes, and any Alpha soror would clutch her pearls till they broke before she said that word! Then where would my precious ladylike reputation go? So, I may be entitled to 'nigga,' but I'm not going to use it. Just like you should keep quiet about all this." Felice spreads her small, fine-boned hands out theatrically toward the windscreen, which shows they are now entering the arid north of Naratrany, eroded red hills dotted with the spreading leafy fans of *ravenala* palms. Of course, she means more than the scene before them, means her entire country: the great island of which Naratrany is a mere satellite, and the fabulously intricate web of its landscapes and tribes.

She adds: "Though, I've noticed already that you've done a decent job of not delving too deep into Madagascar. That's a good thing. No more theories needed! I work with a million foreigners' opinions, and it's a nest of snakes."

"My ambition is to be an eternal tourist," proclaims Shay glibly, as she always does.

"Naratrany's a vacation spot for us highlanders from the capital, too," says Felice, deliberately misunderstanding her. "Kind of the Martha's Vineyard of Madagascar!" She is quiet for a minute, then adds: "But that tourist thing doesn't really work for you, does it?"

"Not really."

Shay downshifts as the smooth airport road, built by grace of the Chinese government, suddenly ends and the Mitsubishi begins trundling down a typical backcountry track composed of orange dust, craters dug by rainy season torrents, the rubble of small landslides down slopes denuded by slash and burn. This morning the two friends are in search of a remote sacred tree supposed to be on the trackless northern coast of the island. It is rumored to be as large as the much-visited ancient ficus, planted by an early Sakalava queen, that occupies an entire bluff outside the port town. But their quest for the tree is just an excuse to wander, to enjoy the early freshness of the air, the beautiful skies of the dry season that have not yet turned brazen with midday heat.

They pass through plantations of ylang-ylang owned by a rich Karan Indian, the strange gray-barked trees pruned to bend down like arthritic

knuckles, giving an eccentric fairy-tale look to the rolling hillsides. They
edge around herds of humpbacked zebu driven by ragged child cowherds
who shout greetings and wave their sticks in the air through the clouds of
dust. They pull over to squat and pee in the bush, shaded by trees hung
with monkey ladder vines bearing giant seedpods worthy of Jack's bean-
stalk. They pass through villages so unused to traffic that the villagers have
spread cloths in the road covered with drying turmeric root, gleaming like
crude gold in the sunlight.

Felice props her small feet on the dashboard, contemplating her lacquer-red
nails and a delicate silver ring on her second toe. She has on round tortoise-
shell sunglasses that look like something Hepburn might have worn in *The
African Queen,* and Shay teases her for having tied her hair up in a print
wrap that suggests an amateurish take on a Ghanaian style.

"Well, we Merina don't have our own head-tie tradition," retorts Felice,
adding with a mischievous glance at Shay: "We tend to have good hair . . ."

"Felice, I give you official permission to say 'nigga,' but you can't talk
about 'good hair'! My sister and I suffered for years with my high yellow
great-aunts telling us: 'Girls, your hair is a mixture of "good" and "bad"!'
It infuriated my mother. She'd tell us our hair was beautiful, but of course
we desperately wanted it to be 'good'—just as straight as yours."

Felice giggles. "And when you got to Italy?"

"Oh, so many Italians have nappy heads you wouldn't believe it! And
they are totally into volume!" laughs Shay, patting her mass of crinkled
curls, which she is wearing long these days.

They are talking in English, in relaxed tones but hungrily, about a
topic neither of them can often explore with others. About living in different worlds, straddling continents, about multiple citizenships, about
hopscotching among languages. About how Shay and her husband, Senna,
are raising their son and daughter in Milan to speak both English and Italian, and how Shay has a secret agenda for promoting her own language,
as Senna probably does for his. About how Felice plans to raise her future
kids—in Stockholm, or maybe Atlanta—to speak English and Swedish,
and of course Malagasy.

"Of course, they'll probably turn out to be spoiled third culture brats who will insist on speaking their fantasy version of Ebonics," says Felice, rolling down the sleeve of her white denim jacket as the sun begins to roast her arm.

"It's the language of art now everywhere in the world, even when it's just intonation. Listen to Raydar and the other Malagasy hip-hop stars. Listen to Swedish rap."

"The worst."

"No, the worst is Russian. They have trap music, too."

"Siberian crunk. That could be a thing."

They bump slowly down the road, and Shay starts describing her frustration with her students at the Università Cattolica, where she teaches a phenomenally popular introductory course on Black American literature. "They are so sweet and idealistic, but they don't, can't, have a clue as to the foundation of anger, the background of despair in all these works. What I need is an emotional translator."

They discuss a Yinka Shonibare show Felice saw in Brooklyn, both admitting that they disliked West African wax prints until they began to show up in the context of contemporary high art like Shonibare's installations. But the textiles were created by Dutch traders to advance colonial trade, so—the two women wonder earnestly—perhaps a certain distaste is justified?

Shay's playlist—which ranges from Steeleye Span to the Dungeon Family—tosses up "Valerie," and Felice begins to talk about Amy Winehouse, with whom she is mildly obsessed. She seems personally offended that Winehouse is white. "I just think that incredible voice and those big emotions are too much for her. Too powerful to be natural!" says Felice. "I have never seen such a case of a spirit speaking through a person. It's like a Black jazz goddess—a huge presence—calling out through that little pale English girl!"

"A kind of possession, like a *tromba*? You must have taken part in one! I bet even aristocrats like your family talk with the ancestors."

Felice's chatter cuts off abruptly. "The *tromba* ceremony is a lowland custom, Shay," she says coldly. "It is Sakalava. Not Merina at all." Pulling out her phone, she takes a picture of a flock of turkeys clustered around the concrete stem of an old colonial signpost, where just a few faded letters, "ana," are visible. Then she looks at the map and reads off names: Madirovalo, Ambatofinandrahana. "I don't think we're going to find any sacred tree," she adds, in the same offended tone.

Rebuked, Shay shoves in the clutch. When you have a friend from a different world, no matter how much you have in common, there is still a shadow place where you can't go. On the other hand, she thinks with sudden irritation, Felice needs to make up her mind if she wants people to learn or not learn about her country. And anyway, she's pretty flippant about Black culture in America, talks about it as if it's a damn masquerade party.

Shay reflects, as she has many times, that no one from an African nation can understand the peculiarities of being African-American: the unhealed injury ripped open with every fresh injustice, the ancient crime that lies behind it all. She remembers her father at dinner back home in Oakland, arguing in his dogmatic professorial way that the most pervasive emotional violence done by slavery in the Americas was the loss of names, the amputation of the past.

Shay is so caught up in her internal rant that she speeds up on a curve and narrowly avoids colliding with a wooden zebu-drawn cart rattling slowly along the dusty road. The imperturbable beast comes to a stop, and the carter gives a holler and waves his straw hat, as Shay pulls the wheel to the right and jounces along a rocky washed-out border that nearly pitches her and her passenger through the ceiling.

"Trying to kill me?" demands Felice, scrambling to gather up her phone and bag.

"Just reminding you who's behind the wheel," says Shay demurely.

"*Voilà*—the American imperialist!" retorts Felice, and soon the two friends are chattering and laughing again.

A bit later, they come to a turnoff onto a road with some signs of repair work, lined with dense bamboo as thick as their arms. And, bumping through the tunnel of green shade, they find a hotel Shay has heard talked of.

It is a tiny gem of a place built by a rich young Frenchman and his Vietnamese wife, who set out to create a *Paul et Virginie* fantasy of enchanted beauty in the most improbable setting. There are six thatched teak huts, with fittings from Bali and gleaming Portuguese tile floors, joined by a network of stone pools, where koi flash their coral scales, scattered through a manicured coconut grove overlooking a sugar-white beach facing far-off Mozambique.

The only problem with the place is that the roads are so bad and the seaward approach so difficult that nobody ever comes there. Even the owners have practically given up visiting it.

But through some strange fluke, three or four years after completion, the hotel has not succumbed to the swift tropical decay that has devoured so many other architectural follies on Naratrany. It is kept up with precision by a well-paid staff who reside in a neat cluster of huts nearby, and clearly have some powerful incentive—financial? moral? superstitious?—for keeping it polished up like a shrine.

With wonder, Shay and Felice tour this lonely enchanted kingdom, shown around by an impeccably courteous manager from Fianarantsoa, a shaven-headed Betsileo whom Shay recognizes as the former top barman at Naratrany's sole big resort, dismissed because of some obscure scandal. He greets Felice with pleasure, overjoyed to see another highlander, and is interested to learn that Shay is from California, which he says he has always dreamed of visiting. They view each of the graceful shuttered bungalows with their ikat hangings and gleaming Japanese bathroom fixtures, and then Felice, with her usual breezy air of command, asks the manager to have lunch prepared for them.

Apologizing for the lack of supplies, he seats them at a veranda table set with starched linens and gleaming cutlery and, having donned a pristine white jacket, serves them what must have been part of the staff's midday meal of rice and fish *romazava* with bitter greens. Shay and Felice spoon up the delicious astringent broth and sip crystal glasses of chilled Meursault that has somehow appeared in a sweating bottle properly wrapped in a heavy napkin.

"This is all a miracle," says Shay. "And the wine hasn't even gone vinegary from the heat. We can't manage this at the Red House, that's for sure!"

"They have the ice caves of Kubla Khan," says Felice dreamily.

"No, they just have the fanciest generator I've ever seen in my life. It must have cost a fortune just to get it here. And why? Why this whole place in the ass-end of nowhere?"

"Well, why did Senna build Red House, for that matter?" asks Felice, reasonably.

"People do mysterious things when they think they've found paradise."

"But the owners don't even come!"

"Maybe they just like to know it's here."

After coffee, they pay the manager with a stack of *ariary*, and he asks if they want him to open a room for a siesta, or to set up hammocks for them in the palm grove.

But Shay and Felice decide to take a walk on the wide swathe of beach, where the brazen heat of midday has lessened and the tide has begun to come in in a series of transparent veils, one overlapping another. To add to their delight, they learn from the manager that the sacred tree they were seeking is on a bluff on the very next beach.

"But it is not a very important sacred tree," he says with a shrug.

"Is there a village beside it?" asks Felice.

For the first time the suave manager with his gold earring and sleek smooth-shaven head looks nonplussed. "No. There is no village. Only Franco."

"Who?"

"A mad *vazaha* who lives there."

"All alone?" asks Shay.

"No, with Fatima. An Antemoro woman from the East, with a bad leg and a white eye." The manager hesitates. "Maybe you shouldn't go there, *mesdames*. But probably he will not come out to bother you."

Shay recalls that she has heard something from her husband about this Franco: a drunken recluse, from Rome maybe. And there was something else, some gossip or rumor, but there is always gossip and rumor on Naratrany.

Straw-hatted, barefoot, swinging their sandals, Shay and Felice set off walking along the hems of the incoming waves, in coral sand so fine that their footsteps leave milky clouds in the warm transparent shallows. Tiny ghost crabs, almost invisible, scatter in mincing crowds as they proceed, and the sea breeze of the rising tide ruffles the sea pines that line the deserted shore. Miniature pastel clams emerge and dig frantically back under the sand with each wave, and their shells, thin as babies' fingernails, litter the tide line along with lace-pale twigs of coral.

Out beyond the reef, three fishing pirogues raise their thorn-shaped sails and race southward in the freshening breeze, like ancient vessels passing through from another age. Other than that, the solitude of the two women on the beach in its aloof, sunlit beauty is complete. Strolling along, they gradually seem to step outside the limits of their bodies, feel themselves both far and near, buoyant, floating at ease in the lap of the gods. Shay has felt the same exhilaration as a child playing in the waves that hem the Pacific on Stinson Beach, a wafting sense that the boundaries between light and water and flesh have dissolved; she almost expects to hear her mother and sister calling her, faint cries like seabirds over the wash of the surf. But here she is on the other side of the world, on the shores of the Indian Ocean, adrift in the present.

She and Felice laugh mindlessly, chase crabs, fill their hats with shells, dash into the water and swim just as they are, and walk on, letting the sun and wind dry their clothes.

When they come to a tumble of black-lava boulders that ends the long scallop of the beach, they pick their way up a short path to a low headland, and there indeed is a sacred tree: a giant tamarind, with the gnarled girth of a round table for ten, its vast trunk set about with a barrier of staked *keti-keti,* and its huge serpentine branches, dipping close to the ground, draped with frayed and discolored lengths of red cloth that flutter in the breeze. Beams of sunlight shine through the canopy. The sandy ground outside the fence is scattered with carefully placed rum and soda bottles, offerings for the *tsiny* and other earth spirits who frequent such places. But placed there also, the two friends see, are dozens of shoes: rubber flip-flops, mainly, of the type that the poorest villagers wear. Some are worn out and others almost new.

"Not pairs, but only the left one," Shay says wonderingly. "What might that mean, Ms. Expert on Regional Customs?"

"Some Sakalava superstition," says Felice disdainfully.

"Do you think we should leave a sandal?"

"Are you crazy? Absolutely not! We need them to get back to the car."

A breathless silence envelops the huge tree, except for the wind huffing off the sea and rippling the tattered strips of cloth. But suddenly they hear a woman call out, and, walking around the tree, they enter a clearing with three small, derelict-looking thatched huts standing on bare ground. The usual furnishings—plastic washtubs, a cast-iron brazier, a tall rice mortar, wandering ducks, a black-and-white cat, and a yellow dog—surround the huts. And beside the entrance of the largest is nailed up a large Three Horses beer sign. In the doorway flaps a handsome Richelieu curtain, the coarse unbleached cotton cut out and hand-stitched in an arabesquing design of fish and turtles. And, pushing the curtain aside, a Malagasy woman emerges, limping slightly.

She is neatly dressed in a print *lamba* and a long-sleeved T-shirt, and her thick wiry black hair is parted in the middle and worn in a large braided coil covering each ear, a style foreign to Naratrany. Despite her limp, she is not old: the right side of her deep brown face with its wide cheekbones is unwrinkled, bland as still water, but what grabs the attention and makes one forget all else is that her left eye is wholly blank and filmed with a bluish tissue thicker than cataract, almost like boiled egg white. In her dark face it stands out eerily, looking larger than its size, and hardly seeming to blink, though a gleam of moisture on the cheek below suggests it is constantly weeping. And this blind eye seems to have drawn life and power from the whole left side of her, especially her cheek and neck, which are dramatically disfigured with a webbing of keloid scars, seamed and discolored as old bark. Below this, her torso twists so that the shoulder is hunched and the left leg is lame.

Only much later do Shay and Felice wonder whether this is somehow connected to the single sandal offering at the sacred tree.

"Mula tsara, mesdames!" the woman says, as she approaches them, moving with surprising swiftness. Her voice is hoarse yet vibrant.

Trying neither to stare nor to look away, Shay and Felice present themselves. Then Shay asks pleasantly in Italian, "Are you Fatima? My husband is Gianmaria Senna, and I think he may know your husband—Franco."

"Sono Fatima," replies the woman, with a small, guarded nod.

Shay and Felice ask for drinks, and Fatima leads them to a tiny side yard and serves them warm bottles of Coke at an oilcloth-covered table, then disappears. Seated on a teetering wooden bench, the two friends let the sugary cola run down their parched throats and watch through the moving foliage of the big tamarind the incoming tide fracturing and refracturing its cobalt surface in the leveling sun. The view is luminous and beautiful, but as if a filter has been changed they feel the sudden withdrawal of the euphoria they experienced on the beach.

Something else has taken its place, a heavy feeling of foreboding, and it is connected with the damaged face and figure of Fatima, which not merely excites shocked pity, but seems to convey a cryptic and ominous message. There is, Shay feels, around Fatima and around this quite ordinary thatched hut, with its coarse white curtain flapping in the doorway, a breathless, unsettled atmosphere very different from the simple solemnity of the great sacred tree that stands so nearby. Into Shay's mind, irresistibly, comes the phrase, clear as a printed religious text: excluded from grace.

She glances at Felice and sees that her friend's eyes have taken on an expression of listening and—is Shay imagining it?—dread.

"Oh my God, her face . . ." murmurs Felice. "And that eye . . . I wonder if any doctor ever even looked at it. And her leg—it's amazing she can move around so freely."

"Do you think she and her husband are the guardians of the tree?" asks Shay, who has learned that such trees and their spirits often have acolytes.

Felice shakes her head. "No. I think they have tried to attach themselves. I'm not sure why they are here . . ."

Her words trail off, and she stands up abruptly. "We should go," she says. "We have to get back to the other side of the island. I'm worried about those roads after dark."

Both of them feel a skin-prickling eagerness to get away from that place. They pay Fatima, who in her impassive way also seems relieved to have them depart, and are just turning away toward the beach path when they hear a man's voice from the inside of the hut.

Fatima freezes. At the same time a mottled hand pushes the doorway curtain aside, and the owner of the voice appears.

He is a white man, the kind that Shay defines with the Malagasy word *vazaha,* although the word simply means foreigner, and she herself can also be defined that way. But in her mind the word denotes the kind of tropic-bespoiled white man who hangs out in the Fleur des Îles café and, in Shay's opinion, is far too often a guest at the Red House. Purplish skin eroded by decades of sun, rum, malaria; sparse gray hair yellowed by the relentless ultraviolet of the Tropic of Capricorn; fretful, bilious slits of eyes that in an instant can take on the bold glint of the colonial master who feels entitled to any dark woman in his purview. He wears the usual khaki cargo shorts, but also, open onto his shriveled chest, an exquisitely ironed cotton dress shirt that contrasts oddly with the poverty of the surroundings.

Franco. He comes gaunt-shanked over the threshold of the hut, ignoring his wife, and stops short while staring at the two visitors with almost comical surprise.

"Buon giorno! Bonjour!" he says in an unexpectedly soft tone, with a rather cultured accent. Adding musingly to himself, in a peculiar mixture of Italian, French, and Malagasy: *"Deux madama bé* . . . two memsahibs . . . honored guests to this tree . . . Fatima!" he raps out sharply to his wife, who, however, makes no sign of having heard. "Have you honored them? *Tu as servi? Hai servito?"*

He keeps his small glittering eyes fixed somewhere between Shay and Felice, who stand mesmerized like rabbits in front of a snake; then, suddenly returning to his earlier soft tone, he launches into a startling cascade of words, mainly in French, a harangue that picks up speed as it goes along. "Did she serve you as she should, *mesdames?* Did she honor your arrival, *la Madonna degli Schiavi?* Do you know who that is? The Black Madonna, the mother of all slaves. They call Fatima, daughter of the prophet, *la lumineuse!* But this Fatima is a wretch. Do you see her eye? Did you see her scars and leg, how she scuttles like a crab? Oh, yes, she is my real wife! I took her to the capital one time, and she would never go out, just clung to the heater. She was cold in the highland winter, and ashamed of being broken. Well, that's why I married her! No one in her village wanted her, and a piece of trash just suited me . . . Simple trash. Not like those whores in the port, shaking their asses with beer bottles on their wigs . . . Not like you proud *madames* . . ."

Shay has run into many a drunk on Naratrany island, but never a crazy man. Behind him, she glimpses the woman Fatima making a practiced subtle motion with her head and her good eye, indicating that Shay and Felice should quietly step backward and to the side and melt away on the path toward the beach.

But the remarkable thing about this Franco's unhinged rhetoric is its seductiveness: it has consistency and an underlying logic that tempts a listener to reply. And though Shay long ago learned to avoid engaging with the maddest denizens of the streets and subways of Oakland or New York or Milan, here she feels an irresistible temptation to say something, anything, to connect.

Ignoring Fatima's warning and the pressure of Felice's hand on her arm, she makes an effort and smiles at Franco, and as he draws a breath she offers a pleasant, conventional response, a simple, sociable remark on the beauty of the spot. *"Però, é talmente bello, questo posto! Si stà bene."*

And of course this is exactly the wrong thing to do. As if she has pushed a button, a quick shudder goes through him, his face seems to flatten, his mouth opens wide to reveal a wilderness of crooked dark teeth, and once again he looses a torrent of words in his strange mixture of languages, but in a voice that is quite different, and infinitely worse. Shay is not now or afterward able to define what is so abhorrent about the speech that now pours out of him. Compared to it, the discourse of spirits that she has overheard at *tromba* ceremonies is benign, of high courtesy, worlds apart.

Franco's voice maintains the same soft tone as earlier, but now somehow projects a concentrated malignity so intense that it seems impossible that a human throat could produce it. Soft as it is, it conveys a coarse, almost muscular strength and an eerie kind of autonomy, as if Franco is not so much speaking as having words crawl off his tongue like the toads from the mouth of the evil sister in the fairy tale.

This loathsome speech freezes Shay and Felice where they stand. And there in the clearing between the hut and the sacred tree, it recounts a terrible story.

"Bene?" Franco asks rhetorically, still staring fixedly at the empty space between the two friends, as if addressing an invisible third person. *"Pour nous il n'y a point du bien . . .* there is no good for us, not anywhere! Not for me and this creature." He suddenly whips his whole body around and glares at Fatima, who, still as a statue, looks expressionlessly back at him. Then he whips back to face his captive audience. "Of course," he goes on. "She is the one who disturbs the peace. With her rotten wounds . . . *la pourriture . . .*" He lingers on the word, as if he likes the taste of it, then rambles on. "You might ask how it came about. How did this woman . . . hardly a woman—this . . . thing—get broken? You try to name a name, and it always comes back to *quel maiale . . .* that pig of an Italian priest, with his French aphorisms, and his Campanian accent, and his kissing the asses of the foreign charities . . . and those whores of nuns . . . and the Vatican jackals who barter souls.

"But the worst was this priest . . . this pig who came to Madagascar to save the poor savages but who was soon playing his favorite game, the one that nearly got him slaughtered back in Torre del Greco. This filthy missionary who hung around the villages just to take young girls—children—and rape them in huts out in the bush where there are no roads. No roads, no hope . . . Until the village elders decided that they were going to fix him—catch him out and burn him alive . . ."

To Shay and Felice, the tortured listeners, the voice unfolds the tale as if it is happening here and now. How the village *fokuntany* and other elders choose a breastless young girl, whose task is to lure the priest to his fate inside a deserted granary, which they determine to set on fire. How the plan goes wrong when she is caught by a flaming branch of *satrana* palm that brushes like a fiery wing over the left side of her body. And how the priest manages to dash away unscathed—some say he takes off in the air, like a huge flying fox—while the girl writhes in agony.

"But he gets his reward," declares the voice, with venomous glee.

"Caught like a rat before he can get from Farafangana to Fort Dauphin. And killed in the way the villagers know best, because you can't take a *coupe-coupe* and cut off a priest's head. Not even the worst devil of a priest. So, with poison, the kind the old women make. And I can't say it's gentle! No . . . it takes a long time for him to die. But he's gone now, and no one knows where he lies. Seek, they say, and you will find, but in the desert of thorns, who can find anything? *La pourriture c'est la nature!* Worms have eaten the worms that ate him."

The last few lines are chanted in a low singsong, and then with a sniggering laugh the voice stops short. For an instant Franco shifts his gaze and looks straight at Shay, and she thinks she glimpses something deep in his eyes, an imprisoned flicker of awareness both sane and pitiful. Then all at once his face turns a tallow color; he staggers and begins to crumple forward at the waist like a rag doll.

Fatima, who has stood expressionlessly behind his shoulder for the whole horrible performance, reaches out in a way that is obviously practiced and catches him before he collapses; her strong right arm fastens around his middle like an iron bar.

"Allez! Allez!" she hisses fiercely to Shay and Felice. And to their surprise they find the spell is broken, and they can go. Like terrified children, they charge down the path past the big tamarind tree and, beneath the lowering afternoon sun, find themselves running as if for their lives down the milky beach, where the rising tide snatches at their feet.

They tear through the palm trees, across the hotel grounds, calling out a hasty farewell to the startled manager, then fling themselves into the truck. Here they sit streaming with sweat and breathing hard, as Shay shakily maneuvers out of the hotel gate and back through the tunnel of bamboo.

Only when the Mitsubishi is rattling down the dirt road toward the airport do they speak. "What the hell was that?" demands Shay breathlessly.

"I think that *was* hell!" says Felice, mopping her face with her gauzy scarf. "That was about the worst thing I ever heard in my life."

The two of them are buzzing with adrenaline, as if they've just been attacked.

"We should report it!" exclaims Shay, knowing that what she says is absurd. The rudimentary forces of law on the island have no interest in the ravings of a crazy foreigner up on the remote north coast. Or in the fate of one maimed woman from a distant tribe. And, how much of the tale Franco recounted actually occurred? As sometimes happens on Naratrany, Shay finds herself confronted with different modalities of truth, joined to each other yet separate, like the spiraled chambers of a nautilus.

As their agitation subsides, the two friends fall silent, exhausted but joined in the deep intimacy that comes with a shared shock. Pursuing the last of the daylight, they bump along through the dimming countryside, edging around returning zebu herds. At Madirovalo as the sudden shutter of tropical darkness descends, they give a lift to a quartet of fieldworkers, who jump off at a lamplit market stall farther up the road.

Only when they have passed the old electrical plant humming brutally to itself near the Saint Grimaud turnoff, and then the French cemetery, whose half-collapsed balustrade glimmers in the headlights like a row of broken teeth, does Felice speak up. "Franco himself is the priest from the story!" she says. "That's the only possible explanation."

"Impossible!" protests Shay. "You heard what happened. That foul priest is dead. And it wouldn't make sense. But none of it makes sense. Why would that poor woman tie herself to a monster like that?"

"She's not a 'poor woman,' " corrects Felice, and Shay, remembering the impassive strength of Fatima amid the coils of her husband's demonic voice, has to agree. Fatima is the one who bears the visible signs of suffering, yet somehow Shay knows with certainty—knew from the minute she saw Fatima—that the Antemoro woman, for all her scars, is no martyr.

"They're tied to each other," Felice adds softly. "But who has the real power?"

At dinner back at the Red House, the encounter with Franco and Fatima becomes the sole topic of the evening, in the way that happens when guests are desperately bored with each other's company. The table on the veranda is full of family and friends, French, Italian, and Malagasy, but conversation has lagged until Felice and Shay recount their tale. Senna, an affable host and energetic gossip who keeps abreast of most island scandal, has to admit that he knows almost nothing about the mysterious couple up on the north coast.

He calls in one of the Red House kitchen boys, who comes from a fishermen's village near Madirovalo. When questioned in Malagasy and French, the teenager, blinking with shyness before the assembled dinner guests, says with quiet reluctance that no one knows much about Franco and Fatima, except that some years ago they came from the Grande Île, and that the man is afflicted, and the ugly Antemoro woman is his wife. The boy adds that they take care of the sacred tree and try to run a *gargotte*—a snack bar—but no one wants to go near them.

"Well, was the man a priest?" demands an Italian guest. The kitchen boy shuffles his feet, and replies in a low voice that he doesn't know, but the *vazaha* is sick and he screams and says all sorts of things.

Another guest, a voluble Réunionnais who owns shrimp fisheries all around Madagascar, offers his opinion that it is indeed possible that Franco was once a missionary. He claims that missionaries are notorious for depravity, that he knows for a fact that some of them have whole harems back in the bush. He says no one stops them because there is no law out there.

"*A l'est di Suez non ci sono commandamenti,*" proclaims Senna, as usual misquoting his favorite line from the Kipling poem "Mandalay." And Shay, as usual on hearing it, recalls that it is also the opening phrase of Kipling's darkest story, "The Mark of the Beast."

"Maybe," ventures one of the visiting French doctors, a woman with imposing eyebrows and a long plait, who has been silent up to now. "Maybe the villagers did kill the priest. Just not all of him."

A hush falls. "What's that supposed to mean?" asks the shrimp magnate.

"I mean, maybe they used poison just to destroy his mind. Or even . . . his soul."

A storm of laughing protest arises from the company at the table. "*Oh*

là là—on va bientôt commencer avec les théories de vaudou, des zombies!"
"Funny stuff to hear from a doctor, of all people!"

After that, with something like a collective sigh of relief, the discussion grows more general and much livelier, expanding to touch on the larger ills of mankind—from corruption within the Catholic Church, to the evils visited by kleptocratic governments on rural peasantry, to issues of female empowerment in the developing world. And the tone of the discourse mixes righteous indignation with interjections of the cynical humor that Italians, French, and rich Malagasy deploy so skillfully.

From time to time Shay glances across at Felice and their eyes lock together. They alone, that day, have had the direct experience of hearing the sound of evil pour, twisting and contorting, out of a human mouth, and they know that the heart of the matter is far removed from any of this. Shay feels, too, that her friend is affected in a different way than she herself can know; this is after all Felice's country, and such a revelation must carry with it the sickening sense of intimacy that attends a crime in a family.

As it happens, neither of them finds out much more about Fatima and Franco. Felice and her doctors move on to Toamasina, and though Shay asks her usual fonts of Naratrany information—her stately housekeeper and confidante, Bertine la Grande; her gossipy next-door neighbor, Madame Rose; and Angélique, whose pharmacy, like the Fleur des Îles café, is a nexus for island rumors—not one of them can give her information about the strange couple up north. One night in Saint Grimaud, under the shooting stars of August, she runs into the scholarly Tsimihety priest Père Jobeny and asks him, but even that learned and cosmopolitan prelate is unable to give her any information on missions in the remote east of the Grande Île, near Farafangana.

So the facts remain elusive. Shay, though, is convinced that there is as much truth in Franco's vile narrative as in the material existence of Fatima's scarred flesh and blind eye. But maybe the tale does not recount Franco's own crimes. Or maybe (this is Senna's theory), he is a wandering Tom O'Bedlam, the type of white outcast who always turns up—drunk, drugged, diseased, mad—in the far corners of the world. He could have taken up with another outcast, a woman maimed by an accident, and appropriated her story.

Or perhaps, thinks Shay, he really is the vile missionary who died to the world, and yet somehow half-lives on: condemned, like the Ancient Mariner, to confess his sins to strangers. Bound to his victim, who is also his jailer. *"Madonna degli Schiavi,"* Franco calls Fatima. Does that in some perverse way make Franco the slave?

The truth that haunts Shay is in the sound of the voice that speaks with such coherence and hellish vitality. It conveys the reality of atrocious events involving one woman and one man, but also the universality of an old legend. She can imagine the tale rising like a demon out of the cold dust of the thorny desert to invade Franco's mind and throat, either for revenge or simply because a vessel was required. And that's the single thing she can be sure of, from the whole episode: that at a certain point, for good or ill, a story will tell itself.

A year or two later, news filters through the usual island channels that the strange couple has disappeared. One day during the dry windy season, a column of smoke is seen rising from that angle of the coast, far from any cane fields torched after harvest, and a day later, it is found that the cluster of huts beside the sacred tree has burnt to the ground. The huge tamarind itself is untouched. No bodies are found, but no one on Naratrany ever again sees any trace of Franco and Fatima.

A rumor briefly circulates that a fisherman carried a one-eyed woman in his pirogue to one of the outer islands, where it is possible to take a ferry to the Madagascar mainland. But no one confirms this.

More time passes, and Chinese government-backed investors build a paved two-lane road that joins the north and south of Naratrany. Meanwhile, the beautiful little French hotel acquires a high-speed launch to bring clients by sea from the airport, and actually begins to do business. The hotel owners take over the tract of land where Franco and Fatima had their huts. Appreciative of local tradition, they make provisions for the sacred tamarind, which, duly protected, becomes part of the folkloristic charm of their establishment, even mentioned in guidebooks. Hotel guests stroll down to commune with the huge tree. They sit and meditate in a small rustic pavilion the hotel has erected for respectful enjoyment of the tranquillity of the spot, which, after the fire, seems redoubled. And evidently the villagers of Naratrany, though unseen, also continue to visit, for the number of left-foot sandals at the base of the tree is always increasing.

Noble Rot

I'll let you into a secret . . . I am captain of this ship now, and I am bound to Madagascar, with a design of making my own fortune, and that of all the brave fellows joined with me.

—Daniel Defoe, *A General History of the Pyrates*,
Speech by the Pirate Avery

"It's not about a love affair," says Shay to her friend Orso. On a foggy November afternoon, they are sitting over coffee in a wooden booth at Bar Magenta, surrounded by the polyglot buzz of mothers and a few fathers waiting for their children to pull up in the bus from the International School. It is that borderland hour in the autumn day when the streetlights glow in the early dark and trolleys clatter along striking sparks through the drizzle, and everyone, from office workers to rich idlers, seems to have found an excuse to meet for melancholy discussions of romance. At the Magenta, as in dozens of bars across the darkening city, the full tapestry of sentimental experience is being unrolled in hopes of sympathy and advice: densely entangled configurations of husbands, wives, boyfriends, girlfriends, paramours, prostitutes; hopeless crushes; silly flings; chronicles of cruelty; erotic friendships; *grand amour*.

But Shay feels she has a category outside the usual rubric of love and lust, a relationship she impulsively decides to describe to Orso, whose children go to school with hers, and who is one of her close friends. Orso, who comes from a renowned Milanese intellectual clan, writes an arts column for *La Repubblica* and can display an insight into human nature as finely calibrated as the cut of his inherited Rubinacci suits. Yet when it comes to his own emotions he can be as blind and mawkish as any teenager, and this endears him to Shay. He tells her that he and she get along because they are both anomalies: she, the Black American scholar ensconced, with unexpected ease, in the sometimes vulgar life of the Italian nouveaux riches, and he, the queer aristocrat whose coming out was greeted by his staunchly Catholic family with almost embarrassing enthusiasm.

"It's *always* about a love affair," Orso says, with a theatrical sigh. He adjusts his tortoiseshell glasses on his prominent nose and runs a hand over his glossy bald scalp. "It's a man, right?"

"Well, yes."

"Anybody I know?" Orso went to Brown, and speaks impeccable English.

"No, but I've mentioned him. He is, or was, the skipper of our boat down in Madagascar."

"Ah, your plantation fantasy world!" exclaims Orso, pronouncing each word with disapproving emphasis. The daughters he and his partner adopted are Eritrean, so he is touchy about anything having to do with Africa, particularly since a Fascist branch of his family made a fortune from the cotton trade in Asmara. He continues: "And a spoiled signora having a fling with the skipper is no different from a husband fucking the nanny. Just plain common. I'm surprised at you, Shay!"

"Now don't get nasty before you have the facts. Then you can give me your merciless opinion."

"It will be savage." Orso draws up his spare tweed-clad figure and fixes Shay with a steely gaze.

"I didn't mean you should channel the Grand Inquisitor."

"It's in my nature—the family tree has three of the most bloodthirsty popes. But go on, tell—we have exactly twenty-five minutes until the bus gets here, and then I have to rush the girls to Nonna's house for tea."

Shay drains the dregs of her coffee, dispatches the square of dark chocolate that came with it, then tilts her head and stares off into a murky ceiling corner of Bar Magenta, as if she can see through it to somewhere completely different. "Well," she says. "The story, if you can call it that, begins a few years after we built the Red House, when Senna and his brothers-in-law got together and bought a catamaran called the *Blue Prince*. It's odd to have a boat with a masculine name, but that's how it arrived."

"I'm sure you know that Blue Prince—*principe azzurro*—means Prince Charming in Italian," puts in Orso.

"Yes, but this was in English, and I'm pretty sure there was no wit intended. Anyway, the boat was registered in South Africa, and it came complete with a skipper, whose name was Marius—nickname, Maz. Maz's job was to run the boat for us, our family and friends when we were there on vacation, and in the off-season to take on charters with our bed-and-breakfast guests, and anyone else who wanted to fish around the Mozambique Channel. So for years he worked for us and lived on Naratrany—still lives there, if he's alive.

"I met him when he first got to the island. It was around the end of the nineties; the kids weren't much more than toddlers. It was some time after midnight at New Year's, when everybody on Naratrany seemed to be crowded into the billiard hall in Finoana village. It was raining outside, and hot as hell. You have to imagine a bamboo hut smaller than Bar Magenta: noisy, airless, crammed with young Malagasy prostitutes in their best holiday weaves and their four-inch platforms. There was the usual scrum of European degenerates—their faces all different shades of purple—and a few foreign women like me, everybody there for *l'ambiance*. Crazy *salegy* and afrobeats music, but the quarters were too close for dancing. Senna was off in the crowd around the billiard tables, drinking Dzama rum and watching the local champion Sebastiano playing against a big Belgian tourist. I was feeling suffocated, squeezed up against the bar with some boring Malagasy friends, a Three Horses beer in my hand, sweating in a dress nearly as short as those of the hookers. Mine was white cotton, though."

"I'm sure you looked enchantingly pure and virginal."

Shay ignores this. "So I was thinking that New Year's Eve on Naratrany was fairly grim. I was annoyed at Senna's drinking, and just dying to get back to the house, where I could breathe and hear the waves, and peep in on Augustina and Roby and the babysitter. I could picture them all curled up asleep like angels inside their mosquito nets.

"Just then I saw this French woman, Valentine, make her entrance. She always came in like that—first posing in the doorway like a tough broad in some thirties film. In those days she wore her hair cropped very short and slicked back, and it looked terrific because she had the most feline face I have ever seen, always lit up with a cocky smile that told you she was convinced she outshone any female in the room. She held one of her bony arms out to the side, showcasing the fact that she was dressed up like no one else on the island ever does—not even at New Year's, and especially not on a wet night when the roads are soupy red mud. That night it was a silk bias-cut cocktail dress and a pair of designer heels. I couldn't stand Valentine, but I had to admire her panache: she was much more of a glamourpuss than Marisa, or Giusy, or any of the other femmes fatales on the island. She'd been there for a couple of years, and she had opened a kind of eccentric handicraft gallery in Saint Grimaud, a place where nobody seemed to buy anything. Not that she cared—she kept busy seducing and then dumping most of the European men and some of the women. She generally preferred white lovers.

"Speaking of which, trailing behind her was a new conquest, one of the best-looking men I'd ever seen in my life. Maz. Tall with muscle in the right places, surfer hair streaming past his shoulders, a long sun-darkened face with eyes that were a faded color like smoke, but that seemed to catch on to things quicker than other people's eyes. He eased through the chaos with the kind of hyperalert look that Special Forces types have, at least in movies. Through all the noise I heard the two of them talking in English together, Valentine with her French rich-girl accent—her family owned vineyards, or something—he with an intonation I couldn't recognize. Then she cut him loose for a while, like someone letting a puppy roam. And he came over to the bar for a beer, and after a bit we struck up a conversation; or rather I did, since he wasn't overly chatty.

"Still, I learned a few things. That he was a skipper en route to the Comoros. That he was an Afrikaner, born in what began as Southern Rhodesia, then morphed into Ian Smith's rogue state, then turned into Zimbabwe. And that he had so many Boer ancestors under the soil there that he said 'I'm African' with calm assurance—the first white person I'd ever met who could pull it off.

"Right away I understood that he was one of those very quiet men who, if pressed, can be very dangerous. That he was also the kind of man who picks one woman, and puts himself totally in her power. This was clear from the way his eyes followed Valentine as she slid through the crowd in that slinky dress, swigging rum and dealing out New Year's greetings with her usual theatrical hugs.

"Soon enough, she came back to collect him, and they left the billiard hall, headed for Chanson and the other clubs. And I thought: Heigh-ho, another Naratrany love affair. I wonder how long it will be before he sails away or she kicks him out?

"A few days later, though, Maz went from being an object of idle curiosity to being part of our lives. That was after we decided to buy the catamaran—which, like so many yachts roaming the Mozambique Channel at the time, was for sale, cheap. The *Prince* is a lovely boat: a Mayotte forty-seven, with four cabins and a nice generous layout that makes it ideal for a family to share. And Maz was happy for us to take over his contract. He wanted to stay on Naratrany, because it turned out that he and Valentine were getting married.

"The very next August there was a wedding, the kind of wedding that I'm sure the island never saw before. It was a huge shindig that started out with handwritten banns in Afrikaans nailed up in front of the mairie in Saint Grimaud; then it went on to a ceremony in the tiny Catholic church in Finoana village, with half of the islanders crowding the beach to see Valentine run out into a blizzard of ylang-ylang blossoms. With her usual flamboyant taste, she was wearing an extraordinary gown with a billowing crinolined skirt made out of tiers of finely woven raffia.

"The party had two famous *salegy* bands and filled up the whole garden and beach of the Hotel Chambord with a wild crowd of Malagasy, South Africans, French, and Italians, and after a while, gate-crashers from every village on Naratrany. Everybody who wasn't passed out was still dancing at sunrise, when Maz—he had his long hair in a pirate braid—and Valentine—who had shed her raffia cocoon for a white bikini—roared off in a tender full of balloons. They were taking a friend's boat to go on honeymoon along the coast of Mozambique.

"We were there, of course, Senna and I, sluicing down rum punch and dancing like crazy. Having a great time. Although that party was the first time I overheard gossip about Senna and another woman, some Calabrian bitch who'd been hanging around the Red House—"

"*Il solito stronzo . . .*" murmurs Orso, who considers Senna a vulgarian.

"Of course gossip on Naratrany is like air, it's everywhere and you ignore it, but that rumor touched a nerve. After the party, I was in a bad mood, and it seemed to me then, that all through the ceremony and reception there'd been something wrong. That couple just bothered me: surely a bride shouldn't look so triumphant, and should a groom look so blank? Or maybe I was jealous."

"*Per carità*, it's clear you had a crush on the guy from the start."

"Not really. Like everybody, I thought he was ridiculously good-looking, but somehow he wasn't my type. The thing is, I've always been drawn to men like Senna: a mixture of charismatic, bossy, passionate. The kind of man who makes a whole soap opera about his likes and dislikes. Very Italian. No matter what you think, Orso, you have to admit he keeps life interesting.

"But from the minute I saw Maz at the billiard hall, I felt somehow that I knew him, as if we'd met before. At the same time, he was a complete mystery. He'd been born into what was really the epicenter of white supremacy, the country that—to me and for anybody who grew up in Oakland in the seventies—was rumored to be the land of all evil. In all my travels, I'd never before met a former Rhodesian. And for me at first it seemed like meeting some kind of legendary monster. And you know me, I'm always—"

"Attracted to monsters?" Orso asks in an innocent tone.

"Don't be silly—'curious' is what I was going to say. Anyhow, after his marriage, I saw a lot of him. Every vacation, for eight or nine years, we spent time on board the catamaran—Senna, the kids, and I, along with other family and friends. We sailed to the islands north of Naratrany, and along the west coast of the Grande Île sometimes as far down as Morombe. Maz seemed to know every inch of the Mozambique Channel, every Sakalava village, every tree and rock formation on the coast. He was a great skipper: even-tempered, reserved, incredibly precise, with a kind of gravitas about him that completely eclipsed the fact that Senna's relatives treated him like a servant.

"He spoke a surprising number of languages: Fanagalo with the cook he'd brought with him from Durban, Malagasy with the Sakalava crew, French with Senna and the other Italians. The kids and I always talked with him in English, which I found refreshing, with all those Europeans around. Sometimes when the *Prince* was moored in some bay in the middle of nowhere, and everyone else was off fishing or sunbathing onshore, I stayed on board, reading and occasionally chatting with Maz.

"I'd sit cross-legged with my book in the shade of the awning on the aft deck, while he sat at the helm with his big sun-blackened feet propped up on the wheel. I remember him as always smoking and staring out at the blue-on-blue horizon. There's nothing quieter than a boat just emptied of a group of noisy passengers: the silence is like a church after service. Small sounds just added to it: the wash of seawater as the catamaran revolved on its anchor, the domestic clatter of the cook preparing lunch, the music system—which was usually blaring French and Italian pop music—almost inaudibly playing the skipper's choices: Willie Nelson, Otis Waygood, Dollar Brand. And in this hush it was always Maz who started talking. He'd address me in an abrupt way as if he were continuing a conversation we'd been having for hours already. Whatever he said was punctuated with long silences, and sometimes he'd let off a laugh that had a creaky sound, as if he didn't use it much. Hearing that laugh, I was unable to imagine how he communicated with a woman like Valentine. I myself asked careful questions, and in bits and pieces I started to learn about his life.

"It turned out that he was born lucky, in the country I imagined as being hellish. His family was rich, a dynasty of cattle ranchers and mine owners, and if you look at the records of the Cape Colony, you'll see his surname over and over again. They fought their way northeast from the Cape and, like many of the Voortrekkers, plundered land from the Ndebele. And after that, for generations, they lived like colonial barons in a ranch style that is gone now, like our Old South. You could ride a horse for three days from the gardens of his family's compound near Zezani and never yet reach boundaries marked out by his grandfather. All this he told me without boasting, in fact without showing any emotion at all.

"In this same flat way, he sketched out for me a childhood that was the most exotic thing I had ever heard of: tracking impala and wildebeest; casual encounters with hippos, rhinos, leopards. I remember that his voice warmed up when he told Roby and Augustina stories of raising a litter of orphaned cheetah kittens—describing how heavy a baby cheetah is when it sleeps on your bed, how full of fleas and ticks. He loved animals, and sometimes spoke of rescuing abandoned horses, dogs, and cats, whose owners had fled the country. Of course, he never gave details about why they'd fled, or about the bloody conflict that branched through his whole early life.

"The fact was that he grew up with war as if it were weather. His country went through ferocious convulsions: Matabeleland, then Rhodesia, Rhodesia-Zimbabwe, then just Zimbabwe. The second Bush War was in the background when he went to boarding school in South Africa and learned to sail. He left school and served in combat on the Mozambique border. His brother was killed in Angola, his father was shot on patrol, and as Zimbabwean independence approached, he and his mother left everything they owned and joined the flood of white emigrants to South Africa. They lived in Port Elizabeth until she died of heart disease.

"Maz had nothing left, so he went to sea. He studied for his certification and had no trouble finding work. One of his employers, the rich Venezuelan who sold us the *Blue Prince,* wanted him to come to Caracas and manage a private flotilla. Maz had been mulling over this offer as he sailed the catamaran from Durban toward Anjouan, the passage when he made the fatal stop at Naratrany and fell for Valentine. That was what he called it, with one of his rare lapses into drama: the fatal stop. Though he may have meant fateful. Anyway, I touched off his creaky laugh by quoting him one of my favorite lines from *King Solomon's Mines*: 'Two things I have learned: you can't keep a Zulu from battle, or a sailor from falling in love.' "

Orso looks at Shay incredulously. "I can't believe you, of all people, read that racist stuff."

"Orso, when I was a kid I was crazy about Rider Haggard and Kipling, and all of those period adventure books! They're incredible stories, and my own kids love them too. You learn to spit out the racist parts—like fish bones."

"Non sono d'accordo."

"Well, you and your daughters are missing something. But to go on: as I said, Senna's family—mainly my sisters-in-law, who are jumped-up provincial housewives—didn't show Maz much respect. The worst thing they did was to talk about him at the top of their lungs in Italian, which they thought he didn't understand. I had figured out that he did, but for some reason had chosen to keep it to himself. He'd sit at the helm, his long face blank as a mask, as, in front of him, these women in their gold jewelry and flashy vacation clothes traded witticisms about his looks, or speculated about what he was like in bed. One day at dinner, one of them made such an obnoxious comment that I had to say something. 'You know,' I said, 'Maz speaks excellent Italian.' The group around the table froze, and Maz shot me a single sharp glance, the way a wild animal might acknowledge another of its species. We never mentioned it again, but from then on there was another link between us.

"Not that we spoke often, or ever flirted, though Naratrany is a place where people flirt like they breathe. Our conversations didn't attract attention in the shipboard collection of friends and family, not enough to send up a flare in the mind of Senna, who, like most womanizing men, is extremely jealous. Maz actually seemed matier with Senna than with me: they swigged beer and practically went into conclave about spearfishing expeditions, pored over catalogues of the most arcane nautical gear. Still, every time I was on board, I felt as if Maz and I were carrying on a dialogue, even when we weren't saying anything."

"Oh, come on," says Orso. "You can't tell me that you weren't attracted to him!"

"I could never forget he was handsome, that's for sure. And I wanted him to admire me too, so I made sure I looked good as I clambered around the boat, braided my hair, put on earrings and a crisp white shirt for dinner. That's just normal woman's vanity. But all of that seemed beside the point, compared to our strange intimacy.

"I didn't tell him much about myself. Right at the beginning I informed him that I was from a family of Black American teachers and do-gooders who considered his people, his whole extinct nation, to have been one of the great evils of human history. That my parents had supported Congressman Dellums in antiapartheid activism, and picketed various colleges and corporations about divesting South African holdings. And, on a different note, I told him that I knew my way around a boat because my sister and I spent summers at sailing camp, first on Lake Merritt, then Oakland Bay."

"Did you ever confront him? Discuss anything meaningful?"

"If you mean did I ask for his thoughts on postcolonialism or the hegemonic cycle—no, Orso, I didn't. It's not exactly what you talk about when you're sitting around in a bathing suit. And I had a sense that, if we started in on Nelson Mandela or Mugabe, or who fought on what side, it would be too much. Too much for Maz to tell, or for me to stand hearing. So I guess we censored ourselves, though it never felt like it. After he'd sketched out his life story, we tended to chat about small things: animals, nature, places we'd traveled. He knew I taught at the Cattolica, but he had no interest in literature, or art, or anything that involved me in the world away from Madagascar. Once or twice, as if he were confessing a secret vice, he got onto the subject of land: the glorious expanse of it on the old continent. He found a lot more words than usual as he talked about topsoil and overgrazing, and why goats mean destruction. You could tell he was obsessed with those lost acres of veld and pasture, and it was a little sad to hear him go on about them in the middle of the sea.

"Looking back now, I do regret not asking even one of the obvious questions. What it was like to grow up under apartheid, as one of the ruling caste. What he thought of his ancestors, about their greed, about the blood they spilled and the country they stole. What he thought about Black Africans, about Black people. About me, for instance."

"Well, you were almost certainly the first *donna di colore* he ever had as a boss," Orso interjects helpfully. "It must have been unsettling for him to see you with the money and the power. Having to ferry you around."

Shay giggles. "Like *Driving Miss Daisy* in reverse."

"Come to think of it, you two had a lot in common," continues Orso. "Both of you being, in a way, exiles. Both adrift in Madagascar for no real reason . . ."

Shay ignores this. "Anyway, on Naratrany it was known that Maz and Valentine were deep in love, and, in their peculiar fashion, they stayed that way. While he was at sea, she kept up that crazy gallery of hers, and hung out with her friends. And when Maz came back from a cruise, they partied South African style. It's called jolling, and it is hard-core. But after a few years—starting one rainy season, when the catamaran berthed in the yacht basin—the two of them began to get heavily into drugs. Not just the local *rongony,* but opium from Laos and meth from the Philippines.

"From then on their life fell apart fast, the way white lives can in the tropics. People would find them crawling around on the floor, drunk on Dzama rum, high on whatever chemicals they'd ingested. Outlaw types camped out at their bungalow on Finoana Beach: drug dealers, burnt-out mercenaries, gunrunners working between South Africa and Eastern Europe, all the seagoing riffraff of the Indian Ocean. Village hookers entertained clients up against the big mango tree in their yard.

"Their fights were epic. Once, Valentine—the drugs had turned her into a skeleton, but somehow she was still alluring—stabbed Maz with a butcher knife over some imaginary sin. She was fanatically jealous of him, though she kept up her affairs on the island, and flew back to France when it suited her to meet up with old lovers. Mercifully they had no children; they'd adopted a pair of Ridgeback puppies whom they treated better than they did each other.

"Maz just got quieter, if possible. The chemicals stripped the color from his hair and turned his teeth into what looked like a bombed-out city. We had no reason to fire him as skipper, because he had an uncanny ability to divide his whole existence in two halves. During the cruising season, and for anything related to the *Blue Prince*, he was somehow cold sober and precise as always. I just watched the decay of his good looks and occasionally allowed myself to feel a bit of maternal sympathy for him—which I could sense him silently rebuff.

"Still, our strange intimacy continued. Sometimes we hardly exchanged a word. When we'd moored in one of the deserted bays along the coast, and the others had gone off in the dinghy to fish or sun themselves, I'd read for a while and then say goodbye to Maz and jump overboard. I'd explore on my own with snorkel and fins, following his directions on how to avoid riptides and sharp corals. I'd pull myself out of the waves on some wild beach full of crabs or nesting turtles. I had no worries because I knew that Maz, invisible on the distant catamaran, had his binoculars and was keeping a protective eye out. For some reason the two of us almost always avoided looking directly at each other on the boat, but over distance I felt he was watching.

"When he came by the Red House to discuss boat business with Senna, he'd stop to say hello to me, and show off the good manners of his dogs, who'd each offer a paw. Once when Maz caught sight of me far away down Finoana Beach, he ran after me at top speed, the dogs galloping with him, as if he had an urgent message to deliver. But when he caught up, he just walked beside me in complete silence. And sometimes when I stood bargaining for fruit at the noisy, stinking outdoor market of Saint Grimaud, I'd turn around to find Maz standing at my shoulder. Always without anything particular to say.

" 'Maz has a crush on Mom,' said Roby once, when he was six or seven.

" 'He does not,' said Augustina, who was two years older, but already was perceptive as a grown woman. 'He just likes not talking with her!'

"The kids idolized Maz, though he was strict about shipboard behavior, the stowing of gear and the tying of knots. He was also respected by the villagers of Naratrany in a way unusual for a *vazaha*. He spoke their language, and let their women alone. And he respected their taboos with the naturalness of someone who'd grown up surrounded by ancient cultures. Even my Sakalava friend and housekeeper, Bertine la Grande, who measured all humanity by her own mysterious scale of values, said that Maz was *'bien.'* A good person.

"So the years passed. In spite of the drugs and the drama, he and Valentine somehow made progress in building a future. When Valentine inherited some money, they bought half of a little island to the southwest of Naratrany. They cleared brush and laid foundations for a house, and Maz reckoned that in a few years he could quit skippering and they'd live there full-time. There was a derelict cocoa plantation on the terrain that he planned to revive. The life of a farmer, he told me with one of his rare flashes of wit, would suit him down to the ground.

"In this optimistic period, he was a little more sociable, and he and I sometimes planned ambitious cruises. We pored over the pages of his battered nautical guide, *East Africa Pilot*. The idea was simple: Senna and I and the kids and friends would fly into Mombasa, where Maz would meet us with the *Prince,* and we'd sail down the East African coast. We'd pass Zanzibar and Mafia, then through the Bazarutos to the Comoros, and finally to Naratrany. Or we'd set out south from Naratrany down the west coast of the Grand Île, past a bay that holds a rusted hull that is said to be the remains of a Russian battleship. We would head down to Morombe, where you can take a rickshaw over salt flats to a peninsula where Vezo fishermen live and worship—so people say—a sea goddess. Or we could go north from Naratrany to the Îles Glorieuses, where you can bribe your way past the French military guards and see huge flocks of terns and boobies milling on the sand.

"Senna always opposed these adventurous plans. He liked fishing, not exploration. Only once did we take a cruise that Maz had sketched out with me. With a few friends, we sailed south from Naratrany to one of the most remote of the Radames archipelago, a small pink sand island called Antanimora. Here Senna and the other fishermen took the Zodiac off to a point known for dogtooth tuna. And I, following Maz's directions, jumped off the catamaran and swam the long way from our mooring to the empty shore.

"Then, as he'd told me to do, I started to walk clockwise around the little island. It was eerily quiet and sun-soaked, without so much as a palm tree, just boulders and masses of sea grape. I made my way along the rocky shoreline until I reached a cave in a low cliff. The opening was almost invisible, and guarded by part of a whale skeleton that looked fossilized by time and weather. Maz had warned me not to set foot inside, because it was a tomb of some unknown seagoing people. Their bones and the remains of their pirogues were still inside.

"So I stayed at the entrance in the hot sunlight, leaning on a whale rib that was almost as tall as I was. And I peered in, until I thought I could see vague shapes in the gloom. At the same time I felt something on my face—a slight, cool breath that seemed to come from deep in the earth. When the tide started rising, I stepped away and made my way back to the flat rosy beach, picking up a few shells and bits of coral that I stowed in my bathing suit. On the sand I had the strange sensation that I was the only woman in the world; that I was strolling right on the rim of the horizon, as if it were a tightrope.

"The excursion took a long time, and when I swam back and climbed dripping up the ladder, Maz said, in his flat way: 'I thought I'd have to go get you.'

"I knew he'd been waiting for me, and I felt pleased.

"Senna and his friends called the trip to the Radames a failure, because of murky water in the fishing grounds: nobody could see an inch beyond his mask. But to me it was magical. On the way back north, we stopped on the coast at a bay where a pair of fish eagles nested on the headland. Down below was an estuary lined with dwarf baobabs that looked like figures in a Chinese print. At sunset, Senna and Maz went off in a pirogue with two Sakalava fishermen, and returned with a bucket of mangrove crabs for dinner. They also brought back a spindly sapling with muddy roots that Maz had pulled up for me: it was a young baobab to plant in the Red House garden.

"That was one good time. But after that came a very bad time for Maz: the low point of his marriage, though he never thought of leaving Valentine. He loved her bitterly and without any shame, in spite of her betrayals and their disputes, which got worse and worse. One night Valentine was nearly arrested for an attack with a broken bottle on a pretty Spanish tourist, whom she accused of flirting with Maz. At the same time, there were rumors that she was pushing him to divorce her, because she was obsessed with the idea that he'd somehow steal the property she stood to inherit back home in France.

"All of this craziness of course attracted other bad things. Maz got a serious infection: a big tropical ulcer on his shin, that worked through to the bone. Valentine broke her arm, and ended up with one shoulder in a permanent shrug. The worst thing was that a local gangster, a Goanese, moved in on the little island where they'd invested their savings. When they refused to sell out, he set fire to their construction site and afterward stationed guards armed with Kalashnikovs on their terrain. There was no recourse; all over Madagascar, the rush was on for resort land, and the Goanese had political connections. Word was out, too, that he'd enlisted a famous witch doctor from the Grande Île to work against Valentine and Maz."

"As you do," says Orso dryly. "Just normal island business, I suppose."

"Well, it's an element of life in that part of the world. And I myself have seen some inexplicable things there. Maz was born into it. Though he was white, he'd grown up with tales of *tokoloshe* and other spirits—and, from things he'd let drop, I knew that he believed implicitly in those powers. In any case, his problems just multiplied.

"That January, when he tried to come ashore on his island, he got into a gunfire exchange with the guards. A few weeks later, a terrible thing happened: a young child of the Goanese was discovered drowned. Though there was no proof linking him to this tragedy, Maz was arrested and spent a night in the hellish Naratrany jail. The infection on his leg got worse. It spread through his system and emerged in other places, especially a grotesque tumor running along one side of his jaw; his body seemed to have lost the ability to heal itself. It was around that time that the villagers started to refer to him, in a matter-of-fact way, as someone who was cursed. The Malagasy give great importance to fate, which they call *vintana;* now they watched impassively as Maz's life took on the shape of a myth about hostile fortune.

"This was never the judgment accorded to Valentine; her misbehavior didn't seem to disturb any higher powers. No, it was Maz, her possession, who carried all the weight of bad luck. Senna—he had started to refer to Maz as Man of Sorrows—still paid his salary, and we even posted his bail. But it was clear that his days as skipper for the *Blue Prince* were numbered. We started looking around for a Malagasy captain.

"At about the same time, Senna and I found ourselves going through a bad patch. You know everything about that, Orso, and even the name of the other woman. All spring the two of us were hardly speaking, and in July I found myself completely on my own in Madagascar. That is to say: without Senna, who was off somewhere, supposedly on a business trip. Without the kids, who were in the mountains with their Vercelli cousins. And without companions, because my friend from Boston, who had planned to go trekking in the Ankarana with me, had dislocated her knee. Events had conspired that way. My Malagasy friends like Felice and Angélique, or Bertine, or my neighbor, Madame Rose, were all away, too.

"There were no bed-and-breakfast guests at the Red House, so I was stuck among the few alternate staff, who, of course, somehow knew all about the trouble between Senna and me. Everyone on the island, it seemed, was aware of Senna's philandering ways, which were really no different from the ways of any other European husband there. Still, since it was my turn, it made me an object of amused scrutiny. Villagers and foreigners alike seemed to think I was a fool for not taking lovers of my own.

I wanted desperately to get away from that fishbowl, but the flights back to Europe were all booked for the high summer season. It's always hard to leave Naratrany at short notice.

"I took one chance. The catamaran was undergoing minor repairs, but there was no reason why she couldn't go out. From my bedroom, I could see her, white and shapely, at anchor in Finoana Bay. One day when Maz brought the dinghy over to the Red House beach to pick up some tools from the storehouse, I took him aside. We stood in a corner of the veranda, beside a daybed draped in mosquito netting. From there the view was a long stretch of garden with banana trees and bougainvillea and, still rooting in a big terra-cotta pot, the spindly baobab that he'd brought me a year before.

"I could barely stand to look at Maz. He'd tried to make himself presentable: he had covered the ulcers on his jaw and legs with squares of gauze and surgical tape, had his gray hair neatly bound back in a ponytail, and his patchy beard trimmed evenly, and he wore his usual clean khaki shorts and T-shirt. But still he looked terrible: he was gaunt, his skin was furrowed like pine bark, and his eyelids were weighed down by tallow-colored sun keratoses. He was only in his forties—my age—yet he seemed centuries old. The sight of him reminded me of a line from 'The Hollow Men': 'the broken jaw of our lost kingdoms.'

"Looking and not looking, I said: 'Maz, I need to get out of here, and I want to go somewhere in the *Prince*.'

"Demanding something of him straight out like that felt strange, and yet familiar, as if I were picking up the thread of an argument we'd had a thousand times before. And somehow I knew what his response would be. I wasn't surprised when he looked down at his feet, slowly shook his head, then said in an infinitely gentle voice: 'Can't do it. She has a broken fuel pump.'

"'I know that's not true,' I said, quite patiently. 'Senna said she was seaworthy.' (Actually, Senna had said no such thing, but I knew the *Prince* was fine and that Maz for some reason was lying to me.) 'It doesn't have to be complicated,' I continued, wondering why I had to beg. After all, wasn't I the one entitled to give orders? 'We can go to Mahajanga—that's a straight passage.'

"Maz shook his head again.

" 'Look,' I said, bluntly. 'Things are not good for me here. You see that my friends didn't show up, and that I'm marooned. I've just got to get away. I know it might stir up gossip for us to be aboard with no other passengers, so bring anyone you want, Maz. Bring friends. Bring Valentine.'

" 'It's not possible,' he replied, still in that infuriating gentle voice.

"I lost my temper, and hissed: 'I've never before asked you for help. Not for anything!'

"He was silent for a minute, and then finally raised his faded eyes to meet mine. It was probably the first time we had ever looked straight at each other, and it was strangely anticlimactic. It occurred to me that, like everybody else on the island, he knew all about my problems with Senna— and that they probably seemed like nothing compared to what he'd been through.

"In a voice that dropped so low I could barely hear it, he said: 'If things were different.' Just that, as if it were a full statement.

"And suddenly life seemed hopeless, and I felt that in a minute I'd either burst out crying or slap his face. So I turned and walked away. When I looked behind me a few seconds later, he, in that stealthy Special Forces way of his, had vanished off the veranda without a sound. A couple of minutes later I heard a motor and saw him taking off in the tender for the catamaran moored out in the bay. Fuck you, I thought.

"That evening, the Sakalava kid who crewed for Maz came to me with a package wrapped up neatly in a plastic bag. 'Un cadeau pour Madame Shay—c'est le capitaine qui l'envoie!' he announced in a ceremonious tone, as if he were presenting a gift from a king.

"I opened the bag and found a book: his trusty East Africa Pilot, the same navigation guide we'd pored over some years back, to plan those fantasy cruises. It was an indispensable book, impossible to obtain in Madagascar, one of the few things of his own that was aboard the catamaran. I didn't know what he'd do without it. But I kept it, and that evening I sat up late in my room leafing through the maps, while a sense of comfort stole over me.

"I didn't see Maz again until a week later. Senna had suddenly arrived on Naratrany, begging forgiveness, overflowing as always with declarations of love and extravagant promises of a fresh start; and so, warily, we made peace. It was a heady time, but I was still annoyed to notice that Maz had immediately turned back into the perfect skipper, with the boat ready for anything Senna wanted. It was as if I'd never made my desperate plea.

"After Senna's arrival, Maz came by one night to go over accounts, and with him came Valentine. She was drunk or high. She staggered along with her crooked shoulder cocked under one ear, hair wild, eyes glittering, skin drawn like parchment over her cheekbones. She'd draped her emaciated body in a linen dress that looked like a crumpled couture piece, and standing there on the lamplit veranda, she seemed to me like a figure from a nightmare.

"When I offered them a drink, she burst out in a crazy laugh, grabbed at Maz with her bony hands, and exclaimed, 'I'm just here to guard my beloved husband! He needs protecting, isn't that right, *cheri*?'

"Maz just stood there, expressionless, like somebody looking out of hell."

"But what made him stay with that appalling woman, and waltz around like that in a folie à deux?" demands Orso, drumming his manicured fingers impatiently on the table. Then he adds: "Well, it's clear why. We've all been known to hang on to terrible people and situations. Sometimes you let go, and sometimes you can't." He laughs rather bitterly.

"Maybe it's just fate," says Shay. "It sounds strange but from the first time I met Maz, I felt in my bones that he was paying for something. Maybe for something he did as a soldier. Maybe not even for his own crime, but for the crimes of his family. Or his people. Here is a man who starts out with wealth, power, beauty, and ends up losing everything. Life was just loss for Maz. And Valentine was . . . a conduit."

"I'd call it suicide by marriage," says Orso. "It's more common than you think!"

"Well, actually you can't even call it that, because they really did divorce, the way Valentine wanted. But they never stopped living together. And soon the two of them had a new, insane project: to build a house on a piece of pastureland they'd bought in a village on the top of the highest hill on Naratrany. Word had it that Maz was doing all the construction himself. He'd just returned from having his infection treated in the hospital on Réunion, but it was common knowledge that even the strongest antibiotics had failed. It was too late. Dr. Pau, the Malagasy doctor who is Senna's fishing buddy, said it was amazing that Maz was still on his feet. Yet last year, all through the rainy season, people would come upon him looking like a ghost. Covered in bandages, trudging beside a wooden zebu cart hauling bricks up the steep muddy road.

"By then he'd already quit working as our skipper. Not amicably, either; with a lot of ugly argument, though I can't believe that it was Maz who stirred it up. We were suddenly hit with accusations of crooked dealing, of fudging his contract to cheat him out of a ridiculously large amount of money. The whole thing dragged us into the *tribunal de premier appel*—and lawsuits in Madagascar make the Gordian knot look like a straight piece of rope.

"In the end, Maz remained on bad terms with the Red House. It's a situation like so many others on that fractious little island. This summer I was driving the truck by the port, and I caught sight of him standing at the lumberyard where the big pirogues and the *boutres* haul in logs from the mainland. He was bent like an old man, and in the midday sun his face looked like a skull. We pretended not to see each other, but, as always, I had that distinct feeling of communication.

"Every time I get news from Naratrany, I expect to hear that he is dead. The gossips predict it will be soon. The house construction has stopped. They say he can hardly walk now. The only thing connected with him that seems to be healthy is the little baobab he gave me years ago in the southwest. When it was finally rooted, I had it set properly in earth in the middle of the Red House garden. It still isn't tall, but it has leaves now, and it is taking on that peculiar shape that baobabs have—they always remind me of soldiers at attention. They grow slowly, but I've heard that in twenty years or so it will look just like the trees down on the coast near the Radames."

As Shay has been talking, the coffee hour has flown by, and in Bar Magenta, the atmosphere is changed. The big screen is lit up with a rugby match, a few British tourists are already downing pints of Guinness at the counter, and two old Milanese men are arguing loudly about politics. Outside in the piazza, the foggy afternoon has grown murkier, and it has begun to drizzle.

Shay checks her phone and jumps up, fluffing out her springy curls and looping her bright wool scarf around her neck. "The school bus is in Via Molino delle Armi," she says. "Let's go. I'll pay for the coffee—after all, I did all the talking."

"No, no, *carissima*, that was a thousand and one coffees' worth of entertainment!" says Orso, pulling on his loden coat and preemptively brushing past Shay as he plucks a five-euro note from his wallet and, with a flourish, hands it to the unsmiling Irish cashier. "Yes, quite a yarn," he continues, as he gallantly holds open the brass-barred front door of Bar Magenta for her. "A man and a woman at sea. White and Black. The Tropic of Capricorn. Years of longing. Hints of a mysterious crime, and slow martyrdom in a louche backwater. And, just like in a Tarkovsky film, nothing happens— but somehow all the nothing coalesces into . . ." He pauses, then pronounces dramatically: "eternal love."

"Sorry, Orso, but there was no love involved," says Shay firmly, opening her umbrella as they step out onto Corso Magenta. She sees one of her students from the university loping by, and waves to him.

Outside, the air of Milan tastes like rain and exhaust. Traffic in the wet streets around the piazza fans out into strings of headlights; shop windows full of expensive clothes glow like museum exhibits; shadowy crowds of pedestrians flow by. At that hour, the scene has a melancholy grandeur, the rich dark heart of a European city. No panorama could be more distant from the shimmering coral solitudes of the Indian Ocean. Or from the image of a sunlit bay where a white catamaran rests at anchor, still as a monument.

"Of course there was," insists Orso. "The first proof is that you spent half an hour telling me about it in detail. When I natter on that long, it's always because I have an enormous crush on somebody. The second proof is that although Maz had nothing, he gave you two grand gifts. Just think of it: a baobab tree, and his most precious navigation book. Land and sea. Did you keep the book, by the way?"

"Naturally. It's in my room in the Red House."

"So I rest my case. What else is it but love?" demands Orso, as they stroll toward the cluster of parents and nannies at the bus stop.

"Well I don't know," says Shay, slowing down and looking out from under her dripping umbrella, not at her companion—who has opened his own far more elegant umbrella, with a polished thorn-wood handle—but at the line of headlights along the avenue. "Orso, I'm perfectly aware that there are a million kinds of love. I love Senna, though I have no illusions left about him. I love my kids. And my family. I've had boyfriends I adored, and flings where I was out of my mind over somebody. And as for friendship—what is that word you told me for a polygon with infinite sides?"

"Apeirogon."

"Only you would know that! Anyway, Maz and I weren't lovers, and I can tell you that there is no side of that infinite polygon that fits the connection between us. We were never friends. The thing is that now that he's nearly gone, I feel, not stricken, but somehow under obligation. As if I have to look into what connected the two of us. I thought you'd define it right off the bat, Orso—you're an encyclopedia of relationships. And instead, you old softy, you come up with what sounds like a romance novel."

"Well essentially that's what it is," says Orso, clutching his umbrella as he pulls out an immaculate handkerchief and wipes a few stray raindrops off his bald head. "*Un amore proibito, sotto il caldo sole tropicale*. At least it's not *King Solomon's Mines*!" But then he looks at Shay's face, and softens. "All right, darling, I'll be serious. I confess that, in spite of my immense wisdom, I can't find a category for what you describe to me. So it must remain a mystery." He pauses for an instant, staring past the streetlights toward the Roman Gate, and then continues in a thoughtful voice. "Though I think, Shay, that you might have fulfilled your obligation already: by gathering the pieces and telling the tale. Which I think is a terribly sad one. Also, beautiful."

"Beautiful?" demands Shay, feeling oddly pleased.

"Yes," says Orso, as they walk the last few steps toward the bus stop. "Though I couldn't say why that is." He adds: "But since you so desperately want my opinion, I'll tell you something definite: that island paradise of yours sounds more like purgatory."

Shay opens her mouth to retort, but just then the tall school bus looms up at the corner of Corso Magenta like a galleon at a port, and halts in front of the waiting adults. *"Eccola—la principessina di Papà!"* exclaims Orso, waving frantically as he catches sight of his younger daughter through the window.

Swiftly Shay singles out her own daughter, Augustina, giggling and jostling with other middle school students. And as the crowd of schoolchildren pours off the bus, flooding the rainy intersection with unblemished faces and noisy present-tense dramas, the images of Madagascar—sunlit straits, *vintana,* decay, and death—recede into a secondary frame in her mind.

A few weeks later, when she hears that Maz has died, she thinks that she chose the wrong confidant in frivolous Orso, that she made the whole account—as Orso said—into an adventure tale. But was there anything else to do? Even Maz, for whom silence was an entire language, knew that words, however imprecise, are sometimes required to honor things that are gone for good.

The Rivals

Two loves grew up together,
twin loves:
woe on him who betrays.
Farewell, dear, farewell
foolish love plays tricks,
indecisive love drives one mad.

—Flavien Ranaivo, "Old Merina Theme,"
translated by Marjolijn de Jager

When Floristella catches sight of Pianon on the Red House veranda—the side that overlooks Madame Rose Rakotomalala's jackfruit tree—he gives a martial bellow, charges down the garden path, and attacks his neighbor with a walking stick. And though the two old Italian men, both well over seventy, are ludicrous combatants—Floristella, a diabetic, is ponderously fat, while tall Pianon is skeletal from annual bouts of malaria, so that their skirmish suggests a clash between Falstaff and Ichabod Crane—their energy and passion run high, and no one who witnesses the incident feels inclined to laugh.

The Sennas are back home in Italy at the time, but there are plenty of witnesses to give them a detailed report of the scandalous fight under their own roof, between their resident accountant, Pianon, and their old friend and next-door neighbor Floristella. There is Madame Rose, neighbor on the opposite side. There are gardeners. There are idling workmen from Floristella's snail-paced construction site adjacent to the Red House. There are maids from the Red House, including the Sennas' omniscient head housekeeper, Bertine la Grande. There are Antandroy market women heading up the beach bearing baskets of vegetables on their heads. There is a herdboy driving a string of zebu up the side path from their morning bath in the sea. There is an oyster vendor in a straw pillbox hat.

The maids and gardeners rush to separate the struggling old *vazaha* men while others stop and stare, but everyone shows a notable lack of astonishment. Everybody up and down Finoana Beach and, in fact, all over the island, knows the history of the trouble and the name of the girl at the bottom of it.

Not long before, the combatants were close friends. Pianon and Floristella: next-door neighbors, both men of dignity and substance, as far as it goes in that libertine island atmosphere, where the souls of foreigners grow rotten spots as quickly as a bunch of soft-skinned green bananas. Both of them old settlers who have been in Madagascar since the early years of the country's independence.

Both speak fluent Malagasy, highland and coastal dialects. They've been on Naratrany long enough to have been christened by the islanders with fondly mocking nicknames. Pianon is *Valiha* a long, thin, bamboo zither, and fat Floristella is *Sakav* meaning, simply, food.

Pianon is a notary from Verona, a widower, bony and desiccated from many tropical fevers. He dresses in elegant shirts and trousers tailored, colonial-style, from linen of an archaic thickness, and has cropped white hair, a hatchet nose, and a vast, recondite erudition that is the fruit of a Jesuit education. A passionate amateur ethnologist, he spends his free time consulting missionary archives and interviewing village storytellers for a monograph he is writing on the Sakalava royal dynasties. His present job as live-in bookkeeper and rental manager at the Red House is undeniably beneath him, yet he has grown attached to the space and beauty of the big villa, where he has built up a library, and which he often has to himself outside of peak vacation season. Like everyone else, he is fond of his boss, the boisterous and decidedly nonintellectual Senna. Shay Senna he admires for a degree of learning he is surprised to find in an American woman; he sometimes invites her along on his research expeditions.

No one could differ more from Pianon than Floristella, a Sicilian baron of fallen fortunes who carries his huge belly with the complacent ease of a pasha. In his adventurous youth he was a famous yachtsman and deep-sea diver, whose prowess and seductive charm ensnared the hearts of beautiful women from Capri to Zanzibar. Now that fortune, youth, and good health have vanished, leaving him to a modest pensioner's existence on Naratrany, he still has the grand manner, and is an island personage. His aquiline profile—noble in spite of his two chins—and silver crest of brilliantined hair are a landmark on Finoana Beach, as he holds court daily on the porch of his tiny bungalow adjoining the grounds of the Red House.

There, ensconced on a sagging director's chair, surrounded by a motley array of cats and dogs and even a pet radiated tortoise, he contemplates the tides and changing skies over the Mozambique Channel. He exchanges greetings with passersby, who range from village children to hotel owners, while tapping on a calculator or perusing documents pertaining to a decades-old lawsuit against the Compagnie Bordelaise de Madagascar. On the porch he eats heaping plates of pasta prepared by his faithful housekeeper, Marianne, smokes endless cigarettes, reads thrillers, and doles out wages to the Sakalava workmen who—in starts and stops linked to the fluctuating state of his finances—have for years been at work on a grandiose extension to his bungalow, which he secretly hopes will outshine the Red House.

When Pianon first comes to work for the Sennas, the two neighbors establish a habit of meeting up on Floristella's porch in the cool of the early morning, to drink powerful Sicilian coffee from Floristella's battered pot. For a pleasant hour, as the sun rises and the fishermen set out in their pirogues and Floristella's thin orange kitten purrs on Pianon's bony linen-covered knee, they trade island gossip picked up in that center of all intelligence, the Fleur des Îles café. Sometimes they say spiteful things about a mutual enemy, Kristos the Greek, the most nefarious of Pianon's predecessors at the Red House, who, since being fired by the Sennas, is rumored to be smuggling rosewood. Sometimes their conversations about the crimes and misdemeanors of Italian politicians become discussions of the equally byzantine machinations of the Malagasy government, then take a different tack, become dreamy philosophical musings on the character of Madagascar, of this particular small island where fate has settled them so late in life.

Shay, who likes to put on fins and swim the length of Finoana Bay before breakfast, often pauses far out in the water to observe the figures of the two old men on the porch of the little bungalow beside her own big house and garden. They have a look of harmony that is in keeping with the early-morning hush, the long shadows of palms and casuarinas that stretch across the immaculate curve of beach. When she comes dripping out of the water they call out good mornings and offer her coffee, but Shay feels that if she accepted she'd be disrupting a modest but perfect intimacy.

The woman who does break up the idyll is Noelline. For years she has been Floristella's secretary and mistress, filling the gap left by his indisseverable wife, who long ago grew weary of the tedium of Madagascar and returned to Trapani, where she awaits her husband's twice-yearly visits. Twenty-four and childless, Noelline is no longer young by island standards, and in a land where lovely women are as abundant as grains of sand, has never been a beauty, though she has the almost preposterously voluptuous body of her mixed Sakalava and Ankarana background. The daughter of a seamstress and a ferryman, she has a demure wide face, its teak surface roughened by outbreaks of tiny pimples, a high forehead, and bright shallow-set eyes that miss nothing. She keeps her hair short and stylish, sometimes enhancing it with a waist-length tail of beaded Chinese braids, and her enviable wardrobe consists of tight imported jeans and dresses, purchased by Floristella.

Unlike most of the village women who embark on careers with foreign men, Noelline is educated, has completed two years at the lycée run by the sugar refinery at Ankazobe. She writes a fair hand in French orthography, can use a computer, and speaks good French and Italian. Besides her intelligence, her undeniable energy, and a reputed genius for sex, her greatest talent is one she shares with many resourceful wives and mistresses: an inconspicuous but relentless persistence, the ability to bide her time, to cling without being obvious, and never to show offense.

Over the years Floristella has entrusted her with the keys to his bungalow; the secrets of his defunct business exporting medicinal jungle herbs;
his lawsuit; the erratic construction work on his property; the care and the
pleasures of his swollen diabetic body. Noelline does not live with him,
but resides a mile away in a two-room cinder-block house—luxurious by
village standards, the rent paid, of course, by Floristella—set among palms
and thornbushes in one of the warren-like settlements that sprawl messily
off the only paved road in Finoana.

Each morning she buzzes up to his bungalow on a battered motorbike—another luxury provided by her protector—and offers a cordial
but slightly condescending greeting to Marianne the housekeeper, who
pounds laundry and cleans fish in the small, well-trodden sand yard by
the sea. Throughout the day, Noelline writes Floristella's letters to offi-
cialdom, gives him his insulin injection, eats a bowl of rice and *romazava*,
climbs nimbly astride his big belly during the siesta hour, and sometimes
lingers after sunset on his lamplit porch, patiently listening to his fantastical
musings on how to remake his fortune: he dreams of setting up hotels in
Turkish caïques somehow towed to the Seychelles, or planting oil palms in
the desert near Tulear. She never spends the night.

To Floristella's many friends, she is quietly courteous, especially to Pianon. She absorbs Italian idioms with rapt attention, and laughs appropri-
ately when the two men chat together on the porch. Occasionally, she types
a document for Pianon and sometimes, in the tone of a schoolmistress,
translates for him an obscure term in Sakalava dialect, or explains some
custom, like why it is *fady* for certain young girls to eat chicken.

The villagers know that Noelline has her own *giambillys*, or lovers on
the side, notably a handsome cabdriver from Saint Grimaud, a métis who
is said to beat his old French mother. However, the young woman jealously
guards her position with the Sicilian. On the island she has acquired the
title of Madame Floristella, much to the annoyance of his wife back in Trapani, who has vowed never to revisit Madagascar until Floristella discards
Noelline.

Often when the Sennas drive to market at Saint Grimaud, they catch sight of portly Floristella, conferring with some bureaucrat on the broken, weedy courthouse steps, as Noelline, wearing tight jeans and pointed high heels and clutching a worn briefcase, stands demurely in the background. "There she is, the sly baggage!" says Senna, invariably, and Shay as always protests.

"Don't call her that—she's doing her job! How is she different from any other island girl?"

"Because the other little hussies have kind hearts, but she's a troublemaker, that one. She'll be the death of old Flori, wait and see." Senna loves to rattle what he thinks of as Shay's American prudery with a show of cynical wisdom, and Shay is generally amused. Still, she feels that, as a woman of color, she has to express solidarity with Noelline. What would she herself be doing in the same circumstances?

The fact is, though, that nobody on the island seems to like Noelline, though in general islanders of all colors and classes show gleeful admiration for poor village girls who manage to snare rich white men. No one can explain her unpopularity except to say that, although she isn't beautiful, she gives herself airs. Madame Rose is one of her most vocal critics, but she is embittered because her own husband lives with a Sakalava mistress in Andrakaka. Bertine la Grande, the head housekeeper, simply observes to Shay: *"Elle n'est pas bien, cette fille!"*

"Why do you say that?" demands Shay, though she knows that, in spite of being her closest confidante on the island, the Sakalava housekeeper will never explain further. Bertine has a Manichean vision of the world as divided into *bien* and *pas bien* which has little to do with conventional morality: many an island prostitute is described by Bertine as *"bien."* For mysterious reasons of her own, she calls both Floristella and Pianon *"bien,"* unlike other foreign men. Shay understands that if Bertine defines Noelline, who is from the same village and known to her since childhood, as *"pas bien,"* it refers to something deeper than the girl's ambitious seductiveness, means a deep flaw in her nature visible only to someone with the same origins.

Yet, with a peculiar loyalty, Bertine goes no further in criticizing

Noelline or trying to thwart her actions, even at the height of the drama that the younger woman creates; instead, she stands back with a fatalistic air, as if things must unroll as they do.

And how does Shay herself feel about Noelline? Well, if she is honest, she knows her show of sisterly sympathy is hypocritical, because she, too, can't stand the woman. Noelline greets her meekly with a bland smile whenever their paths cross, but beneath her politeness, in those shallow-set eyes brown as coffee beans, flickers a powerful current of envy and hostility.

The rivalry of Floristella and Pianon begins when Floristella, as was inevitable, suffers a heart attack one hot January night. Alerted by the night watchmen, Pianon calls Dr. Pau and with the help of the doctor and Madame Rose, has the Sicilian transferred by helicopter to the hospital on Réunion Island. His wife and sons rush from Trapani, and later carry him back home.

Noelline; the housekeeper, Marianne; and the groundskeepers are left in charge of Floristella's Madagascar affairs: his bungalow, his pets, his keys and documents, and the weedy construction site out back. Later on, as he recovers, Floristella—forgetting the lessons of history, and his own extensive knowledge of women—sends a request that his friend Pianon keep an eye on things, and watch over Noelline.

Well, as Senna later said, any fool could anticipate what would happen, with Floristella absent for so many months. His convalescence in Sicily is astutely extended by his wife, who is pleased to have her elderly husband back in her hands, out of the infectious atmosphere of whores and decayed colonial dreams that hangs like a fever mist over the island of Naratrany.

From Madagascar, Pianon calls to ask whether Floristella minds if Noelline helps him with some complicated paperwork at the Red House. At that time, Senna is thinking of building a small hotel adjacent to the villa, and Pianon is preparing documents to purchase Madame Rose's rice paddy and the charcoal burners' terrain nearby.

Bertine la Grande later describes to Shay a scene that makes it clear how things are progressing. It is circumcision season, when groups of boys of four or five years old have undergone the procedure all over the island; three days after the operation, Noelline brings a band of little Finoana village boys, her cousins and nephews, down to the beach in front of the Red House, to wash in the sea. They are lured into the water, as tradition prescribes, with singing and splashing circle games. The naked boys wince and squeal as the salt water stings their wounds, and Noelline leads them in playing.

She is wearing a two-piece bathing suit, the kind that tourists wear, a bikini that leaves little about her large breasts and broad thighs to the imagination. And she is frolicking conspicuously as proper village girls never do—decorous girls who enter the water modestly dressed to wash themselves or to fish with a piece of sheeting.

"On dirait qu'elle dansait!" says Bertine sourly. She means dancing like the prostitutes in Naratrany nightclubs, who can move their asses like turbines while balancing beer bottles on their heads.

Bertine sees that Noelline is angling her performance in a specific direction, and then sees Pianon's tall bony linen-clad figure emerge from the garden of the Red House onto the beach. Pianon, who never swims and rarely sets foot on the sand, approaches with his crane's gait—perhaps to make some scholarly inquiry into the chants and songs used in the games. But Bertine sees how his eyes latch on to the nearly naked young woman in the circle of splashing children.

Pianon and Noelline. They are both lonely people, who in a different situation, in a place less strung about with caste, would have done very well openly together from the start. Pianon has lost a wife to cancer and his only child to a drug overdose, and is not inclined to go back to Verona to rejoin the small accounting firm he once ran with his brother. Alone among the foreign adventurers and losers washed up on the shores of Naratrany, he has never annexed an ambitious teenage beauty as a mistress.

Noelline has been estranged from clan and tribe by her curious unpopularity, by her attachment to Floristella, who has devoured her freshest youth, without ever offering to live with her, have a child, or buy her a house of her own. Floristella, whose noble forebears are said to have hunted peasants for sport over the slopes of Mount Etna, has—besides his bungalow and useless building site—only a crumbling sea-girt family palace in Trapani, a tenacious wife, and a mountain of debt from frivolous investments. But Pianon is unattached, and has an Italian pension as well as his position at the Red House.

So, while Floristella recuperates back in Sicily, Noelline begins to spend afternoons working at the computer in Pianon's office at the Red House, and appears at Pianon's side in the pickup truck when he makes his trips to the customs office, or the Banque Industrielle et Commerciale de Madagascar.

Noelline, coming and going on her motorbike, has always had a certain camaraderie with the small army of maids and laundresses who keep the Red House going for the Senna family and their paying guests. Some are girls she has grown up with, and, like Bertine la Grande, they know exactly what is going on. Noelline and her seamstress mother, a tiny woman whose face is the color of a freshly roasted cashew nut, are even seen several times in the Red House kitchen. Everyone understands that in the time-honored manner, she is using magic to entice Pianon, but whether it is simply an aphrodisiac, or a love philter, that she is adding to his food, remains unclear.

By June, when the cold season begins and village infants bound to their mothers' backs wear snug crocheted caps, Floristella has been five months away from the island. Pianon's once-clear and skeptical blue eyes have acquired a submissive, almost doglike expression, and in matters of dress he has become unattractively casual, abandoning his impeccable linens for the tracksuits and safari shorts worn by most old rum-soused foreigners on the island.

When the Sennas arrive from Milan to spend summer vacation at the Red House, Shay is angered to catch sight of Noelline slipping out of Pianon's quarters early one morning, the young woman's usually neat hair standing on end in a way that suggests unbridled rutting. After a decade of sojourns in Madagascar, Shay has developed an ironclad poise and learned to be astonished at nothing, but she is disappointed with Pianon, whom she thought might be the one old man who would not embarrass himself on the island.

"I'll have to say something to him," she remarks severely to Bertine la Grande when the housekeeper reports that the two have been sleeping together for weeks. "This house is not a bordello!"

"I think it is useless to speak to him," says the tall housekeeper. "Speak to her—*la fille*."

But when Shay does take Noelline aside and in her firmest tone tells her that certain behavior will not be tolerated, she finds herself confronted with an enigma. The prow-like bosom and tiny waist, the round face under the Eartha Kitt hairdo, the shallow-set coffee bean eyes, the dulcet voice that immediately agrees— *"Oui, oui, Madame, c'est honteux, je suis désolée"*— all barely mask that blaze of mocking hostility that Shay has sensed before. For a second the American woman, with all her privilege, quails before the Malagasy woman, who has nothing but her wits.

All July and August, Shay observes the progress of the affair. Though no more nights are spent in the Red House, Noelline cleaves to Pianon's side, even showing up in the sweaty, raucous crowd at the weekly Sunday *moraingy* boxing match held in the dusty arena at Betsaka beach. (Pianon attends this popular entertainment to take notes on the ritual insults exchanged by Sakalava and Antandroy opponents.)

One afternoon, Shay returns unexpectedly from an excursion into Saint Grimaud and catches Noelline, her demure mask laid aside, leading the younger maids—it is Bertine's day off—in loud teasing of her elderly lover. Just outside the kitchen the girls have surrounded Pianon in a giggling, clapping, shouting ring as they demand that he throw them a party to celebrate Italy's World Cup win. (The jubilant Italians on the island have been handing out free beer for a week.) Noelline and the maids are hollering that they want Pianon to barbecue a zebu and hire an orchestra, that they want to dance so hard you can see their underpants. To show what they mean, they all start waggling their behinds and chanting: *"Un zébu/Monsieur/Pour voir les slips!"*

When Shay, carrying a basket filled with lengths of Comorean cloth, comes into view, the maids scatter in all directions like ants; Noelline whisks into the office. Leaving Pianon struggling to reassume his dignity. "They are young . . . high-spirited . . ." he mumbles to Shay, who is trying not to laugh.

"Really, Gianfilippo, you shouldn't let them run wild like that!" she says, keeping a straight face as he stands there in his ugly warm-up pants, a dull flush suffusing his bony cheeks.

On the one hand the scene was hilarious: the manager bullied by his staff; the priestly Pianon helplessly aroused by the loud, ribald female crowd around him. Shay has always amused herself by envisioning him as the arid scholar Casaubon from *Middlemarch*, transplanted to the tropics and engrossed not in the Key to All Mythologies, but in an endless history of the Sakalava kings. But now she thinks of his quiet kindness to her children, unswerving courtesy to herself and Senna, and she feels saddened at his mislaid dignity.

"Are you sure this is all worth it?" she asks him quietly, just as her son and daughter come running up from the beach.

Pianon gives her an austere look and replies, *"Le coeur a ses raisons . . ."*

That night in their bedroom, Shay says to Senna, "I think we may need to look for a new accountant soon."

"*Che cazzo*—they never last!" exclaims Senna in annoyance, slapping aside the mosquito net and collapsing on the bed. "I was hoping he would just start chasing hookers like everyone else."

When Floristella returns to Madagascar, in late September, it seems that the affair may die the natural death of countless illicit romances on Naratrany island: everything buried under layers of silence, nothing remaining but a sudden opacity in the eyes of the people who know. But the very evening of Floristella's arrival, Pianon goes directly to his old friend and confesses everything, in the worst possible way.

Yielding to the frailty of the flesh and sleeping with an absent neighbor's mistress is a forgivable lapse by the lax standards of island morality. Running off with a friend's woman is also something that Naratrany has seen before. But confessing such an offense without any particular plan of action, except declaring oneself the woman's defender in a vague chivalric manner, is just foolish. And this is what Pianon does. He does not say that it is destiny, and that in Noelline he has found his dream of love (an acceptable excuse to an emotional Sicilian), but takes an unfortunate middle route: he announces pompously that he and Noelline have made no plans, but that in their newfound intimacy he has come to respect her, and does not wish for her to live a life of misery.

The folly of this! As Senna remarks to Shay—husband and wife are both avidly following the gossip, long distance from Milan—it leaves Floristella not only cuckolded but egregiously insulted, with only the possibility of rage and revenge.

The situation is rendered more volatile by the fact that Noelline begins to act erratically. She abruptly stops her part-time work with Pianon at the Red House, so as not to come anywhere near her official employer, Floristella. With him, she refuses any contact, even to tie up the loose ends of her secretarial duties.

Worse than this, she suddenly starts issuing melodramatic pronouncements: telling anybody who will listen that for years she has been the Sicilian's overworked slave, and that now she wishes to be free. In the opinion of the idlers at the Fleur des Îles, who are following the situation like a television drama, Noelline is overdoing her big moment.

Everyone knows that she long ago offered herself to old Floristella, fighting off other girls, and that she and her mother have since then been living contentedly in the greatest luxury the impecunious Sicilian can afford. For years, he has emptied his pockets to pay the rent of the cinder-block house. Who but he put down the money for her diploma from the lycée, and the typing courses? Where else has she gotten the motorbike, and the satellite dish, and all those shoes? Even now Floristella has done the paperwork properly, and she is receiving correct severance pay.

Yet here she is, going on about suffering, in a way that the gossips opine is suitable only for crazy white women. And the way she brags about her powers of fascination over old *vaȝaha* men, as if every pretty island girl doesn't have the same power between her legs! She even invents a third suitor, a rich German, described with laughable vagueness, who, she claims, wants to take her off to Frankfurt. No one believes this except the two rivals, Floristella and Pianon.

Long vanished are the days when the friends contemplated the sunrise together over *caffè ristretto* on Floristella's porch. Now, morning and evening, Floristella sits in monumental solitude, glaring at the waves while he nurses his Achillean rage.

Pianon keeps inside the Red House, away from the sea. He makes discreet evening visits to Noelline in her cinder-block village house, and takes her on a weekend excursion to Mahajanga. He is filled with bittersweet tenderness at her predictable appetite for fake designer purses and the masses of hair extensions that hang temptingly in the Indian shops of Saint Grimaud. He even buys her a dinner set painted with violets that for years gathered dust on a shelf of Au Bonheur de la Maison. In between her demands for gifts and her dramatic complaints about Floristella, she makes love to Pianon with an explosive intensity that he has never experienced, even as a young man. Throughout his earlier years in the country, he has stayed away from affairs with Malagasy women, but in Noelline's voice, in the touch of her cool, slightly rough skin, even in her greed, he encounters something simple, ancient, and essential that makes his research into history and custom seem unreal as a stage set. He is oddly touched by the fact that she does not even pretend to be in love with him.

Meanwhile, Floristella is overwhelmed with jealousy. He sets up a network of spies led by his housekeeper, Marianne, and bombards Noelline with calls on the cell phone he bought for her in happier times. He abandons pride and begs her to return. Even if it is just for an hour a day. He swears that she'll never again have to give him insulin injections or cut his toenails. She will not have to listen to his rambling theories on politics. She won't have to work at all; she can just sit and keep him company.

He calls a dozen times a day. Finally, when, with her new outspokenness, she threatens to file a complaint, he subsides into an ominous Sicilian calm. Madame Rose reports to Shay, in an agitated phone call, that Floristella is "biding his time, like all maniacs." According to Madame Rose, he

has been heard musing aloud that the beach in front of his bungalow would
be a good spot for a public flogging post, or even a gallows.

Naratrany is, in fact, a convenient place to commit a crime of passion.
A year before, the captain of a Mauritian schooner docked at the yacht
basin vanishes after killing his first mate with a machete. A Belgian
diving instructor who beats his Sakalava girlfriend is waylaid while
riding his motorcycle, and has his skull bashed in with a rock. During
fishing expeditions to the Îles Glorieuses, unwanted wives disappear
overboard, without a trace. Poison is rife, as easy to put into food as
aphrodisiacs. The power of the island gendarmerie is more theoretical
than anything else.

Hassan, owner of the Total-Kianja gas station, reports a conversation
with Floristella where the old Sicilian said he has considered the simple
expedient of flinging a lighted book of matches onto the thatched roof of
the Red House while Pianon is sleeping.

"But that," adds Floristella to the horrified Hassan, "would be burning
down a friend's house to exterminate a rat."

Things come to a head on that memorable November morning when Floristella storms into the Red House garden. He is brandishing an antique
brass-bound walking stick that one of his noble forebears acquired in
Scotland, a blackened thorn meant for tramping across Hebridean grouse
moors. With startling swiftness, considering his bulk, he dashes up the
veranda steps and hurtles toward Pianon, who stands frozen on the wide
gleaming floor before his office, wearing another unlikely European acces-
sory: an elegant pair of fur-lined Venetian slippers.

Heads of maids and gardeners appear around every corner of the Red
House as Floristella flings down a crumpled paper and bellows that he
found some Red House business letters filed away by mistake in his private
strongbox, to which only Noelline has had the extra key.

"This is the final straw, you filthy traitor, you dog!" he shouts, raising
the stick with both hands like a club. "I'm going to smash your skinny legs

and put you in a wheelchair, where you won't be fucking anybody else's woman and plotting against them on the sly!"

"Let's sit down and talk in a calm and reasonable manner!" babbles Pianon, backing away. "I've already told you it was a terrible, a sinful error on my part, and I apologized humbly. In the name of our old friendship. Don't act like this with the staff watching—think of your dignity!"

"Amicizia! Dignità!" howls Floristella. He takes a sudden swing with the walking stick at Pianon, who leaps aside with surprising nimbleness and collides with one of the Chinese side tables. One of Shay Senna's favorite earthenware lamps flies off and explodes in fragments on the floor, to a collective *"Asala!"* from the assembled servants.

Floristella's housekeeper, Marianne, and his handyman race to restrain Floristella, who flings away his stick and launches himself at Pianon, bearing the other man to the ground by his greater weight, and trying to throttle him.

For a second a ring of dark-skinned spectators encircles the thrashing struggle of two old white men, one bony and pale, one fat and vermilion with rage. Then the Red House maids, led by Bertine la Grande, manage to detach Floristella's grip. They pull the disheveled Pianon to his feet and help him to a chair, and Floristella, puffing dangerously, allows himself to be walked away by Marianne and two others.

"I'll see that you get your payment!" the Sicilian shouts as he is hustled past a bougainvillea. "Don't let yourself fall asleep, not even a siesta!"

"You don't understand," calls Pianon, rising cautiously and hobbling to the edge of the veranda. "She's left me!"

"Left you?" says Floristella, pausing. "For that German son of a bitch, I suppose?"

"Not the German. I don't think anyone really wants to take her to Germany. But she won't answer my calls. She won't open her door. It's been three days now."

"Good for you, dirty bastard! Enjoy what's left of your miserable life."

It is true, in fact, that the unpredictable Noelline has abruptly dropped the second of her elderly swains, in a sudden fit of pique that consolidates her reputation as a girl who allows herself emotions far beyond her means.

Word has it that she breaks off with Pianon just after he makes the last payment on the purchase of her cinder-block lodging in Finoana and transfers ownership to Noelline. There is no definite proof of this, but it is clear that her life is transformed. She stops making public laments. She finds work in the offices of the Grand Bleu vacation village, and is soon seen around the island with a new boyfriend: a muscular Tsimihety man, who works for a French yacht charter company. Suddenly prosperous, she adopts a lofty new hairdo of extensions that gives her a Sophia Loren air. She abandons her friendship with the Red House staff, and even acquires a maid of her own, a placid twelve-year-old niece from backcountry Sandrakota.

Many islanders, rich and poor, think she is stupid to cut off such a sure source of ongoing profit as the love madness of two old *vazaha* men. Still, though presumably there are no longer magical philters added to Pianon's meals, the enchantment seems to go on working. Pianon, who has never before given in to the tropical melancholy that leads white men to marinate themselves in rum, now finds himself unable to eat or sleep. Wearing his unflattering tracksuits, he makes his business rounds, walking with a slight limp that makes him look much older. In the Saint Grimaud market crowds, he pauses each time he sees a girl with a high forehead—perhaps inclining her head with the absent expression women have when they retie the *lambas* around their bodies, perhaps tilting her chin to holler at a friend across the square. At such times his angular face looks as if it has turned to stone. He loses all interest in the history of the royal Sakalava, and abandons the project he set up with the scholarly priest Père Jobeny to research legends about the beautiful Queen Binao.

After the fight, everyone thought Floristella would collapse from another heart attack, but he seems undamaged. He has stopped harassing Noelline, but it is rumored that he has offered local toughs fifty thousand *ariary* for an attack on Pianon. He hires two pretty replacement secretaries, young Comorean women with neatly braided heads. He can be seen sitting between them with a bored, distracted air on his seaside porch, perusing the usual documents. In the evening, after he has sent the girls away, he sits on under the yellow light, monumental, oblivious to mosquitoes, slowly eating his way through a heap of spaghetti, his cigarette burning beside him.

At the same time, at the Red House, if there are no guests, Pianon is seated at one end of the long table, picking at a monastic meal of cooked vegetables. Both men go to bed early.

"What is it about that girl?" asks one of Senna's Milanese friends, who hears the tale aboard the Red House catamaran during a New Year's fishing trip. "Who is she, Cleopatra?"

"Nobody understands it!" exclaims Senna, reaching across the deck table to help himself to more fricasseed crab. "She isn't even all that good-looking. But both of those old codgers should get down on their knees—if they can—and thank her."

Senna is as annoyed as Shay is about the scandal and the awkwardness in the Red House, with the whole island gossiping about their accountant, and their dear friend Floristella refusing to set foot under their roof. But being quite a fantasist for a businessman, Senna has his own take on it. When in Madagascar he cherishes a vision of himself as a piratical adventurer, for whom social graces are as superfluous as underwear. Now he pours himself another glass of Three Horses beer and continues: "Yes, that little piece of ass did them the biggest favor in the world: got those two fucking and fighting like twenty-year-olds."

"O, per carità!" interjects Shay, shooting him an exasperated look. Smothered giggles come from aft, where the Senna children are eavesdropping from their perch on the trampoline. They know every salacious detail of the story from their friends in Finoana village.

Senna makes a face at his wife like a naughty little boy and goes on: "Think of it—how often do men that age have the privilege of doing battle over a woman? If it happened to me in twenty years, I'd think it was a miracle."

At sunset on the Epiphany, the day before the Sennas leave for Milan,

Shay walks over to say goodbye to Floristella. He is still nursing his superb anger, sitting obdurate on his porch, immovable as a dolmen. Over the beach, a conflagration of low red rays glares from under a dark cloud bank rippled like the hem of a skirt. The waves are crashing as high tide approaches, and village women returning from work at the hotels pass swiftly like barefoot phantoms.

Floristella—his fat cheeks a sickly map of maroon in the fierce lateral glow—repeats to Shay what he has said before: that he is not jealous or vindictive, that it is a matter of principle. A question of right and wrong. "What is written, is written," he pronounces in a sepulchral tone, as Shay looks at him with compassion. "And those who steal from others will pay."

Shay embraces him, then walks back up her garden path to the Red House, breathing in the scent of jasmine and ylang-ylang, and wondering what life in Madagascar does to white men's brains.

Approaching the lamplit veranda, she catches sight of Pianon sitting primly upright on a rattan chair, right where the notorious scuffle took place. He is discussing with Senna and Madame Rose the cost of installing a *château d'eau* to replace the up-country stream that supplies the beach houses with water. Pianon's eyes are sunken and he is, if possible, even thinner these days, like a dry stalk that the next malarial tremor will break. Yet he holds himself with dignity. To Shay there is something impressive about the way he soldiers on, refusing to speak of his woe, just as there is a certain mad grandeur to the noisy perorations of Floristella.

In some odd manner the two men seem joined more closely as antagonists than they were as friends. Senna, in his usual crude way, has put his finger on the truth: that, near the end of their lives, this melodrama has bestowed on them a kind of magnitude, as if they are a pair of pillars battered by time, holding up the night sky.

A silly thought, because of course the sky needs no support—not the hot star-swollen Madagascar night that leans close over the beach and the villages like the face of a Black girl, tranquil and pitiless.

Then Shay considers Noelline. At this hour, the resourceful young woman is probably already securely closed into her cinder-block house, its shutters barred against insects, thieves, blowing refuse. Perhaps she and her mother are squatting around a dish of rice with their novice maid. Or maybe she is fucking her new man, or getting her scalp greased as she absorbs visions from another world on her satellite television. Or perhaps she is studying accounting, or reading Pascal. Whatever she is doing, she is swiftly losing the bloom of youth that has been her main currency for foreign exchange, growing thick-waisted and iron of countenance, as happens too early to even the prettiest island girls.

You have to respect her, Shay thinks. She's gone far with what she was dealt.

Not much more than a year later, life—or its loyal servant, death—puts a definitive end to the triangle. And which of the rivals triumphs? According to the chattering classes of Naratrany, it all depends on one's point of view.

In the rainy season, Floristella, who has been plagued by dizzy spells, departs for Sicily once again. There, examination reveals that in addition to the diabetes and failing heart, a tumor has infiltrated a lung, and spawned offspring around the huge overtaxed body, even crowding one side of Floristella's stubborn, fantastical brain. His family does not tell him that he will never return to Madagascar, and so he settles into a sunny crumbling wing of his palace in Trapani to begin what he thinks of as convalescence, but which is really a short season of dying.

At the same time political troubles explode in Antananarivo, as supporters of a popular young usurper battle the president's followers in the streets of the capital, torching stores and government buildings, causing unrest even on the far island of Naratrany. And the tourists take off like a flock of startled gulls.

What do politics have to do with the two old men? Well, the hotel where Noelline works closes down—and she, prudent woman that she is, revives her love affair with Pianon. Dressed in a modest blue *lamba*, she arranges a chance encounter with the Italian outside the customs office in Saint Grimaud. It is almost pitiful how simple it is to get him back. Soon she is once more riding beside Pianon in the Toyota pickup that actually belongs to the Sennas, performing wifely actions like buying Sunday *mille-feuilles* at the Patisserie Trois Étoiles.

And by the time the cool weather arrives in May, Pianon surprises everyone by moving out of the Red House and taking Noelline off to live openly with him. Not in her cinder-block house, where she leaves her mother, but in a new construction in a mixed settlement of Chinese, middle-class Malagasy, Indians, and French, on a hillside above the Muslim cemetery. The new house is small, but with stucco walls and European proportions. They install the little maidservant, a generator, Pianon's computer, and a gaudy living room suite from the Indian merchant on the airport road. They also play host to Noelline's uncle, and an array of half brothers, who suddenly materialize from the Grande Île, and who spend their days squatted on the veranda chewing khat with a businesslike air.

Noelline is judged a successful adventuress, but Pianon is thought a double fool for having taken her back. He gains weight and looks idiotic with happiness. Still working at the Red House, he has also taken on some new projects, funded by foreigners who are leveraging the political chaos to buy up land for a song. Pianon has always enjoyed a spotless professional reputation, but now rumors begin to circulate that he is forging documents and bribing village headmen for land they have no right to sell. He is seen in the shabby offices of the defunct sugar company (where, half obliterated by insects and damp, lists of colonial fieldworkers are still tacked to the wall), signing papers with the ruthless Mauritian developer whose nickname is the Crocodile.

Back in Milan, Senna scratches his head and curses over shortfalls in the Red House accounting. Still, Pianon looks unworried; he is always at work, Noelline at his side. Then, one breathlessly hot morning in January, as he stands in his house, telephoning near the window that looks down the sun-scorched hill to the incorruptible blue of Finoana Bay, he turns to say something to Noelline, who is sitting at the computer. The men on the veranda and the little maid in the side yard hear Pianon give a loud cry. It is followed by a crash, and a crescendo of shrieks from

Noelline. When they rush in and turn over his lanky body, he is already dead from a stroke.

Noelline, to her credit, seems genuinely grief stricken, and has two zebus killed for the ceremony. And to the islanders' credit, scores come for the feasting and mourning, even those who had lately led him astray, like village headmen and the Crocodile. Because of the political chaos, most Europeans are absent from Naratrany. The Sennas have to use their connections to the Italian consulate to cut through the red tape and get what remains of Pianon shipped back to his family tomb in the hills above Verona. Intermittently iced, his body has lain for six days at the Saint Grimaud morgue, a cement storeroom behind the police station, and is, as the consul delicately puts it, in a deteriorated condition.

It turns out that Pianon's new house, along with the cinder-block shantytown residence, as well as some prime road-front land, now belong in some mysterious but indisputable way to Noelline. When it becomes clear she is a woman of means, she receives an instant boost in status, and she quickly distances herself from the dishonor that turns out to be Pianon's further legacy. Just before his death, it appears, the *commissaire* had already drawn up a warrant for his arrest on charges of forgery and illegal sale of government land. Had he remained alive, Pianon would have been locked up to eat boiled manioc in the grim colonial stockade that is Naratrany prison. But all ends as he, possibly, would have wished it.

"Così é la vita" is Floristella's only observation when he hears of Pianon's death and disgrace. The words are tossed off with indifference, with a regal movement of his big swollen hand as he lies lapped in threadbare pillows on a huge-wheeled chaise longue on a terrace of his ramshackle palace looking out toward the Aegadian Islands. But for a minute, before he falls back into the morphine haze, his black eyes hold a gleam of savage glee.

The rest of his life is brief. In the afternoons, lizards run up and down the crumbling plaster behind his head, and when awake he stares off across the sunny courtyard that holds a dusty collection of whale vertebrae and sea turtle shells, over a cracked balustrade toward the ferries, the cruise liners, the hangars, the teeming chaos of the port, to the open Mediterranean, almost as pure a blue as the Mozambique Channel.

Night and day they tell him lies—his daughters, his grandchildren, his straight-backed wife with her brusque aristocratic voice—they all say, over and over, that Floristella will go back to Madagascar. To sit enthroned as usual on the porch of his bungalow, gazing out over the strait at the bellying sails of the fishing pirogues and the *boutres* hauling timber from the Grande Île. Through the drugs he listens, and envisions an early scene on Finoana Beach, where he once dragged ashore a pair of hammerhead sharks: himself, Floristella, young, bearded, muscular; his children, blond and small, shrieking with glee as his knife bites through the tough shark-skin and the cold dark blood soaks into the sand. And through the harsh bright smell of the blood comes the scent of the island: boiling sugar, and ylang-ylang. Behind the scene hovers the face of a girl, a young Sakalava woman with a high forehead, staring at him with a sly edge of affection in her shallow-set eyes. Then a blink of brown and blue, a sound of wailing that might be his family, or some cyclonic turn of weather over the Indian Ocean. Then, nothing.

Just four months after Pianon is placed in the tomb in the hills above Verona, the body of Floristella lies in an extra-large open casket in the deconsecrated chapel of his palace—redone in the seventies with ugly murals of fishing apostles—as a crowd of family, former lovers, and friends—aristocrats mingling with sailors, mechanics, market vendors, and the odd crime boss—spill out the doorway onto the seawall. They stand and listen to a tribute in which God is not mentioned, since the old baron was an atheist. He lies in one of the open-necked shirts he always wore on Naratrany, with his big feet bare as they almost always were in life, as around him ring grandiose eulogies. In the crowd are Senna, choking with sobs, and Shay, who stands thinking how she will miss Floristella, how long it will take for the giant presence to dissipate into memory, and thinking also of the less grand sides: how he'd kill palm rats with a sling-shot, and treat her children's coral scratches with rum.

After the cremation, his wife and daughters scatter his ashes in the sea.

Floristella at the very end insists on this, declaring that with the currents he will find his way back to Madagascar.

So, in the end, who is the winner? ask the idlers at the Fleur des Îles café. Is it Pianon, who got the girl, but who died of it, and was sent home putrescent in a stench of crime? Or is it Floristella, cuckolded and robbed of his revenge, but who outlived his enemy—to pass away in honorable peace, in Europe, in a garland of family, friends, and mythmaking?

No one consults the woman who many think is the real winner. These days, Noelline has become an important island personage, who, after her months of mourning—her mother and uncle carefully guarding her two houses—has allowed herself to grow distinctly stout, adopted a pair of nephews, and blossomed into a commanding, wealthy Malagasy matri-arch.

After a few years, she surprises the Italian and French community by opening a big new general store in Renirano village, at the crossroad near the yacht basin, in partnership with a recent arrival on the island, a sheep-faced young man from Bologna who may or may not be her lover. (Her other lovers are said to include a powerful senator and the king of the Saka-lava.) There Noelline sits, magisterial behind the register in the prosperous gloom, with the hubbub and squalor of Renirano market right outside the door, totting up shopping lists for Australian yachtsmen, for rich Europeans and Indians, barking out orders to her nephews, who haul cases of imported gin, soft drinks, frozen chickens, and cartons of laundry soap. Her thick gold chains are laid out for all to see on her handsome, jutting bosom, her eyebrows are penciled in superb arches, and her ever-changing hair exten-sions are the best money can buy.

The Red House does not patronize her establishment, but this is be-cause the Sennas for years have bought their supplies in Saint Grimaud, from the Chinese grocer Fong.

Pianon's beloved library remains at the Red House until Shay decides to donate it to the scholarly priest Père Jobeny; she and Bertine la Grande spend a melancholy hour cleaning rot and insects out of the yellowing vol-umes. At one point, flipping through, Shay thinks of Noelline, observing to Bertine that the other woman has certainly shown character in making a success out of an unpromising fate.

But Bertine's response is predictable: a single terse shake of the head crowned with impeccably twisted Sakalava knots. *"Pas bien!"* she says in a dismissive tone, before picking up another book.

Guess Who's
Coming to Dinner

Lovely woman
The bearing of a queen
. . .
With your smile of serenity
Bearer of mystery
From the height of the hill
You defy churchwardens
Who both classify and muddle
The fabric of your history
From the other side of the ocean
To this one here.

—Esther Nirina, "Lovely Woman"
translated by Marjolijn de Jager

"Well what are we going to do about it?" demands Senna. "We've rented him that room on the beach for two summers now. And he's a good customer, *un bravo ragazzo*. A nice guy, quiet."

Senna pauses and gives Shay an anticipatory flicker of the eye as if he is waiting for his wife to leap in with American aggressiveness and deny the quiet nature of the fat Frenchman, Gilles. But Shay perversely holds back from enacting the familiar choreography and, taking a sip of iced lime water, regards her husband with an air of mild inquiry that she knows is far more annoying. Senna is tired and grumpy, fresh off the catamaran from two days deep-sea fishing off the coast of Ambatozavary, where the savage subequatorial sun has brought his normally indestructible Italian complexion to an inflamed neon glow like that lingering in the sunset sky over Finoana Bay in front of them. Husband and wife are sitting on the Red House veranda in a rare moment of tranquillity, discussing a problem of etiquette. Or is it ethics?

Irritably, Senna continues. "And you know that most of the guests left this morning, and it would look peculiar if we don't let him eat with the family. That's what table d'hôte means, for Christ's sake. But now *she's* here with him . . . Well. It's for you to decide . . ." he says, springing suddenly out of the wicker chair and padding away barefoot over the gleaming dark red floor in the direction of the stairs to their bedroom and the relief of a shower. "After all," he calls over his shoulder, in the tone of one launching a devastating riposte, "you're the lady of the house!" He says it in Italian, and the words resound under the high thatched ceiling: *Sei tu la padrona di casa!*

Shay gives a short laugh and slides down in her chair, folding her arms behind her head and casting her eyes up toward the shadowy beams where a dozen geckos crouch in ambush for flying insects. She's already dressed for dinner, in a long flimsy linen dress from Milan that sticks to her freshly showered skin, damp curls pulled up on the crown of her head, a thick Berber bracelet and no other jewelry: the kind of offhand Euro beach style she absorbed years ago, when she married Senna and became part of the Italian vacationing world.

Around her in the big open space, both veranda and great room, that is the heart of the house, the household staff move back and forth in the evening duties—lighting the lamps, drawing the tall sailcloth curtains that divide inside from outside, bringing mosquito coils, closing bedroom shutters, setting the dining table—that have become ritual in the two decades since the Sennas first came to Finoana Beach. Shay helped establish this, and other domestic rituals. Most of the housemaids, gardeners, and night watchmen have been there for many seasons and can communicate with her in a mere word, a gesture.

Everyone knows exactly what is expected, thinks Shay. *Except, in this case, me.*

Not for the first time, Senna is foisting off on her the task of finding a solution to a dilemma peculiar to Madagascar. In this case, one that makes her feel that she is struggling to negotiate the currents not just of Italian, French, and Malagasy etiquette but of a universal colonial tradition that once seemed to her extinct, but which she knows now is all too alive.

The problem concerns one of their paying guests: Gilles, a corpulent, white-haired truck dispatcher from Arles, who for the last two years has come to Naratrany for March and September fishing trips. Apparently widowed, or separated—though who can say?—he stays for weeks, always with a much younger Malagasy woman, different each time, picked out carefully from the array at the bars of the port. Usually his stays don't coincide with the Senna family vacation, but this time he has arrived early, at the tail end of August, two days before they depart for Milan. And with him is his concubine of the moment, who is the problem.

Shay knows all about Gilles from Hery, the Merina manager who presently runs the Red House bed-and-breakfast business for them. Hery, a gay man with a gently angled face, a musical voice, and a sunken, consumptive chest, says that the Frenchman is the best kind of guest: jolly, generous with tips, fishing all day, out of the way at night—that is, roistering at the billiard hall and the dance clubs. Admittedly, says Hery, he is rough in his manners, a little loud—not at all discreet, as Senna claims—yet he is quiet in the sense that he is benign, causes no trouble. Doesn't get staggering drunk and fall prey to island thugs, no drugs, doesn't go after children. In fact, he is much the best of the crusty old French, Germans, Swedes, and Italians who descend on the island in the off-season, trolling for deep-sea fish, and sex. Gilles picks out one girl immediately on his arrival, stays with her the whole time of his vacation, buying her presents and flaunting her in the clubs, then pays her off generously when he departs.

The Red House pensione, like every other island hotel, has a rule banning prostitution, but no set rules about couples who come to stay. There are only eight rooms, and it is run in an agreeable low-key way, doing most business when the Sennas and their friends are back in Italy. Should the family be there when there are just a few guests, they eat together at the big table on the veranda. Eat well, too: Italian, and Creole, and occasional American specialties (beaten biscuits, key lime pie) prepared by the expert cook Shay hired, a Hova trained in an Italian-run restaurant in Mahajanga. It's part of the relaxed atmosphere of the place that people are so enthusiastic about on websites for travelers who like to get off the beaten track. The Sennas generally enjoy it. They've passed impromptu evenings with charter airline crews, Peace Corps volunteers, Australian yachtsmen, paleontologists in search of Miocene fossils, Malagasy families from the highlands, Indian honeymooners from Mauritius and Réunion.

On this late August evening the dreamy, slightly melancholy end-of-summer atmosphere has suddenly been invaded by the flutter of a question in the air: the uncomfortable query as to whether they should sit down for dinner at the same table with a young Malagasy woman who is not precisely a prostitute, but is certainly paid for her companionship.

Shay is disturbed on many levels: first of all by the hypocrisy of Senna, who styles himself a freethinker. Like most of the foreign men who have vacation houses here, he has visited on his own in the off-season and attended many a dinner given by cronies whose families are far away: rampageous festivities where Malagasy girls from the bars and clubs are part of the company. This Shay knows because Senna tells her—makes her laugh about the scandalous doings he hilariously reports. She doesn't know if she trusts or distrusts his role in this, but at least he tells her.

But now, with his wife present, with Roby and Augustina hosting their classmate from Milan, the framework of his domestic life around him, he is suddenly referencing the old-fashioned European division between haut monde and demimonde. Between good and bad women. It throws a shadow on everything that has gone before. She'd respect him far more if he calmly evoked the unbridled evenings he's described in the past, and simply asked her to agree that no one is unwelcome at dinner in the Red House. Instead of pretending that there is a big decision to make, and that the onus lies on her.

She is further irritated to hear Hery discreetly suggest that they set up a separate table for Gilles and his girl on the little terrace outside of the room that Gilles has rented. A nice table, of course, with flowers: the kind they set up for honeymooners who want privacy. Or, he says, they could simply request that the couple, that night, eat in a restaurant in the village.

Just then her Malagasy friend Angélique, for years the pharmacist in Saint Grimaud, comes by to pick up a stack of fashion magazines, and naturally she pokes her tiny Betsileo nose into the situation, as usual yanking off her angular Parisian glasses and gesturing theatrically with them as she makes her point. *"Oh, mais non, par les cieux!* A couple like that should absolutely *not* dine with you. You shouldn't put your poor children through such an experience!"

"They're not delicate flowers, they're practically adults," says Shay, mildly. "They've seen sex tourists on Naratrany all their lives. Unfortunately. And back in Milan, the International School bus goes right by the afternoon hookers on the corners, so we've had many a serious conversation about women for sale."

"What a disgraceful world we live in! In any case, this is still not a good idea—such a bad example for the maids, for instance. How can they respect a mistress who sits down with bar girls?"

Shay has long been sick and tired of the importance that Angélique and everybody else on the island assign to her role as chatelaine of the Red House. While Senna, as boss, is assumed to be on vacation in Madagascar for healing repose from his mysterious and burdensome job of running the entire business world, Shay is expected to pass her holiday months not as a sojourner comfortably decompressing from a busy Milan life of teaching and translating and chivying her college-bound kids, but as a vigilant matriarch who exerts iron control—even if it is part-time—over the work ethic, health, and morality of her numerous Malagasy household staff. (Why there should be so many, she doesn't know, yet every big house on the island is more like a miniature village.) On Naratrany she is automatically adjudged the kind of woman who—whether she is a white neocolonial or a Malagasy aristocrat like Angélique—is devoted to keeping social, racial, tribal, and sexual hierarchies in place. In many ways this idealized figure resembles the old-fashioned Italian domestic goddesses whom Senna, who grew up in a provincial clan amid the rice fields of Vercelli, envisions when he says *padrona di casa*. However, to a Black American from an academic family in California, the concept has always smacked far too much of plantation life.

Shay has learned to take the expectations lightly, to treat the role with outward respect when she is in Madagascar, privately joking in messages to her sister, Leila, about her sacred responsibilities as memsahib. But tonight, those responsibilities have acquired substance, as if a hologram has suddenly morphed into tangible form. And inevitably her thoughts return to America; her own country standing vivid in her identity, no matter how many years she lives abroad.

She recalls her grandfather's matter-of-fact stories of segregated Washington, DC, where he, as a medical student, walked the tightrope between what was and was not allowed, of the scent of death and blood that hovered around the possibilities of trespass present everywhere: in buses, schools, restaurants, on sidewalks, in the direction of a Black boy's gaze. She thinks of her parents, who marched in Birmingham and Selma, and later spent weekends crisscrossing Alameda County to register Black voters. She thinks of the eager, naïve Italian students in her literature course at the Università Cattolica, to whom she spoon-feeds James Baldwin and Countee Cullen. She thinks of her half-Italian children, whom she has religiously schooled in awareness of the strange fruit that is their American inheritance. She thinks of how she has kept herself conscious of that inheritance, through long, facile years of life in Italy, where social class counts more than race.

And she knows as she has known from the start that it isn't possible to refuse to sit down at dinner with a young woman with dark skin. Though it is not really a question of race. Or is it? She wishes she could consult the one person among her Malagasy friends who would know the right thing to do, the exact protocol: Bertine la Grande. But the housekeeper has the day off, and Shay feels ashamed at the thought of running to her like a child every time there is a problem. No, she must handle this herself.

And so the minute Angélique drives off, Shay tells Hery to set places at the family table for Gilles and his female companion, name unknown.

At eight o'clock the Frenchman comes stumping in on his fat sunburnt calves, beaming and jocular, his arm proudly around the waist of a Sakalava woman of no more than twenty, tall and slender, with a cheap Chinese weave rippling down her back. She is dressed up with the unbridled flashiness that island girls adopt for Saturday night dancing at Mangue Verte, and Chanson de la Mer.

Her appearance is not a complete surprise to the Sennas and their friends, who have all been to the dance halls and marveled at the dazzle of these long-legged girls. A sequined minidress and four-inch platform heels turn this one into a towering apparition of glamour and sex. It's as if a neon sign has suddenly lit up the candlelit veranda, the gathering of casually dressed adults and barefoot teenagers under the slow spin of the ceiling fans. Below the sewn-in Chinese hair, the girl's round face lacks the dramatic sculptural beauty of many Sakalava women, but is good-natured, plucky, with a generous white smile that is oddly remote, as if she is smiling to someone invisible in the far distance.

In halting French she says that her name is Bé, which is an island name of a certain importance: meaning great, or elder, a name sometimes given to the firstborn of a pair of twins.

Bé maintains a patient composure as portly, red-faced Gilles, white hair gelled into ripples, Falstaff belly jiggling in a polo shirt, hauls her around the room as if he's just gotten his hands on a gorgeous big doll. Talking nonstop, with a crude gusto—which, Senna is right, is somehow appealing—about fishing; sapphire mining (he'd like to get into it); South African wines (can't approach the French *goût de terroir*); about the differences between the haughty girls of Antananarivo and the good-natured cuties of Naratrany. He even talks about the sequined dress, which he boasts of having snatched off the rack at Grand Bazaar—right under the nose of the Saint Grimaud notary, who wanted it for his mistress.

Shay receives the couple with an exaggerated cordiality drawn from childhood occasions when she sometimes found herself the lone Black guest at the dinner tables of white classmates from her private elementary school; except now she is in the position of those long-ago, uneasy hosts. Amused by her tone, Senna slips his arm around his wife and pinches her backside as they are headed to the table, whispering, *"Indovina chi viene a cena!"*

Guess Who's Coming to Dinner. Yes, that classic movie also made it to Italy.

Soon, Shay, directing Bé to a place at Senna's right hand, finds herself politely asking the girl where she lives. Then she bites her tongue, because of course it is obvious. The girl comes from one of the shantytowns in the gullies back of the beach hotels, where yellow dogs root through plastic rubbish, and many daughters, like Bé, work the bars as the sole support of their families.

"Ici," replies Bé, with a gravitas worthy of her name. "Here, in Finoana village."

Yes, she is from here, from the very same location on the map as the Red House, yet from a reality so different that it could be another universe.

She does not meet Shay's eyes as she speaks, nor does she do so the whole evening. The only people she looks at, in fact, are Gilles and the housemaids serving dinner—with whom she has already exchanged low-voiced greetings in Malagasy.

Throughout the three-course meal, Shay goes on playing the determined hostess from the old film, itself now part of civil rights history, where Sidney Poitier's face hovers like a Black sun newly risen over porcelain and crystal, and dinner table awkwardness is just the tip of a familiar iceberg of ancient terrors. She's both amused and disgusted to feel her face automatically re-creating Katharine Hepburn's lockjaw smile.

And all the while she's wondering why this has to be. After all, they are a motley group gathered here dining on smoked white tuna, crudités, and curried prawns at the Red House table. Gilles, French; Senna, Italian; Shay, African-American; their friends, Italian Jews; Shay and Senna's children, mixed race and nationality; their schoolmate, German. The ironic thing is that Bé—the young woman whose presence is troubling the gathering—is the only one of them on native soil.

The three teenagers hunker in their corner of the table, a miniature tribe with their healthy sunburnt faces, their expensive tattered jeans, their clear eyes of young people who have known since birth that the good things of the world are theirs. Throughout the vacation, their opinions on politics have been noisy and trenchant, voiced with the absolutism of international kids who have grown up traveling and been rendered un-shockable by the Internet. The Senna kids have many Malagasy friends on Naratrany, particularly Bertine's tall, grave, guitar-playing son, Anse; they keep abreast of Indian Ocean scandal and crime while smoking weed from the Comorean dealers in back of the Grand Bazaar, and feel that their superior knowledge authorizes them to pass dinner hours furiously dissect-ing postcolonial ills.

But now they are as silent as punished schoolchildren, exchanging only occasional scornful glances that deride Shay's forced small talk and Gilles the Frenchman's retrograde political opinions. Are my kids so without resources? Shay wonders. So puritanical? After everything I hammered into their heads?

Her beautiful daughter, Augustina, for example, with her golden skin, Botticellian curls, and pierced left nostril, deliberately blanks out everyone around her, though Shay has counted on some demonstration of sympathy from this daughter who is usually so vocal about women's issues: that she would exchange some words with the silent Bé; at least, with a smile or a glance, telegraph the other girl a message of solidarity. But tonight, Au-gustina, like any other teenager, seems chiefly mortified by the behavior of her elders. The two boys are pretending not to be titillated by the rampant sexiness of the young female guest, arrayed in her tacky finery for the de-lectation of an obscene old man.

Shay sees that all the kids want to be on the side of Bé, but are con-founded at the sight of this child of their own generation—with whom, years ago, they might have played on the beach, along with Anse and other village kids—who is now so definitively set apart, at whom everyone is trying not to stare, whose dark, disregarding gaze sweeps by them like a wind from beyond the stars.

By ordinary standards the dinner is brief, a half hour at most. But it runs on its own circuit of time. And so, seemingly for centuries, the company lingers around the table on the veranda, as ceiling fans disperse the heat, and pungent smoke rises from the mosquito coils, and the two barefoot maids in their blue wrappers serve rice from the mainland and fish from the sea lapping on the beach outside the garden. From inside the garden drift gorgeous perfumes of damp earth and overwrought vegetation, since this is, after all, paradise. That is why everyone sitting at the table has traveled the terrestrial globe to be here. Everyone except for the young woman shimmering in her weave and sequins like some otherworldly creature, the guest who didn't have to travel at all.

Bé eats very little, a few forkfuls of rice and vegetables.

Shay's favorite Francis Bebey mix is playing, but fixed on repeat in the back of her mind are fragments of the Langston Hughes poem that begins "I, too, sing America." The poem that is one of the warhorses of her popular course *Introduzione alla Letteratura Afro-Americana*. Words composed for the peculiar iniquities of her own country, but that ring true in Madagascar tonight.

I am the darker brother
They send me to eat in the kitchen
When company comes...

The meal drags to its close, and after the cook's famous *tarte au coco* (which Bé refuses), after coffee and mangosteen rum (she tosses back a glass), Bé and Gilles leave for their evening out.

"Mademoiselle will spend the evening on the dance floor with her girl-friends, and I intend to sit back and enjoy the spectacle," says Gilles with a grin, giving comic emphasis to the honorific *Mademoiselle*, and giving Bé herself a solid pat on the thigh. "She'll show this old dog how it's done, won't you, *ma puce*?"

Shay reaches out and shakes Bé's hand, and for a moment the girl's hand lies in hers, smooth and cool and unresponsive as a closed lily.

"Merci, Madame," says Bé, in a low voice, still not looking at her. But she does glance around once at the veranda so handsomely decorated with antique textiles and old wooden tools of the kind once used by Bé's grandparents, back when only fishermen lived in Finoana village. *"Tsara,"* she adds almost inaudibly in Malagasy, then repeats in French. "It's pretty. The house, Madame."

Then the short, fat white man in khakis, and the tall, glittering Black girl moving sure-footed in towering heels, step out under the star-spattered sky. In his rented truck, they drive off through the cane fields, down the red dirt roads to one of the packed, throbbing clubs on the beaches or along the port, places where crowds of women like Bé do back bends or squat with beer bottles on their heads, competing for the attention of men like Gilles.

After that, the teenagers adroitly detach themselves from the awkward gathering on the veranda, say their polite good nights, and head off on motorbikes for one last bonfire with their friends over on Renirano Beach.

Shay and the other adults are left marooned on two wicker couches with their drinks, finally able to lapse from French into Italian. Four handsome, middle-aged people, bronzed and relaxed at the end of their long tropical vacation, dressed in expensive lightweight linen and cotton. Old friends, united into something like family by shared tastes, political views, by the gloss of prosperity overlying their lives.

Quickly they run through the usual laments. How disheartening these scenes are. How deplorable the whole situation. How donations to aid organizations hardly scratch the surface. Then Senna, who prides himself on being the enfant terrible of any group, observes with a wink that Bé is certainly not the prettiest of the Sakalava women that old Gilles could have chosen. Though in that dress you definitely got to see what he is paying for. But all in all, he adds, the girl is not badly off, because Gilles is basically a decent sort: the old fellow confided to Senna that he plans to pay the fees for her *équivalent baccalauréat* so she can find a good job. "That Bé is one of the lucky ones," Senna says, and then falls silent. Perhaps he is thinking, as is everyone else, of his beautiful daughter, Augustina, whose education does not depend on her selling her young body.

Silence, in fact, is the remaining mode of the evening, except when the other wife, a jewelry designer, elegant in Indian gauze top and tortoise-shell earrings, leans over and gushes about how expertly Shay handled the dinner. "I must hand it to you, *carissima*. You were superb. I don't know how you managed it!"

This is when Shay's discomfort becomes anger. Much of it at herself, because a tiny part of her was flattered by the compliment. Yet she knows she did nothing worthy of admiration. Small-minded, small of heart, they are—her husband, her friends, and herself—to act as if they'd run some peril, made some great moral sacrifice that evening. In just such a self-congratulatory tone, she thinks, might some Puritan speak, after condescending to sit down with Hester Prynne. Or Tom Sawyer's Aunt Polly, forced by circumstances to dine with Jim the slave. Once again the Langston Hughes poem comes at her, with its wrenching last lines, full of bleak hope against hope that humans can rise above their own nature.

Besides,
They'll see how beautiful I am
And be ashamed —

Have they, any of them, had the grace to be ashamed?

The next day, through the bustle of her family's departure for Milan, she continues to relive the dinner. She parses it through the hours of day-time flight northward over Kenya, Sudan, Tunisia, in a plane filled with European and South African tourists, middle-class Malagasy families, and a few Malagasy-European couples—though none who have the transactional appearance of Gilles and Bé. It seems important to deconstruct and consider, piece by piece, the wrongs that were so obtrusively present on the evening she hosted. Which was the defining ill?

The fact that Madagascar is so poor that sex tourists are a notable part of the economy?

The fact that just the sight of Gilles and Bé together seemed to violate some cosmic law?

The fact that Shay, a woman of color, thought twice about sitting down to share a meal with another woman—no, practically a child—of color?

The fact that the unwanted guest, the girl packaged as cheap merchandise, was the true heiress of the land on which they all sat feasting?

It is all of these things, and something else too, that lies in deep shadow beneath them: a wound whose prodigious length and depth she can just begin to discern, and for which, as far as she knows, the prospect of a cure is as scant as the hope at the end of the Hughes poem.

And even glimpsing it means admitting she is somehow complicit in its existence.

All these things are in Shay's mind as she flies over Tanzania, then Sudan, then Egypt, and finally enters the airspace of the part of the world where old men must be a bit more discreet about buying young women.

And from time to time her thoughts circle back to the scene in her bedroom at the end of the night, when, pulling off her long dress, she says to her husband: "I don't want Gilles back here next year."

"He's an awful vulgarian, no doubt about it," replies Senna, who is in bed, checking his email inside the mosquito net. "But, as I said, he's a decent chap underneath it all. And you know, darling, there will always be men like Gilles."

As Shay looks at him silently, a dark figure half-visible through the veil, he adds hastily: "But you decide. After all—you're the lady of the house."

Sister Shadow

Somewhere, far away, lives the Big Sister.

—Jean-Joseph Rabearivelo, *Old Merina Songs*,
translated by Miriam Koshland

The news leaps out of a void, as news from Madagascar always does. It comes one December afternoon, as Shay sits at her kitchen table in Milan, struggling to contain her exasperation as she helps her son, Roby, correct an American college application essay. She is just about to lose her temper and yell at lanky, seventeen-year-old Roby—who, after urgently requesting her assistance, has been twisting his nascent dreadlocks, listening to *To Pimp a Butterfly,* and texting his International School friends in their patois of Italian and English—when her phone buzzes. It is Senna, calling from the other hemisphere.

"I have bad news," he tells her. "Bertine is dead. The big Sakalava woman. Your Bertine."

As always, the conversation is veiled by static that suggests blowing Sahara sand, electromagnetic particles swirling in aurora australis, the whisper of distance. Beyond the static and Senna's voice there is the faint roar of breaking surf: high tide at Naratrany, eight thousand kilometers south of Milan. He must be standing at the end of the garden where reception is better, near the big tamarind tree where years ago the Senna kids, along with a host of island children (including, she remembers, Bertine's son, Anse), used to clamber and screech like a pack of monkeys. She envisions Senna exactly, a wiry figure positioned beside the seawall, handsome furrowed face and steel-colored hair lit theatrically by the tropical sunset: her husband, who, as he retires from his business in Italy, spends more and more time developing investments in Madagascar. Senna never looks more the part of master and commander than when he stands with his blunt bare feet planted at the sea gate of the tall house he built, decades ago, in a country he has never tried to know. In front of him, on darkening Finoana Beach, a line of silhouettes will be passing: Malagasy household staff, hotel employees, gardeners, workmen, picking their way homeward along the narrow high-tide path that skirts the big beach villas. It is Bertine's path, after her long working days, back to her house in Renirano village. Was her path, that is. Because she is now gone—is that what Shay has just heard?

"Are you listening?" Senna demands through the static. "It was her heart, they say. Nobody knows for sure. She worked yesterday, but she was at home when it happened, in the night. Her neighbors in the village got her to the hospital."

He gives the word *hospital* a derisive intonation. Both he and Shay know the stinking concrete barracks in Saint Grimaud, where rusted iron beds crowd the hallways and the torrential rains of February pour in through holes in the roof. The place where doctors require bribes, whose special offerings include vermin, contagion, sudden death. The Red House officially sends sick employees to the Dominican clinic, but too often the sufferers reroute the money, and accept the misery the *commune* provides.

"No point in you trying to fly down here," Senna is saying. "You know how things go: she'll be buried by sunset tomorrow. I'll look in on the family. It will certainly be hard to find someone to take her place at the house!"

Only now does Shay notice that tears have started running down her cheeks with the steadiness of rain coming in through that tattered hospital roof. Blankly she ends the call with Senna, and tells the news to her son, who is looking appalled at the sight of his weeping mother.

Laying the phone on the table, she dries her cheeks roughly with her palms, and sits for an instant staring across the big apartment kitchen. It is warm and welcoming in the elegantly countrified style popular in Milan, with the battery of copper pots above an imposing La Cornue stove, the willow baskets, the refrigerator plastered with family photos, the walls bright with naïve paintings of village scenes from Madagascar.

On the table beside Roby's laptop, her iPad sits crowded with messages from her Cattolica students. In the last few years she has tried to ease her way out of teaching to concentrate on writing and translation, but her introductory course on Black American literature remains phenomenally popular. They've just reached *The Bluest Eye,* which she swaps in every other year for Gaines's *A Lesson Before Dying,* and as usual the kids have much to say. Outside the windows, the winter twilight glows over Piazza Maria delle Grazie, where the ancient church cradles its Leonardo masterpiece in darkness. Sometimes, Bertine and Shay spoke of Bertine's visiting Italy, to see cathedrals, city crowds, falling snow, and that grand painting. It was a half-jesting fantasy they constructed together, one that Shay was willing to help bring to reality. In a few years, Bertine would say. When her son and her array of young cousins, nieces, and nephews were all settled; when enough work had been done.

As these thoughts pass through her mind, suddenly Roby surprises her by rising from his chair, draping his muscular rugby player's arm around her shoulders, and giving her a clumsy squeeze. *"Mi dispiace, Mamma,"* he mumbles, adding in English: "She was your one friend in Madagascar."

"That's not so!" blurts out Shay, startled and touched by his thoughtfulness, but also stung in some tiny snobbish part of her by the fact that, after twenty years of Madagascar, her sole friend there should be said to be a housekeeper. Though as she says it, she knows her son's observation is accurate. On Naratrany she has grown close to many people, Malagasy and European, but there has never been anyone like Bertine. No one else whose blood seems to flow in the same rhythm as hers, whose existence seems oddly synchronized with her own, in spite of their inconceivably different lives. The news of her death makes Shay feel a peculiar slackening, an uncertainty of equilibrium, as if unknowingly she'd been one of a pair of conjoined twins. And now, down in Africa, the other half of the dyad has been cut cleanly away.

"What's going to happen to Anse?" Roby and his sister spent many a summer afternoon with Anse and his cousins, building campfires on the rocks, and fishing from a rickety pirogue.

"He'll be fine, darling. He's a grown man, remember, and he has a good job with the dive center."

Roby makes an indecipherable noise, his restless green eyes—Senna's eyes—fixed on the laptop screen where his uncorrected essay sits. "It's just wrong how people can just die in that country. Die from nothing."

"Bertine didn't just die of nothing. She had heart disease—at least we think that's what it was."

"Well, did anyone even help her?" demands Roby. Ever since he and his sister, Augustina, became teenagers and took the ills of mankind on their shoulders, they've assumed a condemnatory manner when they speak of the Red House, as they might of a colonial enclave where their parents keep barracoons of slaves. (This disapproval doesn't keep them from enjoying vacations in that same house.)

Senna shrugs off their criticism, pointing out that big villas and hotels are the main source of employment on Naratrany, now that the sugar mill has shut down. But Shay can't endure needling from her kids, whose young lives, to her mind, have been one long lesson in the old Black liberal canon of values absorbed from her own parents. Identity. Respect. Responsibility toward one's brethren. Imparted to her son and daughter with an evangelistic zeal meant to offset what Shay privately views as the primordial Italian cynicism that forms the other half of their legacy. How can they hint that their mother could wrong other people of color?

So she snaps back at her son. "Roby, of course we helped! You know perfectly well that the people who work for us are all properly registered with the *mairie*, and that includes health care. We did everything possible!" With this, she gets up from the table, stalks into the hall lavatory, and slams the door in a way that is the worst kind of example for a teenage child.

Those independent tears start to flow again as she stares in the mirror at her face with its very American mixture of races, the countenance that has defined her throughout her life. Shay's supremely practical mother, the library administrator, once confided a very impractical belief: that when someone in your family dies, your face changes. Small things—the curve of a cheek, the angle of an eye—shift position, not because of ravaging grief, but because of an actual reconfiguration of reality. Regarding herself now, Shay imagines her features look somehow flatter, as if a subtle dimension has been lost. Does that mean that Bertine was indeed family?

The questions hover in her mind as she lies in bed that night. She is glad that Senna isn't there; over the last few years they have been growing apart—for the most part, amicably—and now his extended absences no longer distress her. And tonight she needs solitude, to remember and to grieve. The bedside lamp extinguished, her hand on *The Bluest Eye*, she observes the glow of the Via Ruffini streetlights through the long window. The bedroom, a place of upholstered comfort, with Manzoni drawings, stacks of American and Italian magazines, an eiderdown-covered bed, an armoire from Senna's childhood house in Vercelli, a carefully hung patchwork quilt stitched by Shay's great-grandmother in Raleigh, is, here in Italy, the center of her domestic universe. It's a place that Bertine, familiar with every inch of Shay's sparsely furnished bedroom in that other world, the Red House, could never have envisioned. But tonight, between sleep and waking, Shay feels the tall Sakalava woman as a distinct arrival here in Milan. Undeterred by rules of time and space, she has made the trip of which they always spoke. She has come not as a phantom evoking fear, but as a tranquil, unwavering presence, a still flame illuminating a request for reflection, for setting memories in order. As she herself so often brought order into Shay's life.

And so, who is Bertine? Your Bertine, as Senna has too often called her. He tosses off the words with a jaunty Italian disregard for political correctness, though—or perhaps because—he knows it annoys his wife. It is part of the covert war of values that has gone on for years between them, though he long ago charmed his American in-laws into admiring him as unbiased, earthy, delightfully European. Senna pronounces Bertine's name with the carelessness he uses in speaking of women he considers unattractive. And with a tinge of the distrust a man holds for the woman he knows is his wife's confidante, familiar with all his failings.

Your Bertine. The possessive pronoun is not quite used in the slaveowner's sense, as in the abolitionist novel *Our Nig* (which Shay sometimes assigns as extra reading), but in the casually demeaning way a white American matron, in the 1950s, might refer to her Black maid. The way that rich women on Naratrany—disconcertingly, both the Malagasy and the white—still refer to their servants: *"Ma petite Angeline. Mon Jeannot."* Shay and Bertine could easily fit into this queasy traditional scenario, since Bertine works for Shay. But, as Shay increasingly understands throughout the nearly two decades they know each other, it is impossible to say which of them is really in charge.

In Shay's parents' house in Oakland, a big gold-framed oil painting hangs in the dining room. It is the work of a great-aunt, a Harlem Renaissance painter, and it depicts a French porcelain doll in eighteenth-century court dress, with powdered curls and rouged cheeks with beauty spots. The doll is propped stiffly on a toy chair, but in the darkness behind the chair, the observer can just discern a second, larger, doll: a Black Mammy, standing in attendance. When Shay and her sister, Leila, are little, they are afraid of this looming, half-hidden Black doll, believing she comes to life at night. In her turban and brass earrings, with red lips and eyes gleaming through the shadows, she is more a fetish than a plaything: an almost demonic presence who clearly dominates her frivolous porcelain mistress. Throughout Shay's childhood, that image haunts her.

In her studies, she has observed the roles of master and servant in the work of authors as different as Hansberry, Genet, Twain, Defoe, Faulkner. With her students she suggests analysis of the theme as a key to understanding African-American literature. She has long planned an article on Alice Childress's *Like One of the Family*, a subversive 1950s comic novel narrated in the voice of a Black cleaning woman. But literary tropes and Hegelian metaphysics shed no light on her rapport with Bertine.

Bertine is simply herself. Marie-Albertine Fantokony, nicknamed Bertine la Grande. A Malagasy woman born and raised on the island of Naratrany; a pure Sakalava, of the people who once ruled the western half of all Madagascar. Mother of a son, and former wife of a cane worker, who long ago departed for the Grand Île. Her appearance is a template of her relations, who live tucked away on their smallholdings of manioc and rice in the hills of Naratrany's interior: tall, muscular people, with brown-black skin and round, delicate-featured faces that ordinarily wear an amiable inquiring look, but that, under threat, mask themselves in impassivity. Only five years older than Shay, she seems almost a generation removed, perhaps because of her air of authority, her conservative way of dressing, and the hair that she wears neither straightened nor braided with extensions but bound in six traditional knots, divided with geometrical precision, and protected by an array of enormous hats. Her strong teeth are yellowed from smoking her favorite Good Look cigarettes. Her dark eyes hold a submerged spark, like a torch burning deep in the sea.

To an outsider, Bertine might seem insignificant, a single Black note in the unending song of toil that is the life of the poorest people in one of the poorest countries on earth. For many of the years Shay knows her, she divides her days among three jobs. In the mornings she works as laundress and head housekeeper at the Red House. In the early afternoons, she washes and irons linens at the Rayon Vert, a small French hotel on the cliffs down the beach. In the early evening she returns to the Red House, to give paid massages to the Sennas' family members and guests. Then the two-mile walk back to Renirano village, and the household of which she is the main support. She balances this punishing schedule with a calm, almost nonchalant air, never seeming hurried or out of sorts.

Better educated than most village women, she speaks, in addition to her own tongue, fluent French, some Italian, and even a few phrases of English. She herself has not traveled far: to the windy northwestern city of Diego Suarez, to the sapphire mines on the nearby island of Kely, to her father's ancestral territory on the Grande Île. Still, she is anything but limited: her viewpoint is open and broad, and she has an innate confidence rooted in feeling at all times attuned to herself, to the land around her. Shay—who still has moments of feeling foreign in Italy, and even more so in Madagascar—sees this confidence as the source of Bertine's power.

Shay has felt that power since the early days in Madagascar, when she and Bertine are united by involvement in a household drama that Shay's memory has begun to frame almost as a legend. At the same time, she knows what she saw—and over time she has met other sojourners in African nations who have witnessed similar things: occurrences for which there is no rational explanation. The few people to whom she has told the story are drawn from among these believers; they nod gravely as she describes how in the first years of the Red House, the villainous manager Kristos uses sorcery to try to steal the property, and harm her and Senna. And how it is Bertine who sees the danger and intervenes, bringing magic to fight magic. It's a fantastical story, and, as in *The Arabian Nights,* the final scene is also the opening of a new narrative: the tale of Bertine and Shay.

After the precipitate departure of Kristos, and the completion of the housewarming ceremony, Shay asks Bertine how she can repay her for her help. And Bertine gives her a measuring look—the spark flaring deep in those eyes—and replies without hesitation that she'd like something for her own house. Something important: an aluminum roof. And so it begins in those early years: the give-and-take, the exchange of gifts both immaterial and material. Shay promptly provides Bertine with *ariary* to pay for the corrugated metal sheets that, up until then, Shay has considered the emblem of shantytown misery, part of the squalid improvised architecture of townships and favelas. But for Bertine and her village neighbors, the aluminum roof is a luxury that means protection from vermin, from rain and cyclone winds. It adds value to her home and increases her reputation as a person of substance.

Oddly enough, though Shay often bikes or drives through Renirano village, it is years before she visits the house on which she helped to put a roof. Bertine doesn't invite her, and she doesn't press for an invitation.

This is partly due to protocol, to avoid jealousy from the other Red House employees. But also Shay feels strangely reluctant to see the dwelling where Bertine lives with her son, a revolving cast of nieces and nephews, and an aunt too old to work. She senses herself easing into this connection, the way you do into a serious love affair.

At the end of that dramatic summer of Kristos, Shay bids Bertine farewell and calls her "sister"—a title that Bertine neither accepts nor rejects. But the passing years witness a slow braiding of intimacy between the two women; despite the vast difference between their lives, they share an instinctive loyalty similar to the unshakable bond Shay has with her actual sister, Leila, now a Cal mathematician immersed in a world of vectors and Boolean strings. Can there be such a thing as a sibling unrelated by blood or culture?

Their rapport deepens over nearly two decades of Shay's sojourns in Madagascar. If somebody asks Shay whether she feels at home in the African country where she spends two months a year, she laughingly declares that she's already an expatriate in Italy, and that takes up enough energy— her marriage is registered, her children born, her work centered in Milan, on the foggy Pianura Padana. The other half of her heart belongs to America, her birthplace, whose involute history of flawed idealism, spilled blood, justified crimes, and scrambling ambition shaped her family tree, and her soul. She and Senna have established an unspoken agreement that Madagascar should be considered somehow outside the places that matter deeply for them. On the surface, they view their house on Naratrany with the same sense of complacency and responsibility as well-heeled Californians might feel toward a beach place in Hawaii. But, like Hawaii, Madagascar has its own fabulously complex identity, and is not to be taken lightly. Building on such terrain has consequences: attachments root and expand in unexpected corners, the way that a tough network of sea grapes can cover a whole beach.

Through the years, Bertine is not always present at the Red House; like any other employee she comes and goes, takes leave to help with rice harvests, with family sickbeds, circumcisions, or funerals. But more than any other of the household staff, she is present; and in Shay's memory, daily life on Naratrany is marked off by Bertine's schedule.

In the early mornings, after the bleary-eyed night watchmen have opened the shutters and slid apart the heavy carved wooden doors that block the gateway—pausing before leaving to flirt with the arriving maids—Shay, from her bedroom, can hear Bertine's voice. It tolls softly around the veranda, as she chivies her minions, the younger women, in the unrelenting cyclic tasks necessary to keep up such a large, open-air house in such a climate: sweeping up drifted husks of insects, dead geckos, fallen fragments of ceiling thatch; polishing the red floors with coconut fiber; treating furniture against rot with beeswax and turpentine; battling mildew; chasing palm rats; shooing wandering chickens; dislodging cockroaches and centipedes hidden behind books and cushions. The heart of her realm is the laundry that she and Shay designed after the departure of Kristos. It is a place of order and serenity, with its swept bare earth, concrete washbasins, the lines of white sheets bleaching in the sun, the shaded ironing porch with padded tables and smell of hot starch; the huge latticed airing closet, its shelves stacked with clove-scented linens.

Bertine's authority commands respect from everyone in the household— even the series of temperamental male cooks who dominate the Red House kitchens over the years—endowing her nickname, Bertine la Grande, with the air of a title. House managers (who never seem to last more than a year or two in the Sennas' employ) treat her with caution. If there is a problem with wages or hours, it is she who speaks for all of the staff.

After the midday meal, Bertine exchanges the Red House uniform of floral *lambahoany* and white T-shirt for her own long skirt and blouse, lights a Good Look cigarette from the pack she stores in her oversize cap, and, cigarette in mouth, vanishes into the network of back paths through the cane fields; she is on her way to her second job. Le Rayon Vert is a popular stopoff for French trekkers exhausted by long Grande Île excursions in the Ankarana wilderness or the primeval rain forest of Ranomafana. In dusty hiking boots, they lounge in the tiny bamboo bar, swigging Three Horses beer, swapping photographs of lemurs and chameleons, and arguing about ecology. Meanwhile, inside the guest huts, Bertine silently replenishes their meticulously laundered sheets and towels.

At five in the evening, as the sun disappears behind the headlands, Bertine lights another Good Look and walks down the beach, back to the Red House. As the Red House family and guests return to their rooms to rest and shower before dinner, she begins two hours as a freelance masseuse.

Sometimes as Shay and her family are taking the last swim of the day, reluctant to leave the warm ocean beneath the tumultuous glowing sunset, she catches sight of Bertine approaching along the already darkened shore, silhouetted, but unmistakable in her height and the shape of her imperial cap. The sight of her against the obscurity of the palms and sea pines, a tall moving shadow among shadows, fills Shay with a strange mixture of apprehension and delight.

"Bertine's coming!" screech the children, jumping up and down in the waves and halloing, as if they haven't just seen her in the morning.

"Eccola là!" exclaims Senna, with grudging admiration. "You can set your watch by that one."

In these evening arrivals, Bertine assumes a different role. At the threshold of the Red House, she announces herself as if she were a visitor, calling out *"Hodi!"* in the formal fashion and exchanging pleasantries with the night watchmen. Once on the veranda, she sits down on the couch, and is ceremoniously served a Coca-Cola by the youngest of the evening housemaids. Then she retires to the little garden hut under the kapok tree, which has been set up for massages. With its high padded table veiled in mosquito netting, its pot of coconut oil, its dim overhead light, its wooden bas-relief carved with a procession of naked, faceless women, it is as intimate as a confessional.

If it is Shay's day for a massage, she arrives wearing a pareo, strips, and lies down in front of Bertine. And Bertine spends the next half hour dipping her hands—those strong, fine-boned hands, which, like her feet, are unusually small—into the oil, and healing Shay. Yes, healing, though Shay cannot say of what ills. A spell comes over the two of them, an almost religious focus. Massage is an age-old art in Madagascar, but this is not like other therapies, where tight muscles are kneaded, or lymph urged to flow, or pressure points painfully addressed. No, Bertine's massage seems almost haphazard: perhaps a light circling around a vertebra that suddenly results in a tiny click that, in turn, elicits a deep chuckle from Bertine. *"Hah—ça commence à bouger!"*

Nothing dramatic happens in these massages, which Red House guests sometimes complain are too short, as if she were cheating them even of the minuscule price—a few euros—that they pay her. But the effects accumulate, and Shay finds her body settling almost miraculously into its proper alignment and balance, its relation to the earth and sky. Bertine says she is opening Shay's shoulders, freeing up the center of her back, and releasing what she calls *les nerfs*. Bertine calls everything a nerve, even the heart.

Their conversation on these occasions has the same cumulative effect. They talk constantly, keeping their voices low, because there is always somebody eavesdropping, one of the maids or the Vezo watchmen, though these young men speak little French. As in a petty royal court, everyone in the Red House wants to know what Shay is plotting with her favorite.

Sometimes the two of them are, in fact, discussing the staff. Ever since the downfall of Kristos, this is a sensitive subject, and often Bertine comments darkly on the machinations of certain men and women also working at the house, whom she suspects of plotting tirelessly, with or without magic, to seize power, and steal from the Sennas. In Bertine's strict canon, people are divided into *bien* and *pas bien*. The *pas bien* employees must not be fired, except in extreme cases, but must be closely watched, and thwarted.

At times they talk, sotto voce, about Senna. As their children grow older, Shay has reluctantly become aware that she and her husband have less and less in common; or maybe there wasn't much to start with, except for their two fiercely independent natures. Now, as the fascination of their mutual foreignness wears away over the years, they find they share few tastes and interests outside of family life, and it is easy to let that independence pull them apart. Graver than this, she is beginning to realize that buried deep in their marriage is a permanent incomprehension, a profound disagreement as to what truly matters in life. To Bertine, she simply complains that Senna is testy, domineering, a casual philanderer, a mass of ego.

But Bertine, so earnest about many small things, is dismissive on this topic. *"Ca c'est les hommes, partout"* is her invariable response. Men, everywhere, are all the same. She adds that it is written nowhere, not even in the Bible, that men and women would enjoy living together. She herself has aspiring suitors, but is too busy to take care of a man. In her opinion, Shay should hold on to Senna, as every *bien* woman holds on to her property, by treating him like a child: spoiling him, ignoring his tantrums, pardoning his occasional infidelities, remembering, with affectionate patience, that he is by nature irresponsible and immature. One night, however, late in their acquaintance, Bertine remarks in a reflective tone: "But if you want to leave him, you'll know the right time. You can't leave Madagascar, though. Not after all these years."

Shay can imagine how the massage scene would look to someone spying on them, as is probable. In the weak overhead light through the straw shade, inside the limp mosquito net, Bertine stands tall and imposing in sweeping print skirt and blouse, her hat removed to reveal the gleaming Sakalava knots on her round head, which tilts as she casually kneads Shay, sometimes with only one hand, which looks dark as a root against Shay's bare copper-colored skin. Stretched out on the table, whose spotless white cover also represents the work of Bertine's hands, lies the mistress of the house, helpless as an infant, naked as a worm. Only after Bertine's death does she reflect that, while her friend often saw her bare body, she never saw Bertine other than fully clothed.

On some evenings Shay hears about Bertine's childhood in the rugged interior of Naratrany, where, in the high forest, she was raised by her grandmother, who was a *moasy,* a healer. "She knew everything about plants," Bertine says. "She knew how to give a serious massage; to set bones; to cure illness. People would travel from other islands to get her treatments. She lived to be a hundred and thirty years old."

Occasionally Shay suspects that Bertine might be inventing things;

after all, the Rayon Vert is overflowing with French trekkers who adore fantastic tales about Madagascar. "How do you know that?" she demands once, raising her head.

"Put your head down! I know because my grandmother had a paper with her confirmation date from *le bon père,* the French priest. And also, when she was very little, she began to put a little stone in a glass bottle at every rice harvest. It was what people did to mark the years. When she died, we counted them: one hundred twenty-four. She was always healthy, always looked the same. She said it was because she ate only rice she grew herself. She tried to teach me about plants and medicine, but I was young and impatient to leave the village. I wanted to see what life was like on the other side of the island, where there was a port and towns full of *vaʒaha.*"

Shay imagines young Bertine, afire with curiosity, moving from one culture to another, as her future gradually takes shape. She recalls her own feverish childhood dreams of traveling to every country, of learning how other peoples lived and ate and spoke. It's a restiveness that Shay thinks is signaled in the mixed races of her family tree: the forebears who, desperate for work, or lusting for change, postslavery or postimmigration, encountered each other while scattering around the North American continent like blown seeds. The exception is her father's people, the Gilliams, free North Carolina Blacks who, from the 1700s until after the Vietnam war, lived to themselves on their own remote Tidewater acres. And these inbred, solidly rooted artisans and tobacco farmers were known for their longevity, surviving into their nineties, even past a hundred.

She tells Bertine about them, and Bertine says it means that they were good people. "But you and I won't get that old. And no one on this island will ever again live as long as my grandmother."

Their talks make up a single rambling conversation: organic, epic, stretching over years. Shay rarely thinks of it when she is away from Madagascar, leading her busy life in Milan. Yet when she comes back to the Red House and lies down on the table with Bertine, it is as if no time has passed at all. Changes are marked by Shay's changing body. "You are a little fatter. A little thinner. This ankle will have you limping down the beach if you are not careful. This lump on your left shoulder is a nerve, connects to the heart. Your right shoulder is crooked. Did you do the chair exercises I taught you?"

One time, when they are both in their forties, Bertine remarks, out of nowhere: "Your body is still young." She says it dispassionately, without envy. But in her words Shay finds a stinging reminder that a life without hard physical work represents not normality but luxury.

Bertine herself remains physically much the same, though her large breasts grow slightly pendulous, and her once flawless teeth become increasingly discolored from the harsh Good Look cigarettes. A cough plagues her from time to time, but her health seems good except for a dangerous bout of chikungunya, which sweeps through Naratrany one winter and briefly reduces her to an alarming thinness.

Once she suffers a bad burn on her arm, from an accident with a cooking brazier. Bertine refuses to go to the Sennas' friend Dr. Pau, or to the Dominican clinic, but treats it herself with one of her grandmother's remedies: poultices of wild sweet potato leaves, and a paste of blue clay from the southwest of the Grand Île. Shay, horrified by the ugly wound, returns after months have passed to find it miraculously healed: the skin completely unscarred, fresh and smooth as a baby's—a Caucasian baby's, since the large spot is barely pigmented. Soon it starts to freckle and to return to its normal deep plum. Bertine assures Shay that its proper darkness will be completely restored, adding haughtily that she certainly does not want a *vazaha* arm.

Bertine rarely talks about her troubles. But one day she arrives shaking with distress. A woman from Morombe on the Grande Île has shown up at her house: the new wife of Bertine's ex-husband, and Bertine by the rules of hospitality must host her. She is a woman of the Southern Sakalava, with a soft, wheedling voice; she comes with gifts, but also with a terrible demand: that Bertine's son, Anse, then eleven years old, go to live with the woman and his father in a remote country settlement, scores of kilometers into the interior. The woman is evil, declares Bertine. She has no surviving children, and the only reason she wants her stepson is to enslave him. She will hardly feed him, will work him to death herding cattle and planting rice out there in the bush.

By this time, in her experience with Madagascar, Shay knows that child slavery is a reality. Without hesitation, she goes to the safe in her bathroom, takes out money and a silver chain, and hands them to Bertine to pay for any bribery or sorcery she may need to resolve the problem. Bertine nods grimly. She will do what is necessary. After a few days the stepmother—who with blandishments and extravagant promises has nearly convinced the boy to depart with her—has a terrifying dream; she bolts out of Bertine's house like a dog when a crocodile comes at it. The next day she leaves the island, and Shay and Bertine rejoice.

When do gifts turn into the eternal familial, international flow so well known to immigrants? Shay falls into the habit of sending money via Western Union: the modest amount that will double Bertine's income and pay her son's fees at the Naratrany public schools. Once every two months in Milan, she stands in a seedy, fluorescent-lit office near the Stazione Centrale, shuffling along in a queue of Filipinos, Peruvians, Nigerians, Moldovans, Sri Lankans, all with the strained, calculating look of people supporting too many other people in villages far away.

It never seems enough; nothing does. If an Italian friend is traveling to Madagascar, Shay sends Bertine a skirt or a blouse with twenty-euro notes rolled small and inserted through slits along the seams. When Shay arrives at the Red House in July, or at Christmas, she is always laden with presents for the household staff: T-shirts; lace brassieres; baby clothes; school supplies; soccer shoes; hip-hop CDs. But for Bertine there is a special cache: a gold chain or ear studs, easy to sell to the Saint Grimaud merchants.

This contraband largesse, which no one else in the household notices, which not even Senna knows about, which Bertine receives with solemn thanks, and conceals in her big hat or in a battered *sobiky* basket, induces a low-key confusion in Shay. The giving feels like a blood offering, a payoff for a crime. There is guilt behind her giving, but also a hidden, unholy relish in being in the powerful position of giver. What if, as in a fairy tale, one sister is dirt poor, and the other is covered in jewels? Surely the jeweled sister does well to help the poor sister, or is it just an act of pride? And, because in fairy tales the truth is often occulted, is it possible that the poor sister possesses her own secret wealth, that in the end it is she who is richer?

One summer Bertine tells Shay that she wants to send her niece away to a boarding school run by Ursuline nuns. The girl is thirteen, and beginning to chafe at restrictions, to envy her bold girlfriends, just a few years older, who go out to the port bars, and accept invitations from the shifty-eyed French and Italian men waiting in ambush each day as the girls pour out of the Saint Grimaud lycée. Shay thinks of her own daughter, Augustina, nearly the same age, immersed in her world of gossip, volleyball, music lessons. And she immediately provides Bertine with the fee for two years in the convent, far from sex predators. A hundred and fifty euros, the Milan price of a pair of shoes.

Another year, Shay gets the idea that Bertine should buy a plot of land on Naratrany: she can profit by renting it to a villager who wants to grow rice or manioc. Bertine finds a small terrain already planted with rice and banana trees on the point out beyond the ruins of the old Indian settlement, and Shay smuggles her the sale price. Shay returns to Milan with the agreeable thought of Bertine easing further into prosperity. When next they see each other, she finds that Bertine has bought only half the tract. The other half of the money she has given to an aunt to open a food stall for the sapphire miners on Kely island. This is a smart investment, yet Shay is surprised to find herself swept by a feeling of angry betrayal. It is ignoble, she knows. Bertine is not a child or an instrument of hers. Why shouldn't she act according to the needs and loyalties of her own world?

In all the years of their acquaintance, Shay only visits Bertine at home one time. Though a confirmed Catholic—and, like all other Sakalava on the island, also bound to the old animist faith—Bertine has suddenly joined a new evangelical church. Since the turn of the millennium, as the political situation in Madagascar grows more chaotic, American missionaries have been diligently undermining the twin pillars of Islam and Rome. On

Naratrany, Seventh-Day Adventists and a host of emotive Protestant sects are battling to amass souls. The form of worship that has won Bertine's heart is that of a charismatic church called Cri au Seigneur—Cry to the Lord—which, Shay finds out, is based in Arkansas. The Naratrany congregation is so small that services are held in Bertine's house; and so, after long years, Bertine invites Shay home.

On a blazing hot Sunday morning in December, Shay makes her way down Finoana Beach to Renirano village. She is dressed modestly, and the awkward feeling of her long skirt recalls to her the time, many years earlier, when, dressed with similar ceremonial discomfort, she walked the same sandy route to meet Bertine—on their way to invoke magical powers to save the Red House. It is strange to remember her own ignorance of supernatural matters that for a long time now she has taken for granted.

A right turn from the beach through the mangroves, another turn onto the path behind the tourist shops and bars, past the Muslim graveyard, and she enters a maze of huts coated by windblown red dust, a place where plastic trash, caught on thornbushes, stuck to the trunks of palms, flutters in the breeze like banners for a celebration. Bertine's house stands within a low paling fence, in a carefully swept bare yard, where there are wandering a couple of ducks and an exceptionally fat turkey. Like the others, the house is built of bamboo and palm thatch, but Shay is glad to see that it is larger than the surrounding huts, solid and well maintained, with glimpses of aluminum under the thatch.

The dim room inside, stifling hot, and lit only by the doorway and a tiny window, has the intense atmosphere of orderliness that Shay associates with Bertine. Clothes (including a trio of large hats) and *sobiky* baskets full of possessions hang on nails, and a wooden double bed has been lifted and leaned against a wall. In the center, raffia mats have been spread on the plank floor, and a dozen men and women are kneeling there, crowded together. Half of them are people she knows: market vendors, hotel maids, fishermen, the man who sells octopus to her kitchen. As Shay enters, offering greetings, they rise and part like the Red Sea, gravely regarding her, the self-conscious guest of honor, as Bertine leads her to a single rickety

chair placed at the front right-hand corner. Everyone is dressed up. Bertine
is formal in an elaborate pale blue skirt and blouse, her hair no longer in
knots but braided in spiraling cornrows, joining in a neat chignon. The
minister, an impassive Merina man, is wearing a starched white shirt with
a tie, and reminds Shay of the long-ago pastor of her grandmother's church
in Oakland.

It is, she guesses, nearly a hundred degrees inside Bertine's crowded
house, and Shay struggles not to feel faint as she endeavors to follow the
Malagasy service. She slips into the routine she developed for the many
Catholic ceremonies she has attended with Senna's huge family: following
the congregation in rising, kneeling, or sitting; catching the tonal flow of
unknown hymns; mumbling rhythmically along with prayers.

This works until, after a long sermon that tests her ability to maintain
an air of pious interest, the Malagasy minister suddenly calls out a command. At once, Bertine steps forward and turns to face Shay and the rest
of the tiny congregation, and at her signal, the men and women rise from
the mats, raise their arms high in the air, and begin shaking and wringing
their hands toward the sky, as, at the top of their lungs, they scream out:
"Jesu—Jesu—Jesuuuu!" The sudden cacophony is shocking, uncanny,
for an instant filling Shay with fear, and even a flash of repulsion. Long,
quavering screams of agony, entreaty. The walls of Bertine's house seem to
pulse with the extremity of people whose struggles and anguish, normally
contained under the iron level of necessity, now explode in this heartrend-
ing howl that surely reaches all over the island, and up to the stars that
daylight conceals. Though Shay gets up from her chair, and raises her arms
with the others, she knows that she dare not add her voice. To join in out
of mere courtesy would try the patience of whatever powers watch over
Madagascar.

As the honored *vazaha* guest, Shay knows she is expected to pay for
the feast from the food stall, the samosas, *brochettes*, and pasta that are
Sunday delicacies for the villagers. She will eat a few bites, then politely
escape from the unbearable heat of the packed hut, and make her way
down the beach to the ample cool spaces of the Red House. But she also

senses that she'll go with a feeling of lack: aware that Bertine, in her own house, hurling her voice toward heaven, for an instant accessed a powerful mystery from which she herself was excluded.

This and other episodes convince Shay that Bertine's inner life is, for her, unfathomable. But there is one time when, clumsily, she goes right to the core of it.

It is when Bertine becomes a grandmother. Shay learns of the coming event one August night, when she and Senna and some friends are strolling along the crowded thoroughfare of outdoor restaurants and bars in Fino-ana village and come upon Bertine's son, Anse, uproariously drinking beer at an outdoor stall with his friend Basile, who works as a security guard. Anse is twenty, and recently started work at the dive center for the Hotel Chambord, and Shay greets him with the warmth of an honorary aunt.

The two young men are slightly drunk. They boast to her that they are celebrating the fact that Anse's girlfriend, Titine, is pregnant.

Shay looks in amazement at Anse, a handsome, lanky fellow who has Bertine's plum-black skin, round face, and protruding ears. "You're having a child?" she demands.

"I am a grown man with a job and my own place to live!" he tells her defiantly, and Shay kisses him, wishes him well, and goes on her way, hoping that her own kids don't give her any similar news for a long time.

The next evening she chaffs Bertine. *"Et alors, ma p'tite grandmère!* You didn't tell me Anse was going to be a father!"

They are in the massage hut, already under the veil of the mosquito net, and she sees the other woman freeze. Then she realizes that Bertine did not know. That her son, in fear of his mother's reaction, has chosen her, Shay, as the vessel to pass on the news. And Shay has announced it in this bumbling, disrespectful way. For the first time in their acquaintance she sees the regal Bertine la Grande absolutely stunned, wavering on her feet, seeming to need support. A cosmic dissonance seems to vibrate through the small scene.

Shay grabs her by the arms, and makes her sit down on the high massage table, where even tall Bertine's feet don't quite touch the ground. For an instant the other woman stares in bewilderment at Shay, who is gabbling the story of her encounter with Anse. Just for an instant, and then Bertine's eyes regain their steadiness. That deep submerged spark glows again, lighting a way far inward to a place of reckoning where Bertine weighs the meaning of the new situation, not just for her precarious domestic economy, but in the repositioning of family structure, the framework of ancestors.

"Un petit enfant, une grandmère, c'est pas une blague. C'est une chose serieuse," Bertine says slowly. Not as an intended rebuke to Shay, though the statement itself does painfully rebuke her. Just as a reflection, as if Bertine is talking to herself.

They pause like that for what could be a minute or a year. Two women under a dim light in a small shelter as frail and rudimentary as a crèche. Shay, half-naked in her hastily tied pareo, realizes that for the first time, she is standing in the healer's position, stroking Bertine's shoulder, while Bertine sits weighed down by her overpowering reality. It is the reverse pose of Shay's old family painting of the mistress and servant dolls, and this scene, too, has the quality of a painting: an annunciation, locked in time and to be framed in Shay's memory with the dark luminosity of an icon. Both women are nearly fifty, and though they don't know it, Bertine has just one more year to live. She will welcome a grandson into the world, healthy and strong, and she will work at the Red House until the day she dies.

The last time Shay and Bertine see each other is early on a January morning, just before the Sennas leave for the airport at the end of the Christmas holidays. Shay has given the usual generous tips to the rest of the Red House staff who have gathered on the veranda to bid the Sennas farewell. To Bertine, in front of the envious eyes of the others, Shay presents a basket with a pair of her Thai trousers that Bertine has always admired. Seeded in the folds of the fabric is yet another sizable wad of *ariary* bills.

Bertine is holding one of her indestructible puffy caps, and suddenly, like a magician, she pulls out of it a small bag, one of the quickly discarded kind that flutter bleakly on village thornbushes. She hands it to Shay, and inside is a pair of earrings, the kind sometimes found in market stalls. The earrings are large dangling oblongs of thick glossy plastic, colored deep blue, like the sea in the strait in front of the Red House, or like the sapphires that the ragged miners dig out of the mud on Kely island.

Bertine has given Shay presents before: oily bunches of fresh vanilla beans, hand-stitched Richelieu tablecloths. But never before a piece of jewelry. It is a graceful response to the many gold necklaces and earrings that Shay has rather cynically bestowed on Bertine over the years, to be exchanged for money at the Indian trader's. Shay feels a flash of alarm at the fact that Bertine has wasted money on a present that, even at the village market, cannot have been cheap, but then she sees Bertine's glow of delight.

"I knew blue was your color," says Bertine. "Put them on!"

Shay puts them through her ears, and against her sun-bleached hair and skin speckled from two months on the island, the earrings shimmer. She hugs Bertine and feels that work-hardened body against her own, breathing in her familiar smell of laundry soap and Good Look cigarettes. It is the last time they will embrace.

Shay wears Bertine's earrings on the whole long flight from Madagascar to Italy, but, once she is in Milan, they make no sense at all. They are too tropical for the cold north; not amusing examples of folk art; not exotic enough to be conversation pieces at dinner parties and *vernissages*. She displays them on a jewelry rack in her bathroom, where every morning she sees them with a sense of lightness and warmth.

That spring heralds a chaotic period in Shay's life. The hidden obstruction that has always existed between her and Senna has surfaced after what started as a debate over Roby's college plans—whether, like his sister, he should study in the United States—touches off a bitter dispute about education and snobbery, American versus Italian family values. That summer, for the first time in many years, the Senna family does not vacation in Madagascar, as husband and wife, feuding, have decided to spend time apart. This is not the first time this has occurred in their volatile marriage, but it has an unusually trenchant feeling to it. A French travel agency rents out the entire Red House, week by week. Senna joins old friends to sail from Brindisi to the Dodecanese. Augustina has a research job on campus at Brown, Roby and his cousin Filippo are busing tables on Cape Cod, and Shay goes first to Rome to research the Black actor John Kitzmiller, and then to Oakland, where her father is recovering from surgery. By the end of August, the scattered family reunites in Italy, and Shay and Senna, as is their longtime habit, establish an uneasy truce. In September, Senna leaves to spend several months at the Red House, to oversee a venture into resort construction more ambitious than anything he has ever undertaken. Things are changing in Madagascar, he declares; it is the moment to invest.

Shay remains in Milan. In all these months she has, as always, sent money to Bertine, but otherwise hardly thought about her, until the call arrives with news of her death.

The next day, Shay tracks down Anse—being of the new generation, he has lately acquired a cell phone. In a grief-choked monotone, he gives the simplest explanation of his mother's death: she smoked too much, she worked too hard; she grew old too early, and her heart broke apart. *"Son coeur s'est cassé."*

Shay asks where Bertine will be buried, and is astonished to hear that she will not be laid to rest on Naratrany, where she was born. No: Anse and a group of his cousins will depart that afternoon to take his mother's body on a two-day journey over land and sea to a Sakalava village far inland on the Grande Île, beyond the Sambirano River, called Tanindrazana. It is where her ancestors have their tombs.

"I will visit the tomb when I come back to Madagascar," Shay says. And she is surprised to hear Anse's mournful, distant voice take on a tinge of amusement.

"Non, Maman, there are no roads there. No *vazaha* has ever been in that place," he says. Adding: "Oh, please excuse me for calling you *'Maman'!"*

"It's all right to call me that," replies Shay. "And I'll go there, and find her, no matter how long it takes."

Anse responds with something that sounds like "she said that," or "she knew that"—*Elle le disait,* or *Elle le savait.* It is hard to tell, through the crackling static. She instructs Anse to contact her when he needs anything for himself or his little boy, and then the call ends.

Afterward, Shay goes and looks at the earrings Bertine gave her. When did they turn from deep blue to Black? Certainly the cheap dye is volatile, but she would have noticed before today that the color has entirely departed. She tests it against her cell phone screen to make sure. Yes, the earrings are now black as onyx, black as the twilight over the island, out of which Bertine used to materialize with her unvarying punctuality.

Shay will take them with her when she embarks on the long journey to say a proper farewell. Perhaps she is presumptuous to feel that she is in any way a relation of Bertine. Yet Shay finally sees that in some mysterious fashion the other woman was indeed her twin, or maybe her proxy, standing in for her on the hard path of privation as she herself trod the path of ease. She has always associated Bertine with shadows, but the truth is that they were each other's shadow. Shay was the rootless outsider, whose life of privilege carried with it blindness, pride, and scattershot ignorance, and Bertine was the one who belonged, who saw, and who brought order by naming things for what they were. Who taught her that light and darkness, like wealth and poverty, like foreigner and native-born, are indisseverably joined to each other. As are giving and receiving. Deep in her heart—which, unlike Bertine's great heart, has not been broken by the incessant toil of love—Shay recognizes that this truth is a sister's gift that will last. No matter, she thinks, how many of her own years remain to be counted, like small stones in a bottle.

Elephants' Graveyard

1. To Die in Madagascar

Morte magis metuenda senectus. *Old age should be feared rather than death.*

—Juvenal

A dying man has begged to come and complete his dying at the Sennas' villa on Naratrany. This becomes an explosive topic of discussion one hot January evening at the Red House, where all the houseguests seated around the dinner table are elderly men. None of them, however, are as cruelly stricken in years and fortune as the eighty-six-year-old supplicant—Eugenio Gaber, a once-legendary playboy nicknamed Burton (pronounced Boor-ton by his friends) because of a supposed liaison with a momentarily distracted Elizabeth Taylor on the set of *Cleopatra*.

Tonight being Monday, the Naratrany port bars and the billiard hall are closed, and the men at the Red House table have nothing whatever to do but gossip in a hyperdetailed manner more usual among high school girls. So they pour themselves more rum, and rehash the saga of how Burton, a garment manufacturer who got rich after the war by turning a parachute silk factory into a ladies' underwear empire, went on to become a producer of sword-and-sandal movies and an epic womanizer, who stood out even amid the fierce competition of *dolce vita* Rome. He was notorious for his flashy mane of thick Calabrian hair, his insatiable appetite both for *pasta all'amatriciana* and cocaine, his orgies with Roman society ladies and Cinecittà film goddesses amid the pop art of his Piazza Navona penthouse.

There are endless Burton stories. How he secretly traded places one night with Ava Gardner's chauffeur. How, in his leftist phase, he helped Godard shut down the Cannes festival in 1968. How he risked his life endless times with fast cars and vengeful husbands, survived a helicopter crash, quadruple bypass surgery, and a liver transplant. With all his hair intact, too. But now his luck has run out. The old barracks is collapsing at last, he recently told his longtime friend Senna in a hoarse, thready voice over the phone. And it seems that he wants his last view to be the dreaming azure of the Mozambique Channel, from Senna's pleasure palace on Finoana Beach.

"What does he want to end up here for?" demands Paolini, a filmmaker who spent years shooting documentaries throughout the tropics. "What about his family? His wife?"

"Rachele is his fourth wife, and she's just waiting for him to go," says Senna. "Can't stand to be under the same roof."

"His kids?" asks Gianfra', a grizzled yachtsman, the black sheep of his aristocratic Neapolitan clan, renowned both for his classical erudition and for escaping prison in Brazil.

"They don't speak to him. He never paid any attention to them, and now his money is finished. Neither of his daughters would agree to be a donor for the liver transplant. He had to wait for a stranger to die."

A silence falls for an instant over the long candlelit table, where a parade of carafes full of *rhum arrangé*—ginger, pineapple, vanilla, mangosteen— glitters through the cloud of cigarette smoke. And these worn-out adventurers, who all have picaresque pasts littered with discarded wives, lovers, fortunes, houses, countries, just sit there and consider how awful a father has to be so that his daughters reject him.

"How would he get here? He'd never survive an eight-hour plane ride," says Baptiste, a soft-voiced Frenchman, an artist who has earned unexpected fame as a body painter.

"Oh, he would survive *getting* here," says Senna, draining his rum. "They give him a year, maybe a little more, but you wouldn't know it to look at him. That transplanted liver is giving out, and the diabetes has taken over, but the old devil is full of energy. Still the same dandy as ever, strutting around with the suntan and the silk scarf. And that hair, thick and black as ever."

"Dyed!" interjects Biagio, once a Milanese celebrity hairdresser.

"No, no, Calabrian men are like that, the bastards. Thick black hair until they go into the coffin. Probably keeps growing even there."

The men around the table murmur enviously, and Docle, a former striker for Vicenza, rubs a big hand over his sparse silver locks and says: "So he gets here—then he'll need a nurse—"

Thunderous laughter rises to the high, palm-thatched ceiling, as always dotted with geckos waiting tensely for mosquitoes and moths.

"We can set him up with as many nurses as he needs!" declares Gianfra' with only a slightly guilty glance at Senna's wife, Shay.

Seated at the head of the table, Shay is the only woman at dinner that evening. She will fly back to Milan tomorrow morning, while Senna and his Rabelaisian cohorts remain for at least another two months.

She has been silent through the whole discussion. Sitting there in a composed manner, occasionally being rude enough to check her phone—but she doesn't need good manners with this lot. She claims her space, her position as hostess, with straight spine and sphinx-like smile, giving quiet directions to the staff serving dinner, herself dishing out the *fettuccine ai frutti di mare* with the beneficent air of an Olympian condescending to wait on mortals. Using the detachment she has developed to handle equivocal situations both in Italy and in Madagascar—*I am a distant ship; a tower in Aristophanean clouds*—she studies her husband and his cronies, who have already started to behave as she knows they always do when they have the Red House to themselves.

Somebody asks what will happen if Burton does die there.

"Well, it means a lot of red tape," says Docle, adjusting his flashy steel chronometer with an officious air, as if he were a barrister instead of a superannuated footballer. "He'll have to make arrangements for that beforehand. For shipping the body back. Cremation is against the law in Madagascar, you know."

There is a murmur of agreement. *They* know. Death, with all its intricate regalia of custom and legislation, is their favorite topic. More than sex, or even sports.

These men, these leathery comrades-in-arms, these quondam buccaneers of life, have been vacationing at the Red House for nearly two decades: first with an array of wives, children, girlfriends, and now, in their later years, relying on Senna's inexhaustible generosity to settle in for months of an unending Hemingway-style fishing trip (though no one ever mentions *The Old Man and the Sea*).

They are all retirees, who in the past have in some way distinguished themselves, even moved in grand company. But now their focus has grown smaller, their rituals of leisure repetitive and confining, as if they are all back at school. Like any other group of collegians, they have their private jokes, nicknames, spats, power struggles. And although they are mostly successful and prosperous, there hovers over their fraternity a manifest air of failure, though at what is unclear. Perhaps simply failure at remaining young.

On their endless vacation in paradise, they mess about in speedboats, pirogues, the Sennas' catamaran, Gianfra's plucky Frigate 27, laying waste to the Indian Ocean population of marlin and bonito. In the great expatriate tradition, they follow the unfolding fortunes of football leagues and Formula 1 racing on oversize satellite television screens that glow like beacons through the hot nights and mesmerize clusters of villagers standing discreetly in the shadows. As weeks pass, they grow purple-faced from Dzama rum, and shaky from regularly endured bouts of malaria. They fall ever deeper into the orgiastic pit of gorgeous young Malagasy prostitutes from the island bars.

Over slow-motion games of backgammon and *scopone* through the long afternoons of the rainy season, they swap stories: actresses and models conquered, legendary sports matches rigged, politicians bought off, fortunes made and lost, perils surmounted—that form an epic tapestry of mingled reminiscences and lies. On their cell phones, they peruse every online word of *Le Figaro* and *La Repubblica* and lengthily debate current events. But also—when there are no women their age around to jeer at them—they discuss horoscopes, recipes, health and beauty tips. In twos and threes, they quietly swap worries about blood pressure and ballooning prostates, and about the side effects of the small blue pills they all claim not to take, but which form the bedrock of their liberty.

And of course they derive melancholy enjoyment from the obituaries, which spur them to talk more and more, sometimes with boyish braggadocio, sometimes with crude mournfulness, about the many ways of departing life.

"What do you think, Shay?" demands Biagio—Shay's favorite—crinkling his small sun-yellowed eyes at her in a friendly fashion: "You're the mistress of the household. Shall we let Burton die here?"

It's a formulaic question, asked out of courtesy. All of them know that Senna and his American wife lead mostly separate lives, in one of those unofficial marital arrangements so familiar to all these Europeans, with their Catholic underpinnings. They know Shay comes rarely to Madagascar now that their son and daughter are at school in America. That, since their marriage began some years ago to crack and then crumble, she has mainly laid aside her role of decision making in the Red House.

Still, Shay doesn't mind being consulted. Without a glance at Senna, she replies in a thoughtful tone. "*Ma certamente.* Certainly, poor soul. I wonder why, though: Why would he want to travel so far away from everything he knows? What's here for him?"

A sudden hush falls, and then Biagio responds: "*Ahh—tutto.* Everything!"

"*Et in Arcadia ego,*" murmurs Gianfra'—though the choice of quotation, Shay reflects, is not a happy one.

"You know," pursues Docle, who always pushes things too far. "I doubt that he'll have strength to deal with the young girls of Naratrany. It might kill him right away!"

Biagio gives a bark of laughter. "*Ci metteró la firma!* I'd die that way in a heartbeat!"

Suddenly the men, even Senna, are ignoring Shay, detouring around her presence. As if she has already flown off to Europe to take her place among the distant pantheon of disapproving wives, ex-wives, mistresses, girlfriends, sisters. (Their mothers are all long departed and now inspire worship instead of guilt.)

Only for a second does Senna's gaze, from one end of the table, encounter that of Shay at the other end. Their glances flicker together and then spring apart, like the foils of equally matched duelists who down weapons at once, knowing each other's strategies too well. For a minute she sees him from a stranger's perspective: the jovial host, garrulous, openhearted, his frequent laughter deepening creases in an angular face marked from decades of savage subequatorial sunlight, narrow green eyes parsing life with an intensity she once found irresistible—and other women still do. But she knows that his clamorous extroversion conceals a complex nature that is melancholy, fanciful, full of odd impulses and regrets. Senna is the youngest of his friends, but will be seventy on his next birthday, and though he jokes incessantly about it, she knows that the thought casts him into despair.

Weary of the conversation, she excuses herself and stands up from the table, urging the others to remain seated—Gianfra', with his courtly manners, is already half on his feet. She knows the old lechers are looking her over, and she feels at ease, elegant in the way she intended when she bound her long braids in a wreath around her head and put on flowing silk trousers and a severe high-necked top.

She is aware also, with a twinge of malice, that the sight of her is an irritant to these codgers, who are decades older than she is, but to whom Senna's wife symbolizes old age, and all the women they've left behind. To them, in spite of her American origin and exotic brown skin, she is an unwelcome reminder of home: of lingering responsibilities, and the guilt-fogged landscape of past loves.

In their eyes she is the polar opposite of the girls who now obsess them: young Sakalava and Antandroy prostitutes who throng the island dance halls. Girls who may have seen fewer birthdays than these men's granddaughters, girls whose gleaming dark bodies, always new, always mysterious, always poised at the cusp of adolescence and womanhood, and always—for a very few euros—replaceable, are a path to forgetting the passage of years. But do the men really want to forget? Don't they talk of death all the time?

Shay goes into the kitchen and praises the cook, Denesian, for the chocolate mousse cake, her favorite, which he prepared for this, her last evening. And then, ritually, she scolds him for the huge heap of crab and shrimp shells he has allowed to accumulate in the sink in spite of much admonishment about just this failing. Denesian, a round-faced young Sakalava with a fake diamond earring and a cheeky grin, nods with fake compunction; he thinks her severity is a flirtatious joke. Though the Red House is running smoothly, both for family guests and as a bed-and-breakfast, there has been a noticeable change in morale since the death of Bertine, Shay's close friend, and the superintending housekeeper whose strictness set the tone for the staff.

In the hard fluorescent light, Shay can see that the cook's white uniform is dirty, his eyes are red, and his cheeks bulging with khat—sure sign of the good time coming. The time when the last *vazaha* woman departs, and the fraternity of old men takes over, when they close down the hotel wing and send the house manager on holiday. When the rowdy pensioners trundle in and out of the kitchen, assembling elaborate dishes of pasta and barbecuing gargantuan fish, as he, Denesian, lounges around swigging beer.

The cook's glance strays out the back door, where in the dark yard, near a glowing brazier, Shay can see the kitchen staff squatted convivially around a big communal bowl of rice. She also sees the dim outlines of others, young girls who do not work in the Red House: sisters and friends from nearby villages, possibly some who make their living in the bars, or by giving massages to tourists on the beach.

She knows that after she leaves tomorrow, girls will be all over the place. Combing out their weaves in the bedrooms, squealing and splashing in the swimming pool, dancing on the veranda, sitting at the table, putting their plump dark faces together to giggle and whisper like classmates in a high school cafeteria. Laughing dutifully at the salacious jokes of the old men, making sly comments in their own language that the men don't understand. And Shay has no illusions that her husband, Senna, is not caught up in all this.

"Bonsoir les filles!" she calls out, and the entire group of girls answers her in a sweet chorus from the darkness. *"Bonsoir, Madame!"*

What is there to say? Shay has no grudge against the girls who come to the house for the old men, for she knows who they are: desperately poor young Black women, practically children, scrambling to feed themselves and their families. Like every foreigner with a conscience, Shay has contributed time and money to the endless search for solutions on Naratrany: schools, clinics, craft collectives. Only to run up against the bare stony fact that doesn't require training in postcolonial theory to be understood: that nothing, but nothing, is as directly profitable as fucking tourists for cash.

Shay does not return to the dining table, but walks out of the house along the torchlit garden path to the beach. Her bare feet know every stone that she herself caused to be set in an irregular pattern, the feeling of the sand between them, the prickle of the succulent plants at the borders that she has fussed over with gardeners for many years. The air is full of the suffocating scent of ylang-ylang, with its bitter undertone she knows so well. Near the seawall, the swimming pool glows with eerie soft radiance, and there beside it she sees the outline of a small wooden statue, crudely carved by an island sculptor: a woman with braids, kneeling, quiet-faced. Senna, who long ago bought it by the roadside, jokingly named it Shay. Now Shay the woman glances at Shay the statue, and a sense of presence envelops her, as if the wooden form were a live being waiting to speak. Unconsciously she begins to unpin her own bound braids.

As she pauses, shaking out her hair, out of the darkness come voices: *"Madame? Madame?"*

It is the night watchmen: three or four young Vezo boys. Quiet youths with rusty sun-bleached hair, some still in their teens, who come from starving fishermen's settlements on the remote southwestern Madagascar coast. Born sailors, who read the stars like maps, who are rumored to see in the dark, to believe in mermaids; these are the guardians who patrol the Red House compound all night, clutching crude spears. It is common knowledge that, in dark corners of the garden and in the shadows of the beach wall, they also make love to the old men's girls, who are just the same age as they are—and who can blame them, or the girls?

Over the years, there have been many changing ranks of Vezo guardians, but all are fond of Shay, who gives them extra money for their families and brings them football jerseys from Italy. Tonight, as always when she has the peculiar idea of walking out on her own, they form a silent retinue around her, lighting the way with their cheap flashlights. Shay knows from experience that there is no way to shake them, so she calmly greets them and steps out on the sand.

Another world out here. The clear night sky thick with distant suns, hanging low, like dewdrops on a spiderweb. The mysterious southern constellations, whose outlines she has never learned though she has contemplated them for years from the decks of boats; for her they remain a vague tangle of altar, chameleon, centaur, cross. Armies of tiny crabs scattering at each of her footsteps. The waves starting to slap back in toward high tide like an engine starting and stopping. A smudge of darkness where the Grand Île lies in silhouette across the deeps of the Mozambique Channel. If she turns landward, the narrow pale beach spreads out to right and left like the wings of a seabird. Aligned along the shore, through the shadowy palms and sea pines, shine the lights of hotels and villas. And very close, overlooking the beach, is the great thatched roof and candlelit terrace of her own Red House, where Senna and his friends still sit around the table.

In the stillness between the breaking waves, the men's voices carry, layers of talk and laughter, and she hears that they are still discussing the eternal subjects. Sex—the power and the prowess of their bodies. Death—the final weakness and failure of those bodies. Sometimes they use the same vocabulary to speak about both.

"Well, the moment my heart decides to give me that final little caress, you fellows know what to do. Of course I've told the family, but if it happens here, I guess you all will have to handle it. Just lay me in a wooden pirogue somewhere in the out islands. Some rum, some kerosene, set it on fire and away I go."

"Hah! It's illegal, you know, sweetheart!"

"*Cazzo*—listen to the sad old fucker! He thinks he's a Viking . . ."

Houses, Shay reflects as she listens, have many acts and ages. For the Red House, there is first the honeymoon period, when she and Senna, newly married, enter into a part-time vacation life on the remote shores of Madagascar.

There follows the period of extravagant fertility, when the Red House explodes with the Sennas' small children and their friends: when there never seems to be an end to the animals and pets in the household: goats, chickens, zebu calves, cats, dogs, lemurs, tortoises.

Then comes the time of deepening search for understanding, independence, when the Senna kids are adolescents. In vacation time, the once peaceful house on Finoana Beach is crammed with teenagers from Europe and America; becomes a messy theater of idealism, of desperate romances, of silly political arguments, of dumb experiments with alcohol and drugs, of pointless accidents in boats and on motorbikes, of the chaotic disintegration of old ties.

And now, with a serious yet still undefined rift between her and her husband, has arrived the twilight period: the time of the dissolute elders. Senna himself creates it, with his chameleonlike capacity for reinvention, one year when he is appalled to discover his children grown and himself no longer young. Quickly, so quickly Shay can hardly comprehend it, his Milan company has been reshuffled, and he is deep in business projects in Madagascar that keep him on Naratrany for months. And in doing so he attracts a community of like-minded guests: this ribald fraternity of old white men raging against the dying of their light.

Senna, already once divorced, and with no desire for another messy uncoupling, tries to convince Shay that this is just a passing phase in a long marriage of two people who, it must be admitted, have always had very different ideas about life. Perhaps it is, alas—he muses aloud—that American women possess little comprehension of the flexibility, the almost religious generosity, required in lasting love: how petty betrayals, for example, have no importance. The fact is—he continues—that their love still exists, in a different way, and so there is no need for a dramatic rift. The kids are launched into their international future, about which he once had his doubts, but now approves. Shay has her university work and busy life in Milan, and Senna—well, he has always traveled. And now he hasn't really gone anywhere, has he? He's right there in their family vacation house, where they have all spent so many happy years.

As Shay seems unimpressed, he takes another approach, fixing her with his rueful, entreating gaze. "*Dai, amore,* give us a break—we're just a bunch of sad old guys trying for our last hurrah! Anyhow I'll confess something to you: it's really not that much fun hanging around with those senile playboys. The place is turning into an elephants' graveyard."

Recalling this now on the beach, as the damp sand molds itself to her feet, Shay grows abruptly furious at herself for countenancing such arrant disrespect. Like Senna, she has a dramatic streak, and for an instant pictures herself charging back into the arena of lamplight, into the frayed circle of men with their smug fatalism, and raging like Medea: forcing her duplicitous husband and his buddies to see in her all the women they have wronged. A smile crosses her face as she remembers outrageous showdowns with Senna, and other men; but in the end, what good do theatrics do? At this point in life, she knows that real change comes about with one perfectly clear thought, a single move at the right time.

For months all the unanswered questions have been lining up in a sort of antechamber to her heart. Whether to cut through all the nonsense and divorce Senna in the straightforward American way, or to continue on the misty, equivocal path of separate marital lives so acceptable in Europe.

Whether to abandon forever the Red House and Madagascar. Or to take a different tack: to leave behind the life she has built in Milan, and establish herself permanently on Naratrany, as she has seen determined European wives do. Transform herself into a strict, new-style memsahib. Banish the hookers, kick out the freeloaders, fumigate the atmosphere of cheap sex and morbidity. She understands Senna well enough to know that on some deep Italian level—the level where female sacrifice is venerated—he would bow completely to this kind of domestic coup d'état. But, at this point, does she care enough to do this? All of these decisions devolve on one thing, and that is love, its presence or absence.

She stands thinking these thoughts, with her braids loose down her back, her silk trousers billowing in the tidal breeze, then glances at the young watchmen who are stationed at a discreet distance, talking quietly among themselves in the Vezo language. Youths whose sculpted Black faces and bodies have the same vital glow and divine symmetry as those of the beautiful girls in the bars. Young men who admire her, who have made it clear in their nighttime wanderings under her bedroom windows that they would not be surprised, or displeased, if she behaved with them like the old Italian men do with the girls.

And she has won their respect by never allowing this idea to enter the realm of possibility. Not even so much as by a certain kind of smile or joke. Why? she wonders. Well, because we women are more . . . have more . . . Yes, that is it. What Bertine used to say. We have more to us.

One of the young watchmen points to a constellation in the eastern part of the sky, and says something that sounds like a short song or verse, while the others murmur in agreement. Then the boys all laugh, soft mysterious laughter.

"Qu'est-ce qu'il a dit?" she asks the head watchman, who speaks a bit of French.

The youth clutches his spear and stumbles over the words. "He shows . . . the star that just came into the sky. We call it the woman who waits. The faithful woman who sits in the sky and keeps the fishermen safe. She is watching there at night when we are in our boats."

"And why were you laughing?" demands Shay, in a severe voice she has never used with them before.

"Madame, we were not being disrespectful. We laughed because he said something that was true. He said that the star is like you."

To allay his apprehension, Shay gives an uneasy laugh herself, and then shakes sand out of her trousers and sets off back toward the garden and house. Waiting, she is thinking. What on earth for?

She imagines a deity on a sidereal throne, quiet-faced as the little wooden statue by the pool, looking benignly but indifferently down on the fisher boys bobbing in their pirogues in the starving south of the island. The children of poverty staring up at their lucent goddess, whispering prayers for luck and money that will never be granted. While under the same star, their sisters and their sweethearts, the Malagasy girls marooned in the bars and the foreign bungalows of their despoiled country, flock around the old white men—the dying elephants.

Shay is a believer in signs, and the young watchman's naïve remark hits a nerve. Does it mean that she is barrenly waiting, paralyzed by indecision—as if she stood on the coast, not of Madagascar but of Denmark? Or does it hint at an emerging bond, a profound connection she has never been aware of between herself and this strange country? Perhaps she is waiting for a revelation.

Whatever the meaning, it transforms her mood, as chance occurrences sometimes do. No longer is she fantasizing epic confrontations with Senna and his crew. Nor does she intend to go straight to her solitary bedroom, like a sulky child, baffled and excluded.

Neither, she thinks. Her big decisions will be made in her own time, and on her own terms, but she'll start with little things. She twists her braids around her head, pins them back in place, and, leaving the Vezo boys in the garden, takes a deep breath and walks toward the veranda and the dining table. She will now say a dignified good night to her husband and the others, who in their inglorious fashion are, after all, also waiting for a turn of fate. Barefoot, she steps over the threshold back into the lamplight and the cloud of cigarette smoke. And for an instant the endless chatter of the diners stops short as they watch her arrive like an apparition out of the dark. Graciously she salutes them and turns to go, but suddenly, in a swirl of silk, faces them again. "As for Burton," she adds in a louder voice that makes Senna flinch slightly. "Tell him he's welcome, that I insist."

And then, in a gesture that comes as a surprise to them all, the old men, one by one, raise their glasses to her.

2. Gemini

They resolved to break up pyrating, and no Place was so fit to receive them as Madagascar; hither they steered, resolving to live on Shore and enjoy what they got.

—Daniel Defoe, *A General History of the Pyrates*

Senna does not deliberately set out to transform his family vacation villa into a rest home for geriatric playboys, but nor does this phase of its existence come about entirely by chance. It grows organically out of a friendship, the most important of his life: an illustration of the fact that a longtime amicable bond between two men generally has fewer twists and turns and sudden knots and frayings than that of two women. And so there is a greater possibility of renewal, which sometimes comes about in singular ways.

Gianmaria Senna and Federico Paolini, who now as old men form the nucleus of the raffish off-season company in the Red House, have lived together before: as very young men in Rome. This begins when they share a tiny Trastevere apartment and both work in Italian cinema, back in its dolce vita glory days.

Senna, a blond Lombard escaped from an impoverished Vercelli family of rice merchants, is then twenty years old, too smart for his surroundings, small, wiry, good-looking, fast-talking, electric with ambition. He is the perfect foil for Paolini, the tall, dark, pampered son of a rich Roman film magnate with half of Cinecittà in his pocket. When they meet, Senna has, through a distant relation, bluffed his way into a job as property manager and dogsbody for a neorealist director who is fast becoming a legend. While Paolini works sporadically managing his father's string of movie theaters across Lazio.

It is Rome in the effervescent period of postwar Italian cinema, when the ancient city, still scarred by Allied bombs, has been reborn as the epicenter of the international movie world; where the Cinecittà sound stages and the glittering arabesque of the Via Veneto quicken with a volatile mixture of epic Hollywood glamour and flamboyant Roman vulgarity. In this fluid social atmosphere, the two friends go everywhere and sleep with every possible woman—and for them most women are possible. Legendary movie stars they meet at parties, or on location. Starlets picked up at the industry volleyball games on the beach at Ostia. Rebellious young Roman princesses. Bored mistresses of famous politicians. A beautiful university student moves a desk and typewriter to their apartment terrace and there spends afternoons writing her first novel, naked except for a pair of sunglasses. A Black actress from Los Angeles, often cast as a Nubian slave girl, cheerfully shares the two of them for a few weeks, before running off with a producer. They have a fling with a pair of Sicilian sisters who play sultry Mexicans in Sergio Leone films.

Senna and Paolini get along perfectly, their only disagreement being over who is relegated to the pullout couch bed.

"Laziest bastard I have ever seen," declares Senna, in an affectionate tone, about his handsome friend. "Too lazy even to unzip his own pants for a girl."

"I let Senna have the ones who require attention," says Paolini equably. They never fight.

Sometimes they sit out on their terrace, smoking cigarettes and listening to the noise from the trattoria below—a louche Trastevere place where the cutlery is chained to the table—and spin daydreams about escaping to tropical islands: an infinity of blue waters and pliant brown women. It is their joint fantasy, outshining even the hectic glamour of the movie business.

After a few years, they both have left Rome but stay close; they are best men at each other's weddings. Paolini marries an actress, and goes to work in television, first in Bologna, then in Nice. Senna goes back to Vercelli, marries a rich girl he has known since first communion, and goes to work importing combine harvesters with his father-in-law.

They see each other during mountain and beach vacations with their wives and children; they provide each other with alibis during affairs they have with old or new girlfriends. Their finances reverse positions: Senna gets rich from his agricultural machines, and begins to expand into advertising, and Paolini, who dreams of directing movies, fritters away his inheritance on a series of flops. Suddenly—it is the end of the 1970s— Paolini, in his indolent but oddly decisive manner, departs to make a travel film in southern Thailand.

There, through force of inertia, he remains for months, then years, never again returning to his family or to live in Europe. Eventually divorced, he settles in Phuket and marries a levelheaded Thai woman, a resort manager who manages Paolini as well. With Thailand as his base, he begins to traverse the tropical islands of the world, beginning in the Andaman Sea, but over the years branching out into the farthest reaches of the Pacific, exploring the Marquesas and Tuvalu and other remote archipelagoes, where he shoots documentaries that rarely make money, but to which he devotes the rest of his life.

Senna also divorces and, after a few bachelor years, marries Shay, the American scholar and university instructor who becomes the mother of his two youngest children. Neither Senna nor Shay understands the powerful magnetism that draws them to fall in love, a man and a woman with nearly twenty years difference between them, whose tastes are so different. They can't see that the greatest thing they have in common is an infinite restlessness, a desire to see unknown things—traits that rarely bring lasting marital felicity. Still, they settle in to raise a family in Milan and spend their vacations in a thatched palace beside a cerulean bay in Madagascar. For Senna, who is nothing if not a literalist, has brought his own tropical fantasy to life in the grand manner.

These are prosperous years for Senna, always full of ingenious schemes; among other things, he buys up a derelict provincial printing firm, revives it, and hires Paolini to shoot travel calendars. Sometimes he journeys to join his old friend in his island excursions. No longer young, they are still a picturesque pair: Paolini, tall, impassive as an idol in the Indonesian sarongs he likes to wear, cameras slung on his shoulders, his long graying hair occasionally adorned with blossoms; Senna, compact and piratical in wet suit and Jacques Cousteau sunglasses, knife in his belt, shark tooth around his neck.

When Paolini visits Italy twice a year, he stays with the Sennas in their Milan apartment, stretched out on a couch as unperturbed in his idleness as he is in his hammock in Phuket, watching hours of old movies on television, reminiscing to Senna about the directors and actors they once knew. Shay is not fond of Paolini but knows from the start he is too important in her husband's life for her ever to dislike. The Sennas' children, Roby and Augustina, regard him with awe—so sunburnt and magnificently at ease, a visitation from another climate glowing through the fog of their dark city. Paolini's beautiful Thai wife, Rune, who is brisk and chic and would much rather live in Europe, tours Milan with Shay. The two women attract attention on the streets by their contrasting looks, equally exotic in the eyes of Italians.

Years into their marriage, Rune is diagnosed with late-stage cancer. Hopeless months of therapy, and suddenly she is gone. Paolini, helpless as if his legs have been cut off, hides himself in his condominium in Phuket, suicidal and at bay: dirt gathers and bills pile up, because the woman of his languid tropical fantasies was in fact a brilliant organizer who used to handle everything, from investments to food shopping.

Paolini and Senna are both in their sixties now. Senna's marriage to Shay has frayed almost visibly, like an old silk shawl worn transparent. After the Senna children leave for college in America, husband and wife find that, without the elaborate structure of habit, affection, irritation, and laughter that is family life, they have little to say to each other.

Senna begins to feel bored, restless, old. He starts to invest in eccentric

projects, to travel more, to increase his flirtations—which in the past, Shay, having learned from Italian wives, has ignored—and over these dalliances they have serious fights. But no recent woman has attracted him as much as the island of Naratrany—which suddenly, like a mistress who has long been in the background, has emerged as newly seductive.

Having placed his company into reliable hands, he begins to visit Madagascar in the off-season, to stay in the Red House for weeks at a time, nosing around for business opportunities. It is a time of political instability, when rumors of vast deposits of nickel and heavy crude spawn wildcat schemes. With his usual astuteness Senna acquires swathes of cheap land from the defunct government sugar company and begins to develop spaces for tourism. Shay is included in none of this activity, but raises no objection except for a few sarcastic comments about the aging process in men. Strangely enough her apparent indifference inspires admiration in Senna, part of the baffled awe he has always felt for his overeducated wife. Knowing women, he is aware that there will probably be hell to pay. But for now he has entered a period of reckless self-indulgence of a kind he hasn't known since the time, decades ago, when he first sailed into Finoana Bay and decided to raise up a house there.

With Senna easing back into a semblance of bachelorhood in Madagascar, the arrival of the widower Paolini seems almost foreordained. It takes some doing, though. Over and over, Senna invites him to stay at the Red House. Paolini resists—he's been there on holiday with the Sennas before, and finds Madagascar, he says, far inferior to his beloved Thailand. "The soil is the color of blood," he declares with unusual vehemence. "The beaches aren't as white. The corals look dead. The people—aah—there is something dangerous about them. Africans. Too Black. They'd slit your throat."

"Come on," insists Senna. "In the end, all these hot places are the same—a few shades of brown don't make a difference! And you can't curl up and die there in Phuket. If you are going to be miserable, why not come be miserable here? I have a new project I set up with some friends. It could be very amusing, like old times."

The project Senna describes is an extravagant event that he imagines will establish Naratrany among the vacation paradises of the globe. It is a fashion shoot for an international magazine, a swimsuit edition so famous that whole websites are devoted just to the making of it. Nobody understands how Senna finagled this coup; perhaps through a Spanish media magnate he's done favors for over the years.

And so for a September week, the Red House undergoes a fairy-tale transformation. It is as if the place has been invaded by a circus of nymphs. Some models—American, Brazilian, Dutch—are so well known in their brief flowering into fame that their radiant faces are already familiar. With their stylists and publicists they flood the Red House and nearby hotels, practicing yoga at dawn, blowing out the electrical generators with their hair dryers, fighting with their boyfriends long distance, losing their phones, dashing off to vomit, casually flashing their deiform bodies in the swimming pool.

Madagascar is one of the wilder places the models have ever been, and although they are as cloistered from the real life of the country as a bevy of traveling nuns, they rejoice in the rough edges they can see. Zebus pulling wooden carts, lemurs dancing through the treetops, the patched sails of fishing pirogues, ragged children with shining eyes, distant shantytowns with rusted roofs. They are hardly allowed out at night, but whenever they are, the island prostitutes—who are the same age, and just as beautiful—hover nearby, tense with curiosity.

Of course all of Senna's male friends and relatives have found excuses to fly in, carefully excluding wives or girlfriends, and the presence of pushy Italian playboys makes things feel quite homelike to the models. They generously banter and flirt and dance, most of all with Senna, the host, who has a captivating way of spinning yarns about sharks and of suggesting that he is much richer than he actually is. He hints, too, that he and Paolini have important connections in the film industry.

And so the models, coiffed, made up, adorned in little else but their polished flesh, spread the beneficent fragrance of commercial beauty through the Red House. They reenact every trope of tropical iconography:

frolicking on powdery sand; supine and bronzed by the pool; demure beside market women with baskets of fruit; sculptural in speedboats; draped in nets like freshly caught fish. The photographer is German, and propulsive electro music pounds in the background day and night.

Paolini wanders silently among them, filming with an impassive face as he has done in ceremonies in outermost Oceania. He is not flirtatious or merry, but it seems that he has put aside his grief.

"You see?" Senna says. "You feel good here! Stay. It's not always going to be full of sublime pussy like this, but I guarantee—" He pauses, because he has no idea of what he can guarantee that will make Paolini want to remain alive.

Stretched out shirtless on lounge chairs near the seawall, the two old friends are warming their tough hides in the early-morning sun. Down on the sand in front of them, photographer's assistants hold up huge reflectors as three girls—Russian, Australian, Venezuelan—draped in halters made of wooden beads, pose in the verdant branches of the big tamarind tree, where Senna's children once had a fort. The tree is an important landmark of Finoana Beach, a place where people meet, where things happen; now, in an unexpected flowering, it is full of famous beauties.

For a second the impression flashes through Senna's head that he and Paolini are young again and back in Rome together. Back at the parties, on the sets with the starlets. As if their two fantasy worlds of cinema and tropical seas have finally overlapped and merged. Little about the two of them—he thinks hopefully—has changed since that early time, though Paolini's hair flows silver like a patriarch's around a face weathered into a red-brown mask, and pitiless mirrors show Senna's narrow green eyes set in caverns under graying brows.

"Of course if you stay, you'll need a regular girl," Senna continues to his companion, who is wearily exhaling cigarette smoke, his eyes closed. "A girl from the island. Almost as hot as these models, and a lot cheaper. I'll find you one. I know of one . . . two . . . or three . . . that I think would be fine for you. You can choose. They're good-natured, these Malagasy girls. Clean. They make you feel young, and they don't ask for much. Just a bracelet or a necklace from time to time." He pauses, musing. Then adds: "Rune would be glad to see you feeling better."

"Is Shay glad for you?" demands Paolini, with a rare flash of malice.

"Ah, Shay knows that a man deserves a break. She's an extraordinary woman: wise. We have a perfect understanding. And she's never really liked Madagascar anyway," he declares with false conviction. "Anyway— stay. I have some of the old crowd coming. And I'll give you the biggest room, with the view of the Grande Île."

The tide is starting to come in, and the models up in the tamarind tree are shrieking in mock terror and playfully waving their shapely arms like damsels in distress.

"I'll stay for a few months, and shoot some Madagascar footage," says Paolini, in a depressed tone. "But if I really settle in, I know I'll die here."

"*Che cazzate!*" retorts Senna, watching the nymphs frolicking in front of his grand thatched house, and feeling an intense relief wash over him, as if he's just saved himself. "Don't talk like an asshole. Stay here, and you'll live. Not just live—you'll think you're in heaven."

3. Skin

Art with her bold stigmatizing hand
Doth streaks and marks upon their visage brand.

—John Bulwer, "Anthropometamorphosis"

S hay is visiting her lemur-obsessed friend Kirsten in her house high up in the forest overlooking Finoana Bay when news comes that Baptiste the body painter has been arrested. The generally lax island gendarmes have this time taken action regarding the old French artist's provocative insistence on his work as performance. This time he has been standing for hours in front of a crowd on the shaded sand in front of the Hotel Chambord as he minutely decorates the bare breasts and torso of a beautiful young Comorean girl with a design of the same flowers and arabesques as that of the ornate antique *lamba* she is wearing to cover her hips and private parts.

"He'll cool his heels getting eaten up with fleas and sand flies in the Saint Grimaud prison for a night," says Kirsten, who is from Brixen on the Italian-Austrian border, and has the ravaged complexion and terrible cynicism of European women who have spent too many years in the tropics. "They won't keep a Frenchman more than that. Not even that, if you and Senna pay the bribe. He's your friend after all."

"My husband's friend," corrects Shay tartly, with a glance at the other two women who are lying there by the swimming pool overlooking the luminous vista of Finoana Bay that spreads out from the mangroves far below. They, like Kirsten, are Europeans who have lived long and bitterly in Madagascar, year-round, clinging to their illusions of superiority to the people of the country as a poor exchange for their own savage boredom, their disintegrating health. They've known Shay for years and respect her husband's money, but distrust her as unplaceable on their narrow social scale, a bookish American woman of color who lives there only during vacations.

Shay is aware that they are all wondering maliciously whether she knows, as the whole island of Naratrany does, that the scandalous painter is just one of a court of miracles that has formed at the Red House, and made it a center for debauched old men to drink and whore. That her husband, Senna, the jokester and libertine, with his grand plans for island supermarkets and country clubs, is the ringmaster of the whole group and can barely be bothered to conceal the fact when his wife and family are there on holiday.

Yes, Shay knows. With a cold smile she looks levelly back at the two women, pleased that she has a life outside Madagascar, and that the sun has not wrecked her face and her spirit, as theirs are wrecked. Whatever corrosive truths she may be harboring inside are hers alone to deal with, she thinks, in her own time.

Kirsten's ring-tailed lemurs are beginning to honk and leap around in their big bosky cages, flashing their magical eyes, and calling out to their wild forest brethren as feeding time approaches; Kirsten herself issues a barrage of shrill directives in a mixture of French and kitchen Malagasy at a Sakalava houseboy bearing a big plastic tub of rice and bananas. Shay winces at her tone. She admires her friend as one of the few people on the island truly interested in Madagascar wildlife, the magnificent, doomed community of mammals and amphibians existing nowhere else on earth. However, Shay sees that living year-round on the edge of the jungle, with these rare creatures rescued from deforestation, has left Kirsten slightly deranged. What is it about this country, she wonders, that turns foreigners mad?

Returning to the subject of the body painter, Shay shrugs and says carelessly: "He's no criminal. But I don't like his work, and he needs to respect the laws of the country. So I think we'll leave him in jail."

But she knows that when she returns to the Red House she will almost certainly find Baptiste, as always, at her dinner table, sharing a laugh with her husband and their friends, perhaps describing his near arrest as a hilarious adventure. Senna is too proud of his own powers as a mover and shaker on Naratrany to allow one of his houseguests to be taken into custody. Bribes and blustering will have been deployed with his friend the *commissaire*, and the incident will become one more tale to recount over after-dinner rum.

Baptiste the body painter is quite a personage. Before he becomes a fixture at the Red House, Shay has come across his work in magazines: beautiful female and male models whose skin has been decorated in a trompe l'oeil fashion that extemporizes on the style of the dress or the setting, sometimes blending the models into a background of forest or urban streets, sometimes ornamenting them in an improvised blend of unearthly patterns more dimensional than the best tattoo work.

Shay tries to like him. Like so many Red House fixtures, odd ducks drawn by her husband's extravagant hospitality, he first appears as a paying guest, seated on one of the Chinese chairs at the long dining table on the Red House veranda. Initially he seems unobtrusive: a small slightly stooped figure of a man well into his seventies, with a soft, cultured voice fluent in Italian, English, and other languages besides his native Parisian French. He is bald and deeply tanned, with a small, carefully tended gray mustache and goatee, and round gold glasses. The goatee, and especially the glasses, gives him an air that is half psychoanalyst, half midcentury bohemian: through the lenses, his eyes gleam black, intensely intelligent and aware. Emphatically not the eyes of an old man—and not necessarily, thinks Shay, the eyes of a good one.

Senna, man of impetuous enthusiasms, is enthralled by the new arrival. His own picaresque life is thrown into the shade by the experiences of this quiet artist, who lives by his odd expertise. No one doubts Baptiste's history:

that he has known shamans in Mongolia; studied designs with tattoo masters in New Zealand and Japan; worked with henna artists in Morocco; absorbed the spirit of rococo from a Neapolitan master restorer; and apprenticed in cosmetology with a makeup director from the Comédie-Française. When he arrives in Madagascar for the first time, he is on his way back from the Sahel, where he visited the supreme body painters of Africa, the Wodaabe.

Wherever he goes, he practices his craft: in countries where faces and torsos are rigorously covered according to law, he decorates hands and feet. His method is unvarying: he creates a design and paints it on the skin of a model—a man or woman at the height of physical perfection—sometimes working over a whole day. Then the ephemeral moment of completion is captured in photographs, and swift as passing memories, the paint is washed away.

Shay talks to him at that first dinner, and finds him unsettlingly intense but quite conversable, one of the few of Senna's friends who ask about her work. When she tells him about teaching African-American literature, he wants to know what interests her most as a scholar. "I think it has always been exoticism," she says, throwing the truth out almost idly, as she does from time to time.

"*L'esotico,*" he repeats. (They are speaking in Italian, a language native to neither of them.) "*Soggetto particolare, e curioso.* And what does the exotic mean to you?"

"Artists and writers trying to process other cultures by rendering them ornamental and harmless. It has to do with surfaces—not so far from what you do."

Baptiste really looks at her then. "I paint the surfaces of people's bodies," he says evenly. "But the result is never superficial."

Shay feels she has insulted him. Quickly, in her best social voice, she asks how one develops a passion for painting on skin. And Baptiste describes a scene for her from early in his career, when he considered body painting a banal cosmetic craft, something to pay the rent. The job is for a fashion magazine; the subject a teenage model whom it is his job to transform into a statue, a crumbling stone maiden covered with moss, who will be posed for a photo shoot in the garden of an old château. The model has to stand still, hour after hour, and if she moves under his brushes, he shouts at her. He is quite young himself, still married to his first wife, a Danish photographer. When, after a long time, he has finished the model's face and torso and is working his way down her long legs, he hears a sniffle and sees tears rolling down the girl's gray painted cheeks. Sees this with rage at his work ruined, and also with a sudden overwhelming surge of love for the art that can make a statue weep.

"And how did you get her to stop crying?"

"Ah, that's a secret I'll never reveal," says Baptiste, with a smile that for some reason sends a chill down Shay's spine.

In the years following this first visit, Baptiste comes and goes on his travels, more and more often ending up in Madagascar. There is something about the country, and about the island of Naratrany, that peculiarly appeals to him, he who is familiar with so many far corners of the earth. He basks in Senna's hospitality at the Red House. He enjoys the young beauties of both sexes on the beaches and in the villages: country girls, prostitutes, *moraingy* boxers, dockworkers, who are always ready, for a small fee, to serve as his canvases. He becomes quite a member of the household, appearing both when the Senna family is present, and when Senna is there out of season, with his fraternal circle of friends.

On the August day when Baptiste has his brush with the Naratrany forces of law, the Sennas' son, Roby, a junior at Williams, happens to be in the Red House after a summer spent in restaurant work on Nantucket. The painter apologizes profusely for the upset, and as a recompense for the Sennas' help, playfully offers to paint Roby, who is preternaturally good-looking and acting moody after a breakup. Impulsive like Senna, Roby accepts the offer. Senna thinks it's hilarious, a great idea; Shay is somehow repelled by the thought. But since her son chose to say yes, she goes along with it.

So Roby, his body shaven like that of a fetish boy, and wearing an abbreviated Italian bathing suit from Senna's younger days, spends the greater part of a day perched on a high stool on the front porch of the guest cottage overlooking the beach, as Baptiste, absorbed and frowning, limns an intricate design on his model's face, torso, and arms. The design concocted by the body painter, after a study of Roby's features and the long dreadlocks bound at his nape, is an elaborate improvisation on Maori and Polynesian themes, with a few Tlingit motifs woven in: in honor, Baptiste murmurs, of Roby's American side. To Shay's relief, Roby—who, like every other college student, knows his way around cultural appropriation—gives a sour grin at this nonsense. It would be hard, Shay thinks, to paint a skin map of Roby's true lineage: the complex mixture of West African, Irish, English, and Algonquian heritage that results in a Black family like her own, and the solid generations of Lombard peasants who make up Senna's people. Much simpler a trumped-up heraldry.

As always, Baptiste's work becomes a performance; observers gather on the sand in front of the Red House. Looking out from where she sits in the garden, Shay is aware of how much the beach has changed from the early days when Roby and his sister were tiny, tumbling half-naked on the sand in a scrum of village children, the great thatched roof peak of the house rising behind them, the only building visible beyond the palms. What was once a salt-white arc of empty beach is lined with hotels, cafés, and other big private villas, and the blue expanse of Finoana Bay, which once held a few fishermen's pirogues, is now dotted with catamarans and speedboats; cruise ships pass by in the distance. In the crowd of onlookers are German and Russian tourists from the hotels, Malagasy people from nearby villages, even a Japanese travel photographer. Senna, beaming with paternal pride, chats and jokes with everyone.

Shay feels a growing distress as she watches her beloved son, with Senna's features and her own tawny skin, turn into a spectacle. To her there is nothing lighthearted about it. A vampiric artist whom she instinctively distrusts is openly, lingeringly, touching her child.

Yet, deep into the afternoon, when the painting is completed, she has to admit that Roby, decorated, has become something more than a handsome youth—has become strange and magnificent. Paint on skin can offer more possibilities than tattooing, and Baptiste has invoked a kind of magic in his transformational art. Roby's face is barred with indigo, his body intricately ornamented like that of an idol, with nets of shadow and light over his muscles that make him half some creature camouflaged in forest leaves, half a totem with powers drawn from everyone's, and no one's, cultural tradition.

The foreign tourists applaud, their phones out and recording. But the Malagasy—people from Finoana and Renirano villages, who have known Roby since he was a baby—look at him and turn away quickly with fixed smiles: the kind of smiles, Shay knows, that they use when a foreigner clumsily makes a huge breach in decorum, or blunders into an act of sacrilege. She realizes that no Sakalava or Antandroy person who works in the house has ever warmed to Baptiste, as sometimes happens with frequent guests. No, they look through and around him, as if he doesn't exist, just as they do with Jean le Dragon, the notorious conjurer from Ambanja who sometimes, laughing and chanting his nonsensical patter, wanders up and down Finoana Beach.

Baptiste takes pictures for his records, then packs his materials away, as quiet and self-possessed as ever. But Senna, caught up in the excitement of the crowd, is giddily proud of his son. He shouts out witticisms, flirts with the pretty Japanese photographer, takes dozens of snaps on his iPad and phone. He tips two Sakalava fishermen to bring in a huge old six-person pirogue for Roby to pose against, before the sun gets too low on the beach. He calls out directions to his son, who has unwillingly allowed his transformation to be completed by the addition of a twisted Balinese pareo that just covers his backside.

But Roby finally rebels, beckoning to his mother. "I'm sick of this," he whispers to Shay. "I feel like a total dick. I'm not a fucking model. I'm not doing it anymore."

"Just make Papà happy, and pose against the boat."

"No. I'm done," Roby says stubbornly. For an instant he looks at his mother and she sees that he knows everything, as children always know: witnesses the destructive friction between his parents, and how that connects to something more profound, perhaps to a deeply embedded error that lies beneath his family's careless holiday life in Madagascar. And though this is no solution, her heart lifts.

"Well then, go wash it off. Go!" she tells him. And instantly—she can hardly believe it herself—her son walks quickly through the crowd, which parts for him; he moves faster and faster until he passes the beached pirogue and is running, running in a confusion of shouts from his father and whoops from the spectators. A painted figure, like a fugitive character from a myth, he dashes into the ocean, dives under, and stays there a long time. When he comes up, shaking his long locks like a wild creature, water flashing off them in the low afternoon sun, the paint is nearly gone from his face and shoulders.

The spectators cheer. Shay bursts into laughter, but Senna lets out a string of curses. His face is dark with fury, and he glares at his wife with such pure rage—but for what?—that she realizes things will never be the same between them.

But Baptiste, who is cleaning his round glasses, looks over and gives her a little nod of acknowledgment, almost of respect, as if she'd outmaneuvered him at chess. And for some reason Shay wonders whether this man would have offered to paint her body when she was Roby's age. Assuredly. And now? She glances down at herself, bare-legged in her beach dress. Still good to look at, but certainly no longer with the youthful perfection into which the body painter allows himself to trespass, with the excuse of his art.

What does that matter? Roby did the right thing, and as she looks at him striding out of the waves, grinning sheepishly and wringing the seawater out of his hair, clean-skinned as the day she bore him, she feels for a minute like the mother of a hero.

2.

The episode of Roby's body painting marks a new phase for Shay and Senna. The long story of their love and marriage has always been full of stops and starts, dependent on dashingly improvised bridges over differences in temperament and culture. Through the years they've even congratulated each other on their daring unconventionality, their talent for muddling through. But now they must acknowledge that a bourn has been crossed; they've entered territory where the subtle fabric of loyalty that binds two people together across decades of common life has dissolved like a morning mist. And they are left blinking on opposite sides of a nameless gulf.

Shay and Senna don't speak of this revelation, but like many another couple they communicate it in other ways. They stop making love, and even a casual touch becomes fraught. They speak of little but practical matters dealing with their son and daughter, the family nucleus that holds steady long after conjugal love expires. Their gazes, accidentally crossing, generate that unique embarrassment that arrives when two people who have found their way far into each other can no longer recall the reason why.

When the summer vacation ends, Shay goes back to Milan, sees the kids off to school in the States, and evades her worries by plunging deep into work. She makes changes to her reading list, adding Nella Larsen's *Passing* and two little known 1920s stories from *The Crisis;* she takes on more translation work than she can manage, including a French to English rendering of *Le Mulâtre* by the Creole playwright Victor Séjour. Adrift in thoughts on the multifoliate family tree of Black literature, she rides her bicycle back and forth from Via Fratelli Ruffini to the university, relishing the inimitable Milan street fashion and the clammy autumn chill of Saint Ambrose's ancient city, where through two decades she has learned to feel at home. Why should she ever have to think about Madagascar?

Senna continues to travel between Milan and Naratrany, spending ever longer periods away. He jokes that he plans to spend his days sitting in the sun and fishing; but Senna can no more retire than sprout wings. Like Shay, he is constantly at work. Madagascar is opening to the contemporary world, and he continues to seize hold of the frontier possibilities offered by the times. With his peculiar mixture of impulse and shrewdness, he acquires a failing ylang-ylang plantation that happens to abut a future power plant financed by the Chinese. With an old friend, a Karan In-

dian, he invests in a fleet of minicabs that begin to replace the old Renault
taxi-brousses. He travels to the capital and establishes friendships among
the Merina aristocracy, who hold the real power, and gradually begins
to connect to the shadowy fonts of wealth that lie beneath the surface of
nations like Madagascar. After much haggling, he buys the house of his
longtime next-door neighbor Madame Rose Rakotomalala, and begins to
transfer the Red House bed-and-breakfast business there.

More than ever, Senna is starting to relish the privacy of the villa he
built so many years ago. Though he himself is never idle, he enjoys the
company of the retinue of idlers he has attracted there: friends who have
begun to take the place of family.

Shay's no-nonsense sister, Leila, in Berkeley, and her American friends
all urge her to wake up: to make a definite move either toward or away
from Senna. But she does nothing, and this inaction is approved by her
Italian friends. The atmosphere in Italy—the lulling Catholic incense of
sacrament and sacrifice that permeates every facet of even secular life in
that timeless country—encourages the idea that two people can live for
years, even for all eternity, in a dead marriage. Because of Senna's travels
for work, the two of them have always had independent lives, and so Shay's
existence in Milan these days is much the same as always: working, social-
izing with friends, connections with her children and family in the United
States, a few flirtations that keep her vanity burnished, though she has little
inclination toward love affairs, whether as anodyne or as payback. Senna
covers his part of the bills and keeps abreast of family matters.

Meanwhile Baptiste has become the star of the gang of comrades
her husband has assembled in the Red House. The body painter's work
flourishes. He attracts fashion shoots and art journalists, and his presence
increases the prestige of the Red House, which presents a show of his
photographs with a reception attended by local politicians and the king of
the Sakalava. Senna loves hosting him; the presence of Baptiste puts him
in touch with the artistic dimension that has attracted him since his boy-
hood experience in the world of cinema. In his phone calls, he occasionally
seeks to revive complicity with Shay, to entertain her with outré tales of

the models the body painter brings to the house: exquisite young girls from remote districts where not even French is spoken. One Betsimisaraka model had never sat on a chair, never seen a knife and fork. Shay listens coldly to these anecdotes, a small part of her wondering just when she is going to lose patience.

For months she keeps the Madagascar situation at a distance, until, like many another wife, she is confronted with unconfoundable reality in the form of social media. The image she can never unsee is a group photo featuring Senna and his cohorts, but not the usual Hemingway fantasy shot in which the beaming pensioners pose on the bridge of the catamaran as they hoist a giant, phallic marlin toward the lens.

Instead this is a scene captured in the Red House garden: a lineup of gray-haired men under the tamarind, the giant tree that has witnessed so many curious events over the years. As if in a frieze, four of them frame a central figure: a beautiful and very young Malagasy woman. Her face and body—breasts barely covered by a strip of fabric—are painted with an intricate running design of hibiscus flowers. On her right stands Baptiste, with the ceremonious indicative hand of every artist displaying his work. On her left side is Senna, caught in one of the theatrical poses he loves: holding up the thick stalk of an elephant ear plant, so that the umbrella-size leaf shades the girl's head.

Shay's heart seems to change location, beating up somewhere deep behind her tongue as she sits down at her kitchen table in Milan and contemplates this image. The girl—it will be a miracle if she is past eighteen—seems familiar: maybe she was one of the Sakalava urchins who once waved and shouted at her from the shanties as she drove by in the truck: *Bonjour, Madame Shay!* Perhaps she has been fished out of the penniless young crowd of kids who dance in the road outside of the island clubs.

But this is not just any casually chosen model. No, great pains have been taken with her appearance and her pose. She is a gorgeous apparition, not only painted with a maze of swirling pink blossoms that suggest the fullness of love and life, but also garlanded: her hair, plaited in the style village women adopt for solemn occasions, is crowned with a wreath of hibiscus appropriated from the bush Shay herself planted, years ago. With languid composure, the girl looks directly into the lens, while Senna, in the padronal position, shades her with the big leaf in a manner recalling the famous photograph of Picasso holding a parasol over the regal head of Françoise Gilot. Shay sees instantly that the gesture is no joke. It is a pronouncement. There is no doubt about it, not to Shay, who reads on her husband's face a familiar look of possessiveness and fatuous pride. This girl, who stands there with the simplicity of a newly created Eve in the garden of the Red House, is a woman who wields power there, the power of a lover or a mistress.

Shay is swept by a wave of jealousy and rage that in an instant obliterates her carefully fabricated notion of a marriage of distance and tolerance. She shakes her head, rubs her eyes to loosen blocked tears that burn like acid, grits her teeth, while through her head stampede all the usual furious but practical soap opera questions. *Who is that hussy? How old is she? Who posted that fucking picture? Did the kids see it? What does that son of a bitch Senna think he is doing? Declaring independence? Declaring war?* Shay scans her husband's face with ferocious curiosity. She picks up her phone to call and scream at him, but then she puts the phone down. First she must decide what the crime is, and whether it's a crime at all.

One thing about Shay is that, even in the grip of the Furies, she can step away from a situation and consider it from another angle, as if she stood on a far planet. Her family and friends have always found this trait unnatural, and Senna, who relishes a good tantrum, sometimes mockingly calls her "Tedesca" for her supposedly German-style self-control. Shay has always ignored the gibes, and calmly goes on following an instinct that springs from a central part of her, the part that likes to contemplate life at the instant she lives it.

For a short span of time, as the March afternoon darkens beyond the windows of her kitchen in Milan, she sets aside her anger and her pride. She switches on some music—Fela Kuti's *Shuffering and Shmiling*—and sits examining the bright colors of the photograph that has traveled through her iPad screen to invade and change her world. Simple phone capture though it may be, she has to admit it is an extraordinary image. Like all great pictures, it hints at other pictures: there is Gauguin, of course, but also something of Botticelli about the floral maiden, something of Rousseau in the flat background foliage. The pattern that the body painter has applied to the brown skin of his human canvas has nothing to do with the designs of Madagascar and everything to do with the decorative tradition of Europe—and this subtle dissonance adds allure. Just so, the fake tribalism of the design the artist painted on her son, Roby, managed to express something deep and powerful.

But the most extraordinary thing about the photo is how it flips the convention of certain pictures that have always fascinated Shay: the Olympia paintings, she calls them, where a Black person is present in a shadowy subservient role. Here, though, the Black woman in her vivid efflorescence commands the scene. And seeing this, Shay feels, even through her jealousy and anger, a grudging sense of solidarity with this unknown girl. Rising in Shay's mind is the eternal Naratrany question: *Don't the island women have the right to take what they can?* And with it follows the next question, faint and reluctant, the kind of question that will repeat itself over sleepless nights: *Is this girl stealing something I really want to keep?*

Still studying the screen, Shay moves her gaze to Baptiste the body painter, and at him she pauses, enlarging the image until she can even see the spatters of color remaining on his thin arms. His eyes behind the round glasses are, as always, unreadable. Suddenly she feels an irrational hatred toward him, as if he, not her husband, is the one publicly betraying her. But at the same time she acknowledges the mastery present in his work, which she once thought trivial. She recalls their first conversation, and sees how the wandering artist has flung back a riposte to her careless remark, brilliantly displaying, with offhand malice, just how surface decoration can reveal deep truth. Her problem—pressing, now—is how to respond to the message conveyed in paint that is already washed away.

4. Blue Period

Blue is the color of longing for the distances you never arrive in.

—Rebecca Solnit, *A Field Guide to Getting Lost*

Months pass, many of them, and Shay does not return to Madagascar. The packed schedule of her own ever-increasing work and the American college calendars of Roby and Augustina make it easy to let slip the decades-long Senna family custom of spending winter and summer vacations at the Red House on Naratrany; to let it go, as if it were only part of the natural evolution of a family whose children are fast becoming adults. This is not discussed, just as no one talks about the fact that, while three of them—mother, daughter, and son—are spending less time on the island, one of them—Senna—has withdrawn from life in Italy to spend most of his time there. For all of them, Madagascar has become not just the nostalgic lost land of childhood holidays, but also the country of secrets and silence.

Though Shay is physically absent from the Red House, she revisits it in dreams. Wandering the oneiric borderland between the mundane and the fantastic, she doesn't always see the shining sweep of Finoana Bay, or the tall thatched house Senna built and presented to her when they married.

But she feels her location there as migrating birds sense the magnetic fields of the earth.

Often the central point of these dreams is her Red House bedroom: the airy blue and white chamber with the four-poster bed, the old Chinese chest, the three antique *lambahoany* hanging on the wall and swaying in the breeze from the ceiling fan. The bedroom where for years she sleeps with Senna in sunburnt conjugal intimacy, sometimes with a baby in a bassinet veiled with mosquito netting beside them, sometimes with a restless toddler cupped damply between their bodies. The bedroom that the Red House servants have since the beginning called *la chambre de Madame,* which, after a decade passes, becomes really hers alone—when Senna withdraws to sleep in his fishing hut twenty meters away down the garden path.

Senna's hut is a dank, comfortless split-bamboo construction attached to the diving equipment shed, stuffed with maps, books on fishing, papers and old photographs, detritus of his bachelor past; Senna only adds a single bed with a cheap mattress from the Indian merchant along the port road. In the family, the joking excuse for the move to the hut is that Senna's blocked sinuses are so bad after his diving expeditions that Shay has exiled him to where the crash of the waves can drown out his thunderous snores. The joke, too, is that his late-night excursions up the garden path to make love with his wife in her room are common knowledge to the rest of the household, almost ceremonial, like those of a sultan to his favorite. In Milan, of course, they share a bedroom like a normal couple. But in Madagascar, the division between them is on display well before it becomes a fact.

In the big bedroom, the focal point is a large painting on the wall, one of Senna's early presents to Shay. It is a genuine curiosity, a four-by-two-foot oil on canvas, edges damaged by insects and humidity but otherwise remarkably intact. Senna found it rolled up in a heap of rubbish at the shack of Pinceau Fantastique, the painter who lives on the side of the road outside Finoana village. Pinceau—foreigners know him only by this ambitious *nom d'artiste,* Fantastic Brush—is a taciturn young Sakalava man who occasionally works decorating hotels. But he mainly earns his bread with souvenir paintings for tourists, small bright canvases of fishermen in pirogues, which he displays pinned up like laundry on a cord suspended on two sticks in front of his doorway. He smilingly refuses to say where he obtained the big unsigned canvas, but it is clear that he bought it to cut up and reuse, and that it was painted long before he was born.

Clearly inspired by the Picasso masterpiece *La Vie*, the anonymous Malagasy artist has created a scene in deep shades of blue. It shows a man and a woman, gaunt, and longilineal in the El Greco style of early Picasso, but with complexions darker than Spanish and features that are clearly Malagasy, perhaps Merina or Betsileo. The standing male figure is skeletally thin and nearly naked, his lower body hidden by the seated figure of the woman, who is clothed in the timeless draperies of art—garments seen in real life in Madagascar. Cradled in the woman's arms, almost hidden in the folds of cloth, is a sleeping infant. A family portrait? A nativity? The man and the woman look out of the frame with bleak expressions, and there is a haphazardness to the pose, as if the characters are unrelated and have been swept together by a catastrophe. In the background, rendered with inexpert perspective, is an open illuminated doorway framing a small silhouetted figure; whether it is male or female, arriving or departing, is impossible to tell.

With its formal European structure and its Malagasy look, the scene always suggests to Shay the sorrowful romanticism of young aristocratic Merina poets like Rabearivelo: French-educated geniuses, strangers to their own traditions, writing in the early twentieth century in the language of the colonizers who hardly acknowledged them. Certainly it is an odd and complex picture to find on the wall of a beach house. Once or twice she has thought of bringing it back to Italy, but it is clear that it is meant to remain where it is.

The melancholy hues of the blue painting saturate the atmosphere of her present dreams of Naratrany. They are all unsettling. In one she has to sleep curled up on the beach, like a stray dog. Another time she is at the outdoor market in Saint Grimaud, haggling for rotten fruit. Once she is blocked from the Red House by Senna's old man friends laughing like hyenas and circling the garden in a conga line. Once she is pursued by an angry giantess rising out of Finoana Bay: the figure of Bertine la Grande, dead three years. And in one dream she looks into a mirror, and finds her face unrecognizable behind painted designs.

These dreams make her think of Pinceau Fantastique, though she hardly knows the artist, has no idea if he still lives by the roadside. She recalls the one time she did have a conversation with him, when he described his periodic retreats to his family's remote village on the Grande Île, near Daraina Forest. He went there to clear his head, he said. There he got his best ideas for his pictures of fishermen.

"In the forest?" asked Shay.

She recalls how he looked at her with an expression of infinite patience in his seed-shaped Sakalava eyes. "Madame," he said, "sometimes it is possible to be in two places at once."

Phantasmagoric visions may invade her sleep at night in Milan, but in the daytime she avoids any thought of Naratrany. She lets the gray foggy dome of her Italian urban life close down around her. She has taken on still more work, an online course with students in Bari. Has changed her hairdo—begins to wear carefully highlighted raveled twists wrapped in vintage Como silk scarves that give her a glamorous Afro-Euro look. She is leading the accelerated social life that a near-single woman with money and decades of friendships in that interesting city can lead. Gallery openings, concerts, dance classes, gastronomic weekends in the Langhe. Impromptu dinners in the big kitchen of the apartment overlooking Santa Maria delle Grazie; Shay's specialty is polenta with *spezzatino,* which her circle of Italian and American friends concede she cooks as well as any Milanese. Efficiently she handles the details of family life—tuition, the family chat, nagging reminders, funny things she finds online, innocuous postings of fishing pictures from Senna. He returns to Italy for the Christmas holidays, which Roby and Augustina are pleased to spend with their parents, not in Madagascar but skiing in the South Tyrol.

During his stay, Senna and Shay are civil to each other, even shyly considerate, like two teenagers who are trying to conceal a developing crush.

Except that what this husband and wife are concealing is the end of love. Quietly holding on to their secret, they share their bed without touching, keeping apart not with bitterness but with a kind of courtesy. Strangely enough they are both able to sleep, each one clutching silence as if it were a new partner.

In public, Senna behaves like any other husband whose career takes him far from home. He paints an amusing anecdotal portrait of the hard work he is doing in impossible circumstances. He is transforming Madame Rose's former house into a small luxury hotel, and he is involved in far too many other construction projects on the island. It is worthy work, he declares, bringing jobs to a place where there was never anything but sugarcane. But how hard it all is! How difficult it is to get construction done in tropical heat while dealing with the assorted taboos of Malagasy workers, and satisfying the limitless greed of the local bureaucrats in the *faritany* offices. How tedious are his many friends who camp out off-season at the Red House, busting his balls with their old men's depression, their endless sponging, the squalid and predictable situations they fall into with local girls. A tragicomedy, he says, laughing. The whole thing wears him out. It is ridiculous that after a lifetime of toil in Italy, he should have had the bright idea of pursuing business in that primitive place.

Shay knows that the Madagascar scenario Senna sketches out for her, his children, his family friends—himself as a reluctant laborer amid the grotesqueries of the tropics—is as much an alternative reality as her recurring dreams. Still, she doesn't confront him.

After all, they both know how serious it is. Their problem became public and irrevocable when the picture surfaced of Senna with a Malagasy girl adorned in hibiscus like a bride. After Shay looks over the photo, she calls Senna and rips him, but even when she is yelling through his lame excuses—his insistence that the whole thing was a joke, that Shay knows what Naratrany is like, that he hardly knows the girl, she is one of Baptiste's endless stream of models—she feels that both of them are wearily acting out an old scene.

So over the Christmas holiday they keep quiet. Just once, in the mountains, when Shay and Senna find themselves alone at a window seat in the hotel bar, sipping coffee and grappa after a day of skiing, Shay says: "You know, eventually we are going to have to make a decision."

They are watching daylight fade on the crags of the Pizes de Cir, waiting for the kids to come trudging up with their snowboards. At Shay's remark, Senna's narrow eyes abruptly flicker to attention like an old cat's. He leans his elbows on the table and grins at his wife with the look of rueful, rumpled honesty that used to topple all her defenses long ago when he was courting her, and that over the years she has seen him use with his mother, his business partners, even his children. The familiar litany pours out: *"Solo tu mi capisci . . . una fase particulare della vita . . . mantenere la famiglia . . ."*

"Are you in love with her?" she interrupts.

Senna looses a theatrical sigh. "What nonsense!" he says. After a pause, he adds: "Shay, *Tesoro*. There is no 'her.' And after so many years, you know that Madagascar is just a fantasy. Nothing serious happens there."

There are a number of feelings to feel just then, but she looks at him for an instant with pity.

When the holidays are over, Roby and Augustina fly back to the States, Senna returns to Naratrany, and Shay once more plunges into her work. She ignores a number of texts, calls, and emails that arrive over the next few months from friends in Madagascar, and even from staff at the Red House. But she does check Facebook and Instagram.

Social media has taken root on the island and spreads fast like everything else in the tropics: first just among the rich, and then to any villager with access to a cell phone. And suddenly everybody has access— sometimes ten Naratrany kids share a single phone. As the millennium advances, the median age of the population in Madagascar is somehow just eighteen, and there is an explosion of teenage tech-savvy expression, even in villages where indoor plumbing is unknown. The earliest posts might be selfies proudly displaying a bunch of bananas or a pirogue full of fish. But the phenomenon soon morphs into tropes familiar worldwide: GIFs lifted from Hollywood, Nollywood, and Bollywood; kids in goofy poses beside motorbikes or Jet Skis; risible exchanges in teenage text patois mixing French and Malagasy; outdated hip-hop signifiers like gold chains, low-slung pants, and backward caps; girls performing passable covers of Rihanna and Beyoncé.

Meanwhile, Senna's pensioner friends post pictures of the innocent tropical recreations of their sunset years. Fishing, eating *pizza margherita* in Saint Grimaud, playing cards on the Red House veranda: images for the reassurance of their families back in Europe, who have all seen *Best Exotic Marigold Hotel*. But their photographs too often contain hints of another reality: the intrusion of a smooth brown arm or a smiling young female face.

At Easter, the Grand Relais Chambord (formerly just the Hotel Chambord of Vatolampy beach) inaugurates its new golf and tennis club, and trio of restaurants, with an extravagant bash of fireworks and international deejays, guests flown in from Paris and Cape Town and Dubai. Senna— one of the investors in the ambitious venture—halfheartedly invites Shay to fly down, but she abstains. Afterward, videos and photos of the party reveal to her the village beauties of Naratrany mixed in among the foreigners and Malagasy celebrities. Once again Shay sees the nameless girl, no longer a floral apparition, but wearing a modest pink dress and standing beside Senna. She is not the prettiest of the young Sakalava women, Shay decides: she has a large jaw and a sprinkling of acne—she is, after all, a teenager. But she has a presence, a placid solidity to her that indicates grit, a determination not to be treated lightly. Hovering at her side in the crowd as if he just happened to end up there, Senna looks pleased with himself. To Shay, his permatanned face appears eroded by long years and crude appetites, and for the first time he seems to her like an old white settler, destined to be in Africa forever.

March, April, May. More anxious messages arrive from the Southern Hemisphere.

From Celestine, the Red House assistant cook: *"Madame, quand tu viens?"* Accompanied by a trail of heart emojis.

From Madame Rose, who has now retired to the capital, but who keeps abreast of Naratrany gossip: "It would be wise, *ma chère,* for you to come down here and do a good housecleaning!"

From Anse, Bertine's son: *"Maman Shay—tu ne viens pas en Madagascar?"*

Senna himself continues to call, with his usual contributions to practical family matters, and his usual lies about his life of hardship in the tropics.

Shay has the semester off, and has been traveling since Easter. A conference at Case Western. Visiting Roby and Augustina in Providence and Williamstown. A stay with her sister, Leila, in Berkeley. Research in Paris. The kids, too, find themselves much too busy to visit their faraway old vacation house. Summer jobs. Internships. Music festivals. Travel with friends. It's as if they have all deliberately stepped into limbo to keep themselves far from the country that was once so familiar.

Shay has an idea that the family might spend Christmas on Naratrany, but can't bring herself to make the usual travel arrangements. After all, she is on the island night after exhausting night, stumbling through her dreams. Waking up in the mornings, wherever she may be, feeling as worn out as the shoes of the dancing princesses in the fairy tale. Though she won't admit it to herself, she lives with a breathless sense of anticipation that grows heavier with the steadiness of sinking barometric pressure before a typhoon.

And then, in early November, the tension breaks. As so often happens, the shift is heralded by a phone call from Madagascar. With the usual interference, the granular rasp of distance over Mozambique, the Sudan, Egypt, the Mediterranean. Shay can never afterward recall what Senna's voice sounds like when he says the words that change her life. *Is it shamed, penitent, fearful, guilty, defiant? Ever so slightly proud?* All she can sense—and perhaps it is just her own perverse reaction reflected back by the stars and desert dust and sea winds—is a strange relief.

He confesses to her that at seventy-two he has fathered a child with a young island woman—with the girl of the painted flowers. The woman has a name, of course, but Shay refuses to hear it.

And, just like that, her denial evaporates and her dreams colored by the blue picture cease. As if a last piece of a puzzle has been placed, or the last day of a calendar crossed off. An Advent calendar, because after all, at the center of things there was—as there so often is—a nativity scene.

5. That Old Island Tale

Il est une fleur sur l'océan.
Il est une fleur rouge sang.
Palpite ce sang dans mes veines,
Roule le temps, emporte ma peine.
Il est une île rouge sang,
Elle attend, elle attend . . .

—Christiane Moreau-Phocas, "L'Île Rouge"

In Madagascar, everything speaks. Not just people and animals, but trees and rocks and individual islands and rice fields and lagoons and houses; and ancestral spirits, who offer oracular opinions just like pushy relations everywhere. Naturally, this kind of discourse goes on all over the world, but in big cities, with their incessant mechanical babble and jumble of human fates, it is hard to make out the quiet voices of inanimate things. But in self-contained places, like the great African island with its blood-colored laterite soil and hushed atmosphere of geological antiquity, there is much that is discernible to anyone who pauses to listen.

Shay has come to know this over the years she has spent vacationing in the country. She has also learned, through dreams and flashes of insight— even when she is at home in Italy, thousands of miles away—that time and distance make no difference if a communication from Madagascar is for her. She revisits this knowledge in the tumultuous days after her estranged husband, Senna, confesses to her that he has fathered a child with a young woman from Naratrany.

After the rage, the tears, the screaming, the nauseatingly practical talks with Milanese lawyers, the days in bed with her head under a pillow, the agonizing expanse of conversation with her angry and bewildered son and daughter, her indignant sister in Berkeley, her stepchildren and in-laws—aghast as only rich Italians can be over a possible glitch in an inheritance—there comes a quieter time, when she begins to feel a story pressing to be heard. A Madagascar story, though that's the last place from which she wants more news. It is not a quaint myth or ancestral legend, not, as she might have expected, a message from her truest Malagasy friend, Bertine—though she knows Bertine, if she were alive, would advise her to listen. No, it is the most unwelcome of tales, recounted by an annoyingly omniscient voice from the future: that of the young man—her husband's son—who will grow from the infant born to the young Malagasy woman.

When the tale becomes insistent, Shay has left Milan to spend a month in a borrowed house in Santa Fe, a place she fled to because it is far from any landscape she knows. Its southwestern topography is entirely different from the Pacific coast where she grew up, the East Bay with its fawn hills and jumbled cityscapes, the transcendent loneliness of its shining bridges. New Mexico feels unlike any region of Italy, her second home—and is surely, of all locations, one of the most remote from the Indian Ocean. Day after day, she sits in front of a picture window in an adobe cottage isolated enough on its hilltop to count as a hermitage, observing the slow march of cumulus clouds over the high desert. But as she does, she can't help but see that the reddish New Mexican landscape with its powerful aura of spirit life, its bloody palimpsest of tribal and colonial conflict, bears a haunting resemblance to the highlands of Madagascar. So one afternoon, seated in a ranch chair covered by an old Navaho blanket, she finally surrenders to the eerie sensation of a voice addressing her from within.

"Le fait de ma naissance," begins the young man (Shay imagines him as sounding quite pompous, communicating in flowery rhetorical French like Malagasy Catholic dignitaries she has met). "The fact of my birth in the second decade of the new millennium causes a commotion on two continents, the way extracurricular births in a royal household do. Think of

it: my father the rich Italian, already an old man, with a family respectably established in Milan—but still a pirate at heart, an irrepressible adventurer settled into a dissolute life with the crew of aged libertines gathered at his Red House. My mother, the girl Virginie, just nineteen when I am born— though she lies and tells Senna she is twenty—daughter of the woman from Soalala who lives up the hill from the Finoana village market. My mother, so beautiful and of such a strong nature, that from the time she is small it is clear that she will be the one to grab good fortune for us all.

"The Italian family is thrown into convulsions: outrage, mourning, howls of betrayal, moralistic scolding, bitter emails and tearful phone calls, anxious family meetings about whether I, the late-blooming intruder, will be recognized under Italian law. Questions circulate as to why I should have been allowed to be born at all.

"But the Malagasy family—and there are many of us!—rejoices, because my advent in the world means a lifetime of prosperity. Not just the trinkets that a casual girlfriend may get, until an old man's fancy picks a replacement from the endlessly renewed horde of maidens. No: an income, and a house—not the Red House, but our own ample cement-block dwelling in Finoana village, complete with satellite dish. A motorbike, maybe a car. An indisseverable link of kinship to one of the wealthiest men on the island.

"My arrival on the scene is encouraged by my grandmother Ayesha, herself young enough to be Senna's daughter, who, like other mothers in poor places, urges her daughter into bed with the rich foreigner. And when there are early signs of my existence, Ayesha guards her daughter's secret pregnancy like the most precious of investments. When my father finds out, I am already an ineradicable fact, floating like an astronaut in my teenage mother's belly, child of two worlds combined. As was inevitable. As is only fair. You can't just come into a country, build a big house, and take what you want. The country comes into you as well, into your blood. And so the land you set out to plunder ends by plundering you.

"And I will grow. I'll grow up tall and beautiful, with my mother's skin and my father's eyes, and I will go to the school for rich men's sons in the capital, and to the university in Italy. I'll meet my half brothers and sisters and the rest of the family spread across the world far from Madagascar—and please don't be surprised if I include you too, Madame Shay. Though it is true that you will be old when I reach my majority, and my dear, impetuous father will be long gone. *En tout cas,* whatever transpires, I intend to have my share of the Red House. Because that is the right thing and you know it, *Mère qui n'est pas ma mère*—Mother who is not my mother."

These last words resound in Shay's head, making her wonder if this is what it feels like to be a schizophrenic. Or a mystic. But now that she has permitted herself to hear the strange monologue, she feels better. Settled, with an odd sense of appeasement. At some point the sun has gone down, and she sits staring out over the sea of scattered lights running up into the Sangre de Cristo Mountains. But what she envisions is a landscape not in New Mexico nor yet in Madagascar. In her mind she sees a sweep of coastal plain in the southeastern United States, where centuries ago her American family narrative began, where the bones of her ancestors lie in lost slave burial grounds and the forgotten cemeteries of free Negroes. Tidewater country, the lush flatlands of the Virginia tobacco belt, an expanse that in Shay's imagination is dotted with big plantation houses like galleons on the Spanish Main. In each great house, at the side of a white master, a white mistress rules a community of Black slaves and deals with the rage and humiliation that consumes her at the growing number of slave children with the features of her husband. A troop of chattels who are also relations: proof that, over time, all boundaries become fluid.

From such mixed origins come the generations of Shay's bloodline, with their tawny brown and high yellow skins: house servants and freedmen whose descendants spread across the country in the great Black American migrations and who, through ambition, struggle, and luck, attain affluence and privilege but never forget the old tales. In her comfortable bourgeois childhood in Oakland, absorbing her parents' truths, she learned to condemn the ancestral masters who raped female slaves, to feel disdain for the plantation mistresses whose men betrayed them, and above all to know compassion for the enslaved women who were taken, and for their children born between cultures.

So is there any possibility that she could truly hate a Malagasy woman in a situation that echoes that early story? A Black woman—not a slave, but with freedom curtailed by poverty and circumstance—who has followed one of the few paths that life has opened to her? And even in Shay's torturous position as betrayed wife, could she ever despise a child born out of such an encounter?

Shay sees the irony in how her own fate, shaped by her privilege and her restless heart, brought her, the product of Africa and Europe, first to Europe and then, willy-nilly, to Africa. It would have been a lifetime adventure just to make her way into the marrow of a country like Italy. But fate leads her still further, to a position that is almost a burlesque of that of the plantation ladies she always scorned: mistress of a colonial-style household in an African nation, where a troop of Black servants labor for her comfort. There's no doubt that the Malagasy people employed at the Red House see their work as desirable. But through years of her Naratrany holidays, she never shakes the sensation that her leisure is built on old crimes.

In the early days of the Red House, she finds herself dangerously exposed to the spirits of the terrain where it stands. She quickly learns to believe in those spirits, to see that she and the other foreigners there are dancing on the surface of powerful mysteries. Her response has been to cultivate a lukewarm relationship with Madagascar, a relationship she knows, deep down, is incomplete, deliberately detached, based in guilt and fear—unworthy of the people and place. It is an attitude in no way superior to that of Senna, who, for his part, has always viewed the country as his personal playground; as if it were indeed Libertalia, the fictional pirate colony that has captivated Western imagination since it was first born from the pen of Daniel Defoe.

Shay recalls an episode early in her marriage when she and Senna are camping in the Mitsio Islands, three days' sail northward from Naratrany. It's her birthday, and Senna has given her an antique Malagasy bracelet, one of the twisted silver cuffs that freed slaves once wore. The two of them are exploring a beach where tall pleats of rock rise like giant organ pipes from a stony shore, and come upon a crevice in the headland; it leads, as they have been warned, to a cave that is an old Sakalava tomb forbidden to outsiders. Irreverent as always, Senna scoffs at Shay's hesitation, and ducks inside.

This is how Senna does everything, directed by the gusts of his own caprice; this is how he sailed into Finoana Bay and decided to buy up a tranche of beach; how he met Shay and promptly started to court her. Soon he emerges from the cave, urging her to take a look: there is light enough, he says, to see skeletons. Shay feels positive that it is wrong to enter, but he mocks her lack of daring, and she wants to impress him.

So, reluctantly she approaches and puts one foot inside, where her sun-dazzled eyes see nothing but shadows. And then out of the darkness erupts a *faraka*, a monstrous wasp, pursuing her like a heat-seeking missile. She dashes away, and dives into the sea, which for a few nightmarish minutes actually grows rough, as a cloud suddenly blocks the sun. When she finally clambers back onto the rocky beach, she finds that the waves have torn off and carried away her silver bracelet. Senna finds the wasp encounter comic and the loss of the bracelet annoying, but Shay knows the episode was a warning. About abuse of hospitality. About the need for respect. The word *desecration* comes into her mind. This single incident illuminates the hairline fissure between her and her husband's views of the world, a division that runs far deeper than their differences in race and nationality, and that will only grow wider with time.

The person who offers a map for how she should be in Madagascar is, of course Bertine—Bertine of the many faces: sister, housekeeper, healer, judge, guide. Through years of conversations behind closed doors, Bertine gives her directives on how to connect. *"Tu dois toujours revenir à Naratrany,"* she tells Shay, over and over again. "You must always come back here, because by now you are joined to the house and the people. But you can't live here always, because that would not be good for you. So you are with us, but not with us. Like how *le patron"*—her slyly mocking term for Senna—"bought the land and built the house . . . but doesn't really own it."

These sibylline pronouncements often baffled Shay, but now, in the light of the crisis in her life, they start to make sense. Could they allude to the age-old paradox, the fragile equilibrium between insider and outsider, *vazaha* and *teratany*, that the prophetic voice of her husband's son suggests when he addresses her as "Mother who is not my mother"? Slowly she starts to consider whether there is a way to live intentionally—with a modicum of principle, if not grace—in the space between different worlds.

To friends and family in Italy and the United States, she only says that she and Senna have separated; that after Santa Fe she is going back to Milan, to take up her life and plan her future steps. She says nothing about Madagascar, for she has not decided anything. With Senna, whose frequent, guilty calls she occasionally answers, she always has the same conversation.

"What are you doing?" he asks.

"Thinking."

"Do you want me to come there?"

"No."

"Don't let the kids turn against me."

"They're still speaking to you, aren't they? That's my doing."

"We shouldn't make any hasty decisions."

"Don't dare say 'we.'"

"You can't think I *wanted* this? I told you over and over it was the worst kind of accident! I just wanted to feel—"

"You don't need to run through the full mea culpa."

"If you could just look at this with some compassion. Or at least irony. You were always so good at—"

"Don't start, or I'll hang up. And one more thing: I don't want her and the child living in the house until everything is worked out."

"That will never happen—what do you think I am?"

"Unfortunately, I know."

"I guess it's no use saying—"

"No use."

"Then I'll say this: you'll always be the mistress of the Red House, Shay."

To which she makes the ritual reply: "Fuck you, Senna."

As the winter passes, the long silent days of light that she spends watching snow melt on piñon in the New Mexico high desert finally afford her enough peace to plan a few steps further on. She will, she decides, return to Madagascar, if only once. She'll take the overnight flight from Milan to Antananarivo. Arriving in the dawn, she will see from above the nakedness of the Grande Île, so lush when she first saw it two decades ago, now largely stripped of its primeval forests by human greed. From the capital she will fly to Mahajanga and there hire a Land Rover and driver—and bodyguards, too, because there are bandits on the roads—and make her way north toward the bleak Ankarana region, where the cuspate limestone crags of the *tsingy* grin at the sky. It will be a grueling trip, four or five days of spine-shattering off-piste tracks.

Near Ambanja, they will turn east and follow the bush paths to Tanindrazana, the tiny village where Bertine's tomb is located. Shay will pay her respects at that tomb, with whitewashing, with offerings of rum and packets of Bertine's favorite Good Look cigarettes; with the blood of a slaughtered zebu, if that is what is required. And then she will travel back to the coast and take the one-car ferry over the Mozambique Channel to Naratrany. When they get there it should be nearly midday.

From the port at Saint Grimaud she knows the way. A slow drive up the pockmarked concrete drive from the bustling pier. Past the port bars and dance halls. Past the lumberyards where *boutres* with patched sails deliver hardwood ravished from mainland forests, to decorate the big hotels. Past the colonial governor's mansion, which some ambitious foreign investor is starting to renovate. Along the ruinous Haussmannian boulevard, where zebu still graze amid the memory of planted hedges; through the swarm of minicabs in the chaotic market square; past the unchanging Fleur des Îles café, where the drunks and money changers will look up and wonder what well-heeled tourist has come to town. Past the prison, and the pizzeria, past the gleaming fortresslike supermarket opened by Senna's associates. Past souvenir stalls selling raffia baskets and counterfeit DVDs of the movie franchise *Madagascar*, which Shay has never known any islander to watch.

Then over the river, where as always Sakalava women squat pounding their washing on stones; up the road past the French cemetery, and the Adventist church, and the elaborate wrought-iron entrance to the country club and condominiums that Senna and his partners have conjured up out of the old cane fields. And so through the countryside: bamboo huts, manioc patches, overgrazed pasturage, billboards advertising fast food and vacation resorts with names citing heaven and paradise. To turn off, finally, at Finoana village, where the street vendors are settling down for siestas and the sleepy prostitutes have just emerged to comb out their hair in doorways.

She'll send the driver ahead with her bag and she herself will alight on the beach, so that she can approach the house on foot as she has so many times before, across the blistering sand, in the white-hot noon. As she walks, she will squint out over the coruscating blue of the bay, across the reef and deeps to the silhouette of the big island, where she has just tended a grave. As always, she'll overhear the whispered dialogue between land and sea, now filtered through the chatter of tourists sprawled on plastic lounge chairs.

Soon above the fringe of palms and casuarinas will rise into sight the tall thatched roof her husband caused to be raised so many years ago. Minutes later, she'll step through the sea gate into the Red House garden. There she'll experience the usual realization that the place never looks quite as idyllic as she remembers: the pool is slightly murky, the wooden statues seem battered, the lush jumbled foliage of tamarind, baobab, kapok, vanilla, banana, and hibiscus appears unkempt in spite of all gardeners' efforts, as if the old jungle were seeking to reconquer the terrain. Or is it just that the garden is cluttered with memories and ghosts?

Word will have traveled of her arrival and she'll greet the staff, who, astounded, will flock out of the side courtyard, where they are having their noon meal. *"Madame. Madame!"* Some she knows well—Denesian, Celestine, and others of Bertine's generation—and some are new hires. None of them will have seen her, or any foreign Madame like this:

tramping in sunburnt and dusty, wild, knotty hair pulled back with a bandanna, dressed in travel-stained khakis, looking worn out but with an air of accomplishment about her, as if she'd just returned from mapping an unknown continent.

She'll cross the veranda to the long dining table where Senna and his guests sit at lunch around an encampment of serving dishes tented with gauze fly covers. Senna, flabbergasted, will try to grab control of the situation with one of his theatrical salutations—*E arrivata la regina!*—as she walks up and coolly greets him. She will ignore the tableful of gaping old men, as if they were just a collection of sun-weathered skulls propped on sticks. But she will greet the young Sakalava woman, Virginie, quite probably seated at Senna's side; greet her with the dignified composure that might be expected from a wife who, however estranged, still wields power in the household. Formal recognition between the older and the younger woman: an almost biblical gesture that won't soon be forgotten, even when the names of Senna and his friends have faded into the fabric of anecdote that forms the chronicles of Naratrany.

Senna will rise mechanically from the table, calling for another chair. But Shay will remain standing as she makes the request for which she has traveled over land and sea. *"Fa' mi vedere. Montre moi,"* she'll say in Italian, and in French. "Show me."

It will be the Malagasy woman, Virginie, who understands her even before Shay finishes speaking, who will get up and lead the way to a far corner of the veranda, a corner that Shay knows from her own children's infancy to be the breeziest spot for a napping infant. And now once again there is a baby carriage—flashy-looking, probably a special order at the new supermarket—an exotic sight in this land where infants are still mainly bound to their mothers' backs. But these thoughts will melt away, as Shay fully engages with what she is doing: the simple act of traversing the familiar expanse of shining floor, whose oxblood color once unnerved her as a bride. A processional of a few seconds that seems, as in dreams, to last forever. An act which every person in the household has gathered to gawk at, but in which Shay feels completely alone.

This isolation will suddenly be history as she reaches the carriage. Here, Virginie will draw aside the mosquito netting and reach inside, then hold out to her a small bundle, like a gift. And Shay, feeling the Red House beating like a heart around her, will for the first time look into the eyes of the child.

Note from the Author

Red Island House is a novel about foreigners in Madagascar; its viewpoint and its "voice" are those of an outsider looking in. Any reader interested in investigating true Malagasy voices will discover one of the richest literary traditions of any African nation. It ranges from the ancient national epic poem *Ibonia*; through the beauty and wit of classical proverbs, *kabary* discourses, and *hainteny* love poetry; to the early modern masters, such as Ny Avana Ramanantoanina, Jean-Joseph Rabearivelo, Flavien Ranaivo, and Jean Razakandrainy, who writes as Dox; to contemporary poets and prose writers such as Esther Nirina, Lila Ratsifandrihamanana, Jean-Luc Raharimanana, and Naivoharisoa Patrick Ramamonjisoa, who writes as Naivo. For generations, Malagasy literature has been available to international readers mainly in French, one of the two official languages of the country, but in the last few years it has become more widely translated for an anglophone public, as in the anthology *Voices from Madagascar* (Center for International Studies at Ohio University, 2002). At the forefront of new publications are Naivo's sweeping historical romance, *Beyond the Rice Fields*—the first Malagasy novel to appear in English (Restless Books, 2017)—and, more recently, Johary Ravaloson's subversive and mythic modern retelling of the prodigal son narrative, *Return to the Enchanted Island* (Amazon Publishing, 2019). As an American seeking to know more about Madagascar, I immersed myself in many of these works, and included brief quotations from Naivo, Rabearivelo, Renaivo, Nirina, and Christiane Moreau-Phocas in my novel. Without their inspiration, I could never have brought *Red Island House* to life.

Acknowledgments

Red Island House was a complicated novel to write. It began as a series of stories seen from different points of view and set in different parts of Madagascar, based on notes from my travels to the country over the last few decades. Only years after composing the first drafts of the earliest stories did I see that they could actually become part of one narrative, centered around a single, fictive Malagasy island; a house; a character. I would hardly have made it through this process without the vision, faith, patience, and warm generosity of a number of people: my agent, Amanda Urban, who has been a transformative force in my writing life since we were both practically kids; Kevin McCarthy, who was there for every single dimension and detail of the novel; Marie Sandokony who, in the most unforgettable way, taught me about Malagasy traditions; Ruggero Aprile, whose in-depth knowledge of Madagascar provided unique inspiration; Courtney Hodell, the remarkable independent editor who has an almost preternatural sense of the shape of a good story; Deborah Treisman, whose precise and sensitive handling of my work that appears in *The New Yorker* filters through into how I view everything else I write; at Scribner, publisher Nan Graham and editor Valerie Steiker, who, along with the rest of the team, showed me what it is like to feel truly valued and understood at a publishing house; my daughter, Alexandra Fallows, whose good taste and professional insight helped me shape the book; my son-in-law, Thijs Leegwater, whose video skills helped me overcome my fear of the lens; Joan McKniff and Mark

Gettes, who shared with me their vivid memories of the country; my son, Charles Aprile, who helped with historical details; my brothers Alan and Lloyd, who patiently helped me sketch out Shay's Oakland childhood; and Dan Boeckman, who lent me the most beautiful house in Santa Fe, where, gazing out at the Sangre de Cristos and listening to the travel adventures of Dan's mother, the dauntless Elizabeth Mayer Boeckman, I suddenly had an idea of how to finish the novel. As every writer knows, words—the tools we use incessantly—are weak vessels to convey profound gratitude, but words are all we have. So, thank you. Thank you all.

About the Author

ANDREA LEE is the author of four previous books: the story collection *Interesting Women*, the novels *Lost Hearts in Italy* and *Sarah Phillips*, and the National Book Award–nominated memoir *Russian Journal*. A former staff writer for *The New Yorker*, she has written for the *New York Times Magazine*, *Vogue*, *W*, and the *New York Times Book Review*. Born in Philadelphia, she received her bachelor's and master's degrees from Harvard University and now lives in Italy.